© Brian Joseph Davis

EMILY SCHULTZ is the cofounder of the literary journal *Joyland*. Her previous novel, *Heaven Is Small*, was named a finalist for the Trillium Book Award alongside books by Margaret Atwood and Alice Munro, as was *The Blondes*. She lives in Brooklyn with her husband, Brian Joseph Davis.

The inspiration for *The Blondes* was a Gucci ad in a *Vanity Fair* magazine, featuring murderous-looking blonde women. Emily's story about her masquerading as a blonde was featured in *Elle* magazine. A blog post from Emily entitled Spending the Stephen King Money went viral.

emilyschulz.com

Additional Praise for *The Blondes*

"Like the literary love child of Naomi Wolf and Stephen King, *The Blondes* examines our cultural attitudes about beauty through the lens of a post-9/11, high-alert nightmare. The result is a spellbinding brew, both satirical and deeply satisfying."

—Helene Wecker, author of *The Golem and the Jinni*

"Sharp and fluid and legitimately disturbing. A thinking person's nail-biter." —Ben Loory, author of *Stories for Nighttime and Some for the Day*

"An energetic, startling novel. Emily Schultz is a writer with a deadly sense of humor. You laugh one moment, you're frightened the next. As unsettling as it is funny, *The Blondes* had me hooked from an early line: 'The neighbors have finished burning the hair.' How could anybody not read on from there?"

—Peter Orner, author of *Last Car Over the Sagamore Bridge*

"Emily Schultz gives new meaning to the term 'femme fatale' in her apocalyptic, darkly satirical new novel. . . . A gripping and unsettling story . . . It's a scarily realistic state of affairs."

—*Toronto Star*

"*The Blondes* takes you by surprise and keeps on surprising."

—Andrew Pyper, author of *The Demonologist*

The Blondes

The Blondes

EMILY SCHULTZ

Picador   A Thomas Dunne Book   St. Martin's Press   New York

THE BLONDES. Copyright © 2012 by Emily Schultz. All rights reserved. Printed in the United States of America. For information, address Picador, 175 Fifth Avenue, New York, N.Y. 10010.

picadorusa.com • picadorbookroom.tumblr.com
twitter.com/picadorusa • facebook.com/picadorusa

Picador® is a U.S. registered trademark and is used by St. Martin's Press under license from Pan Books Limited.

For book club information, please visit facebook.com/picadorbookclub or e-mail marketing@picadorusa.com.

Designed by CS Richardson

The Library of Congress has cataloged the Thomas Dunne Books edition as follows:

Schultz, Emily, 1974–
    The blondes : a novel / Emily Schultz. — First U.S Edition.
        p. cm.
    ISBN 978-1-250-04335-1 (hardcover)
    ISBN 978-1-4668-4146-8 (e-book)
I. Title.
    PR9199.4.S394B566 2015
    813'.6—dc23   2014042873

Picador Paperback ISBN 978-1-250-08169-8

Our books may be purchased in bulk for promotional, educational, or business use. Please contact your local bookseller or the Macmillan Corporate and Premium Sales Department at 1-800-221-7945, extension 5442, or by e-mail at MacmillanSpecialMarkets@macmillan.com.

First published in Canada by Doubleday Canada, a division of Random House Canada Limited

First published in the United States by Thomas Dunne Books, an imprint of St. Martin's Press

First Picador Edition: April 2016

10 9 8 7 6 5 4 3 2 1

To Henry

And Beauty draws us with a single hair.

⁓

ALEXANDER POPE
The Rape of the Lock

PART ONE

ONE

WOMEN HAVE STUPID DREAMS. We laud each other only to tear each other down. We are not like men; men shake hands with hate between them all the time and have public arguments that are an obvious jostling for power and position. They compete for dominance—if not over money, then over mating. They know this, each and every one. But women are civilized animals. We have something to prove, too, but we'll swirl our anger with straws in the bottom of our drinks and suck it up, leaving behind a lipstick stain. We'll comment on your hair or your dress only to land a backhanded compliment, make you feel pathetic and poor, too fat or too thin, too young or too old, unsophisticated, unqualified, unwanted. For women, power comes by subtle degrees. I could write a thesis on such women—and I nearly did.

Don't get me wrong. I am one of *them* too. I've had stupid dreams, and you yourself are the result.

You: strange seven pounds of other.

Here you are, under my hand, swimming in blood, about the size of a turtle. I know my voice must sound far away, muted, like someone talking under water. Maybe it's crazy that I'm nattering on, having a conversation with you when you aren't even born yet, just tumbling and turning in the big cloud of my abdomen. You can't possibly understand . . . Still, this is where I've got to. I'm here in this cottage in the woods and the snow— stuck here, really, because Grace has taken the car with gas and left me with the one on Empty, and how far can I walk in this state? To be honest, I don't know what else to do. So I talk.

Let me tell you where we've been over the past few months, baby. You'll never understand, but let me tell you.

Right now, I can see our neighbours outside the window and through the trees. They're the only people other than Grace whom I've seen in nearly three months, always from a distance and only sporadically—perhaps they aren't home all the time, or don't go outside any more than I do. There are just the two of them. I can see the red of her coat and the blue of his. I only know who is who by their heights. I can smell the smoke that's rising up, the stench of something singed. Even through the closed door and the window glass I can smell it. Like sulphur. I smelled it the first day I came here, but there was too much happening then for me to think to ask what it was, and Grace probably wouldn't have told me anyway. She had her own troubles—and I . . . I was just looking for Karl.

Now I know it's the smell of hair. Burned hair. It flares up quick and bright, and then it's gone in a breath of dark smoke. Before Grace left she was shaving hers and flushing the trimmings down the toilet—although where does it go except to the septic tank? Our neighbours are even more cautious than Grace. If any of them had seen what I've seen, they wouldn't worry. They'd know that disease comes or it doesn't, and if it comes, there's nothing you can do to prevent it.

Just as I can't prevent you growing inside me, little baby, my skin bulging more around you each week. I can't stop your growing, can only watch and wait. I'm sure that Grace has left me here all alone on purpose, that this is a power play in the ongoing sad tale of the fallout from my affair with her husband. She's left me in this, their second home, with all their things— and still I have nothing. She must know that to be alone out here at this stage in the pregnancy is more dangerous for me than anywhere I've been.

It doesn't seem that long ago I was in New York. I remember the day I found out about you: I lugged the weight of a suitcase behind me, down four flights of stairs at the Dunn Inn. There was no other way to move between rooms. So I had packed up everything I owned and taken it down to the check-in desk to check out—and then check back in again. I would have to heave the case up those stairs again when I got assigned my new hotel room. The stairs were steep, narrow and twisted, the green banister caked with paint from being retouched many times. My calves knotted as I descended. Forty pounds of suitcase behind me, handle sweaty, as I shifted my laptop bag on my shoulder. It was always with me then, like a growth, a clumsy but permanent part of me. Down I went, down, the wheels of the suitcase sticking on the fireproof carpeting. I lost a shoe on the landing and had to wriggle it on again before the suitcase bumped me down to the next step.

For a legal reason I didn't understand, the hotelier wouldn't let me keep the room for more than fourteen consecutive days. I hadn't been in Manhattan long enough to know about squatters' laws—that if they let me stay longer in one room I could deem it my permanent residence. I'd been in New York only fourteen days times two, and was moving for the third time already.

I had started out in an apartment—an old railroad flat, just a room for rent—but it was overrun with roaches and roommates. The bugs darted up along the shower pipe in the tub in the morning, and we rinsed them down before we stepped into it. One of the girls was a student, the other a stripper (although it was never said). How they knew each other—or even if they did—I have no idea. I had found the place online, sight unseen, a bad idea. All of our rooms were one after the other, with me in the middle, and not even a window. I didn't sleep for the first two days—it was ninety degrees and the air in the room was so dense. Of course, the student had the least privacy of all: her space was not really a bedroom so much as a cot and a desk in a screened-off dining area that the stripper and I had to walk through. The third morning I saw two rats in the alley, scuttling from one garbage heap to the next. So I found the Dunn Inn in Chelsea. It was overpriced but clean. And now I was moving from one hotel room to another as if playing musical chairs at a birthday party. I've always hated birthday parties.

But the hotel was quiet, and I didn't have to sign a lease, so I stayed. It was close to NYU, and I could go in and out at night as I pleased. I admit it was kind of thrilling to be right in Manhattan, even though I didn't have many places to go. The courtyard that my rooms—plural—looked onto was still, as if not in the city at all. It made me meditative and I found it easy to think about my thesis, my excuse for being there.

I remember the landlady asked me, "What is it you're workin' on?"

She was really the concierge, but I preferred to think of her as my "landlady," perhaps as some sort of dodge around the fact that I was living in a hotel, not an apartment. Was it even a real hotel, or just a flophouse? I wasn't the only occupant, but the halls had a transient feel. A few tourists, a few students.

Bent over behind the desk, looking for my new key, the landlady wasn't really waiting for an answer. I was about to try to explain "the study of looking," also known as "aesthetology," when I found myself staring at the top of her hair: a permed and dyed chestnut head. Redheads are an interesting group- ing, and one I'm quite familiar with. We've been labelled by society as cold but competent. A study back in 1978 found that 80 percent of those surveyed expressed a dislike of redheads; the same test group ranked the skin colour of redheads the least desirable of eight hues. Of course, 1978 was a long time ago—I wasn't even born yet—but here was my landlady, who had chosen this colour of her own accord. A red-brown, really. The colour of squirrels. Her sister, with whom she ran the place, was dark and I was sure my landlady's hair was naturally the same colour. She was bobbing around near an ancient computer she used for the bookings. Beside her was a stack of business cards that doubled as breakfast vouchers at the coffee shop next door.

"It's an essay on what women look like and what we think they look like." *Aesthetology*, or the study of looking, began when the Harvard School of Anthropology created an advanced course of studies in partnership with Empire Beauty Schools as a way to increase female enrolment in the sciences. It was still a buzzed about subject last year, and I selected it as a banner for my studies explicitly to attract a particular adviser. Also known as Professor Karl Mann. Also known as your father. Also known as Grace's husband.

The landlady came up with the key. "Three-oh-five. Don't forget to undo the *tap lock* with this one," she said, holding up one of the two keys. She spoke with a thick Brooklyn accent even though we were at Seventeenth Street. She meant "top lock." We'd had a funny exchange around that phrase the other time I switched rooms, where I said *what?* and *sorry* and *pardon?* and she kept repeating herself until something clicked and I figured it out. When I first arrived, she had also asked me if I needed to "pork" my car. I told her I didn't have a car, then mulled over the phrase all the way upstairs to my room.

She handed the keys over the partition between us. I remember being relieved I wasn't on the fourth floor anymore—there was no elevator in the place; it was a long, steep climb every day; and I suspected they'd put me there to give me the exercise. In spite of this, I'd lost no weight since my arrival. And every time I got to the top of those stairs, my chest would heave like an old engine.

"What we look like?" the concierge asked, a hint of distrust in her voice. "Like, you study advertising or something?"

"Yeah," I said with some resignation. "Like advertising."

"So you make ad campaigns?"

"No. It's complicated. I just look at them."

"They give you a degree for that?" she asked.

I nodded. "Communication Studies, PhD."

That's when she told me there was someone in three-oh-six. She told me that I'd *hafta* share the bathroom, that it was in the hall between our two rooms. "But it's only for the one night. She'll be out tomorrow."

I said fine, and the landlady slid me a form. I printed my name, then signed it in cursive for her: *Hazel Hayes.*

A smile played across her lips when I passed the document back, and she said, not derisively but as if it had only just occurred to her: "Maybe *I* should go back to school."

She was a decade or more older than me. I thought her name was Natalie, but couldn't have said for sure. I still don't know. Let's say it was. I forced my lips up at Natalie as if I'd never heard that kind of response to my thesis before. "Maybe!"

It pays to be polite. Especially to someone who brings you clean towels.

It's surprising what the mind remembers, and what it forgets.

My new room had velvet drapes, peach. The light came through, giving the white space inside a soft, womblike glow. It felt hidden, and I immediately liked that. The bed was the same as the one in my previous room, a double with an old gold frame and a quilt, and beside it was the same basic round table that would become my desk. I had bought my suitcase in Toronto's Chinatown for twenty-two dollars before I left for New York, and now I unloaded it once again and placed my things into the dresser. The drawers were not deep, but I didn't have many clothes, so it worked out. When I was done with the clothes, there was nothing left in the suitcase except the paper bag with the drugstore initials. I'm sorry to tell you I didn't remove it. Not then.

Instead, I flipped the suitcase shut and unzipped the side pocket, where I had stashed some of my books and photographs. I had a fabric CD case, full of sleeves that contained DVDs people had given me or I had downloaded over the years. Schlock and art movies kissed inside the plastic sleeves. I wish I still had them, but the government seized them. They're gone now, like everything.

I also had the journals. They contained articles with titles such as "Beauty's Moral Majority: A Meaning-based Explanation for Complexions Used in Advertising," "Barbie's Secret Plan for

World Domination," and "Metaphor in the Microprint," which was an examination of metonymic progression in beauty product ingredients—i.e., how to come up with a comforting phrase for "includes placenta" or "exactly like Preparation H but for facial use." Things I hoped to reference in my own work. It's strange to think how, only a few months later, they seem hopelessly archaic.

In the side pocket of that suitcase were two photographs. I hadn't taken them out in my last room. Bringing the first was an accident—or at least, not my choice. My best friend, Larissa, had presented it to me when she drove me to the airport in Toronto. *Presented* is the only word for it. The way Larissa gave gifts always made them seem bigger and grander than they were. This photo had been housed in a cheap dollar-store frame but gift-wrapped in expensive Japanese paper.

"In case you need something to stare at in New York besides the brick wall of the building next door," she'd said, which, I have to admit, turned out to be not inappropriate.

I peeled back the paper to reveal a photo of the two of us. Grinning, we were sitting on the same side of a booth in an upscale Toronto diner called the Swan. My eyes were slightly red from the flash. Hers were very blue. She had her hair in a slick ponytail that spilled gold threads over her shoulder, her face slightly turned toward me. It was last summer—oh god it *was* just last summer . . . I could tell because my hair was still four inches above my shoulders. In a white flowing tank top of Indian cotton, Larissa looked diaphanous. In a red-checked shirt I looked both lumpy and stunned. In spite of hair that is an obsessive, salon-created, middle-of-the-road mud brown, I've never been able to wear the colour red. I'm not sure why I persist in attempting it.

I've always wondered why people who love you do that to you—give you photographs where they look beautiful, you not so much.

I thanked her and reminded her that my place would have wireless: I could look at her photos online anytime I wanted. She squeezed my hand and kissed my cheek and said, "I know, but still," and I thanked her again, shoved the photo in the side pocket, and didn't pull it out again for twenty-eight days. It wasn't that we weren't good friends—she really was my best friend—it was just that she had no idea what was going on in my life, and I didn't know how to tell her. We'd grown apart. She had her husband and toddler son, and I had—

What I'd do to have that photo back now. It was from a better time.

The second photograph was no accident. The image was of Karl. Just Karl. You'll need to know about him—but what can I tell you? I took the photo on my cellphone camera and went to the trouble of printing it out—as if to convince myself he was real, tangible, could occupy physical space. It hurts me now to know the image is out there, somewhere in the world, but without hope of recovery. I imagine Karl's face inside a file folder, or a box with my name and number on it, or buried in a recycling bin that hasn't been emptied in months.

Karl's photo had no frame, and I remember laying it over the glass of the one of me and Larissa, where it fit very well. I moved around the hotel room, holding the photo in one hand, yanking open the heavy peach curtains with the other so the daylight flooded in. In the photo Karl's in his office, staring up at the crammed bookshelves, not at me. When I close my eyes, I see him there, as if he still inhabits that space. He had known I was snapping the picture, but at the last second he'd looked away, up, as if something of great importance had distracted him.

I lay down on the bed with Karl and, beneath him, the photograph of Larissa and me. The light was coming down on his face perfectly, which was why I had gone to the trouble of having the photo printed. There are many pictures of Karl here in Grace's cabin—but not my Karl; they're of a Karl I don't really know, someone else's Karl. In the photo I snapped of him, he looked thinner than usual, younger, his hair more brown than grey, chin pointier as he craned his face upward. He usually wore glasses, but he wasn't wearing them in that shot. A white shirt, tucked in at the waist, concealed a body I knew by smell, touch, and taste, one that was whorled with small brown hairs, dotted with pockmarks, scented with sweat, semen. I shouldn't say this to you, but all the way in New York, so far away from him, there flared in my nostrils a musky smell with an underlying tang of time and neglect. Just talking about it now I can almost smell it still, and . . . Why did looking at the photo conjure such a physical response? I felt panic rising in my throat like bile, and I swallowed it before it turned into a weird repulsion-desire. Karl was complex. My feelings for Karl could change quickly then. Now . . . well.

I placed the photo of Karl on the dresser and turned back to the suitcase. I couldn't neglect that paper bag from the drugstore forever. I'd already avoided it for two days.

Clutching the paper bag, I opened the door to the hall. A black-haired, trench-coated woman was standing opposite, cursing under her breath and struggling with her room key, an immense backpack hunched on her thin shoulders. My neighbour in 306, the one the landlady had mentioned. I didn't say anything, just shoved the bag behind my back and stood there, blinking. I hadn't run into many guests in the twenty-eight days I'd been living in the hotel. When I had, it was usually in the stairwell or downstairs at the check-in desk. There were some foreigners who made apologies in stilted English as we shuffled past one another, and a gay couple returning from a night of clubbing, speaking too loudly then suddenly silencing their giddiness as they rounded a corner and realized they weren't alone. This woman was different—our two rooms were joined by an intimate hallway, about the size of a closet. At the end of it sat the bathroom, which, now that she had arrived, we were to share.

"Didn't mean to disturb you, just can't quite . . ." the woman began, and then the top lock turned. "Oh!" She laughed. It was a guffaw that was almost musical. She leaned into the room, pack-first. "Let me—" There was a thud like a body falling. "There."

"It's all right," I told her. She had a golden complexion and small dark freckles like someone had flicked black paint at her. She had a wide everything except for her frame: wide nose, wide mouth with dimples at the corners, thick lips, large eyes. Or perhaps it only seemed that way because her neck was so thin and her hair so dark, coiled, and choppy.

I told her I hadn't known she was there and gestured to the open restroom door.

"Of course!" She grinned. It caught me off guard, and not just because of what I was about to do. "At least now there's space for you to get by. I'm Moira, by the way." She held out her hand.

I looked at it. I was holding the pregnancy test in my right.

Either she sensed my urgency or I struck her as weird, because she moved inside her own room, muttering, "Sorry, sorry, of course, of course."

I tried to smile, but it was too late. I do that quite frequently, you'll learn once you meet me: fall out of beat with others and respond too late. I'm not awkward, really. I just take an extra moment, that's all. I hope it's not a trait you'll inherit.

Moira missed the smile. She'd bent down for the gigantic rucksack at her feet.

"I'm Hazel," I said as I sidled by.

"Hazel, Hazel," she repeated from inside the room, as if she were storing the name for later. "Hello, Hazel."

I went into the bathroom and closed and locked the door. It didn't take the full minute the pregnancy test promised— more like fifteen seconds. A little pink cross marked the place my life as I knew it ended.

Never had the colour pink so disturbed me. I'm sorry. I'm so sorry, but it was the colour of girlie drinks and girlie-drink puke, peeling sunburns, and Grandma's bathroom. The pregnancy test was called First Response, as if an emergency were already waiting for me inside the pink box. Little pink firefighters with little pink ladders waiting to climb up me.

The oblong pink window of the test contained a plus sign. My urine had seeped across and revealed it, like some kind of secret code. I felt I had not been pregnant before that moment, although of course I had. I'd been exhausted and short of breath, falling asleep early, waking late, becoming increasingly greasy-skinned, and intent on chowing down New York bagels and pizza slices on every corner. My symptoms I had attributed to travel, to my new environment, and perhaps to "low-level depression," a phrase of Larissa's that felt more comfortable than labelling what I'd been feeling as heartbreak. At that moment, though, I realized my true label: wholly and undeniably pregnant.

How can I say this? And yet I am saying it—the thought of a fetus inside me clung to my mind like a brown swimming leech, which was probably about the size of you then. I thought about my body breaking open and tearing down, and something screaming and bloody the size of a football emerging, and I fell to my knees—yes, fell—and vomited into the toilet. I had just peed into it, and the smell of urine combined with regurgitated breakfast made me heave again, but this time nothing came up. I tapped the handle and flushed it all down.

I sat beside the toilet feeling nothing, hearing nothing, seeing nothing—because I was crying, although I didn't compute that until a light rap came on the door.

"H-Hannah . . . ?"

It was my new neighbour.

"You all right in there?"

I scrambled up, wiped my sleeve across my face, looked at my watch but couldn't make out the numbers. My glasses. I found them and pushed them back up my nose. How long had I been in the bathroom? Five minutes? Ten?

Another rap at the door.

"Hazel," I corrected my neighbour through the door. My voice sounded shredded. "One minute."

I began running water frantically—off with the glasses again—and splashed it on my face, grabbed the folded white towel from the bar. I looked terrible. *This may very well be the worst impression I will ever make on anyone*, I thought—which of course is hilarious now—and then, oh dear . . . I laughed. But it was, you know, like a hiccup, and I threw up again, right there in the sink. Bagel is not a nice food to barf.

When I came out, there she was, hovering in the little hallway, a narrow, pinched expression on her wide face. She had ditched the trench coat and wore this short-sleeved sweater that was the colour of an old tennis ball. It seemed tatty, but later I'd realize the texture was only because I'd left my glasses on the sink again.

"It's—it's not my business," she stuttered. "I mean, I don't even know you, but are you okay? Can I get anything for you?"

I shook my head. I could feel how dreadful I must look, how my eyes burned. "It's all right. I'm just pregnant," I said nonchalantly, shaking my hair back.

She looked past me toward the bathroom. "Why don't I get someone from downstairs?"

"Sorry if you heard me in there. I didn't mean to disturb you," I said.

It was then that her gaze seemed to fasten on to something, and I turned and recognized the oblong shape: I'd left the pee stick sitting on the bathroom cabinet.

"Oh," she said in a voice that was suddenly squeaky, and I realized for the first time that she was maybe a little younger than me. "Oh, Hann— Hazel. Hazel, why don't you come in and sit down for a minute?" She gestured me into her room, and even though I had forgotten her name, strangely, I found myself stepping over the backpack and inside room 306.

The neighbours have finished burning the hair. I can still smell it, hanging in the air like a thick sheet. Brown; it smells like the colour brown. The smoke goes quickly but the odour lingers. I don't see the man and woman now—not even from here at the kitchen window, which has the best view past the hill and that row of evergreens. They've gone back into their own cottage.

When do you develop your sense of smell? I think Larissa told me that babies practise breathing while they're still in the womb. At his mid-term ultrasound Larissa's son was also practising sucking, and had placed his small, transparent thumb up next to his mouth. She had a black-and-white image

of that one taped to her fridge. But I don't know if breathing
and smelling are related in the womb.

You know what I'm going to do? I'm going to go over to
that neighbouring cabin tomorrow if Grace hasn't come back,
and I'm going to tell that couple my situation. A pregnant
woman alone out here? How can I be a threat to anyone?
They'll have to help me. I did go banging on their door once
before, but that was at night and they didn't answer. I'll try
during the day, when they can see me from their window.
They must have a car. If they have a car they'll have to agree to
drive me to a hospital when I go into labour. Ordinarily anyone
would, right?

TWO

I FORGET WHERE I WAS. Oh, yes: I was telling you about the day I found out about you, which was also the day of the first attack.

I was telling you this hours ago, but it is night now and I feel so alone out here. Earlier you were very active, wriggling around under my skin, bumping under my hand, but now you've gone still inside me—as if you've fallen asleep. When you're moving I feel less alone, as if you're real, or almost real. These days, even though I haven't met you, you feel more real to me than people I've known. Like Karl. Because I can feel your movements, can feel that you are here.

I hadn't realized how much I've come to depend on Grace. I hadn't realized how vulnerable night can make me feel. It helps to keep talking.

Moira wasn't from New York either. After she invited me into her room and helped me onto the bed, she disappeared. She'd been gone about five minutes before I thought about getting up off her bed, which was quilted, like mine, and returning to my own room, but my head was like a weight suspended on fishing line, gently swaying, and I realized I shouldn't budge for the time being. I closed my eyes. I felt a vague vertigo. Or maybe I was having a panic attack. I'd never had one before. I opened my eyes and found I was staring at Moira's rucksack. I can still picture it. It felt very satisfying, stabilizing, to look at, slumped in the corner where it was, a metal frame extending from the top of it, buckles and zippers and pouches puffing out from the sides. It was khaki green, a nice calm shade in the dim room. My entire acquaintance with its owner had totalled about fifteen sentences strung out over ten minutes, and still Moira had left me, a stranger, with every item she possessed.

She'd run downstairs to alert someone that the bathroom needed cleaning and to fetch us cups of peppermint tea from the café, which she assured me would calm my stomach. She was buying the cups of tea from her own pocket, and meanwhile there I was with all her things in a bag. I couldn't get over the trust Moira was showing me. It filled up my eyes, and when she returned I was still crying, the grey-green blur of the backpack swimming before my vision.

Moira set the cups on the bedside table and disappeared again. "Here," she said, right before she vanished, as if I were supposed to take something from her even though she'd left the room. When she came back a few seconds later, she silently extended a roll of toilet paper with one hand. I could vaguely see my glasses, folded and held gently, in the other. I wiped my eyes with a few squares of the tissue and blew my nose louder than I meant to, then reached for my vintage tortoise-shell glasses and felt the frames perch heavily over my burning cheeks. Embarrassment had begun to set in.

"Drink this," Moira told me.

I took the hot paper cup in both hands.

The cleaning person was opening the door to our little alcove to go into the bathroom. She was a petite German woman who spoke little English but would thump her breastplate heartily and proclaim, "My job!" dipping her grey-blonde bob, every time I had tried to apologize for the tub that wouldn't drain properly upstairs on the fourth floor. Moira shut the door and we were alone in the room together.

"I threw it out," she said abruptly. At first I didn't know what she meant. Then she added, "The test."

"It was positive, though?" I looked to her for confirmation. I couldn't quite believe this stranger had touched something I'd peed on. She was still standing in front of the closed door, as if she wasn't sure she should sit down with me, even though she had before she went to get the tea, had sat right there, hip to hip, a hand making slow circles on my back, saying, "It's okay."

Moira gave a vigorous succession of head nods, biting the bow of her lips, as if she feared I might shoot the messenger. Then she held her cup of tea in front of her face but didn't drink from it, just kind of clutched it there as if for warmth, though it was certainly warm enough in the room. Her thick, dark eyebrows rose. "You have a boyfriend?"

I told her no. At forty-six, Karl was too old to be anyone's boyfriend. "Well . . . sort of," I amended. This was more than I'd told even Larissa.

"Where?" Moira asked, which in hindsight was a logical question considering we were in a hotel, but at that moment I got goosebumps from her seeming omniscience.

"Canada. Toronto."

"Then that's where you should go," she said.

She came over and sat down beside me. She was tall but slender, and when she took up space on the bed, it was no more than if a cat had jumped up and perched on the mattress. She said I should phone the father, that I didn't want to go through this alone.

I hunched my shoulders. "It's kind of—" I stopped talking to drink more tea. The weight that I'd felt in my head had sunk to my stomach, and I realized it wasn't anxiety but guilt. "Complicated. I would go through it alone there too," I told her. "He's . . ."

I fought the term *married*, weighing it in my throat, staring at the closed door of this stranger's room. *Attached* sounded like a chemical compound. Like something bleachy, strong. *Committed* made me think of the mental hospital. Then there were other terms, like *partner*, *husband*, *wife*, that sounded like bondage. In the end, I just let my words trail away, and Moira didn't seem to notice.

Eventually she deposited me back to my room. No—*deposited* is the wrong word. Moira said kindly—she was very kind—"Maybe you should go and give him a call."

I figured this was code for "Get the hell out of my room."

She walked with me to the door of my room, a foot outside her door, of course, and there she touched my elbow and said simply, "Don't worry." I remember those two words because they felt solid as stones gripped in either hand: *Don't* and *Worry*. She turned and disappeared into room 306, and a second later I heard the backpack as it was heaved and dropped onto her bed, presumably to be unpacked.

I closed my door and sat down on my bed.

I meant to call him. I have to tell you, baby: I was *going to*. I want you to know that I did, at least, think about it. And then, there I was two hours later. I simply sat unmoving until feeling overwhelmed me and I knew I had to get out of that room.

There's a map of New York inside my head. The streets are in white and the buildings are in yellow and the bridges with subway lines stretch red over the blue Hudson. But I also have a three-dimensional memory of the city. There are the stone buildings with small faces etched into them above doorways, and I remember the way the buildings cut the light six storeys up. There's the black corsetry of fire escapes, a symphony of car honks, and the way all the florists and corner stores arrange their carnations and lilies on pedestals with bows, as if any given weekday is as important as prom night. There are the children at the nearby elementary school, dressed and styled like they are priming to be in indie-rock bands. There is a thin girl in a tank top, leaning out an apartment window, smoking her cigarette for all eternity. I can't remember anymore the exact day I saw her—but the image is still there, lodged in my brain. The thing about going to a city not your own is that everyone looks like someone you know, but they can't possibly be. There's that sense of strangeness mingled with déjà vu. Then there are the people I would see standing on street corners—earbuds corded into cellphones that glowed in their palms—looking disconcerted and full of intent at the same time, as though waiting for directives to be beamed down so they could know where to go and what to do next. And after work, the streets would fill with the skinniest, most beautiful women—all teetering along, looking as if they might burst into tears, as if a morsel of food hadn't passed their lips in twenty-four hours, as faint and sad as Shirley MacLaine in that 1960s Billy Wilder movie *The Apartment*. And truthfully, if it weren't for the illness and the events that soon followed, I might have come away from New York with this floating, movie-inspired view of the city forever in my mind.

That day I found out about you, I headed out into those streets. I sat for a while in Union Square, which always seemed like more of a circle to me. I loved it best on weekends, when there were vegetable and fruit stands. During the weekdays it was just another park, with people sitting around its edges, stabbing at things in Styrofoam containers, and pigeons pecking at every speck on the sidewalk, and someone handing out flyers for the coming apocalypse, and skateboarders shooting down the steps in disregard of the tourists. Usually I took a perverse pleasure in watching the debt clock tallying what the nation owed so silently and with such dizzying speed, but that day I wasn't seeing anything.

A couple on the bench next to mine had begun to quarrel. He was black and wore a fisherman's hat. I remember the brim was turned down and I thought he looked fashionable. His knees were pulled up, his elbows draped over them, lanky, hands dangling, and his white sneakers were braced against the bench. I can see things like this, little moments, crisp and still like photographs, when I close my eyes. His companion was a chubby white girl with very black hair and red lipstick, and maybe a pair of striped leg warmers over her Converse sneakers, even though it was plenty warm out. I had stopped there to scroll through the numbers on my cellphone, and I paused at Larissa's name, then at my mother's, and finally at Karl's, before flipping back to the menu screen. I'd been meaning to buy a New York cellphone, but I had so few people to call that I'd procrastinated on the expense, which meant my signal had to bounce all the way back to Canada. A mere three minutes of roaming fees could buy my dinner, I told myself.

"What you want?" the boy asked the girl. He repeated it several times and she wouldn't look at him or answer, her arms folded across her stubby body. "I said, what *do* you want?"

"I don't want nothin'," the girl snapped, and she stood up and made a big production of straightening her cargo purse before she walked away, the skull patch on it bouncing off her hip. He looked at me, and I looked back, apologetic for women the world over. His mouth made a straight-line smile, as if saying he'd had better days. He had small acne bumps across his cheeks—and I realized neither he nor his girlfriend was more than nineteen. He lifted himself off the bench and loped after her like he wasn't in any hurry to catch up but would eventually.

"Call me," I said to the phone, quietly. "Call me. Call me." I stared at that goddamn phone the way I used to stare at objects the summer I was eleven, the summer I thought I had telekinetic powers. It didn't warble, burble, vibrate, or sing. Wouldn't you know the cold black object just sat there in my palm, ticking off the time? I dropped it back in the side pocket of my bag and stalked off in the same direction as the young couple. With every step, I wondered where the fetus was located inside me. Did it slosh to the right or the left? Did it bob between my hips like a thimble in a tub of water? How big was it? Was it just a tadpole still?

I felt incredibly naive, unfeminine—un*female*—not automatically knowing these facts, and a wave of heat overcame me. I vaguely recollected a series of pink illustrations from some textbook, imagined a seahorse or dinosaur shape, with alien eyes, about the size of a cashew. I sat down again before I had crossed the park and swiped my short sleeve across my forehead to mop up the sweat. As you will eventually learn, I overheat when I'm in crisis. I added another shade of pink to my list of pet peeves: sex ed.–pamphlet pink.

Eventually, I got up off that bench and kept walking, and after a while I found myself in a hair salon in Midtown. By then I had decided I didn't want you. How do I explain this? Especially if you can hear me. If you can understand. But you *can't* understand, can you? I'm just a voice. A hum.

It's a rational thing. I'll tell you all my reasons. I didn't want to be a single mother. I had no income. Sure, I had an MA in Culture and Communication Studies, but what did that really mean? I was a PhD candidate living on a ticking grant clock. I could probably find employ back in Toronto, something dull but for which I was qualified: a job in media or arts, copywriting, maybe the CBC. God, how we all wanted to work at the Canadian Broadcasting Corporation! It was practically upper-middle-class welfare. I was qualified to teach, but even sessional college jobs were rare. I could get a job doing some kind of marketing, or maybe just secretarial work. But the idea of raising Karl's baby when I wasn't sure how I felt about Karl made me feel small, both as a woman and as a human. The idea of raising *any* baby was bewildering.

I'm not sure exactly how I came to my conclusion about you that afternoon. It just seemed that with each step one thought replaced another, and by the time I found myself sitting in the swivel chair of a stylist who didn't speak a lot of English, I had run out of ambiguity.

"Fix it," I instructed, pointing to my roots.

"What you want?" the stylist asked, cocking her head, oddly echoing the words of the teenager in the park.

What *did* I want?

The stylist was middle-aged, her own hair a lustrous black without a strand of silver, blown into a bob, smooth and straight around her face. She held up hanks of my hair and then let them fall again, watching. Then she watched in the mirror as she repeated the gesture. My hair was dull, she told me. This was a surprise to me because New York's water was softer than Toronto's, and I had thought my hair was healthier than usual. But she gazed at me like she had known me all my life and the way I had treated my hair was a true disappointment to her. She shook her head. "So dull."

I thought I might cry.

I had heard a lot of hair tips over the years from my mom. I had followed none of them:

- "Put your leisure time to work on your hair!"
- "Before washing, brush your hair. The shampoo will not rinse out properly if your hair is a bird's nest of tangles."
- "Combat dry hair with a beer rinse."
- "Your hair is your family's crowning glory, so invest in a good conditioner."
- "Rub mink oil into your hair to add shine and sparkle."
- "A touch of olive oil will curb your dandruff problems."
- "Head massages stir up circulation and improve the scalp for a healthier head of hair. If the skin is tight it usually means you are rundown or tense."
- "Instructions for washing: Rinse with warm water. Rinse and rinse again. When you're positive you've got all the soap out, rinse again. Rinse until your hair squeaks.

If the hot water won't last out through all these rinses,
be brave: the last rinse can be icy cold—which gives
more shine."

I was never sure how an eco-girl was supposed to cope.
As for scalp massages, if my head was any indication, it
seemed I was always rundown and tense.

"Colour it," I choked to the stylist. I took off my glasses
and laid them over my knee. I wiped one eye with my fist, and
some mascara came off on my knuckle. I wiped my knuckle
on my jeans. I put my glasses back on. "Colour it," I said
again, stronger. I tilted my chin at the stylist as if daring her
to object.

"Oh-kay," the stylist said, as if thinking, *It's your funeral.*

My hair has always been slightly bushy, with a coarse,
brittle texture, and it was this, I thought, more than the colour,
that she was reacting to. White people's hair is supposed to be
fine, like cornsilk. My hair came from my father's ancestors,
who, although I never knew them, were apparently as Scottish
as border collies. It was sheepdog thick.

The stylist went to a cabinet and took out that book all
salons have, the one with loops of hair in a myriad of colours:
black velvet, ebony, sable brown, umber, chocolate, walnut
brown, ash brown, mahogany. I used to love playing with them
when I was a kid in my mother's hair shop. The stylist flipped
quickly through the browns. Then came auburn, orange-red,
ginger, copper, radiant red, flame, deepest scarlet, merlot,
purple orchid, violet, plum, indigo, azure, and even flamingo

pink. And then there were the blondes. Though I'd never been one, I knew the names by heart: sahara, desert ochre, dark blonde, goldenrod, luminescent blonde, honey, chamomile, chardonnay, silver blonde, white blonde, and finally, platinum. Back and forth the stylist flipped the book.

"Brown," I told her, sheepishly. "Just a mid-brown. This colour." I showed her the ends of my hair. The roots, on the other hand, were the shade of spaghetti marinara.

I had never seen a woman over forty wrinkle her nose, but this woman did exactly that as she looked at me in the mirror. I watched her hold up the book and select a rusty strand to hold next to my roots. "This one," she said, and nodded.

I craned my neck to look her in the eye. "Brown," I insisted, but even I could hear some hesitation in my voice.

The stylist next to us looked over. She was younger than my stylist. She said something in Korean. Then she looked hard at me and said, "Go back to your natural colour. It's right for you."

I didn't say anything more. The stylists had won.

The older woman whipped around and started mixing up the colour on a side counter. She threw a vinyl smock over me without even a glance at my face.

She was going to strip out the colour that I'd put in. At least the bleach burning my eyes meant I could cry in public if I wanted to. I had lots of reasons to cry: Karl Mann wouldn't leave his wife. We had slept together only five times. Karl and his wife had slept together how often? Fifty-five times, three hundred and five, one thousand and five, ten thousand and five? I imagined them fornicating into infinity. I saw them floating nude through the chamber of their clean white bedroom, like astronauts untethered from gravity, stray limbs tangling like ribbons, indulging in upside-down acts of love-making.

It was just before Labour Day weekend, and the younger stylist had propped open the door of the shop. A fly came in and landed on my pant leg, then another. I jostled my knees and they lifted off, zipped around the salon, then returned, settling defiantly on me.

Karl and I actually slept together six times, if I counted the night in his Mini Cooper, when he had begged me to masturbate for him just once, then give him a hand job, just a hand job, then cried afterward while I rooted around in my purse for a package of Kleenex to clean up. I usually didn't count that one. I had seen men cry before. My dad, when I was really young. But watching Karl cry was different. He was too tall for that car and the space felt small to begin with. He was a married man, and he wasn't mine, and I wasn't sure why I got crying Karl while *she* got stoic Karl. And he didn't just tear up and hold his fingers across his eyes like my dad had. No, when Karl cried he blubbered like a hundred-and-seventy-pound baby. I had never seen anything like it. His whole forehead wrinkled up. There were more wrinkles there than I'd ever seen in one place, and Karl's emotion seemed to surge upward through his whole body as if the cacophony, and his soul, would emerge out the top of his head in a big mess. A volcanic eruption. It was like watching someone orgasm, but uglier. Ours was an ugly affair. And now the flies were back, four of them, big black ones.

"Shoo," I said, "shoo." I shook my knees and they took flight, only to return a minute later. In the mirror, my hair looked positively white, fuzzy with the bleach. I had taken my glasses off, and they lay folded on the vanity. My stylist came over to check on me. She gave me a magazine to swat the flies away, but the flies kept returning.

If I were to try to guess when *it* happened—this thing, this strange thing, *your conception*—I would say the fourth time. And that's what I sat there thinking about, in that hair salon, sweating under that smock. Even now, I still think it was that fourth time.

Karl had shown up at my place unexpectedly. It was close to eleven at night, a Friday, and suddenly he was at the alley door, standing on the fire escape, his drunken face on the other side of my window. I was straining Kraft Dinner for a late meal. I dropped the strainer and the pan together in my sink and sprang halfway across the room I was so surprised. Drops of hot water had splashed my wrists, and they burned, but I said nothing, just wiped my hands on my shorts. I don't know if shock always leads to good sex, but in that case it did. That he'd come to me was thrilling. Watching him move through my space, touch my things, was more of a disinhibitor than alcohol or the weed no one ever shared with me.

That night, I felt as if I filled my entire body for the first time, was as present as I could possibly be. The only time I'd ever felt even close to that way before was in a women's history elective in second year, when I'd sat behind a girl named Catherine Lee—I knew her name only because she raised her hand a lot, and the professor would call on her. And every time she raised her hand, her scoop-neck shirts would gap and I'd stare straight down her perfect back at her black bra straps. I don't know *why her*, but when she did that, especially if she leaned forward to get the prof's attention, I felt as if I would burst out of my own skin. It might have been the fact that she didn't care if her bra showed, that she'd seemed to have a sexuality all her own—I certainly never felt like I had that. Even the couple of men before Karl that I'd messed around with had been like experiments in tactile sensation and physical mechanics rather than fulfilling contact. And until that night in my apartment, Karl had also been an experiment.

I fell on Karl and kissed him in the hallway. He was about to use my bathroom to urinate but somehow I pinned him against the doorway, and in spite of his condition, we began, right there, standing up. I remember I got the feeling almost right away. *That* feeling. It's one where you feel limp and full of adrenaline at the same time, and your head is suddenly a black-and-white movie, and you can hear the ocean crashing a thousand miles away and radio static and snatches of songs at full volume, and there aren't any words for it. It wasn't exactly the sound of violins, but . . . I hadn't felt anything like it before with Karl. Maybe he sensed it too, because he got nervous and stopped.

"We shouldn't," he said.

But then we went into my bedroom. *Professor Karl Mann*

was in *my* room. He was breathing my air, and then his hands and his hair and his scent were in my sheets; he was leaving behind his skin cells; he was trailing a finger over my books and saying something innocuous, and out of the dresser drawer I pulled a condom—the only one I owned, procured two years before from the university women's centre along with a safe-sex instruction kit. I threw the condom on him, and we finished what we had begun. But because I was still going, could have continued indefinitely, was having my first orgasm with him, he stayed inside me with the condom on after he'd already finished. That must have been when it happened.

In that Midtown hair salon, I shooed the flies away again.

Karl had always seemed delicate. He was tall and thin— much thinner than me. He had a long thin face, and long thin fingers, and a long thin penis, which I didn't love but also didn't mind. I had made a lot of noise that night, which I hadn't done before. Because we'd never been anywhere where I could. Except the one time at the cottage. *This cottage.*

But that was early on in our relationship and I was too nervous to make much noise then.

At my apartment, it was different. It was mine and I was comfortable there. I couldn't tell if he liked it, my being loud, or if it bothered him. He called having an orgasm "getting off," which I found alienating, impersonal: *Did you get off?* I felt a little ashamed, and I remember I walked around my room, cleaning the place up, because I couldn't look at him.

A little while after that, we mixed the cheese powder and milk into the Kraft macaroni and ate it cold. "This is just awful," he said, laughing, and I hoped he meant the instant macaroni. I thought he did, but I knew he was upset with himself for coming over, for staying too long, though it had been only an hour or so. He said he was going to go. No, *had* to. Had to go.

He kissed me at the top of the fire escape, his clavicle against the top of my head when he hugged me. It was the second week of July. The smog of the city felt like a blanket on our shoulders as we stood in the open night air and said goodbye. Then he was going down the steep metal stairs out the back of my place, and because I knew his feet must not fit entirely on the slats, I watched him as he descended carefully from the second floor. I wanted him to look back, and when he got to the bottom he did. He grinned for a second, like a seventh-grade boy in spite of the wrinkles around his mouth, like he had accomplished something. His glasses were in his pocket, and he looked younger with the streetlight from the alley streaming across his face. The fragrance of the Magic Thai restaurant downstairs was belching out the back door into the heat. The moment felt perfect, reckless, floating, and I thought to myself: *Remember this.*

Remember this—and here we are, and I have.

And then he ruined that moment. "I wish you could be my girlfriend," he called up, still grinning, as if he had said something profound or beautiful. As if he had said, "I love you." He turned, and I watched his tucked-in blue shirt drift away through the dark. A large wooden bead tumbled in the back of my throat.

It was that time, then; that was when you happened. I was punished for my desire. (The fifth time, although it was the last, was lacklustre, unmemorable.)

In the salon, six flies stuck themselves to my jeans and I felt like a freak, like Pig-Pen from Charles Schulz's *Peanuts* comic strip. The stylist came back, and the flies took off; they only wanted me. The ammonia climbed my nostrils, a scent that I could taste with each breath, it was so astringent. My eyes still burned and I still wanted to cry—and I would have, if I hadn't already been cried out. Karl was old and pathetic and sad, and I had been attracted to all those things about him. I "got off" on them. I writhed against his sadness.

I remember the tug of the stylist's hands as she checked my hair again, parting the sections and rubbing at them with latex-gloved fingers. Eventually I was done. She gestured me over to the shampoo chair, where I reclined as she washed out the rest of my disintegrated colour. Then she applied the dye almost tenderly with a brush, smiling at me and talking to the other woman in Korean. My stomach had a gaping feeling in it, but I couldn't tell if it was nausea or hunger. In retrospect, I probably shouldn't have been around all those chemicals in my state.

When the stylist had applied the colour and rinsed it again, and dried and styled my hair, and it was all over, I looked like a self I hadn't seen in a long time. Against my mother's wishes, I had been dyeing since age fourteen. The stylist had taken an inch or so off and my hair was gently bobbed. It lay just below my collar: a brilliant orange, the colour of lilies. I didn't know how I felt about it.

"Pretty," she said, moving the hair around my face, adjudicating me.

I had staggered into the cheapest-looking salon I'd passed, but of course it still cost more than I had, this thing I hadn't wanted, but that, well, filled the time. I pulled out my credit card and paid the woman.

It was just after three and I was on my way home—*home* being a relative term—when the first incident happened.

Businesspeople were striding along the sidewalk past me, weaving and streaking into each other, a blur of hosiery, patent leather, pinstripes. I felt bright as a Christmas ornament with my new hair, which was really my old hair. It wasn't far back to the Dunn Inn, but I was walked out. I would ride home, and do what made the most sense: call Karl. The academic feminist part of me felt defeated: devastated by biology, I had run out to get my hair done as a balm. As I descended into the white-tiled corridors of the station for the F train, the gluten and cheese of a pizza slice shifted inside me, and I wondered, too late, if I should have opted for something less heavy.

My feet, the shape each made on the stairs as I descended: I remember watching them. I remember clinging to the rail as I tried not to be rushed by the impatient crowd behind me, a knot of hollering high school boys. I was about to sit down to wait on the one bench seat remaining when my guts roiled.

I put my hand out for one of the posts. I drew a quick breath—*hold it down, hold it down*—and stared at the ceiling, my eyes tracing the pipes. *Aspergillus* and peeling white paint. The dark station was hot and smelled of urine and sweat, which only made the closed-in feeling worse. I swallowed, and shuffled slowly between clusters of other waiting passengers, over to the trash receptacle. It seemed the logical place to be for what I thought—feared—might happen. I placed one hand on the bin. Where normally I wouldn't have touched it, now I was leaning on it. If anyone noticed, no one seemed concerned. Given the time of day, almost everyone was young, oblivious. Nearby, some schoolgirls in kilts and sneakers were pushing each other's shoulders and laughing. Upstairs, a lady busker with a karaoke machine was crooning into a microphone. The Supremes: "Baby Love." Slightly off-tempo, a high, reedy voice tumbled down the stairs, the words just reaching us. My eyes watered. I swallowed. My newly coloured hair fell forward, forming a curtain between me and my surroundings. Through it, I saw her.

Something about her pace drew my eyes. She was ambling along the yellow stripe of the platform opposite. Under the fluorescents and through the wall of black posts that divided our two tracks, I watched her. My face was tilted almost sideways, so that everything seemed off, skewed, yet I couldn't help focusing on her. She had a slight lumber, as if one side of her body were heavier than the other. Her left leg seemed to drag a little. She was wearing a red power suit, sneakers— puffy, bright white Nikes—and her Barbie-blonde hair touched her shoulder-padded jacket. She had the chiselled chin of an older woman who maybe had had some work done, though truthfully she was too far away for me to make this observation. Maybe I'm remembering pictures I saw later, when the whole story surfaced. A white bow was knotted at her neck. Again, I probably didn't notice that at the time. What I did notice, though, was that her movement didn't match someone so put-together, long strides that lagged as if her feet weren't behaving. Maybe, I thought at the time, her odd gait came from wearing heels all day—except she wasn't carrying any, and not even a purse. Then the truth dawned on me. I knew the insane well from my home in Toronto, a city that had a grand scheme of integration alongside gentrification; condo towers had been built practically on top of what was once called the asylum—all just a couple of blocks from my old apartment. Living there had taught me how to identify crazies from a distance. It's funny but I was almost grateful to the strange woman in that moment, because she gave me something to think about besides myself, something to focus on as I fought the second wave of nausea. She had almost reached the end of the platform when it happened, quickly and—I hate to say it—almost gracefully.

A girl across the way, about the same age as the schoolgirls beside me, was holding a heavy backpack and corded to an iPod. She had turned to peer down the tunnel for the train. She was standing so close to the edge. The blonde woman loped up to her, seized her by her shoulders, brought her face into the girl's hair, as smoothly and easily as if they were old friends embracing. The girl let out a shriek, and my head snapped up on my shoulders, my heart racing. By then the blonde was holding her at the edge, the girl's body seeming to dangle there on the lip of the platform, her dark backpack and dark hair nearly hanging over those black tracks. Then the blonde businesswoman reared back, the white bow of her blouse suddenly blurred by blood. As she reeled she dropped the girl abruptly onto the tracks. The girl hit the metal with a frank thud, and the shrieking stopped. Just like that. The pack with its weight fell over the girl's head.

Upstairs by the turnstiles, the karaoke lady kept warbling for quarters to an anemic music track, oblivious. It was some old show tune—maybe "Happy Talk" from *South Pacific*, I think now.

On the opposite platform, figures rushed away from the scene like a herd moving together from danger.

A woman on our side yelled for someone to get the attendant. All eyes were on the girl, though, and in contrast to those on the opposite platform, our crowd seemed frozen. I know I felt that way. For several heartbeats I just stood there.

Then cellphones came out into palms, and people punched into them, some reticently, some frantically. The punching continued for what seemed like forever, but no one lifted a device to an ear. Lack of reception. A couple of the high school kids didn't even bother trying to phone; instead, they held up their devices and calmly filmed.

An older gentleman in a suit rushed forward from our platform, hand out. "Here, here!" he yelled. The girl on the tracks had pushed herself up on her hands now and was struggling to regain her feet. But she didn't look in his direction. Her iPod. She still had her ears stopped with music. Behind her, the blonde was laughing, a kind of chortle that woke up my body and propelled it toward the tracks. The next thing I knew, I was kneeling beside the man in the suit, and both of us had our hands out. A third guy joined us. I could feel the LEGO-like bumps of the safety strip digging into my knees.

"Let them work it out," a voice said behind us. "They probably know each other."

I couldn't freaking believe that. Farther down the platform, although I can't say for sure, I thought I heard the words *cat fight.* The people behind me were muttering, rationalizing. I turned and—I'll never forget this, although it was just a split-second glimpse—saw a barrel-chested guy about my age pushing an oversize hero sandwich into a mouth not large enough to encompass it. This guy, he stared at the scuffle, chewing as if he were at a main event. A pair of mirrored sunglasses hung from the collar of a T-shirt that said, in letters so large I caught them without trying, *Just Pretend I'm Not Here.* He kept chewing. It makes me shudder even now. I turned my head quickly back, heat prickling through me.

The girl, by this point, was limping across the rails, bleeding from her shins through her white socks, which were also streaked with dirt. Because I was the one on my knees, closest to her level, it was my hand she reached for, and as I leaned out, I felt one of the men next to me slip his arms around my waist to give me support and balance. The suited man reached out and grabbed her other hand. Her hands were small. Her eyes dark, full of fear. I could feel her breath wrench through her in small gasps, and I caught the tinny smell of her saliva. Then she kind of . . . Yes, she put one foot against the wall to spring up, but her fingers—her fingers were slick with sweat and slipped from mine, and she fell.

There was a stomping sound—the blonde had jumped onto the tracks. She was wearing those white trainers on her feet, so she crossed the gap quickly, and the girl too was now moving quickly. The girl grabbed the lip of the platform with one hand and the suited man's hand with the other. She swung a leg up and her sneaker glanced the yellow safety stripe before it slid off. The blonde had her by her skirt's waistband, and the girl was going from us—going, slipping away. We watched as it happened. The whole platform watched. The two women stumbled, tall and short, blonde and dark, old and young, struggling, over the closest tracks and onto the other set. The girl, she was fighting all the way, and she managed to jab a fist upward into the blonde's throat, but the blonde had her now by the hair—I mean fistfuls of it—and was dragging her, a mad determination on her face.

Then there was a light in the tunnel, coming closer on our side.

One of the men still had his arm around me, something I didn't realize until he pulled me back, hard, and we landed together on our butts on the platform. A huge simultaneous shout went up from the crowd on our platform, and I didn't know why, except that the train had pulled in. The guy and I just sat there blinking at each other. He'd had his arm round me the whole time, but I hadn't even looked at him before that moment. He was short but beefy, wearing a Mets ball cap.

"What happened?" I asked.

"I—I don't know," he said.

If I close my eyes, I can still hear his voice and see his face. He had clear brown eyes and a crewcut with a bit of gel at the front beneath the cap. He wore a white T-shirt with a small gold cross on a chain.

The train doors started opening and people were climbing off. We were lost in their legs, and they didn't seem to understand, pause, or stop. It was such a mess. Someone stepped on my hand and it hurt, and I had to skitter backward, crab-style. Then we heard it. I could see it on this guy's face the exact second I heard it: the thundering.

Somewhere behind our train, somewhere we couldn't see, a train was coming from the other direction.

The guy beside me swore in Spanish. He and I both stared at the tracks. We could see windows through windows, the second train through our train. We could see the shapes of people riding on the train like an ordinary fact. Red shirts, blue jackets, white skin, brown skin, backs of heads, hands wrapped around poles.

"I had her," the older man in the suit said as he regained his footing against one of the posts. "She was right here." He held out his hand to us, peering at it. He looked like any businessman. He had silver hair on his knuckles and a thick gold ring with a tiger's eye or topaz embedded in the middle.

"I had her," he said again, and he continued to say it, staring at the hand.

The young guy said something in Spanish again, then glanced around us. "My bag . . ." He became distressed. He must have put his knapsack down. It was gone, long gone. You wouldn't think he would care at that point, but he got up and began to jog down the platform, weaving, glaring at those he passed as if he would recover his bag from them then and there. But the crowd—our original crowd—had meshed with the exiting passengers. Some were left, I guess, standing in shock, while others had already boarded the train. I could still feel the guy's arm around my waist where he had grabbed me to try to help, yet there he went, already disappearing up the stairs, taking them two and three at a time.

Our train pulled out, and when it did, it left behind the train on the opposite tracks. At first I saw nothing—I guess I was looking for blood—then I saw the thin white string of wire, just a piece of it, twelve inches or so, the cord of the iPod headset lying nearly under the silver body of the train. I couldn't help it. My gaze fastened to the small round earbud, no bigger than a penny, and the other severed end. That was when I threw up.

Maybe the acrid smell of human vomit had more effect than violence, because the platform cleared quickly. By then, two cops had swung down the stairs. Beside me, the older man in the grey suit was still saying, "I had her . . ."

He was going into what had already become a story. Some onlookers gathered in one area of the platform to talk over one another and continue to be part of the scene. Vultures. The high school girls were gone, I realized, in spite of wearing similar uniforms to that of the girl who had disappeared on the tracks. But the submarine sandwich guy was still there— although, wouldn't you know, the sandwich had vanished.

A lady cop was bellowing, "If ya witnessed the incident and have something to report, please wait. Otherwise, we ask that ya go about your business!"

New passengers were arriving, coming down the stairs, people who had no idea and were impatient to get where they were going, asking what had happened—*was it a flasher?*—or slinking with skeptical glances away from the commotion toward the non-puke part of the platform.

And then I had a terrible thought: *Eventually that train, that train right there, is gonna move.* And probably not even eventually, but soon. I didn't want to be there when it did. Every part of my body said, *Go.* I found that my purse was still strung over one shoulder, between my breasts, and before the officers even glanced in my direction, I stumbled up the stairs and out into the daylight, saying, "I need air. Excuse me, pardon me. Sorry. Excuse me."

Someone said, "Ma'am!" behind me, and it might even have been the lady cop, but I just kept going as if the voice didn't apply to me.

I remember walking so fast I was practically running, past dollar stores that sell postcards of the Chrysler Building and coffee cups with pictures of the Statue of Liberty. I stalked through rush-hour intersections like a seasoned pro, and cabs and limos burst forth from one-ways and honked. I flew up my street like a kid chased home after school, up the stairs to the fourth floor before I remembered I was now down on three, and finally managed to get my key into the door, and landed face down on my bed. Through the parted velvet peach curtains, evening bled a gentle stain of light. I must have lain immobile for an hour or more. Then I curled onto my side, and stared at the sky above the courtyard until it greyed and sleep crashed into me.

THREE

THERE ARE WORSE CIRCUMSTANCES in which to be born, my little womb-raider. This is what I tell myself. You will not be a child of war, for instance, just a child of plague. You'll be *Babe of the Plague*, like a character in an old horror movie such as *Children of the Corn* or *Child's Play 3: Look Who's Stalking*. You see? I still have a sense of humour. If I think too much about the pandemic, I become frightened, and I worry that you can feel my fear, that fear is in the blood. That's why I'm going to keep my sense of humour, keep talking, keep moving around this little room. Until Grace comes back, *if* Grace comes back—and I wouldn't blame her if she doesn't—I have all the time in the world, and nothing left to do but this.

For a while after I found out about you I was making lists of names—not that I can imagine you ever having a proper birth certificate. And not that I can imagine you being alive long enough to learn your own name. But the lists were a welcome distraction. At one point I toyed with Carlotta, after Karl, but then I decided you should have an identity all your own. When I say your name, I want you to feel there is only love behind it, no conflict. There should be no trace of the dead or the damaged hanging over you.

Every time I come up with an option these days, it sounds like a dog's or cat's name. Or the name of a Southern belle. Or else it's Scottish, and am I really going to saddle you with my ancestry when I don't even know my own father? Hippie names are out, because do you want to be named Ocean, Sapphire, or Harmony after age twenty, if by some miracle we all live that long? At that point, you might as well sign up to be a stripper. Gender-neutral names are off the list too, because I can't think of a single one that rolls off the tongue.

If you survive, the world you grow up in will be one that has experienced intense panic and distrust, violence and hysteria—though that's a loaded word. I don't think I would have used it before this past year. But now? All of us living with a disease that affects only girls and women? *Hysteria* is so bang on.

As outrageous as the news reports were, and the solutions and proposals of their talking heads, I miss them. We lost our cable signal the fourth week after I arrived here at the cottage. Grace had just finished putting on her makeup and had sunk into Karl's chair. I remember I was heading into the bathroom when she shouted out, "Fuck me, fucking, come on, you lame little ass-wipe, come on—"

I came back out immediately to see what had happened. Grace jabbed her fingers over the remote, got up and toggled buttons, but to no avail. The television remained—and continues to remain—blank.

Grace is so paranoid. Before we lost the signal, she'd already cancelled the mail and her magazine subscriptions, because even though the mailbox is out by the road and therefore safely away from the house, she saw a woman driving the delivery truck one morning. She freaked, saying, "What if that woman becomes contagious? What if she comes up to the door to ask for a signature for something?" And so Grace used the wall phone to call the post office in town.

Just like that, news of the outside world disappeared and Grace replaced television with drinking. She had a case of wine and a few bottles of whisky stashed around the cottage, as if she'd known that day might come. There are still a couple bottles left, and sometimes I'm *tempted* to take the edge off, let me tell you. But I won't. I won't, for your sake. I offered to go into town and get the newspaper or ask someone what's happening in the world—maybe buy us some milk other than Carnation canned, fresh bread instead of frozen, restock the eggs—but Grace just shook her head. "And take my car?" she'd asked haughtily, begging for argument.

She told me to take some of her vitamins in the medicine cabinet "for the baby." I guess it was big of her to share them, all things considered. I have to take two a day for you to get everything you need, though I didn't tell Grace that. The contents don't have the amount of folic acid required, according to the pamphlets I got from Nurse Ben, forever ago now. To be on the safe side, I pop one vitamin every morning with dry cereal and one at night with supper, which tonight will be canned green beans and maybe a hot dog from the freezer. I am in the heartburn stage of the pregnancy, but you need the protein.

You want to go outside, my little goiter? Have a look at that satellite dish? If we could get the TV signal back, I'd feel so much better—maybe the panic would stop. Maybe someone on that illuminated screen would say something smart for once, about what is causing the Blonde Fury and what is being done to contain it, and everything would click into place.

Too high. But I think there's a ladder in the shed.

Rickety thing. This would be great, just great, if I fall off this stepladder in the snow and hit my head. That'd be a crazy way to go out after everything we've been through.

I shouldn't have done that. The satellite dish was icy and I tried to chip away at some of it with an old broom handle, but I didn't think about what it means to stand on a ladder and work above your head while carrying a giant kettle on your front that weighs an extra twenty-five pounds. Yes, I'm talking to you. You're like a little pasta pot. Fuck, I don't believe this. Still no signal.

Well, I guess there's nothing to do but continue telling you my story. Our story. Lucky you.

All the New York dailies carried articles about the subway attack. The news was up on their sites only hours after the incident had happened. In some cases it was the lead. This shouldn't have surprised me, and I guess it didn't really, but still. It made me feel numb.

The papers said that by the time the police arrived at the station, the worst had already occurred. They said that a seemingly unprovoked attack had left Eugenia Gilongos, seventeen, dead. Eugenia. That was her name. It is a beautiful name. But for the reasons I've already noted, it won't be yours.

Eugenia's photograph seemed to spring from my computer, taking up half the screen. It was eerie, a two-dimensional school picture—eerie to have seen the real girl, grasped her hand. She was younger in the photo, and her hair was different. She was wearing a band behind her bangs and her hair was curled. She had on an Oxford shirt, maybe the same kind as she was wearing that day, her school uniform. She wore a small pendant, a heart or a cross or something. She was smiling, a shy smile. I could already imagine the tribute page in the high school yearbook. I scrolled down my computer screen to avoid looking any longer.

The woman who attacked Eugenia had not yet been identified, but the articles included her photo. It's funny how a photo stays with you. Sontag said, "Images transfix. Images anesthetize." Aesthetology would agree. And there, as evidence, was the grainy surveillance image of the attacker: a smear of pixels, a tight mouth and chin, waves of hair. Police were urging the public to come forward to identify her.

The first report I read confirmed that Eugenia and her attacker had perished beneath the oncoming train. Police said the girl died instantly. Those of us who had tried to help were referenced as "strangers"—"Strangers attempted to pull the teenager to safety."

The man I'd taken for a businessman was quoted. He was a lawyer in his fifties named . . . Hoagland, that's what it was. And he said much the same thing he'd said on the platform, as if he'd become stuck permanently on those words: "I had her. She caught my hand, but then she slipped away. I grabbed her again and then she was gone—just like that. I can still feel her."

The article was written in short, clipped sentences. A statement of facts.

Eugenia's parents, Mr. and Mrs. Gilongos, were Filipino. She was their only daughter. She'd gone to the Fashion District with her friends after school. The reports speculated that she had parted ways from the other teenagers before the attack occurred. She was an honour roll student. She was Catholic, and very involved in her church. She also played volleyball for her school team and loved dancing. She had a younger brother who was quoted saying something about her belief in God, that she was with Him now.

Witnesses gave conflicting reports about whether the teenager and her attacker knew each other, but police said it was unlikely given the age discrepancy and cultural differences. What else can I tell you? Apparently some witnesses said the woman had first hugged the teenager, then pushed her onto the subway tracks. The detective called the incident "strange." I remember he said that the person who had done this might have been emotionally or mentally unstable; there was no way of knowing at such an early point in the investigation. The tone of the reports was both cold and indignant, the way articles of that sort always are; there were statements about how young people should be safe at four in the afternoon. The MTA advised passengers to always stand well back from the tracks, to remain alert and aware, to disable audio devices while in transit. Most of the articles speculated that the attack might stir discussion over MTA safety barriers.

You have to remember this was before anyone knew that the attack would not be an isolated incident.

Another article claimed that the women were together, that the older woman had "helped Gilongos onto the tracks" and "joined" her there, and that police had not yet ruled out an association between them. Still another claimed that double suicide was a possibility. Gilongos had been "embraced, then thrown," "dropped," "lowered," "punched," "forced," and in one report, quite accurately as it turned out, "bitten and tossed away."

Late into the night I was swimming in information, none of it illuminating. Eugenia was elusive. She liked cats and her favourite subject was math. I wondered, *Is this how we summarize a human life—with cheap speculation and lists of hobbies?*

It was then that Moira reappeared. I heard the outer door to the alcove scrape open, followed by footsteps. A weight paused in the hall, and then came a soft *rat-a-tat* tap.

"I saw your light," Moira said when I answered the door. She had an instrument case with her. She looked tired and smelled faintly of juniper, likely the after-effect of several gin and tonics.

"Come in," I urged.

She did, but lingered just inside the door and didn't set down her case. She was wearing a long dress and strappy sandals. The lights in my room were blazing, and I realized for the first time that she was black, or more likely half-black. I'd been too self-involved before to notice.

Moira said she'd just wanted to check how I was doing.

"I think I'm in shock," I told her.

She nodded and said that was natural. Then she asked if I had called "him" yet, and I realized she meant Karl. We were talking about two entirely different things. I reached over and flicked the laptop shut. I didn't want her to see it. I had unburdened myself to her enough already.

"What's that?" I pointed to her case.

"Glockenspiel."

"Will you show me?"

Moira held the case out and pulled at the edges, producing fold-up legs. She opened the case, and it was now a stand. Two sets of slim metal bars gleamed inside. I wasn't sure about the difference between a xylophone and a glockenspiel, and I admitted as much to Moira. I told her I'd thought that the glockenspiel had tubes hanging from it. Although I supposed it was wrong to engage in small talk after everything that had happened that day, I found myself doing it without guilt.

"Now you're thinking of a marimba," Moira said. "Xylophones are wooden. Glockenspiels have metal bars. Marimbas have the resonating tubes. They're more for orchestral performances." She told me she had one at home, but not a good one, since a good one cost as much as a piano.

I asked Moira where she was from.

Buffalo and Richmond, she told me. Her parents had split and she lived with her "mum"—which is how she said it, with a soft *u*—but sometimes spent summers with her father in Virginia. Moira did a lot of travelling. Drifting, she called it. I remember that I felt a flicker of excitement—now I had met someone while travelling, and that meant I was a real traveller too. Moira had studied music in school, and she performed with various art groups and experimental ensembles, mostly in galleries. I could hardly believe she roamed across the country by herself. When she was in Buffalo she tended bar because it was flexible and she could easily get away for days at a time. She'd had just the one performance in New York, so far—"And it paid," she said. I remember her raising her expressive caterpillar eyebrows in amazement at this. She said she would be back to play again in the city in a couple of weeks.

I told her I wished I could've seen the performance and asked if she would play something for me.

"The glockenspiel makes a pretty penetrating sound," she said, and made a worried shape with her mouth. It was after one in the morning on a Thursday. But she'd been standing behind the instrument, as if about to play, since I had first asked her about it. "I'm sure there are other guests here, aren't there?" she added, uncertainly.

I didn't say anything as Moira turned and closed the door

to my room. She picked up the mallets. Her face took on a look of concentration.

When she struck the first bar, it was as if a bell had been shaken in the small room. The song progressed, flute-like and tinkling, almost a lullaby. She used hard, quick-moving mallets, and eased from the vibrating bars a timbre that reminded me of running water. Blue-green was the only way to describe the sound, and reclining on the bed, I closed my eyes. A few moments later, the song became more percussive. The floor shook with thumps from an irate neighbour. The instrument hiccupped a couple of final notes, as if Moira wanted to fit them in, then stopped suddenly.

I opened my eyes.

"*Glockenspiel* literally means 'hitting of one body against another.' Well, actually that's not true," Moira amended. Her voice was softer than before, perhaps from concentrating on the music. "It means 'playing of bells,' but the hitting definition is in there somewhere too. Germans!" Her eyes were downcast, fixed on the gleaming instrument.

"That was . . . breathtaking."

The corners of Moira's mouth curled into a wry, half-hearted smile. "That song's called 'Plastic.' Usually the glockenspiel is amplified and I use a delay pedal."

It took me a second to realize that she was apologizing—that she felt the song hadn't sounded quite the way it was supposed to, that I'd somehow been cheated.

I laughed, the sound startling me. "Call it whatever you want," I told her. "It was great."

Sometimes, Moira told me, she played with art-school bands. She listed a flurry of names—none of them recognizable to me. As she tucked the mallets away, a gold cord caught my eye. Attached to one end of it was a shape the size of a dollar coin, slightly thicker, flat and shiny. The apparatus lay in a crevice of the case. It reminded me of Eugenia's earbud.

"I've been thinking of aborting," I told Moira from the bed, where I was still sitting akimbo. "What's that?" I gestured to the cord.

"This?" She held it up, the gold circle dangling. She didn't seem fazed by anything, and I decided I really admired that about her. "It's a contact microphone. It catches the sound directly from the instrument's body." Moira efficiently inserted the contact mic back in its place. "I have a friend in Brooklyn. She might be able to help you find a clinic. She's been here a while. In Williamsburg. I don't know if she knows these things or not, but she might." She closed the case. "What's your last name? So she can get in touch with you?"

"Hayes."

Moira repeated it. "Hayes. Hazel Hayes. *H-A-Y-E-S*?"

I nodded.

I had noticed she did that: repeated things, or sometimes said them out of sequence, like that morning when she'd told me "Here" before she brought me the toilet paper to wipe my nose. I wondered if it was a musician thing, something to do with timing and thought processes. Or maybe she was just a little drunk and tired.

I thought about the fact that Moira hadn't told me not to abort. She hadn't offered advice either way.

"Have—?" I began. "Have you ever—?" I let the words hang.

Even if I'd had the words right then, whoops and hollers interrupted me from the window. It was noise carrying from the gay bar on the street out front. A man with a shrill voice screamed, mock-seriously, "Come on, bitch. I dare you, I dare you!" It was that time in the morning when people had drunk or inhaled too much and were being pulled home by their friends.

Moira gathered her hair between her hands and pushed it back behind her neck. She peered at me. "Wait . . ." She gestured vaguely, one hand extended, moving in circles. "Something's different. Glasses—no, you did have those this morning." I could see her squinting, cataloguing me.

"My hair."

"How was it before?"

"Brown."

"Brown, brown. And now you're red. Here—" She came around to the front of the glockenspiel and reached toward me. She plucked a lock of hair between her fingers. "It's coarse, but not as coarse as mine." She let the section fall.

I told her I had used lye once to tame it. The first time it straightened my hair and gave me slick baby-doll locks. The second time it gave my hair a plastic texture every time it got wet, and strands broke off when I tried to run a comb through them. My mother had cried to see me. Eventually I had shaved all my hair off in one go.

"Wash it as infrequently as possible, or use conditioner instead of shampoo," Moira said, nodding.

I didn't tell her my mom cut hair for a living. I didn't tell her about the eggy fumes of perm solutions that were the smell of my childhood, or that I had heard every piece of hair advice there was as if it were gospel.

"The other thing you can do is gather it in a ponytail and just wash the outside strands," she continued.

Then, as if the alcohol had caught up with her, Moira swayed and moved away. She retreated from the bed and closed up the glockenspiel for the night, as if putting a bird to sleep by covering its cage. "I'm sad to say I leave early tomorrow morning." She folded up the legs of the makeshift pedestal and snapped them into place so that the whole contraption was just a briefcase again. She held out her hand to me, and we shook. She had calluses on her fingers.

I suppose if Moira hadn't stopped by my room that night I might have phoned someone, crying, to talk about the pregnancy, the girl I'd seen killed. I might have had less pride. But Moira calmed me. When I look back it's easy to hypothesize about the course my life might have taken. I might have made it back here sooner, and Karl and I might even have worked things out, one way or another, together. But who knows? Maybe if I'd left the city sooner, I'd have wound up somewhere else, the wrong place at the wrong time. Maybe I would have contracted the virus myself. Maybe I'd have landed in one of those wards Moira later told me about . . .

Because, as it turned out, the second attack had already occurred.

I woke the next morning to find a business card lying on the grey carpet, just inside the door. It had been slipped under. *Moira Clemmons*, it said. There was a website address and a woodcut image of a glockenspiel in green ink. On the flipside she had written in ballpoint pen, *My friend in Brooklyn,* and an email address. She had big, neat bubble penmanship, the kind that popular girls have in tenth grade. I ran my thumb along the edge of the paper stock, then tucked the card into my wallet.

I was at the New York Public Library when I found out about the second blonde incident. I couldn't concentrate on my thesis, though I'd gone there with that intent. The entire time I'd been in Manhattan I'd been flipping through magazines, stopping at spreads by Gucci or Bulgari, and writing down random phrases such as *The machine of gender, Beauty as its own language, The wealth of youth, The "wet look" of women in fragrance, Nautical-scarved superwomen,* and *Androgyny in advertising in the age of HIV.* I had three dozen scraps of paper with these nonsensical snippets on them. The thesis was a year in progress and I still hadn't written anything beyond scraps. Let me tell you, what I'd write now would be much more cohesive. Women and vanity? Ways of looking at women? After these past seven months every human left on Earth has become a women's studies major. We women matter. We are the discourse on a twenty-four-hour news cycle because we are dangerous.

But back on that day I was browsing the newspapers instead of writing my thesis. I quickly found a more comprehensive article about the subway attack. Coworkers and associates had identified the blonde business-woman. Her name was Alexis Hoff. She was forty-eight, an advertising executive. Her assistant reported that she had torn a whiteboard off its stand and thrown it at a trash can before storming out around two-thirty that afternoon. Her face had turned haggard and her eyes bloodshot. Nothing had prompted the outburst, and those who witnessed it had assumed she was having a personal problem. Her assistant said that Ms. Hoff had breezed in "acting like her usual self" that morning, but by noon had asked for Tylenol for headaches and had begun mumbling nonsensically. She had passed on lunch, saying she had no appetite, and had "seemed a little edgy or paranoid," but the assistant had not thought it his business to ask if anything was wrong. A fellow ad exec had expressed his grief at the—and I quote—"bizarre incident that resulted in the loss of one of our finest." The company's official statement was that although Ms. Hoff certainly could have a powerful presence, the company had never seen her act violently—that the acts she had been accused of, if indeed true, were highly out of character. They could only assume she had been delirious and in need of medical attention.

Ms. Hoff was a Harvard graduate, and spent her free time with her two Weimaraners, who were her pride and joy. She was close with her parents, who declined to comment. Her sister said, "We're grieving. You need to know Alex was a good woman." I remember that quote was highlighted in a big call-out font: *She was a good woman.* "She wouldn't harm anyone," the sister continued. "This is not her fault."

It made me feel cheap: reading about the previous day's incident, like a tourist of tragedy. Beneath the table I pushed my hand along my belly to quell my nausea.

News of the second attack was buried, and it was a while before I discovered it. Titled "Blonde Fury," it was not much more than a bit wedged between local shootings, arrests, train and automobile accidents, and ads for the New York Diamond Exchange. That catchphrase, *blonde fury*, wasn't widely used yet—or not that I knew. This was the first time I saw it.

The previous evening, at six o'clock, in an upscale Midtown hair salon called Humble & Tumble, a client had brutally attacked her stylist. Halfway through a bleaching session, the stylist had been blinded with his own chemical potion. Three other hairdressers rushed to subdue the client, who grabbed a hot flatiron, yanked it from the wall, and began beating them with it. One stylist was rendered unconscious by a forceful blow with a hairdryer. Police arrived after the stylists and their other clients had hastily left the premises. The attacker was easy to identify by her erratic behaviour and the purple vinyl smock still fastened around her neck. In apprehending her, one of the officers sustained minor cuts and lacerations. Two stylists were treated for minor burns and released, but the main victim was still in critical condition with chemical burns to his face and eyes.

So now it was blondes, plural.

My eyes raced to the top of the page, where the day's date was printed. I walked out of the DeWitt Wallace Periodical Room, down the hallway, and outside as fast as I could without making Security nervous. On the steps, under the disapproving gaze of a stone lion, I fished my cellphone out of my bag. I had already missed two calls from an unknown number.

The first message was from Dr. Wanda Kovacs. We had arranged to meet several times already, but she always cancelled at the last minute via email—something that needled me. She was a busy woman, and one of the few contacts Karl had given me when I told him my plan to apply for funding to go to New York. All he had said about her was "An amazing woman." The rest I'd had to research on my own.

Kovacs possessed a BA in Cultural Studies from Trent University, an MA in Psychology from Cornell, a PhD in Semiotics from Brown, and apparently a soft spot for Karl and for Canadians. Although I was frustrated with the number of times she'd managed to cancel or delay our meetings since my arrival, I'd had no recourse but to persevere. Her tone in emails was always tepid. She was doing me a favour and I was highly aware of it. And now, in an unforgivable fog, I had been the one to miss our appointment entirely. I had believed it was the following day. I'd lost a day, I guess, when I found out about you. Or lost it somewhere between the discovery of you and the subway accident. Or maybe it was a psychological block on my part. I mean, looking back I have to ask myself: How had I gone to the library to work on my thesis on the exact day I was supposed to meet the one contact I had in the city *for* my thesis? There's a name for this kind of slip. I'm sure of it. Freud coined it. *Parapraxis*, that's it. The rest of us call it a major fuck-up.

Kovacs's second message said she was sorry but she was leaving her office. It was nearly one in the afternoon and she'd been expecting me for an hour and a half. I quickly dialled the number she'd left.

"Doc–tor Kovacs," she intoned. Academics who referred to themselves as "Doctor" when they weren't in the classroom made me stutter. And this one drew out the word longer than necessary as if to emphasize her station.

I panted out apologies. "Dr. Kovacs, I'm—I'm so sorry."

To my surprise she responded, "That's all right, dear." I could hear her voice softening with effort, the "dear" tacked on stiffly but not unkindly. "What's happened?"

To my even greater surprise, I realized that my rib cage felt too tight for my lungs. Her answer had been a response to the fact that I was crying.

"Oh gosh," I blubbered, sounding for a moment like my mother, "the subway attack yesterday, the woman and the girl—Eugenia. Have you read about it?"

"I saw it on the news," Dr. Kovacs replied warily.

"I was there."

"I see."

There was another pause. I remember thinking there might be a gap in the connection. Then I realized Kovacs was adjudicating my excuse and measuring the quantity of her own put-out-ness. I watched three Yellow Cabs whoosh through the intersection while I fought to breathe normally.

I must have passed muster and landed in the sympathy pile, because Kovacs finally said, "How awful. Did you have to give a statement?"

I turned away from the traffic, covered one ear with my hand. "Y-yes," I stammered around the lie. "I've just come out of the building," I told her. I *had* come out of *a* building—just not a police station.

"I see," Kovacs said again.

She arranged to meet me at a café near NYU.

Political communication, international communication, communication theory, feminist studies, media and minority, the making of icons, media and activism—thinking of these topics gave me a bubble in my throat, made me choke. I could recite Dr. Wanda Kovacs's areas of interest by heart, yet I had no idea how my thesis fit with them. She had written a much-lauded book on how the beauty ideal repressed the brunette, *Louis B. Mayer and the Making of the Blonde Icon: The Repression of Jewish Identity in Early Hollywood.* Now I had to impress her, and did I even have my notes? I had made them two days earlier, *by hand*, in preparation, but when I dug in my bag there was no spiral notebook. I had intended to type up and flesh out the notes the day before. There were reams of them on that old laptop—about fifty Word docs on different topics, all as disjointed as the individual phrases I had scrawled while flipping through magazines—but I couldn't show Kovacs those. Of course I had an earlier draft of something I'd prepared for one of our meetings that hadn't happened, but the last time I'd looked at it, the thesis had seemed insipid and wandering. Now, standing in the sunlight, I said to myself, *I need a phrase, just a few phrases that will sum it up*—something, in other words, that would stun and dazzle.

I was now bringing up balls of old Kleenex from the side pocket of my laptop bag, crunching them under my glasses, against my eyes, and swiping at my nose. I'd never been so emotional. Before I knew it I'd found *Karl Mann* in my phone's directory and dialled. I just needed to be told what to say. A line, a phrase. What was my thesis about anyway? Calling my thesis adviser at a time like that was *advisable*.

"Hello—" a high, flat female voice said, and I stopped, frozen. I'd done something I had never done before: phoned Karl's home instead of his cell.

"Grace and Karl aren't here right now . . ." the voice continued, to my massive relief.

I let out a breath, and cursed myself for having punched the number into my phone directory.

"If you have the Collingwood number, you can reach them there."

Them? She referred to the two of them in the third person? Yes, she did. She really did. Grace freaking Pargetter. Because I hadn't met her yet, she was a different Grace then—faraway and pristine. As soon as I heard her voice, I could see her blonde, choppy haircut and her axe-like face in my mind, even though I had spotted her only once before—way down at the end of the hall in front of Karl's office, leaning her weight back on one brown heel. The *wife*. I stabbed the cellphone off and experienced what was perhaps my finest New York moment. I paced to the curb, shot up my arm, and hailed a Yellow Cab, praying it would not get stuck in traffic and drain me of the meagre funds in my wallet.

Thankfully, it did not. Rush hour would have been another story, but even so, taxis cost less in the Big Apple than they do in Toronto. That's right, you're kicking. You know that this is something you might need to know one day. If we ever go back to civilization. If we survive.

I know. I promised you I wouldn't do this again, but here I am, outside in the cold. If I can just get the satellite dish to turn, I feel like the signal will come back on. It's worth trying. Steady, and . . . Shit, it's cold. If I can use my glove to— What's that sound?

The mail truck. *Oh.* Why is she swerving like that, like she's drunk, like— It's that same delivery woman. Damn, I can't believe it. Grace was right. Yeah, yeah, baby, I know. I'm going. I'm climbing down. Slowly, carefully. We're going to run back inside. Look at her go. Holy frig! It's like she isn't even seeing what's in front of her. She just took out the neighbour's mailbox as if she were driving over a soda can. That must be what I heard before. I'm surprised she hasn't wound up in the ditch. Don't wind up in the ditch, please don't wind up in the ditch—I don't want to have to make a decision about whether or not to help. Good, just go. Go. Wow.

We can't get a signal out of the satellite, but if *that* isn't another kind of signal, I don't know what is. And don't worry, baby, I'm not going back outside again—not today, anyway.

FOUR

HERE'S WHAT I SHOULD TELL YOU about Dr. Kovacs before I get to the story of our meeting: the thing about Kovacs is that she did try to help me. But here's the other thing: if I hadn't met her that day, I wouldn't have been so angry with Karl. And if I hadn't been so angry, our lives, mine and yours, might have taken a different path. That said, it's easy to look at the what-ifs or trace an alternative route after the fact, isn't it, my little hatchling?

Kovacs, sitting in the booth of the restaurant that day, had the bearing of someone who had been waiting half the afternoon and had reached her last shred of patience. I remember how her mouth turned downward in a slightly constipated way. Here was this tall woman, chiselled chin emerging from a sleek white-blonde bob, white eye shadow and black mascara highlighting dark eyes. Dramatic, my mom would have said. Kovacs's long manicured nails were wrapped around a half-empty glass of red wine. I stopped partway to the booth. She hadn't spotted me yet. In the black-and-white photo on her department webpage, she'd looked silver-haired. I hadn't anticipated that she would be blonde. Although her head had clearly been assisted to such levels of luminosity, there was no doubt that she was naturally blonde. This is what gave me pause: I wasn't sure what a blonde would make of my thesis. Would she find that it perpetuated stereotypes, even though I was attempting to dismantle them? (Most models in advertisements are blonde—or they were back then.)

I also had a hard time marrying this woman in front of me to her work. Kovacs's thesis focused on the early men of Hollywood, how they—insecure about their Jewish culture, concerned about class, and about appearing aristocratic—turned away from the thick-tressed, dark-haired beauties of the silent film era to the blonde starlets, who would pervade pop culture ever after. They selected small-nosed, pale-skinned lovelies as a standard for the silver screen, and any mark of originality was cut away, surgically removed or dieted off with the help of doctors on the studios' lots.

One of the men she wrote about was Louis B. Mayer, who grew up in Saint John, New Brunswick, the son of Russian-Jewish immigrants. By the age of seven he was a full-time scrap collector, supporting his family by salvaging and selling odd pieces of metal. Kovacs's description had made quite an impression on me; I imagined a small frame tottering through cobblestone streets and dirt lanes, forty pounds of odds and ends hanging on the child's back. Mayer was a constant truant from school, lugging sharp, unwieldy objects in a red metal wagon. In my mind, he took on the shape and grubbiness of an eighteenth-century London, England, bone-collector or rag-picker. In spite of his dedication to his work, he was mocked by his teachers and beaten by his father for being overly ambitious. Silent films arrived in Saint John in 1897, and Mayer, age twelve, was enthralled by them. Scrap sales would give him the means to sign the cheque on his first theatre, then a chain of small theatres in the American Northeast. In—let's see, was it 1918?—1918, only twenty-one years after viewing his first silent film, he would open his first production, starring Hedda Hopper and Anita Stewart, having realized that making films to put in one's own theatre would yield a higher profit than simply securing a film from a distributor to show. That same year he moved to Los Angeles, and soon the studio MGM was born, and with it, the star system.

Tell me, how do I remember all these facts when I forget the names of actors I once liked? That's the life of a Cultural and Communication Studies major, my little grub. Pure facts and chance of memory. Some of us are better at it than others. Or maybe it just goes to show you how diligently I studied Kovacs's work. She had a fascinating way of telling the stories of the silent film stars who moved into talkies—the dark-haired leading ladies such as Greta Garbo, Norma Shearer, Joan Crawford, and Hedy Lamarr. But in the '30s and '40s the movie business turned away from anything "ethnic." Now came the blondes: Anita Page, Jean Harlow, June Allyson, Lana Turner, Ingrid Bergman, Janet Leigh. Even indisputably striking women like Ava Gardner were under threat: MGM attempted to manipulate her into erasing her chin dimple to render her into a more generic, from-the-mould beauty. She refused.

No wonder I was shocked to discover the author of this essential tome was of that very class of beauty she seemed to disdain. Or maybe I was simply afraid of beautiful people. Maybe that's what my thesis was really about, and why I hadn't been able to put my thoughts down in words.

Kovacs looked up and saw me hovering a distance from the booth. She rose as I approached, and put her hand out to shake. My grip was sweaty and soft. I fumbled with my bag and sat down.

"Well, what has Dr. Diclicker sent me?" she said, bemused.

"Ex—excuse me?"

"Sorry. Dr. Mann." Kovacs waved a hand. "Diclicker. Diclicker *was* his name, such a long time ago. He changed it, you know, during his master's. After Mann, the German novelist—"

"Thomas Mann?"

"No. Heinrich. Wrote a novel called *Professor Unrat*, which was adapted into Germany's first sound film in 1930, *The Blue Angel*. It was Marlene Dietrich's first major role. Karl wrote his master's about it, before moving on to that . . . Howdy Doody shoot-'em-up stuff for his doctorate."

Karl's thesis was *Self-Aware Masculinity in the Late American Western*.

"But Dietrich was always *my* territory, hmm." She paused. "I wonder. Do you think our Karl was competing with me or trying to impress me? I guess he just didn't want to be Dr. Dick-lick-er." She stressed each syllable. "I cannot fault him."

I *had* known Karl changed his surname. But he'd never told me what it was originally. He'd said, "At a certain point in your life, you have to make a break with the past to become your own person." I tried out his name in my mind as if trying to fit a square peg in a round hole: *Karl Diclicker, Karl Diclicker, Karl Mann.*

I opened my laptop bag and set up the computer on the table between me and Kovacs. I remember she whisked her wineglass far to one side, as if concerned I would accidentally topple it.

A waiter came and I asked for a menu.

Kovacs told me to have a drink with her. "It will settle you," she said, and the matter was decided. She ordered another glass of red for herself, though she hadn't finished the first.

"I'm really not sure I should drink," I protested, but the server had already turned away.

"It sounds like you've been through a lot, dear," Kovacs said, but the "dear" again struck my ear as glacial.

I told myself this was the way accomplished women her age spoke, with distance and sheen. She had a slight accent, and I suddenly recalled Karl saying that she was Polish, that she had come to Canada at sixteen. Now the fact that Kovacs was blonde made sense.

"Let's not start with that." Kovacs indicated the computer with a wave of her hand as if it were a distasteful thing.

I nodded for the second or third time.

She squinted at me and asked me how old I was. "Twenty-five?" she guessed. She didn't wait for me to nod or correct her, and I wasn't about to. She asked me where I'd studied. No, wait—I remember she made an assumption, asking if I'd studied entirely in Toronto. She said the word *Toronto* with some disdain, as if even the name of the city was off-putting.

"I did my BA in Communications in Windsor, Ontario," I told her.

"I know that Windsor is in Ontario. I lived in your country for seven years, hmm." She tacked on *hmm*'s for emphasis. Everything about her had emphasis, from her eyeliner to her phrases. "There it sits, across the border from Detroit. Such an *absolutely* ruined city."

The drinks arrived and she finished her first glass efficiently but elegantly and handed it to the server.

"Windsor," she said, attempting to find the conversation's thread again. "Windsor. And then you moved to Toronto and became acquainted with our Karl."

I nodded. I drank. I reflected that I ought to put more effort into what I was saying if I intended to impress her. Which is funny. It's funny because of how little it ultimately mattered.

I told Kovacs that I liked her book, that I admired its *writerliness*, that it was a crucial work "full of salient details," a phrase Karl used when he was excited about something he'd read. That it was "chatoyant and layered." I was about to launch into how I might reference it in my own work when her look stopped me. She seemed vaguely offended. She cocked her head and her hair swished. It was so shiny, I remember. "Which one?" she said.

I immediately realized my mistake, but I plunged on. "*Make—Making of the Blonde Icon*."

"Ah, the Mayer." And she waved a hand carelessly. "I've had a new one come out."

"I see." For the record: that information hadn't been on the department website.

"Yes, yes, the *New York Times* reviewed it last week, somewhat favourably." She grimaced. "You do read it, don't you?"

I made a mental note to begin buying the paper regularly instead of scanning it irregularly online or in the library. In preparation for this meeting I'd read four hundred and fifty pages on Louis B. Mayer and 1940s Hollywood, even though my own interests were much more contemporary, and Kovacs clearly wasn't impressed. I attempted to plunge into my thoughts on the work anyway. I told her she had "made real the generalizability of beauty." I guess I was thinking if I could say the right thing, prove how thoroughly I'd pored over her book, she would warm to me. But she stopped me again with one look. Actually, it was a looking away. A television was mounted above the bar, its sound turned down. I stopped talking when I saw what was playing.

A jumpy handheld image filled the screen, something recorded on a phone camera. It was shot from the street through a window. It showed a woman in a salon with a purple smock around her neck. Vaguely, we could see a table inside the room, and an elaborate hanging ornament or lighting system above it. The woman was gesturing, clearly agitated, and a man was trying to grab her arm and subdue her. She was tiny. Her hand shot up, grabbed the hi-tech lighting system, and yanked it down on his head. He slumped to the table and then the image shook as if the cameraperson had stumbled backward. I wondered why the cameraperson had begun shooting the scene anyway, but later when I watched it online there was audio and you could hear the woman in the salon shrieking. At any rate, there was a burst of pavement, as if the person recording the scene had decided to retreat, then another image sprang up, this time showing the door of the salon. It was a large overhead hairdryer, I realized, that the woman had pulled down on the man. It wasn't an old-fashioned gun-style dryer like the kind my mom used, the kind I'd imagined from reading the clipping that morning, but something far heavier.

The footage showed several people—men and women— racing out of the salon and out of the frame. The woman followed, half her head covered in white. Bleach. Her mouth had a strange downturn, like she was in pain. She was Asian— Thai, although I didn't know that then. The camera moved as the operator seemed to realize running might be wise. The footage cut, and a news anchor began speaking silently to us.

When I glanced back at Kovacs, she was scrutinizing me.

"You have been quite affected by the accident, haven't you?" Kovacs reached out and patted the back of my hand. "Why don't you tell me about it, since it's in the forefront of your . . . *hmm?*" She gestured to her temporal lobe with her pointer and her pinky finger.

"I have," I said, echoing her syntax.

I recounted what I had seen, and when I finished, I realized my glass was empty and the waiter was replacing it with a second full one. I shouldn't have been drinking, of course—but you'll forgive me, won't you? Many things have happened that weren't meant to.

Kovacs must have been on her third glass, and in stark contrast to the rest of her, her teeth had begun to grey. "Dreadful, dreadful . . ." she murmured. "A dreadful thing." But then she briskly changed gears and said, "Well, shall we?"

It took me a moment to realize she wanted to talk about my thesis. I popped open the file I had prepared the last time we'd planned to meet. It would have to do. I would have to forge on, even though I hadn't eaten enough and the wine had numbed me. I began to read straight from the screen.

"Listen, Hayes," Kovacs interrupted almost immediately, "if your thesis exists only on computer, it doesn't exist. You must know which issues are your focus. Forget the file. Tell me." Her long fingers punctuated the air, waved away my words.

"Okay. It's called *Through a Screen Darkly: Vamps, Tramps, and False Consciousness in Female-Marketed Culture.*"

"Is that really what you want to write about?" Kovacs boomed. The café had begun to get busy with after-work traffic and we had to speak up now over the clatter of plates and the whir of the espresso machine. "I lived through the '70s. You didn't. Don't you think falseness *can* be powerful?"

Aesthetics isn't simple politics, Kovacs said, and she tapped her glass with one fingernail. Why, she asked, did I think she continued to maintain her blondeness at her age? It brought a person things: flattery (she tapped the glass), attention (tap), sexual attention (tap, tap), power (tap), and with power, money (tap). If you come from very little, why give up any privilege? she asked, reclining against the deep red cushions of the dark wood booth.

I had the distinct feeling we were done talking about me and my thesis. Kovacs looked fatigued, and quite a bit older than she had when I'd walked in. I decided that she must be older than Karl by a few years, that he must have been in first year when she was in third or fourth. But just as that occurred to me, a sly smile appeared on her lips.

"Tell me," she murmured, reclining into the cushions, "does Karl's cock still kink to the right?"

"Excu—excuse me?" I stuttered. I felt hives climb my neck. I could tell I was as bright as a tomato.

"Come now," Kovacs said, sipping her wine. "It's an honest question. I thought it, and I asked it. It is what I was honestly wondering . . ." She smiled, tilting the rim of the glass so the last of the liquid swirled lazily around the bottom.

There was a terrible pause, and then without even knowing what I was going to say, I opened my mouth. "Beautiful women," I said, "are full of anger over their privilege. They use deceit as a kind of trade. They receive more attention than other women, and want to be the centre of attention at all times. It's an addiction. And like all addicts, they're controlling and abusive, full of insecurity and rage."

"Oh my," Kovacs said. I think she bit her glass a little. "Is that really what you think? That—*therapy speak*?" Then she waved a finger at me, and peered at me with her dark eyes slit. "Now I see you, Hazel Hayes. Now I see you, Hayes. I see you in there. You were hiding." She set the glass down and we both looked at it rather than at each other. She slid it this way and that on the table like a cat with a mouse. "This is personal for you."

She brought her hand up to her temple and held it there, covering one eye. "This headache, it's the wine. Forgive me . . ."

I raised my arm and signalled the waiter. Paying the bill was the least I could do, given what I'd said. But Wanda Kovacs wouldn't hear of it. Her credit card was on the table before the bill had arrived. The server took it, and as we waited for his return, I shut down my laptop and managed to stammer a weird roundabout apology.

"Please," Kovacs said. "It's been . . . fun." That's the word she used. *Fun.* "You're not at all what I was expecting. You are not like the girls Karl usually sends me."

It was as if she had spit in my face or called me "full-figured." I looked away; I didn't want her to know how she had affected me.

I stared toward the bar. A young woman in a halter dress and heels was arguing with our waiter. She gestured, posture loose, waving an arm at the vodka selection behind him. Bottles of Absolut Citron, Absolut Pears, Absolut Kurant glowed on a sturdy wood bookcase, lit from below—bottles and cocktail glasses round and clear as snow globes. The waiter ignored her. He ran our bill and brought it over. The woman rapped her knuckles on the counter and leaned so far back on one heel I thought it would break. The receipt slid onto the surface between Kovacs and me, and the server dodged away to another table. Kovacs signed it with a flourish and collected her purse.

"This headache," she said again, circling two fingertips against her temple. "I should know better than to start a long weekend this way." I was reminded that we were beginning the Labour Day break—it was almost six months ago now. "Hayes . . . Hazel—" She found her feet, towering to her true height, and extended her hand to me. I took it briefly and briskly. "Nice to meet you. Really." She seemed to mean it.

Kovacs teetered out onto the street and I let her go, watched her fumble for a pair of sunglasses, fit them on her face, veer to the left. I slowly gathered my things and then cloistered myself in the bathroom, where I ran the taps, splashing water on my hot face. *This is personal for you.*

There was a sudden thumping from inside one of the two stalls. The pink door vibrated—a tinny quaking, as if someone had punched it from the inside. A woman's voice cursed repeatedly. I remember thinking how strange it was, how she must have known I was there because I had been running the faucet. Slow and wine-sodden, I stared at the door in the mirror. The paper towel tore off loudly as I wiped my hands quickly and prepared to leave. The door to the stall flew open and the woman, who was about my age, wobbled out on peek-toe heels. She had an anchor tattooed on her ankle and bright red lipstick, and she looked drunk. She was the one who had been standing at the bar earlier, when Kovacs and I were talking.

When she saw me, she froze as if she'd been caught at something. She was tall and pink-skinned with a short tufted hairstyle the colour of vanilla ice cream—one of those girls who'd gone all the way with the retro fifties look. I remember having a fleeting thought that she was in the wrong bar for it—I would have expected to run into her someplace where pictures of Elvis hung on the walls.

My mother would have approved of her style choices—I remember thinking that too. My mom always said that if a girl was going to wear her hair short, she had to wear more makeup to show she was still all girl. Liza Minnelli, Anne Murray, Mary Lou Retton, Jamie Lee Curtis, Tyne Daly from *Cagney & Lacey*, Demi Moore when she cut her hair—these were the short-haired women my mother admired. According to her, even Annie Lennox, although mannish, had the good sense to put on some blusher. My mother gave some of her clients a short haircut where she used a curling brush and blow-dried the hair straight up from the brow. "Go big or go home, that's my motto," she would say.

I was standing there when the girl suddenly reached out and punched the lid of the garbage can. It swung on its hinge, screeching. I backed away, grabbing for the door handle, but the girl pushed past me, mad-eyed. I fell and my tailbone hit the tiles hard and I yelped. The door clunked me in the temple as the girl clawed it open and tore out of the tiny room.

I sat there crying. I didn't even try to get up. A few minutes passed, and then the waiter tentatively knocked on the door and stuck his head in.

"I'm all right," I choked, and brushed myself off.

He offered me his hand anyway and helped me to my feet, saying that the establishment had removed the strange girl—as if he cared more that I might press charges than whether I was hurt.

I've been sitting in Karl's cabin, looking out this window, thinking about the affair that led to the creation of you. There's nothing outside but snow and trees, and little bushes that might look like animals if you let yourself think so. But the thing that I'm thinking about my affair with Karl—or about any affair, I guess—is that the relationship is based on absolute disconnection.

You know there are things you can never say to the other person in an email because someone else may find it. You know you can talk on the phone, but only during certain hours of certain days. And even then, your number is there, multiple times, in the phone's memory if anyone were to check. The more you and the other person communicate, the more likely you are to be caught. You have memorized the schedule of a person you don't even know (your lover's partner) and certainly don't like. Every time you touch the person you're involved with, you wonder if it will be the last time. There's a finality to everything you do together. Everything is a first and a potential last. You may do it again, but the kernel of doubt means you've already been jettisoned, become disconnected. I knew this the first, second, third, fourth, fifth, and sure, let's count the hand job in his car and say sixth time with Karl.

But knowing it also excited me.

If I hadn't actually met women hurt by dangerous relationships with men, I at least had a plethora of examples from television shows, films, and novels to draw on—everyone from Hester Prynne and her scarlet letter to Lana Turner in *The Postman Always Rings Twice*. Was there ever a female adulterer, or "other woman," who met a desirable fate? Nina Simone sang about the loneliness of the other woman and how she cries herself to sleep. Tess in *Tess of the d'Urbervilles* is cast aside not for her dalliances but for admitting to having been *raped* before ever meeting her husband; *The Great Gatsby*'s Daisy Buchanan ends up stranded in her rich but empty life after her lover, Jay Gatsby, has been murdered for her crimes; Janey Carver in *The Ice Storm* loses her son while she lies fetal after the shameful canoodling of a key party. The film of *Doctor Zhivago* features Julie Christie as Lara, attracted to and repulsed by the same man, eventually attempting to shoot him. In Catherine Breillat's *Une vieille maitresse*, Asia Argento plays the used and abused Vellini, ruined by her love, good for nothing but sex with one man. Literally, all she can do is screw him; there's nothing else in her life. Then there's Catherine Deneuve in Luis Buñuel's *Belle de Jour*, a prostitute by day but frigid housewife by night. Her husband is shot when her rough-trade lover tracks her home, and she winds up caring for an invalid the rest of her days.

None of these were marvellous ends.

But back to Karl: the thing about Karl was that he needed me like no one else needed me. He was absent-minded, caustic, and sad. Yes, you should know this. It's possible you'll inherit these traits too. And yet he managed to accomplish so much. I heard of Karl while doing my MA; other students spoke of him as if he were a character in a film, someone with whom they all shared an identical experience. There was a rumour that he had been part of an art performance in the early '90s where he lay on a gallery floor and a woman knelt over him and urinated on him. Addy and Jude told me that they had seen the footage—even though it wasn't online anywhere.

When I met Karl, I was surprised by how unremarkable he was. I had heard he was known for his eccentricity, for wearing his hair up in a fountain over his forehead like the film director Jim Jarmusch. But when I met him, he was going through a buckled-down, respectable phase. He had jettisoned his shiny shirts and anoraks and replaced them with plain button-collar fare. He had applied for the position of department head and cut his hair. Although he was tall, to me he was always slightly diminished in comparison to the description I had been given of him.

That first day, I found him in his office. The door was open, the telephone was ringing, and he was standing on a chair, endeavouring to retrieve a slim book from beneath a stack of film canisters and other books piled sideways and every which way overtop. I was attempting, late, to get into a seminar he was teaching.

"Ah! Could you take these?" he asked when I poked my head into his room. That was our first exchange. The absolute ordinariness of it strikes me now, considering how things went. He began handing me book after book to hold—there was no place else to put them. The shelves that ran along one side of the small office were crammed with double rows. And there were even more books where there were no shelves. I watched his knobby, hairy knuckles moving across the rows. How they flicked and snapped as he dropped volumes into my hands. *The Little Black and White Book of Film Noir. Simulacra and Simulation. Hegel's Phenomenology of Spirit.* The telephone kept ringing. *Illness as Metaphor. Against Interpretation.* After it had ceased ringing, there would be a pause and it would begin again. Roland Barthes's *S/Z.* "Damn phone. Could you . . . ?" Karl asked from above, removing another book, a film canister pressed tightly to his body under one arm. He was still a dozen or so books away from the one he seemed to actually want. I set my stack on the floor and hopped around it to the telephone.

"Dr. Mann's office."

"Uh . . . hello. Is he there?"

"Y-yes," I said into the receiver to a confused young woman. "But he'll have to call you back. Would you like to leave a number?"

It was his teaching assistant. I took the girl's extension.

In the meantime, Mann—which was how I thought of him then—had descended. "What am I going to do about this mess?" He peered at the tower of books he had passed down to me. It was as if a garbage can had been turned upside down and its contents dumped out. He set the film can down on the desk. It had come open and loops of brown were spilling out.

"What's the book?"

"Oh . . ." Mann looked at it as if surprised to see it in his hand. "A lend from a former student." He told me he had thought it was a gift—and when people send you something by mail, you assume you can keep it, don't you? He tossed the volume onto the desk atop the film can and ran his hand over his inch-long hair. Then he squatted and grabbed half a pile of books, heaving them up against one wall. He toed the other half, using his leg to push them flush against the shelves. I noticed he wore brown shoes and old-man dress socks, even though he wasn't, you know, ancient.

"I'm so sorry to impose," he said, "but could you . . . ?" He indicated another stack, one he must have brought down before I came to the rescue.

The book on top of the pile was a blue-bound edition with text on the spine only. I tipped it sideways and stared at the title, stamped in gold foil: *Phenomenology of the Cowpoke: Self-Aware Masculinity in the Late American Western.* I opened it and saw that it was by *Karl Mann, PhD, University of Minnesota.* It didn't look like it had been published so much as bound, perhaps by Mann himself. I wondered what had taken him to Minnesota, and what had brought him back again.

Karl put out his hand, and I closed the cover and handed him the thesis. As he tried to find new places for the volumes we had unshelved he made hemming and hawing sounds in the back of his throat—like Kovacs, it occurs to me now.

Five or ten minutes later, he said doubtfully, "Well, this can't be the permanent spot for these, but I've taxed you enough . . . I'm sure you have better things to do. What did you say your name was? Could you—?" Mann gestured for the message.

"Hazel," I answered, handing the message across the desk, where he was fussing with several of the film canisters we'd moved, trying to stack them on a narrow shelf above his desk chair.

"I'm going to put these over here for a while and then I'll forget to move them again. They'll fall on my head one day. That's when I'll remember they're here!" He peered at the stuff with contempt. It was an astute assessment; later I'd find out that's exactly what would happen, time and time again.

That office was snug as last year's sweater, packed tight. A little room with no window, it was filled with files and findings: books, DVDs, audio cassettes—audio cassettes, even!—VHS tapes, magazine file boxes, at least two Rolodexes, a bottle of wine, milk crates of records, a dusty antique typewriter sitting on a case with a broken handle, a whole shelf full of cowboy figurines and wagon trains and ceramic cacti. A lacquered suit jacket made of stretched bread packages hung on a valet in the corner, the word *Wonder* emerging from plastic lapels and pockets, the whole held together by blue and yellow bread-tie buttons: a sculpture Mann had obviously purchased without having a place to properly display it. A dusty cowboy hat hung by a cord from a nail in the drywall. Oversize framed artwork was stacked against the wall, the front one a drab square of kraft paper declaring in blown-up typewriter font:

```
is     was
```

The overall effect was more that of an installation than an office. Right there, that should have told me about the dynamics between Karl and Grace. I never saw their condo, and she's never talked about it, but I imagine it looks quite different. His stuff would have been relegated to his office and other distant places.

Mann extended one hand and took the phone message without looking at me.

"I'm trying to get into your course, and I need your signature," I said.

He ceased straightening and put up a finger, studiously taking in the message. "I am so *very* sorry. I know this must seem unprofessional, but I have to return this call. It's just been one of those—"

I nodded.

But the call did not seem urgent at all, judging from what I could overhear. While Mann and his assistant spoke, I removed a stack of books from the only other chair in the office and placed them to the side. Then I sat and waited for Mann to finish. When he had, he looked around the office again and said in a tight voice, as if he might cry, "I don't know if I can be of any help—"

I was jolted back to reality by his pinched tone and suddenly wondered if I should have left the office during the call and given him his privacy. But it was too late for self-doubt. And all I needed was his signature.

"Walk with me," Dr. Mann said. He was now pale and sober-looking. He came around the desk and picked up my bag for me, an act that made him difficult to refuse. He told me that the Starbucks line was long at that time of day, and that he hated standing alone. "I'll buy you one and catch you up on the two classes you missed."

You must remember that less than an hour earlier, Mann had known nothing about me except that I had willingly entered his office. But now I was rearranging his books, listening to him complain about his teaching assistant's confidence (or lack thereof)—the same teaching assistant he had just signed me up to take a course with—and waiting with him in line because he couldn't face standing alone.

"You look about the same age as my assistant, and you seem to have a fair sense of self-assurance," he said, giving me a glance up and down. "It will be good to have you in the group."

While we were in line in the café his chest pocket became illuminated by his cellphone, and for a second, with the light showing through the thin fabric, I had the impression that he had a blue electric heart. Then he took the device out of his shirt pocket, frowned at it, and extinguished it.

Later, after we returned to his office, Mann picked up a stray DVD collection he'd forgotten to shelve. "I want you to have this," he said, pressing it into my hand like a gift. "I think you'll like it. You seem like you might go for the Neo-Victorian Betacam-ness of it. It's from the '60s. Let me know what you think."

It was a three-disc set of *Dark Shadows*. And it wasn't a gift, I would realize later, when he casually asked me three times over the course of the next two months if I'd ever seen it. It was just something he liked that he didn't have a place for.

This is why it should not have surprised me when Kovacs implied that Karl Mann had slept with a dorm's worth of students, then sent them to her—for what? A man who gave things away without thinking about them and couldn't stand in line by himself . . . No, it should not have surprised me.

But it did.

Did I honestly believe that in his twenty-odd years of teaching, I was the first female student to stumble into Karl Mann's office and somehow manage to interest him? The first to stand too close to him in his cramped little space? The first to pity him? The first to believe my love would save him from middle age and mediocrity?

Honestly, I did.

Following my meeting with Dr. Kovacs, I thought several times about dialling Karl's number again—but then I would hear *her* voice repeating that *they* were at the cottage. Instead I returned to my room and reread a journal article called "Don't It Make Her Brown Eyes Blue," about the practice of matching models' eye colour—naturally or by digital alteration—to product packaging. I also wrote numerous emails to *our Karl*.

One of the emails, maybe number ten or thereabouts, was cribbed from a movie I had once made him watch—the only one he did at my insistence. Ironically, it was about a man having an affair, but with his own wife:

> K.—
> Once, I felt like an old used rag. And you, you were like a piece of rotten fruit on a windowsill. And it was great.
> H.

Another one of the emails—my twelfth attempt—made me shake. I could hardly believe the depth of my own rage, and yet I felt a hundred times better after writing it. It was like running down a hill—how your feet get away from you, and you're going so fast you think you'll trip and roll, but in the end you just keep running, and you stand at the bottom looking back at where you've come from, chest heaving, an incredible fire inside you. I got away from myself and something propelled me that was but wasn't me. I deleted that note. It scared me to have the words exist.

I sent none of the emails, but retained them (all but number twelve) in my Drafts folder as proof of my suffering should future anthropologists ever haphazardly stumble upon my laptop and develop an interest in the life of Hazel Hayes.

It was because of that anger I didn't phone him. It was because of that anger I didn't tell him about you. I was paralyzed by it. And in the midst of that paralysis I found out, finally, the truth about what I'd seen first-hand without knowing it. I found out about the Fury.

For forty-eight hours or so after my meeting with Kovacs, I had forgotten about anything but Karl—I had even managed to push the subway incident and the news report about the woman in the hair salon to a remote corner of my mind—and I had quit logging into my social networking sites. I was worried about what I might post. Finally I emerged from my rage long enough to log into my computer and check if, in the two days I'd ignored the site, I might have suddenly become popular—and that's when Larissa began to instant-message me. She popped up immediately.

I was reminded that I hadn't spoken to Larissa in weeks—not since she drove me to the airport for my flight to New York. **You there?** she wrote.

I typed that I was.

Then: **Cut off all my hair** popped up on my screen. **It's terrible . . .**

I didn't understand. What was the big deal? She'd cut it short before. I wrote back: **Sienna Miller circa *Factory Girl* or Nicole Kidman circa *Birth*? LOL.**

I thought I was being smart to come up with those hair/movie references off the top of my head, but Larissa didn't respond right away. When she did, she simply typed: **The plague.**

I sat for a second with that piece of information. I couldn't tell if Larissa was going to say more. On the phone she usually talked nonstop, which made sense since most of the time her only conversational outlet was a two-year-old. But the icon onscreen didn't appear to be moving.

What plague? I asked reluctantly.

What are you on? It's everywhere . . . There was a pause as Larissa broke the line with a hard return, then continued, **People hysterical here. Totally.**

There was another pause and then:

Two attacks in Toronto, one in Ottawa . . .

Her letters filled the screen, ellipses marking how quickly she was typing, an indicator there would be more to come. So I sat and waited, not sure I believed what she was saying.

More in the UK, Switzerland, Finland, Sweden . . .

They're talking pandemic . . .

Oh, and Latvia!

Everyone keeps going to hospital . . .

Jay insisted I get rid of my blonde . . .

So I did . . .

But nothing we can do about Dev.

They say infants are more sceptible.

Susceptible! She corrected her spelling.

He is pretty dark but we are so worried.

They still haven't said if boys can be affected, or just girls & women.

I peered at the letters like they were some code I'd found on a scrap of paper on the street.

Thank god you are safe—brunette already! she typed.

You there? she typed.

She may have had to type it a couple of times. I remember

the heat that engulfed me as I stared at her messages. **What are you talking about?** I finally wrote.

Then she wrote, **Oh god, Haze, turn on your TV.**

I hadn't turned the thing on since taking room 305. Hibernating from reality, I had not wanted to see any news. Now I flipped from channel to channel until a news anchor finally filled the screen. She had hair like Hillary Clinton's, though she was half Hillary's age.

"Tell me, Ted," the woman said to a man off-screen, "as far as experts can tell, is the disease affecting blond and bleach-blond males?"

The next shot featured a man in a suit on the Brooklyn Bridge, its trademark steel wires visible in the shot, the illuminated Manhattan skyline behind him. "Amanda, are you there?" he asked. He had puffy, serious eyes.

The anchor repeated her question, and the view switched to split-screen windows of the two of them.

"No men have been affected yet by what has been called, by some, the Blonde Fury. Others have called it Gold Fever, Suicide Blondes, or California Rabies. But whatever its name, it *is* serious." Behind him, the reporter said, we could see the location of the most recent attack. There was footage of a bloody bicycle helmet. It was only a couple of hours since a male cyclist had been brutally assaulted after offering assistance to a female cyclist who was unknown to him.

The anchor pressed Ted, the reporter, for details, staring out at the audience as if she were asking all of *us* to reveal what had happened.

I sat on the edge of the bed, my palm sweating around the remote control.

"Amanda, it was a Good Samaritan act gone wrong. A cyclist *spun out, then raged out.* Witnesses say the woman cyclist appeared shaky, then, I quote, 'spun out' while crossing the bridge on her bicycle at around seven this evening. A second cyclist, victim Owen Worthington, dismounted his own bike to offer assistance. That's when the woman flew into a fury and attacked him." Apparently at some point Worthington's helmet had come loose, and the woman grabbed his head and bludgeoned him against the rails. "We don't know much," Ted said, "but we do know that like all the other attackers today, the woman was blonde."

I listened without moving as Amanda explained, "The Blonde Fury can affect women of all cultures—with both natural blonde hair and hair that has been stripped to blonde or salon-created. Scientists are being consulted, and although they caution that it is too soon to offer a causal explanation, some *believe* the lack of melanin is what is leaving women and girls vulnerable to this particular disease."

Amanda and Ted continued to discuss other cases, including that of Eugenia Gilongos and Alexis Hoff from my subway attack. And in the window on my laptop, Larissa continued writing to me:

Did you find it? The whole thing is so surreal . . .

Five attacks in NYC and 6 in LA . . .

I would phone but Jay is on it . . .

You there?

Haze?

My hair felt like barbed wire between my fingers. What was orange but a variation on gold? Red-gold. A thing ablaze.

Owen Worthington had been admitted to New York Methodist Hospital, where he was placed in critical condition, and had since succumbed to injuries, the news anchor, Amanda, was stating in the background. "He is New York's fifth *rage victim* of sixty worldwide." Beth Barrett was the name of the female cyclist who had attacked Worthington. The reporters were still using the word *alleged*—*alleged* attacker, *alleged* disease—even though Beth Barrett had also succumbed to injuries. Shortly after her attack on Mr. Worthington, she had been struck by a transport truck. Barrett, Worthington, Hoff and Gilongos, others too—these would be the celebrities of the coming plague, and their names would soon be bandied about as frequently as those of politicians, musicians, actors.

The news show continued: it was believed nearly two hundred women had contracted and died of the virus, with the largest concentration in the Netherlands and the second largest in the United States. "Scientists and doctors are working to—"

I'm here, I typed. **I bought a ticket home.**

Meanwhile the TV was cautioning women with blonde hair—whether Caucasian, African American, or Asian American—to shave it to the skull or dye it a dark colour. There were no reports yet on how the virus affected women with mid-toned hair, such as myself, or how it affected men.

Bought just now? Larissa questioned. I guess she thought I'd gone online right then and snapped one up. **Toronto's crazy too.**

Bought it yesterday . . . I typed. **Home on Monday . . .**

It was true: between bouts of rage I had made an appointment with my doctor in Toronto, whose receptionist said I would be in fine time to "discuss my options." It was the one meaningful thing I'd done since my meeting with Kovacs. Which meant the only person involved in my dilemma whom I hadn't phoned was Karl.

Immigration is nuts—they're locking it down, babe, Larissa informed me.

Ever since Larissa married Jay two and a half years before, she had developed a habit of talking to everyone as if they were her nearest and dearest, adding *love, dear,* and *baby* to each sentence that fell from her lips. I suppose it wasn't so different from her teenage pothead days, when every sentence had a tacked-on *man.* But *babe* meant something very different to me right then, and the word did not comfort me. I knew that Larissa had undergone a "procedure" of her own when she was young—but that was *before.* Before Jay. Before-before. It's hard to ask advice about such things from a happily married young mother at any time, but especially in the middle of an international pandemic.

Still, I was working up my courage to tell her about you, but as I hesitated, my attention drifted back to the news. Ted on the bridge seemed to have disappeared from the broadcast. I watched anchor Amanda bobbing her stiff flaxen head at another man in the studio, a sober expression fastened on her pert face.

Someone behind the desk on TV joked dryly, "And, Amanda, you'll be getting rid of *your* goldilocks?"

"I can see a stylist waiting in the wings right now. To all the ladies out there, remember: it's just hair. I'm Amanda Cristobel," the anchor closed half-heartedly.

You're wondering how I can recite all this from memory, aren't you? Don't forget—this is what I *do*. The language of television is my work. It's my language. And that moment was also a singular one. Everything changed in that moment. Larissa told me to turn on the TV—and nothing has been the same since.

The chat window on my computer chimed. Isn't it strange how we live in a world where inanimate things beep and burp at us, asking for our attention like a crying baby? Larissa had to get off the computer, she typed. Her son, Devang, had just asked her where his mother was. She'd told him she was his mother, and he'd said he hated her. He only loved his mother who had hair. She typed **LOL but not really!** I knew this was the kind of thing she would cry about later at a party when she'd had too much to drink.

She promised to phone me in a couple days, and we both signed off with Xs and Os. After she had logged off, I looked at the updates friends and peers and near-strangers had posted online for everyone to see. One group tended to be earnest and aghast, buzzing about the plague and posting links to petitions and news groups, but just as frequently people were carrying on discussions about their cats, favourite foods, season premieres of television shows, alcoholic beverages, where they were going that night or with whom. The meaningless pitter-patter flickered steadily past like tickertape.

I took out my map of New York. The attacks had been building in the past two days. The epidemic, though still nameless, had been announced the previous day when I'd been walking around with my earbuds in, listening to music, writing emails I had no intention of sending.

Now I found there were a few images I couldn't get out of my head.

One was of Dr. Kovacs exiting the bar. She'd teetered slightly and veered out of my sightline. The next day I had sent her a veiled apology masquerading as a follow-up about how our talk had motivated me, but it remained unanswered on her end. Maybe that's why the image came to me. But I quickly dismissed it: I was just being paranoid.

The other image was of a woman I'd seen in Central Park. After buying my flight home at a wireless café, I'd gone to sit on the hill and watch the joggers, the women who run with SUV strollers, pushing them like they're made of paper, their chests jiggling in sports bras and tankinis. A woman who wasn't attired for jogging came around the corner. I remember she was ordinary looking, fiftyish, vaguely churchy. A speed walker, maybe. She was wearing a floral blouse, beige safari shorts and sports sandals with socks, and she'd muttered something, then weaved to the side of the pavement. There, she announced loudly, "I've just got to get this out of my system." She might have been talking to me. She bent to the curb, her pear-shaped butt in the air, and attempted to vomit, pushing her fingers down her throat, though by that point I had turned my face away. The sounds she made were gut-swirling, and I quickly moved to a new area of the park. I hadn't noted her hair colour.

Worst of all was the memory of the woman in the bar bathroom who had punched the stall and the garbage can, then knocked me down. Now I felt myself breaking out in hives, worried she'd infected me. As she'd passed, had she scratched me with one of those manicured polka-dot nails? I checked my arms and examined myself in the mirror. Nothing but the flush of fear.

I spread the map out on the bed and X'ed the subway station where I'd seen Eugenia pulled onto the tracks—I couldn't bring myself to say the word *die*, as the idea of seeing a human die was too much for me then—and the intersection where the hair salon bleach attack had happened. Those two had occurred within an hour of each other on the same day, twenty blocks apart. The Brooklyn Bridge incident had happened three days later. Larissa was wrong to say that there had been five attacks, then; the number stood at six. A quick spin on the internet revealed the other three New York locations: one in Park Slope, one at LaGuardia Airport, and one on the G line subway in Brooklyn, somewhere between Lorimer Station and Long Island City.

The attack in Park Slope occurred when a real estate agent pulled down a set of kitchen shelves in a house she was showing, then turned on the startled buyers, scratching a man and biting a woman before throwing herself out of an upstairs bedroom window and breaking her neck. The injured couple had been quarantined and placed under observation.

The airport attack involved a flight attendant. She hadn't attacked anyone in particular, had simply thrown a fit and attempted to overturn a row of benches far too heavy for her stature. She'd been Tasered by airport security and placed in custody before being transferred to hospital, where she remained. The subway scuffle had a hero, one the media nicknamed the Big Guy from Bedford-Stuy. He'd stepped in when two women began to brawl on a moving train. The first woman, a blonde, lit a cigarette on the metro car. Another woman told her she really shouldn't smoke there—or, as witnesses said, pointedly but politely requested that she butt it out. The smoking blonde flew into a rage, pulled out the other passenger's hair weave, and burned the woman's cheek with the cigarette. The Big Guy from Bedford-Stuy intervened, single-handedly pinning the attacker to the floor of the subway car until police and medical help could arrive.

Four of the women were white, the one from the hair salon incident was Thai, and the LaGuardia flight attendant was black with bronzed hair. Two were pushing fifty, three were in their thirties; one was a scant twenty-two. What they had in common: sex, hair colour, and class. They were all middle– to upper-middle-class. But those were only the attackers—the world was just starting to realize that there must be other victims who had succumbed and died in suicides or accidents. And scientists were starting to investigate whether the attacks were indeed the result of a virus rather than a phenomenon of mass hysteria.

Media reports claimed the Fury had something to do with melanin and also with the double-X chromosomes associated with being female—as if that lonely Y that left men vulnerable to male-specific diseases, such as hemophilia, was in this case a shield. Genetic scientists began searching for an allele that might be attached to the Y chromosome, protecting males while females were left vulnerable. Or maybe they were searching for an allele that would attach only to the second X—I wasn't sure. After all, it had been a long time since I had heard the word *allele*. I had taken one "bonehead" biology class to meet my undergrad degree's requirements, and even then I was lucky I got a B. The most interesting fact I learned that year was that a true calico cat—a tricoloured one, with orange, black, and white—can only be female because the colour trait attaches to the X chromosome. A female cat has a base colour of white and then two colour alleles (black and orange) that can attach, one each, to her two X chromosomes— black on the first X, orange on the second X. A male cat can be only the base colour (white) and one other shade (either orange *or* black, but not both), because he has only one X to take the allele.

All this ran through my mind, but then I shook my head: it was ludicrous to think of cats at such a time. The room felt hot and stuffy, so I went to the window and heaved it open. The courtyard below was still and empty, giving no indication of a city in crisis. That seemed so wrong to me. I felt there ought to have been an uproar I couldn't have missed, even with my headphones on, even walking around in a self-centred fog. In a window across the way and up a level, a man's white-shirted back was pressed to the pane, as if he were standing and watching something across the room, or perhaps watching some*one*, having a conversation. I noticed that there were black smudges across my line of sight, so I pulled off my glasses and blinked at them. Mascara was speckled on the lenses, and this seemed so ordinary it unsettled me. That everything should be the same; that such little things should still matter. I pulled up my shirt and used a corner to rub the lenses before replacing the glasses on my face. I don't remember if I cried. I don't think I did. I probably should have.

The thing about disease is that it's based on connection. What connected those six X's, those six women in New York, to the ones who were now statistics in Los Angeles, Miami, Atlanta, Toronto, Ottawa, Stockholm, Frankfurt, Amsterdam, London? I asked myself that question as if it mattered. The truth was, I couldn't do a thing about the answer, much less about what was to come next.

FIVE

THIS MORNING, EVEN BEFORE I DRANK the instant coffee that is making you kick, I wandered up the road to have a look at the neighbours' place. It was about 9 a.m., which I thought was a reasonable time to go knocking. But their car was gone. There were fresh tire grooves in the snow, backing out of the drive. And there was blood in the snowbank along the road— maybe some animal. Maybe that dog Grace and I saw a few weeks back, the one she calls Alf. Maybe not. The mailbox that the postal woman knocked down with her vehicle was still lying there, toppled in the ditch. I don't know what that means, and I don't want to speculate.

I walked up the yard until I could see the living room windows. They're plastered over with newspapers now, and they definitely weren't before. I went up on the porch and stood there and read the news stories, taped overtop of one another, some half-hidden. A few reported the usual small-town fare about failing local business, but the headlines were enough to give me some idea of the state of the world. For example: the British R&B sensation Shelbee Brown, who died of the SHV while I was in the Women's Entry and Evaluation Centre, had a final album released posthumously. A review, reprinted from a larger paper, proclaimed, "Shelbee Brown's soul is still haunted, and it comes through in her croonings and stylings as if reaching us from the other side. Although she could not possibly know what fate awaited, these songs are testament to the times that took her life. This voice comes from somewhere beyond."

The album sold a million copies in the week of its release—and knowing that reassures me. Things continue normally. People are buying and consuming, turning up the dial while driving in their cars, surfing the Internet and inputting their credit card numbers to own a little piece of culture. If I were anywhere but here, I would likely be caught up in all of that too.

I started to read a local news piece about current cases of the virus—and then I got spooked. It was so quiet. So I ran all the way back here, and you woke up inside me, and I ate a whole can of peaches and a freezer-burnt toaster waffle, and drank that Nescafé, black, to steady myself.

The good news? "The Simcoe Muskoka District Health Unit has no new cases of the SHV virus to report today. Last Wednesday, two cases of the virus were confirmed in the Barrie area, however." That from the most recent paper in the window—February 23, just a few days ago. Although I had to ask myself: What about that delivery woman? Is she an uncounted case? Or next week's case? What about the blood down there along the road? And why have the neighbours left in such a hurry?

Still, *no new cases*—even if it doesn't hold true—is a good sign. I've decided to read it that way.

I suppose if I could find someone to beg gas money from I could head back to Larissa's place in Toronto—but Larissa has problems of her own, and how can I expect her to take care of me? Especially after I took off on her like I did. I could try to sell Larissa's car rather than let it sit right where I cruised it into the driveway on fumes. But almost no one drives past this place, so even if I were to clear the snow off and write on the back window with a bar of soap, how fast would it sell? Still, I could try. I *will* try if Grace doesn't come back soon. With a couple thousand dollars I could get myself back to civilization and put myself up somewhere—at least until you come.

Unlike Grace, I didn't drive all this way up north to get away from the virus. I came here for Karl. I was only five months pregnant back then. I drove down several wrong roads where the houses were black smears, hunkered down behind fence posts and evergreens, hiding under snow. Driving with one eye exhausted me—the lens in my glasses was gone, and if I'd been pulled over by the cops I'd have been sunk. I had no licence or ID on me. I was wearing a half pair of specs and driving a car that belonged to someone else. All the way here, I travelled in the right-hand lane so as not to go too fast, also to align myself with the white stripe that outlined the road. The left side of the road was a grey whirl. I couldn't say who or what passed me. I was in Wasaga Beach, nosing up and down laneways, going slowly and craning my head to see, trying to retrace by memory the path I'd taken with Karl, using pine trees as landmarks. A hamburger stand. Horses wearing blankets, standing in the snow. An Esso station. A bait shop. The car got stuck on a bend where I'd slowed down, uncertain, and as I spun the tires I thought that might be it for me—all she wrote. The needle in the gas gauge had sunk below Empty at least ten miles ago. I gunned it to eighty. Then I turned the wheel just enough and the tires jostled into new ruts, and I was free. I jolted forward, braking before I hit a snowbank, and the cabin was right there: tucked in among the trees, a light shimmering beyond the branches.

I felt my heart jump in my chest. What would I find inside? I didn't know it was going to be just Grace and me. Grace and me for two and a half months, and then she'd go too—disappear, seemingly without preparation, without taking anything with her. Disappear the way women seem to, the way everyone seems to now. Blip, and we're gone.

Grace shovelled out the driveway before she drove off in Karl's Mini. I don't know how I missed hearing the scrape of the shovel, but I get so tired these days because of you, Hazel Junior. So tired that sometimes I sleep as if someone has poured concrete on top of me.

Shush, don't kick. Don't push your little claws into me. Shush, shush. You think you want to know, but you don't, little one. You don't want to hear what I've seen. Still, I'm going to tell you—if only to keep sane while I figure out what to do.

After I found out about the Blonde Fury, I thought I'd better colour my hair again. I bought the dye at the same drugstore where I'd bought the pregnancy test, only this time its shelves were half vacant. There was an inventory girl with dark blueberry hair who stood in front of the selection with a clipboard. She had loaded all of the Blondissima and Super Blonde into a shopping cart, presumably to be trucked away into some back warehouse, out of customer eyesight. I reached out a finger and ran it along the remaining choices, as if touching the boxes would help me. When you get to know me, you'll find out I have to touch everything to convince myself it's real. I touch everything. Except people. Your father, an exception.

Brown Sugar, Toffee, Pecan, Cedar, Acorn, Walnut. In the cardboard panel on the boxes that showed the results, and on the dingy hair loops attached to the shelves below, they all looked the same shade.

"I went for the darkest," the employee said. "Don't take chances."

A Japanese girl in jeans and pumps ran down the aisle, squealing, followed by a friend. The first girl, who had her whole head bleached white-blonde with the exception of her naturally black bangs, grabbed the last box of Ebony. In contrast, her friend had one or two stripes of blonde floating in her dark hair. She stood scanning the shelves as though another brand in the same shade might present itself to her.

The employee informed us that in addition to the mid-browns I'd been browsing, there was still Ash Brown. Chocolate and Black Brown, on the other hand, were all out. "We'll have more in at the end of the week. Sorry," she said. "Distributor can't keep up."

The two girls beside me seemed to be debating whether they would share the box of Ebony. Meanwhile, I went with the Ash Brown. Is an ash tree darker than a cedar or a walnut tree? Hair-colour names had ill-prepared us for questions of scientific classification. I noticed the two Asian girls kept their distance from me. There were still boxes of Pomegranate and a lone box of Auburn on the shelves—I guess because they were closer to brown—but the lighter Henna Red and Ginger, and other red shades more closely resembling my own natural colour, had been cleared away in the inventory girl's cart.

The woman at the till was portly and had long hair pulled back in a barrette on top of her head and hanging down her back, part straw-coloured and part silver. She confided that she thought the panic was a lot of nonsense, that no one knew what caused the sickness and she wasn't buying the hair-colour story. She'd had her natural shade her whole life. People were always telling you what to eat, what not to eat, what to avoid, what might be dangerous. "Like cancer," she said. "They don't know. But it's your $10.99," she added. It seemed to take an unfathomably long time for her to ring me through. My stomach groaned and a few paces behind me, the two young Japanese women giggled and nudged each other. My eye lingered on the magazines beside the till. "Singer Shaves Head Again," one of the covers proclaimed. And, "This Time It's for My Kids, She Says."

Outside, the streets were abnormally quiet, especially for a Saturday. People were going about their business, but with reservation. Drivers sounded their horns less. I saw several blonde women in jogging suits and also an ice-blonde hipster. I gave them a wide berth. Two of them glared at me, and the third didn't notice. A small group of people had gathered outside a corner eatery that sold stone-oven pizza. They were staring up at LCD screens positioned inside the glass facing out. Normally the screens showed ads of happy people jamming their mouths full of hot, gooey pizza, but for once the screens had been tuned to a news station. A cold, quivery feeling burst through me: the owners had conceded something more important than sales was happening. Together, these strangers—these strangers and me—read the closed captioning at the bottom of the screen.

Woman in quarantine shows signs of "Gold Fever."

"They put it in quotes," a tall man in a business suit said to another man in a suit. I couldn't tell if they were together or just bound by the fact that they both wore ties. "Because it hasn't been named officially. Names of diseases have to be registered. All these names are just ones the media made up."

"That true?" the other guy asked.

Authorities are now able to track the progression of symptoms, which are indeed similar to rabies. The public is advised to be wary—and here the prompter went into a list of symptoms—*of women with raised voices, acting violently . . .*

Lumbering, limping, exhibiting imbalance . . .

Flailing or throwing any object . . .

Grimacing, displaying a downturned expression . . .

"We're not allowed to have downturned expressions?" the girl beside me muttered. "I mean," she said a bit louder but still to me, "what if we're just worried? In a bad mood? PMS?"

Several heads turned from the screen to look at her. It must have made her nervous because she ran her hand back through her hair. She was pale as an elephant's tusk.

"What?" she said.

The smell of pepperoni floated over us, and people passed by, ignoring the news to get their lunches.

"You're still blonde," a guy in cargo shorts pronounced. "That's not real smart."

The girl said she was a model. "I just got a big gig—what would you do?"

The businessmen looked at Model Girl sympathetically but said nothing. Money was their language.

The TV told us: *The public is advised not to assist women who appear to be in crisis. Contact can lead to the spread of this disease.*

Above the news captions, a smiling blonde continued silently delivering some other report. A portion of the screen showed rain, and another portion followed cars creeping along the Jersey Turnpike.

—

Does trauma make people go through a purge-and-binge cycle? I found a deli, where I ordered a sandwich the size of a hubcap and probably heavier. I took the plastic basket to a table for two and sat alone, eating. It was almost lunchtime and the place was starting to buzz with human traffic. Two undergrads at the table beside me were lingering on a long wooden pew strung with little tables. They were picking at their food rather than eating it—the same way they probably pretended to read for their courses but only skimmed, pretended to drink more than they did, and get laid more, and do drugs more. I knew they were university students because because they were talking about what they wanted to compose for a creative writing class. The boy was cute and dark, and he squirmed in his chair complaining about how fat he'd become even as he pushed his chips around. I remember him stressing that, because it was a ludicrous suggestion. He was wearing a T-shirt with a drawing of an octopus swallowing a businessman, gripping him in its multiple-tentacled arms, dress shoes dangling. I couldn't decide if the girl was his best friend or if she wanted to be his girlfriend. She was preppy and back-to-school clean.

"It would be set in Paris in the 1950s and it would be, like, a love triangle thing, because, you know, I'm writing it," the boy said.

The girl asked him if he'd feel comfortable reading something like that aloud in class and he said no, that was just it, he could *never*. That's why he hadn't written it.

Yeah, yeah . . . the radio sang above us. *Nobody feeds you like your mama.* A feminized begging blues updated with a grinding bass track by the then-still-living pop sensation known as Shelbee Brown.

The girl had an excuse for not having a single idea about what to write for the assignment: her mom had called her in crisis over the blonde thing. The girl rolled her eyes. The boy clucked how sweet it was that her mom cared. His parents hadn't phoned him, he pointed out.

"But you're male. Like you have anything to worry about." The girl crunched potato chips loudly around her words. "After they announced it, all these girls in my dorm were crying. People were, like, locking their doors, locking each other out, as if it's already in the dorm!" She tossed the crust of her sandwich down angrily. "They're making this big thing of it later today. Like our brother residence is coming over and they'll shave and dye the girls, to try to take the sting out of it, make it, I dunno, sexy or fun. Like it's the new frosh week or something? It's so lame. I'll probably go."

The boy cocked a finger-gun at her and told her she should *so* go. "Boys doing hair? I'm there!" They laughed.

"Is this blonde?" the girl asked, touching her hair. The boy squinted as if he were really assessing it. I snuck a glance. If I recall, it was the colour of peanut butter, mud mixed with honey, golden olive, neither brown nor yellow. *Mousey,* my mother would have called it, not that this rich New York University girl would ever have set foot in my mother's partially wood-panelled salon.

"Get a handsome one," the boy told her.

Yeah . . . the radio moaned. The girl nodded, then started to cry. As the song ended, she drew the back of her hand across her face, like an overtired little kid. I looked away.

As I finished my sandwich, it occurred to me that the news captions on TV had all been directed at men. There was nothing about the symptoms women should look for in themselves.

"You changed it again. . . ." Natalie, the concierge at the Dunn Inn, nodded at my hair, which was back to basic brown.

My things were packed and I was paying her in advance for the amount owing on room 305.

Her hair colour was still the same, chestnut. She told me she had liked mine before, when it was bright "like nasturiums." "This epidemic . . ." She shook her head. While she was waiting for the machine to process my credit card, she said, "You know who doesn't have to worry about this thing? The juice." She whipped up the receipt and patted it onto the counter. "Of course, I shouldn't say that, because maybe you are. But my parents were Sicilian, so we're like the juice."

"Sorry? Pardon? Maybe I'm what?" I stared at the receipt, pen in hand.

"Jewish," she said. "This epidemic passes right by them like it has its turn signal on. Except for one or two blonde ones I read about in Israel. It's gone the whole world over. Almost as bad as swine flu."

"No, I'm not Jewish," I said, and signed the receipt.

"Well, too bad you're not. They're lucky—they're mostly safe. My sister's after me to colour this black like hers, but then we'd look too much alike."

I had a professor in Toronto, Dr. Jacques, who said that the first thing you noticed about a person was their hair. That you didn't see their face; you saw the way the hair framed the face, and recognized the person from this. That's why when someone changed their hair colour or cut it drastically it took you much longer to recognize them. Maybe Dr. Jacques was right. I hadn't looked closely at the sisters' features as they Windexed the door windows or slapped keys onto the board behind the desk, but now I saw clearly that they were twins.

"Y'all got it in Tor-on-to?" Natalie pronounced every syllable, the way I had when I'd first moved to that city three years before. Three and a half years ago now. I had quickly learned to say it *Tronna* like everyone else, like something slick that you slip on walking down the street. Like dog shit.

I told her that from what I'd heard we did, and that I was only going for a short visit. I'd be back in a week or two. I'd make a room reservation online like I had before. I didn't know if I was telling the truth or not.

"Just show up. We'll take care of ya," Natalie said, and punched the yellow bill onto a stick. "Tourism'll be down with this bug goin' round."

At last I sent one email—number twenty-nine—to your father:

Karl—
Flying into Toronto on Monday. I know it is short notice.
However, it is important that I see you.
Hazel

When I got up at five the next morning for my flight, I found
a response from Karl. He'd sent the email after one, which
I thought meant he'd been waiting till Grace was asleep.
Now I know that she goes to sleep religiously at eleven.
Beauty sleep, she calls it. He hadn't even bothered to use
capital letters. You don't forget an email like that, even if you
forgive it:

hazel,
little hectic here. definitely can't do Mon. or Tues. things are
always insane the first few weeks of September with school,
you know that. but we'll see what we can work in. I trust
you've been in good hands with wanda and your thesis is
coming along.
karl

It was composed so that someone else could read it and
not smell a whiff of joined crotches or anything else between
us. At least, that was my impression. It was from his personal
account, not his university one. The last sentence was a
statement, not a question, as if he didn't want to know how the
thesis was.

I remember I went into the shower and took longer than I should have on a flight day. I lathered my legs but then put the razor down. I wouldn't shave because I wasn't going to sleep with him, even if he made time for me in the end. The lather ran away in the shower stream like milk. I threw up twice and brushed my teeth twice. The thought that Karl was already seeing someone else crossed my mind, but then Grace's face chopped through my brain. Had Karl been noncommittal with me out of anxiety? Or out of pride? I considered writing back the very basic "I'm pregnant," but when my hand reached the laptop I found myself shutting it down. I wish I had written those words though. I still wish it. I wonder what it might have changed, if things could have been saved.

I stashed the laptop in my shoulder bag and left the Dunn Inn, pulling my suitcase as quietly as I could down the steep carpeted stairs. In the foyer a large bottle of sanitizer had been placed on the occasional table. Because I wasn't expecting it, I almost knocked it over with my suitcase. A markered sign read:

DUE TO THE OUTBREAK, PLEASE
SANITIZE YOUR HANDS BEFORE ENTERING—
EVEN IF YOU THINK YOU'RE NOT AT RISK!
HELP US HELP YOU
KEEP YOUR VISIT GERM-FREE.

THANKS DUNN INN MANAGEMENT.

I liked the way the last line read, as if the Dunn Inn was congratulating itself for putting up the sign.

I remember pale daylight and industry floated beyond the windows of the AirTrain, which glided over parkways trim as golf courses, parking lots with trucks backed into loading docks, and strangely, a pond with ducks and swans. Three uniformed guys—maintenance, or maybe ground crew—jostled near me, mumbling and joking as they rode to work. They were a few years younger than me, and wore their plain navy uniforms with a sexy haphazardness. With the smallest gestures, they'd found ways to stylize their homogeny. One had the collar open a button, a white undershirt showing, a chain at his throat. Another had bought his belt oversized and it hooked back through the loops twice. I can picture it even now: the exaggerated length seemed phallic. The third wore his pants a shade lower than they were meant to be. Their day was just beginning and they were already hopped up on sugar and hormones. In contrast, I'd had only one coffee and was seriously yearning for another. One of the guys took his automatic clicker from his pocket and pointed it out the window, attempting to lock or unlock his car in the parking lot as the train glided by. His friends ribbed him for thinking it would work from that distance.

But sometimes we do things just to see if we can. I know I have.

As the train skated deliberately around on its track and the doors opened and closed silently at terminals that weren't mine, I thought of Karl that first time we kissed in his office. There were a few of us who tricked him out to the pub for beers with us sometimes after class, though you should know he seldom drank more than half a pint. In his defence, I guess it must be said that we weren't high school kids hanging out with our teacher; we were twentysomethings, thirtysomethings. Seeking out someone twenty years our senior had an illicit vibe, but only because it seemed as if we were getting away with something. We sought to impress him and occasionally topple him with our more current trivia.

Once, at Karl's insistence, four of us jammed into a room in the Media Lab and watched *Alien*, which as a Cultural Studies major I was supposed to adore, although maybe I would have liked it more if we had still been living in the 1980s. Karl argued, with himself, about whether the character of Ripley should have appeared in her underwear at the end of the film.

"When this came out, it was a fierce debate, whether it was conventional sexism on the part of Ridley Scott, who just wanted to show Sigourney Weaver in her skivvies, or if it was humanizing to feature a heroine in her underwear and in fact sexist to automatically assume it sexist." I'd noticed Karl frequently used words like *fierce* around his gay students. He craved acceptance.

That was followed by an episode of the American *Queer as Folk*, because it was shot in Canada and Karl had never seen it. Jude was the one who had insisted that Karl couldn't possibly teach us without having viewed it, that it had been a ground-breaking show, and he ought to grasp its importance.

But that particular night Jude and Addy had gone, if they had even been with us at all. It was often just me and the boys. In any case, I was the only one left in Karl's office. It was eight or so at night and Karl asked if I *puffed*, which was his word for getting high. It was October, not this past October, but the one before. I had been stoned only a few times and not for a long time. We went out and walked across the quad, passing the tight white line of a joint between us. He had seemed younger to me in that moment, hipper. The world was as leafy and rich as the smell of the weed. The air seemed to ring without any noise. I became aware of Karl, his clothes, the brown buttons on his jacket, his knuckles, his fingertips as we moved alongside each other. When we went back inside, the office seemed small and I felt as if my lungs had feathers inside them. I was standing too close to Karl—whom I still called Mann, or Dr. Mann—and I knew it.

He was leaning on the edge of his desk, and I was maybe six inches away from him when he said, "What are you waiting for, a spanking?"

"Are you being inappropriate with me, Dr. Mann?" I asked, but I was smirking. I didn't have much going for me, but I could smirk. Boy, could I. "Go ahead. Spank me, Dr. Mann." I looked at him like I didn't think he'd dare—and I didn't—but part of me also knew he would.

I moved a little closer, about an inch or two away. And then he said, "All right, then," and grabbed me around the back and pulled me to him. Let's just say I went very easily over his lap. I was wearing a dress and knee socks, and I felt the skirt ride up slightly on my thighs.

"You're a very bad girl, Hazel. You have potential, but you must learn to apply yourself." His voice was soft, with a hitch in it.

I let my hair fall over my face, and I looked at the floor, which was dusty. For a second I wondered if I was really over his lap, or just imagining it because of the weed. Then I felt his hand land with a forceful slap on my right buttock. I gasped. We both laughed. I turned my head and looked back at him. My big rump arched over his lean hips. I liked the way it looked, like a Jan Saudek photograph. Through the thin black cotton of my dress I could feel him, hard against my belly. Then Karl glanced at the door, which was open. Maybe that's all it would have been, one playful moment, something inappropriate but easily smoothed over the next day and forgotten, had I not got up, gone to the door of his office, and looked down the dim hall in either direction. I closed the door and returned to my position.

That was how it started. The next week Karl agreed to be my thesis adviser.

SIX

HOW MANY STORIES AM I TELLING YOU? I wonder if Grace has gone all the way back to Toronto, and if she has, whether the city is functioning as usual or collapsing in ruins.

I can imagine Grace going back to her and Karl's condo. She may have left it because there was too much of their life together there—but at least it doesn't have me in it, toting around this big lump of you. A constant reminder. I wouldn't blame her if she doesn't come back. When I came here, I thought I was driving toward something, but when Grace came here, she was driving away from everything. She abandoned it all, including her job. Just walked away. Maybe the money is running out . . . Karl never cared about money, which made me think he had plenty. But you never know. I can see him and Grace keeping everything separate, right down to the bitter end.

It's hard for me to imagine that they were in love once, hard to imagine Grace as young as me, flirting, playing. Hard to imagine Grace happy with anyone or anything, including Karl. I can't imagine them running out to do something as permanent—or perhaps simply spontaneous—as marriage.

If I recall my third-year philosophy course correctly, Schopenhauer said, "Boredom is just the reverse side of fascination: both depend on being outside rather than inside a situation, and one leads to the other." Schopenhauer also wrote, in *Prize Essay on the Freedom of the Will*, "A man can do what he wants, but not want what he wants." Although, if I recall, sometimes that second *want* was also interpreted as *control* or *determine*: "A man can do what he wants, but not determine what he wants." Yes, that's it, and although I never heard the name Schopenhauer on Karl's lips, both these ideas strike me now as being very true to Karl.

It's dark now, the kind of dark where there's nothing, where the world could cease to exist on the other side of that hill and you wouldn't even know it. It was only half an hour ago that the sky was holding the light among the branches, like water cupped between fingers and palms. Now it's so black out there, even the memory of light feels distant. You can hear the silence. It's like the sound of your own blood.

I don't know which terrifies me more: the effects the virus has had on the world, or that it could circle invisibly and descend upon us in the first place.

———

Because it was a Monday morning flight, the terminal was packed. I quickly realized that people were waiting in line as if they didn't know how to use the self-serve machines. I got my boarding pass from an abandoned automatic kiosk. I weighed my suitcase, and watched it sail away from me on a conveyor. Time was on my side, but there were still two more lines to navigate before coffee and the gate. People were muttering with dissatisfaction and nervousness, the way they do in those situations. The sound travelled upward into the metal beams.

In the check-in line, I stood beside a ratty-looking traveller. She had on a pair of bright pink Doc Martens and was wearing pins that said *Drink Fight Fuck,* and *Know Your Riots.* Bold of her, I thought, to wear them through Security. As the Doc girl and I shuffled forward, we passed an ownerless knapsack.

"Is that yours?" I asked her.

She shook her head.

I looked around at the people in our line, which doubled back and forth on itself, and I started to think *bomb.* I was about to gesture to a security officer when a lanky white guy with a beard loped over, plucked the knapsack up by its handle, slung it over his shoulder, and ducked under the rope into line. He excused himself past several people and joined his friend farther up.

After our boarding passes were scanned we entered Security. Mascara and lip gloss already in Ziploc baggies. Shoes off, clogs purposely worn for speed. No belt. Laptop out of bag into grey bin. The officers waved us forward and pushed us back like traffic cops. Next to one line they had erected an easel that said: ALL BLONDES MUST USE THIS LINE. Below the English, it said the same thing in several languages: Spanish, French, Italian, Chinese, and Arabic. A female officer was going through our lineup, pulling out the blondes, and waving them over to the other area.

A blonde middle-aged woman insisted she wanted to stay with her male business partner and asked the officer if the partner could come with her.

The security officer nodded and gestured them off.

I couldn't see where the lineup went; it verged away from ours, seemingly into another room.

I walked through the metal detector without incident. On the other side, a black female guard ran the hand-detector over my clothes, and as she did so, she asked me how I was feeling. Had I had any pain or headaches lately? I told her I felt fine and she stood aside. I picked up my possessions and sunk my feet back into my shoes. An officer wearing blue latex gloves was feeling the lymph nodes of the *Drink Fight Fuck* girl. The girl was standing very still and I didn't recognize her at first because her khaki jacket and Docs were off; a chipped pink toenail showed through a hole in one of her black fishnet socks. In spite of the rubber gloves, the guard seemed to be holding her gently between thumbs and fingers, the way you might before you kiss someone. It was almost tender.

In my mind, what happened next is almost orderly. Every detail is in sequence, just like putting one foot in front of the other. But I have a feeling that when I try to say it out loud, it won't come out that way.

I was about to spend my last six dollars on a coffee. I was standing at the coffee counter and had just reached the front when the sound floated toward us—a faint roar from the direction of the gates. Everyone looked. Two security officers jogged past. Their hands cupped the tops of their weapons.

I tried to order my coffee, but the barista was staring off over my shoulder. That was when a gym bag flung with force knocked over a rotating bookstand beside us. People were running in our direction. Instinctively, the people in our line dispersed, ducking under the ropes and scrambling back toward Security, that barrier we'd all been so anxious to clear. Beside me, a man dropped his recently acquired coffee on the floor and grabbed his wife by the hand, yanking her away, her cup still sitting on the counter.

It was The Blondes. And that's what we called them after that day, as if their violence had instantly had resulted in a new social class.

There were seven or eight of them, all flight attendants, moving quickly. Wearing navy blazers, they tore through the airport's wide aisles. One of the attendants grabbed a boy by the shoulders—he looked about twelve—and flung him directly at a security officer. The two collapsed to the floor, boy and officer in a tangle, and the blonde kept coming. Her hair was untucked, pins dangling. It spilled over her uniformed shoulders. I saw all of this, but I also experienced it as a blur, commotion, little bits and pieces.

A golf cart driven by security officers spun around the corner. It was going at top speed and it knocked out one of the Starbucks line posts with the corner of its bumper.

You see, I'm not telling this right. It sounds comical, even to me. Part of the difficulty has to do with the fact that they *were* very beautiful women. But more than that, I can only say what happened, only repeat a sequence of events. There's a sound to terror, which is the sound of human reaction. A jumble of voices, all shouting and muttering.

People had plastered themselves to the walls; some were crowding into stores. The bookstand next door began cranking its gate shut, sealing off the area with a curtain of metal bars. Some travellers sat, stunned, on benches, as if continuing to wait for departure. Others were gathering their things. Everything happened fast. It's only when you try to tell it that you slow it down and it sounds absurd.

One of the cabin-crew members snatched a cellphone from a bystander's hand and hurled it. Far off down the aisle, another of them had grabbed an old woman by the hair. I watched as she yanked the woman along, her victim's stockinged ankles dragging until one foot caught in the leg of a seat at the end of a row. The elderly woman used it to her advantage, to hold herself back. I looked away before her ankle could snap; instinctively, I knew that would be the outcome. When I glanced back the woman had been dragged a few more yards before something worse happened, which was that chunks of her scalp tore off in the flight attendant's hands. The blonde looked at the spongy patches and then cast them away, leaving the old woman sprawled and bleeding on the carpet. All around me rose a din of awe and horror.

The security guard driving the cart stood up and administered a Taser, an electric arc materializing between him and the aggressive flight attendant. Another guard leapt out and chased down one of the other psychotic crew members. Picking up a deserted window-extension pole that had been abandoned by a cleaning cart, the blonde spun in circles, her hands and the pole held out as if everyone around her posed a threat and she didn't want to turn her back. The officer grabbed the pole, twisted it from her, and brought it to her throat, expertly subduing her against the wall. Everyone was shouting.

I realized the coffee shop was trying to crank down its "Closed" barrier, so I put both hands on the counter and heaved myself over it. I banged my shoulder on the barrier as it came down on top of me, and tore my knee on the espresso machine. Something sharp cut into me, but I barely processed it. Hot liquid from a left-behind cup on the counter spilled everywhere. The surface slippery, my body skated off it heavily onto the floor. I landed on a syrup bottle that went down with me but thankfully didn't shatter. I remember the barista who had been about to serve me was screaming, as if I were a threat, one of *them*.

"Get out! Get her out!" she kept shrieking to her co-worker, backing away.

"Take it easy," I told her. I struggled to get up off the floor. I adjusted my glasses, which had been knocked askew. She stopped panicking pretty quickly, and we watched through the thick, transparent plastic of the barrier as more carts of airport staff arrived and began directing the human traffic out of the area. These new officers were wearing white surgical masks and gloves. They must have been directed to protect themselves first.

One of the blondes made a mad chase after a woman with a stroller who had started to run. The pink-faced toddler in the stroller opened her mouth in a wide wail. She was followed by a female officer in a bulletproof vest who sprinted down the long aisle. We all jumped back as the officer grabbed the blonde and crashed with her into the plastic shield that separated them from us. The window rattled and rolled as they bounced against it. Cheek first, the flight attendant was slammed into it repeatedly—the officer just kept jerking her. The blonde had this twisted expression, smeared against the safety glass in pink lipstick and pancake makeup. We watched her tooth hit the barrier and her lip crack open. Blood was painted back and forth with each movement as the officer—who was no taller than me, five-one or so—single-handedly subdued her. She slapped cuffs onto the struggling flight attendant's wrists, a knee firmly planted in her back.

The blonde, feverish, made eye contact with us and I felt everything around me fade. From her nostrils and mouth, breath steamed the glass and spittle flecked it. The cop smacked her against the barrier again, as if for show, or maybe because her own adrenalin was up. Dinging the barrier was the flight attendant's name tag. *Morgan*.

A sound crept through the Plexiglas—not a scream, more

of a moan. One of the baristas gripped my shoulder as if to pull me farther back, although we had already flattened ourselves against the sink.

Several security staff approached, and together they lifted the blonde and carried her away, enough of them that she could no longer struggle. "Watch that mouth doesn't bite!" the take-down officer yelled.

Someone began reading the woman her rights. Then another officer shouted, "Save it, Burroughs! Her brain's bleached. She can't hear you."

They were already inventing slang. I stared at the blood patch on the scratched plastic where the woman had been.

Inside the coffee area, one of the baristas started hiccuping and exclaimed something in Korean. The other barista asked, pointing, "Why?" I followed her gaze and saw that out in the gate zone, another of the blondes was rocking an empty security cart, her face flushed with effort, her brow furrowed with anger. There was no reason for her actions that we could see. No one had come near this woman and she had nothing to gain by concentrating on the act. Yet the cart flipped onto its side, then with another push, over it went. I felt a vibration through the floor up into my banged knee. That was when I looked down, aware for the first time of the throbbing; a trickle of blood had seeped through my jeans.

"You should go with them," the barista who had screamed when I first came over the counter said to me. She pointed at a line of passengers who were being escorted, presumably to safety, by airport staff.

"I'm not leaving here."

She started to say something about Starbucks regulations.

"You are hurt," said the other. Her green apron had the name *Mae* pinned to it. With shaking hands Mae yanked several times at a first aid kit high on the wall beside the menu board.

I tried to wave her away, saying it was nothing.

Mae jumped up on the back counter and, kneeling there, pried the kit from the wall. When she got it open, she dug out scissors and bandages. She insisted I sit down on a stepping stool, then rolled up my pant leg and swiped at my knee with cotton and peroxide. My eyes watered and I bit my lip. The other girl got on the phone with someone, maybe a manager, to try to find out what they were supposed to do. Her one-sided conversation came to me in snatches, like something on the radio. As soon as the peroxide cleared it became apparent my knee was worse than I'd thought. A good chunk of skin had been gouged out, and the joint was quickly swelling.

From where I was sitting, the counter blocked my view of the rest of the airport. I could only just make out events occurring above it. There was a marble-green line of laminate separating us from them, and even now I'm grateful it was there. We could hear shouts. The final two blondes were being violently subdued.

"Where were you going?" Mae asked as she poured iodine on a swab.

"Canada," I told her.

"I hate to say, but you may not get to Canada today. They will keep you here. I think so."

She was young with flinty eyes, her black hair pulled back in a butterfly clip. I remember her hands were still shaking. It occurs to me now that taking care of me calmed her, and maybe I knew it then too, because I let her.

The other barista was on the phone again, speaking in Korean this time.

Mae tried to tell me I needed stitches but couldn't find the word. "You need . . ." she said, and made a sewing motion with her hand.

I assured her I was okay, but she took scissors and clipped several lengths of medical tape, which she kept hanging from individual fingers before retrieving a clean white gauze pad from its package with her other hand. The colour of membrane, the lengths of tape hung and fluttered. Mae had a brave face but she continued to shake. She called me an athlete for being able to jump the counter.

"What's going on out there?" I asked her.

Mae glanced over her shoulder. I could make out the blue backs of security officers standing in a circle, their heads bent down, one speaking directly into a walkie-talkie, and I knew—dead, or alive but Tasered—they must have had the blondes on the floor.

Mae turned and lurched over my shoulder, vomiting into the sink.

When the area had been secured, an officer in a face mask came over and rapped on our window. We were drinking coffee, which felt wrong, as though we were charmed house-wives at a bridge game, sipping and standing around speculating on what would happen while health officials sealed off the gates and EMS workers removed the four covered bodies and a dozen injured travellers. But we were wobbly. Mae and the other barista, Kate, and I had reasoned we should have something to steady our nerves, especially since we had no idea when we'd have the chance again. Mae was very focused and clear-headed that way. Kate was nibbling on a biscotti when the officer knocked, and she jumped. The biscotti crumbled, half of it falling to the floor.

"Stop what you're doing," the officer said, the words muffled through her face mask.

Mae took another sip.

"Stop!" the officer commanded, and gestured for her to put down the coffee.

"They think it's . . . it's contaminated," I stammered.

We looked down at our cups.

We were led out, and right away the coffee stand was sealed behind us. The security officers were fewer now, intent on escorting the remaining employees and passengers. Emergency workers in bloated yellow hazmat suits moved into the gates, circling and pointing, like astronauts discovering the moon for the first time. Once past the newly erected, vacuum-sealed plastic sheeting we could see these figures floating, ghostly. I was forced to leave behind my shoulder bag with all my identification, laptop, and cellphone. It was still sitting at the base of the counter, where I'd set it down or dropped it before jumping over. The blood patch on the barrier was just a few feet above it.

We were taken out an exit to a trolley already packed with wide-eyed, silent people, and trundled across a flight strip, where we were isolated in an aircraft hangar. On the way over, I watched a young boy playing a pocket video game. His small thumbs tapped across the mute buttons, and he frightened me with his concentration, his ability to meditate on something else. Beside him, his mother was gaping at something over my head. I turned and looked but there was nothing but a bank of grey clouds.

We were met with clipboards, then handed questionnaires and pens. The questions asked if we had come into contact with blood or saliva. How close had we been to an infected person? Had we touched or been touched by an infected person? Did we have any injuries? Did we feel any signs of illness? I wondered if it was a standard form or if it had been written and copied that day, specifically for our situation. We had to write down our names and addresses, where we were going and coming from, our birthdates and Social Security numbers, the names of our closest relatives, any medications we were taking. We were told that the welfare of the country depended on our honesty.

As at any airport, our luggage showed up an hour and a half later. It took ten minutes for the armed guards by the mammoth doors to open them, or perhaps decide to open them. We could hear them orchestrating that process while someone else collected our checked and X'ed boxes. Finally, a man in a see-through suit towed the luggage in on a string of carts. He got out and began unloading our things into a pile, none too delicately. When he had unloaded half of it, someone approached the suited man, touched his shoulder, and gestured for him to leave the carts and get out. He unhitched the final carts from the back of his vehicle, so that half the things lay in a heap and half sat neatly on the skid, then he drove out the way he'd come.

Someone shouted through a bullhorn that we would be permitted to claim our personal items. Most of the carry-ons looked the same, grey or black with zippers and wheels. People walked over and dug through them or climbed onto the still-bundled carts to pick up cases that did not belong to them, sometimes opening them up and re-zipping them, before finding the pieces they had arrived with.

I found my laptop bag under a hard-shelled orange plastic carry-on. My wallet and cellphone were still there, but the computer, when I tried to turn it on, flickered and brought up only a dark grey screen. I couldn't say whether it was because of my own treatment of it at the coffee stand, because of the man who had unloaded it, or because of another traveller desperately searching for his own bag, throwing others aside without regard.

Not everyone had cellphones, and near me a senior-citizen couple in retirement pastels were asking a face-masked official if we would be allowed to make phone calls.

"Whoever you need to reach already knows you're going to be late," the official said. "We're world news."

When they pressed her, saying that was exactly why they needed to call—to let their daughter know they were all right—the official became stony and said she couldn't make any promises about communications. After she moved away, I extended my cellphone and told the couple they could use it if they kept the call short. They thanked me profusely but in the end couldn't get reception. Someone a few feet from us looked over and said that too many people were trying to phone at once. The airwaves were jammed. The couple passed my cell back to me. I tried Larissa and my mom—both had known I was flying—but the phone just said *Searching* . . .

The day moved in sluggish waves. When we'd first arrived, some people were crying and rocking, covering each other's shoulders with jackets. As the morning wore on, those people resigned themselves while others who had held it together began to break down. Several teenage girls with smudged mascara were leaning back to back in pairs, providing a brace for each other while sharing earbuds. Japanese businessmen—five or six of them—crouched together in a circle, weight on the balls of their feet, hands hanging between their black-suited knees. They were facing one another, as if they were having a board meeting, though none of them spoke. Some people had neck-support pillows and were resting against them along the walls; every once in a while someone would take his pillow over to someone else who seemed to be breaking down and in greater need. Although it wasn't comfortable, people stretched out on the concrete. A few security officers engaged in crowd control. When a guy tried to urinate in the corner, they grabbed him and stood talking to him with puffed-out chests. The message: *Sit down and hold it.*

Other security officers, many of whom had been caught in the fray, lounged together on the ground at one end of the hangar. They'd been put at risk now too, I guess. They had coffee, which they were sipping from Styrofoam cups. They had a whole urn between them, and a few people drifted over in that direction like seagulls toward a picnic. When they came back again—to sit down on their suitcases or against the wall—they were empty-handed. It wasn't long, though, before people began complaining and arguing. Some minor yelling matches broke out here and there: people smacked the backs of their hands and wanted to know about reimbursement. As the din rose, a woman with a bullhorn shouted that food had been generously donated to us by a pizza chain. It would arrive in an hour or so. It was eleven in the morning, and we had been in quarantine for almost three hours.

"We're doing our best here, people!" the bullhorn-woman informed us brusquely.

A handsome Indian man, who looked a little like Larissa's husband, Jay, approached her and we could see them having a serious conversation. They went back and forth, then she nodded and lifted the horn to her mouth again. It was likely some of the food would be vegetarian, she declared, and she expected there would be milk and juice for the children, as well as soda, but of course she had no idea of quantities. Children would be fed first. She asked that those who did not have dietary restrictions leave the vegetarian portions for those who did. Another woman came and took the horn from her and gave the same speech in Spanish, halting here or there, the button on the horn giving her trouble. It felt like a sombre, official potluck party.

Again, we waited.

Eventually a woman with a drill sergeant's bellow read out a list of names, mine among them. Reluctantly I left Mae and Kate, who were slumped together holding hands, Kate with her eyes closed. I had noticed that officials were occasionally making rounds with our forms and taking people away to the other end of the hangar. Now I hobbled after the other injured parties to a makeshift station where those who needed medical attention could get it. It was essentially a group of clean sleeping bags covered in paper sheeting and spread on the ground in front of an ambulance. I was ranked as low priority. I stood at the line's end on my bad knee, shifting my laptop bag around on my shoulder, and wishing I'd left it with Mae and Kate. High priority was clearly in the ambulance. I stood for a long time before I was allowed to move up to a "waiting seat" on a sleeping bag.

When it was my turn, the medic undid Mae's handiwork and briskly cleaned my knee. Behind a pair of protective glasses, her eyes were a watery blue, and beneath them were pouches like pockets. Like everyone I saw that week, she had a skin tone that didn't match her hair. It was fire-engine red, and I wondered if her pharmacy had run out of brown.

Through her paper mask the medic told me to brace myself. I was in for six stitches.

EMILY SCHULTZ

The woman next to me was having her fingers splinted. She had broken two knuckles trying to close another woman out of the bathroom stall where she had been hiding. She didn't even seem embarrassed about it.

My medic commented that a number of the injuries were crowd-related. The broken-knuckle lady said she'd heard rumours of two trample victims. I told her I'd seen them carried out.

Shaking her head, my medic exclaimed, "Good thing it wasn't a Macy's sale." She said it to distract me right when she was sticking me with the needle. I didn't laugh. I bit my lip. I watched the green thread zipping under my skin, tattoo-like.

The woman getting her fingers splinted said, "It's bioterrorism." She said she'd been reading an article about it that very morning in the limo to the airport. She stared blankly at her hand as her medic looped it up in gauze.

Her medic said through his mask that every time something happened at the airport, people would yell "the T word." He had a pleasant voice. The medics were trained to be cheerful in emergencies, I think.

"It's a big place," her medic told her. "Sometimes things just happen here. It's not always terrorism." He tied the end off and told her she was done. Then, squatting, he looked at my shin and watched my medic go under the skin a fourth time while he waited for another patient. The line of injured people had run out and they were about to start a new line, I guess. I found myself staring at the broad, good-looking face above his mask, and I said, "I think I'm gonna be sick."

"Hold it down," he instructed me. The softness that I had liked about his voice was gone.

"Hold on. Tying off," my medic said, and I felt a hard tug on my knee. We were two stitches short.

The male medic grasped my head and he and his partner lay me down on the ground. "Are you experiencing any pain? Dizziness? Do you have headaches?" he interrogated.

"No," I gasped, rolling onto my side to fight the nausea. I had noticed that lately I felt sick when I ate too much or too fast, and also when I hadn't eaten enough.

"Were you nauseous before the attacks?" the female medic asked, a flatness in her voice. They were a little bit afraid of me, I guess. Afraid that I would contaminate them.

I told them I was pregnant.

"Shit," my medic cursed. "Green sticker here!" She pulled her mask down slightly and yelled it again, louder, over her shoulder. Someone in the ambulance came running over with a sheet of stickers, and above me they ripped a tab off and a hand came down and thumbed it onto my shirt. "You didn't put it on your form," my medic chastised me, glancing over my questionnaire, her mask back in place.

"I didn't think it was important." The nausea was gone; fear had taken its place.

The female medic left abruptly and I could see her and the sticker-runner back by the ambulance, speaking to someone else in an EMS uniform and gesturing.

"I didn't think it was—" I said again to the other medic.

"Of course it is." He took my hand and yoked my arm around his neck. He told me that *we* were going to stand now, that we had to get me out of here. "Being in this area could still infect you," he told me.

He walked me over to the far end of the hangar, near where the officers were. It wasn't easy going because he was about six-two and my knee was swollen. One of the officers got up and gave me one of two chairs in the place; the other chair was back in the medical area.

"Sheppard is arranging transport for you as quick as she can." The male medic tapped the green sticker above my left breast. It already had a signature on it across a white stripe, and a UPC code. "This is your clearance if anyone asks. Wait here."

I felt like a piece of produce. A melon, to be precise.

The medic went back to his station and a cheer went up at the far end of the hangar. The pizzas had arrived. I could see stacks of thin white boxes being driven in by a figure in a hazmat suit. Another flatbed had trucked in a couple of port-o-johns, which were being erected along the far wall. Two, it looked like, for a crowd of three hundred.

Sheppard of the Radio Flyer–coloured hair jogged toward me like a stout but fast-moving tank. My laptop bag swung from one hand, a set of forms in the other.

It occurred to me that I wouldn't see Mae or Kate again.

"My friends—" I said to Sheppard, as she pressed my things into my hands. Then I realized they weren't really my friends, just two young women I'd imposed upon. Maybe on other days they weren't even friendly with each other.

"I don't know who you were with, dear," Sheppard said through her mask. "But if they come searching, I'll tell 'em where we sent you." She turned and trotted back toward her station.

A Jeep came promptly for me. It sounded its horn, and the officers let me out of the hangar through a side door. My driver wore a face mask, gloves, glasses; his hair was covered by a surgical scrub cap. I was taxied silently and speedily across the tarmac, where we were met by a minibus.

I climbed up into it and took my place among six or seven women, all much further along in their pregnancies than I was. Some barely fit in their seats. I've read somewhere that you aren't allowed to fly after seven months, and now that I'm at that point myself, I can say that most of those women were between five and seven months along. But at the time they sure looked huge. Maybe they loomed large also because they eyed me suspiciously—I had kept them waiting, or possibly even brought them back from the airport's far reaches. The driver put the vehicle into motion and we rolled out, trucking across the tarmac to a roadway, then curving around the airport before exiting and heading back toward the city.

PART TWO

SEVEN

LISTEN, BABY, THIS IS HOW LIFE WORKS. It's one thing and then another, and sometimes they go together, and sometimes they don't. I sound like my own mom when I say that, but these days I'm finding out maybe she knew a lot more than I ever thought she did. I got sprung from the airport because of my condition; if I hadn't been pregnant, or hadn't admitted to it, I'd have been back there in quarantine for three more days. There are reasons you're still here, but they aren't the reasons you think. I'm getting ahead of myself, though.

I remember the minibus let us out in the parking lot of a long, low building made of pale brick. There was a real estate office across the street and a fenced-off lot containing vehicles and scrap metal, the kind of spot where construction might be about to happen. There was a grade school and a Sunoco station. There were modest, very uniform houses with TV antennae and satellites, a KFC wafting its delicious deep-fried garbage in our direction, and billboards for cellular phone companies depicting cute animals at peace with technology. It was a place where people lived, and we had come to infect it.

Given my indelicate state, I was off the bus before the other pears, who were in various states of waddle. A woman in a pink uniform exited the low building and jogged over. She came right up to the bus and offered a gloved hand to the women, helped them down slowly, telling them, "Don't rush. Careful there. Take your time," and "I got you." The driver just sat there. Apparently it was not in his contract to help pregnant women, or at least not during an epidemic. I watched the other women's swollen ankles descend, their shirts ride up, their abdomens bump against the door's rubber seal as they turned sideways for the final step, firmly grasping the stranger's chalky glove. I took up the rear, and in we went, stopping to sanitize our hands at a dispenser like kids lining up at a drinking fountain.

I saw that one of the women wasn't pregnant but in fact had an infant snuggled so tightly against her bosom in a scarf carrier that I'd just naturally mistaken it for being part of her. The carrier was beige and one of the infant's feet made a small claw shape against the material, as if against a membrane, as though it wanted to break through. I remember how I stared at the toe impressions.

We filled out more forms inside. The same woman who'd helped the swollen ones off the bus brought us a bowl full of rinsed apples. We sat there, munching, ticking off boxes, and watching a silent LCD screen report on the place we'd just come from. We learned that the others were being kept in quarantine in the hangar for three days. The disease was thought to have a two-day incubation period. One of the women watching began to cry. Her daughter and husband were still in the hangar. She cried and ate at the same time, tearing great chunks out of the red fruit and crunching the white pulp. Another woman handed her a tissue from a box on an end table. The first woman thanked her and used the tissue to wipe the juice from her fingers, ignoring tears that were spilling down her cheeks.

It turned out that three of the pregnant women had partners in the hangar. One was on business, and one was coming from a funeral and hadn't wanted to fly at that stage. The woman with the sling freed her breast and fed the bundle before it could issue more than a few plaintive squawks. Even these were much too big-sounding for the shape of the thing that made them. Pink mouth and pink nipple latched together until the white orb of the woman was all that could be seen. The others chatted about due dates; about where they were from and where they were going; they asked about possible names. They complimented each other unfailingly, even when the names were terrible. They asked anything to avoid talking about the obvious: the reason we were together. I asked nothing and no one asked anything of me. The nurse called us one by one from the room.

After I had been seated in a small office, I asked the nurse what they would do with us.

"Do with you?" she repeated.

I asked if we'd be sent back to the airport.

"I don't think so. I mean, I really can't say. But I imagine if you have the sickness, they'll isolate you, and if you don't, they'll send you home."

She closed the door, leaving me alone with my sweat, which began to drip from my hairline down my neck and back, and behind my knees under my jeans. I hadn't realized it would be so easy to tell if we had contracted the disease. Didn't they have to wait for the two-day incubation?

The doctor came in and smiled weakly. She was younger than I had anticipated. She began talking right away.

"Antibodies bind to foreign invaders called antigens. They bind to them and neutralize a virus. Essentially consume them," the doctor told me, as she must have told the others. That was the simplest thing she said. She kept talking, but I felt as if waves of static were zigzagging between my ears. The doctor held her forefinger and thumb apart, then pinched them together, as if there were a substance between them and she was checking its viscosity. I got the impression that something was supposed to stick to something else. She wanted to measure the antibodies, and somehow this would tell her if I had contracted the virus by showing her if my system was reacting in a binding fashion.

"So if it sticks, that's a good thing?" I asked.

The doctor made a face I couldn't interpret, continued to explain in language I didn't comprehend. Apparently, this procedure was called an ELISA test, like a woman's name. She told me what the letters stood for. She just kept talking, but none of her words made sense to me.

"There are other tests we could do," she finished, "but this one is faster, cheaper, and more objective."

"It's a better test." I felt reassured.

"It's a more objective test," the doctor reiterated, as if she didn't want to commit to anything.

"I see." I asked if I was paying for it. No, she said. I signed the forms consenting to the test—or was I only saying I understood the test? The government had brought me here and the government was paying for it: maybe they didn't need my consent.

When we were done, I said, "There's something else I have to ask."

The doctor said she'd be right back, then we could talk. She left swiftly and returned less swiftly.

The doctor came back, sat down, and gave me the same smile she had before she ran the test. How fast was the test, I wondered—could she know the result already? If she did, she said nothing.

"The thing about this pregnancy . . ." I tapped the desk with one fingernail and watched my finger instead of her eyes. "I don't want it," I told her.

"I see," she said, a slight hitch in her voice. She asked me if I knew where I was.

"About ten miles from the airport . . . ?"

"Yes, Jamaica, Queens," she said, but that wasn't what she meant. She told me the name of the medical centre. Then she said it a second time, stressing *Saint*.

The centre was Catholic, a family practice.

"If it were up to me personally I would arrange service for you," the doctor said, as if we were talking about a transaction like renting a car or hooking up my cable. She said that these were not her beliefs, but that of course the policy wasn't up to her. She had to respect her workplace. She recommended a clinic in Midtown and said she wasn't going to note the conversation in the file.

None of our antibodies were binding—or perhaps all of them were. In any case, the group of us was given a clean bill of health and we were put back on the same bus we'd come on. It dropped us at the AirTrain/subway depot. Those who had places to stay in New York headed back into the city. Those who didn't, went back to the airport in search of flights out of other terminals, or to try to gauge what had happened to their partners or families.

I suddenly felt so tired I thought I might collapse. I stopped at a stand in the subway and bought a large bag of cashews and a package of M&Ms. I ate them both in handfuls, which helped a little. Then I rode back to the Dunn Inn, where Natalie's sister, whose name I didn't know, said she couldn't give me the same room. She checked me into Moira's old room, 306. I had been away for only twelve hours.

I hauled what fragments I still possessed upstairs. My checked luggage hadn't come on the cart into the air hangar, or if it had, I hadn't been able to locate it. So I was left with a broken laptop and the clothes I was wearing. I lay on my back on the blue quilt and, cradling the heavy room phone to my ear, dialled my mother. She started crying as soon as she heard my voice. She said a bunch of dumb, slightly incoherent, vaguely racist things about terrorism, and I said, "I'm all right, I'm all right," again and again, as tears ran down the sides of my face into Moira's quilt.

I loved my mother, even if she was racist. I loved that she hiccuped when she cried. In that moment, I loved everything about her. I loved that she'd grown up during a time when girls rolled their hair on soup cans to achieve curls instead of using a plug-in iron. I loved that she had met my father in a disco, and that she still called it a disco when everyone else called it a club. I had been conceived who knows where— maybe in the bathroom there, maybe in the back seat of his car, maybe at his apartment, maybe in my grandparents' home. I'd never asked. I even loved that the conception had happened in Windsor, a city that was like a grubby-kneed little sister to Detroit, a working-class town where sloppy unions transpired in alleys after last call and people looked the other way.

These are your grandparents I'm talking about now. And they met in an honest-to-gosh discotheque, like the kind I used to read about in the French textbook at school. *Allez-vous à la discothèque? Gaston et Gabrielle vont à la discothèque.* Dad had been tall with flaming red hair that went straight up, an open shirt collar—you couldn't miss him, Mom always said. Sadly, I got his hair and her height (or lack thereof). His last name was Urie, but she gave me hers, as if she'd known from the beginning it wouldn't pan out. That's a good thing, because to me Urie sounds like *urethra*, and imagine the teasing I'd have faced all through school. They were married briefly, then divorced, then together off and on. He'd come around again and again as they tried to work it out and be a family, but I'm about five in the last memory I have of him— eating ice cream outside the Dari DeLite on Howard Avenue, dirt from passing trucks making the chocolate swirl gritty— and then he was gone like something that had melted. That's my creation myth.

I told my mom I might need some money, a few hundred. I didn't tell her what it was for, and she assumed it was for the replacement flight to Toronto to see my thesis adviser. She'd never understood what I studied, but she knew school was important. She said she'd check with Richard about the money, but that the hair salon was going gangbusters since the Blonde Fury had broken out. "Went and broke out," that's how she worded it. When I asked what colour her own hair was, I heard the neck of her beer cluck against the mouthpiece. "Purple as a baboon's butt," she sputtered.

It would cost me a fortune to tell the story of my day all over again, so I reminded my mom to phone Larissa and fill her in. Then I hung up. For a moment I thought about emailing Karl. But the computer was broken and I doubted he was worrying about me yet. I wondered how long it would take for him to link what he knew of my travel plans to the national disaster.

———

I didn't always feel so tenderly toward my mom—your grand-mother, not that you'll meet her. It required catastrophes to coax that feeling out of me, to make me let go of grudges.

My mom changed after she met her boyfriend Richard, became happier, more settled. When I left for Toronto and grad school, I really didn't know what would happen to her. We'd been so set in our routine, and without me . . . well, I didn't think there would *be* a routine. I thought she would slide down-hill. But Richard came along and he effectively took my place.

Before him, about five years ago, there was Joe. He was just some jackass who looked like Mr. Clean and took my mom to suburban taverns, but when he and my mom broke up, she got drunker than I'd ever seen. I counted her beer bottles the next day and she'd put back eighteen. She'd been on a bad streak to begin with. Before him, she'd worked her way through a group of linebackers turned line workers who liked to drink as much as she did. She and the new one, Joe, had been going together about four months, which might have been a record for her around that time. He dropped her out of the blue—but not really, because he was a hothead and any little thing could set him off. She accused me of having a thing with him.

I remember we were in the Head Start salon. God only knows why she felt like she had to clean the shop at that moment. She used the water spray bottle that dampened children's heads during haircuts to wet the vanity. She swiped at it with a paper towel. Then she said, "He didn't like you hanging around. He said you were too old to live here. He didn't like you, you know."

"Oh, I know," I said, and I pulled the shampoo and conditioner bottles down from the shelf that she'd asked me to dust.

She was already unsteady on her feet. She'd been planning to sharpen her scissors, but she must have realized she was wobbly because she set down the scissors on the vanity next to her vodka glass and sat in her own styling chair.

"You didn't say something to him, did you?"

"I try to say as little as possible.".

She appraised me, her mouth scrunching. "You didn't do it, did you?"

"Do what?"

"*Fuck him.*" She leaned forward in the chair and stabbed her cigarette out in the ashtray. "Ya fucked 'im."

"Like I would!" I paused. "I don't—I haven't fucked anyone, Mom."

She said, "Oh, that just figures," but her tone and her facial expression softened. Then she put her scissors in the drawer and lit a second cigarette.

Later that week, Ruth, the majority owner of Head Start, walked in with bags of new hair rollers.

"This one's still a virgin," Mom said, gesturing at me with the comb.

"Well, that's no surprise," Ruth said, without raising an eyebrow.

I loved my mom, but I didn't want to be like her.

———

I took my laptop to a shop where they said it would take a few days to fix it, and they couldn't promise a full recovery. So for a while I bought newspapers and watched television to follow the outbreak. It took three days to locate and retrieve my suitcase from the airport.

In the meantime, I bought a package of plain white Hanes Her Way from the drugstore, even though they made me feel seven, and a couple of sports bras, and some kilts and cords and blouses at a slightly malodorous Salvation Army. I handed over these articles to be laundered for eighty-five cents a pound. I knew that when I got them back they would be passed over the counter to me on paper-covered hangers that declared: WE HEART OUR CUSTOMERS. As the shop owner took my clothes and his wife wrote down my name for the tag, they smiled widely at me. I wondered briefly if they did *heart* me to some extent, if commerce between people was a type of love. At the very least, our exchange felt more honest than any of mine and Karl's.

The cleaner was not far from my favourite deli. The creative writing students I'd seen before, the boy and girl, were there again. And this time they had a friend with them—a girl with her head shaved and a shiny red headscarf tucked in on itself around her scalp, old Hollywood–style. They were sitting at a tall table with stools, and were easy to spot among the businesspeople. The place was busy and I had to wedge myself in behind them to eat at a narrow ledge. The former peanut-butter-haired girl was now sporting jet-black tresses. She looked like Snow White.

I remember the skinny boy told jokes where every punch line ended in a zombie-like groan, one side of his mouth turning down, one hand lagging behind as he turned in his seat. "How many blondes does it take to invade an airport? Anhhhh. Anhhhh." He groaned eight times before announcing the punch line: "Eight! What does a blonde say when she bumps into you on the subway? Anhhhh. How do you know if a blonde is having an orgasm?"

"We're still blondes, you know," the shaved head put in before he could groan again.

"Blonde at heart," the original girl seconded. They ripped into a shared bag of potato chips and ate loudly, without reserve.

"Anhhhh," the boy groaned. His T-shirt sported a thought bubble with no text inside it.

I picked up a discarded newspaper near the garbage bin. It had a headline announcing the naming of the blonde virus. Scientists had settled on SHV, *Siphonaptera Human Virus*, after fleas, which they believed were involved in transmitting it to women who were vulnerable to becoming hosts. "When the insects blood-feed, the parasite enters the bloodstream of the host." The hitch in this case was that not all those who came into contact with the virus were likely to carry it or succumb to it. Some, like men or women with dark complexions, even if bitten by an infected flea, would show no signs of illness or transmit it to others. There was a sidebar with illustrations of other anthropods that had been vectors for diseases. Mosquitoes: dengue fever, yellow fever, human malaria. Fleas: bubonic plague, murine typhus, and tapeworms. Ticks: Lyme disease.

Tsetse flies: African sleeping sickness. Triatomine bugs: Chagas disease. Bats: Coronavirus such as SARS, rabies. Just reading the names made me itchy.

A related story described an attack outside a Planned Parenthood. "A chain of life became a chain of death this week. A group of anti-abortion protesters had linked arms to block women from entering the medical office when one of their own turned against them. The young woman, silently affected by the virus, arrived with her church group to participate in the demonstration. From within the chain she began screaming, then acted out violently, resulting in broken arms for two of the other protestors and the death of a church leader, Reverend Randall, 48. The name of the attacker, age 17, has not been released." I scanned the article, then rolled up that section of the paper and pushed it away. The travel section touted vacations to Cuba and Mexico. Large ads featuring bright blue skies beckoned me to say *sí* to Cuba. Meanwhile, I noted, Finland, Denmark, Sweden, Switzerland were bursting with SHV cases and in lockdown, travel-wise.

The students hadn't made up by the time I left the deli. I went back to the hotel and made phone calls, waiting through an hour or more of voice recordings before a woman told me that I would receive a credit for my missed flight, but that international travel was still cancelled. This had been a Major Event, the woman said, repeating it again as if it were a corporation's version of a personal day. If I needed to leave the country, she suggested, I should fly to a nearby city, such as Boston or Pittsburgh, then try again from there—contingent on there being no more Major Events. Because I still didn't have my computer and couldn't book a ticket online myself, I phoned a Flight Center. I discovered that by the time I added the cost of the flights—the one from Boston or Pittsburgh to Toronto would come out of pocket—I would save nothing with the voucher. I asked about Detroit from JFK, thinking I could get Mom or Richard to drive the half hour across the U.S.–Canada border to pick me up. But to travel in the next two days, even with the credit, would cost four hundred dollars more than my original flight. I told the Flight Center rep I would think about it and call her back.

The issue for me now wasn't whether the abortion was worth an extra four hundred; it was whether including Karl in my decision was. Fundamentally, I felt he had a right to know I was pregnant. At the same time, I didn't think he had any right to choose what would happen. Is that a contradiction?

On the one hand, I wanted him to say that he would leave Grace and we should have you together, but at the same time I didn't want to hear him say those words, because a cheater cheats—that's one thing you know when you start sleeping with one. Worse than that, by now I knew I didn't want to be tied to him even for a minute. The fact that he would send me to Wanda Kovacs had permanently changed how I felt about him.

I remember there was one other time my feelings toward Karl had irrevocably changed: we were buying cheese in St. Lawrence Market in preparation for our weekend at this cottage. He purchased the same kind twice, from two different stands, because, he said, the second one was better. When I told him he'd already bought that kind and why not a nice havarti or Edam, he insisted there was no comparison. I remember thinking, *Oh, so that's who you are.* I wasn't going to stop flirting with him over a block of cheese, of course, but the exchange had niggled at me for months.

In any case, I decided to stay in the city and deal with my dilemma there.

Within a week, *National Geographic* ran a fold-out colour map charting the attacks and outbreaks. New York had a bright red circle over John F. Kennedy International Airport. Land was shaded red all up and down the West Coast, starting in Los Angeles, which had the greatest concentration of cases and incidents, into Las Vegas, and up to San Francisco. Florida was like a sunburn, as were all the major cities and most of the southeastern seaboard. In Canada, outbreaks were concentrated in Vancouver, Toronto, Ottawa, and Halifax—port and business cities. Calgary had a lone single orange freckle. Likewise, all of the middle American states and cities were fairly empty—a muddy landscape of brown, blue, green.

Siphonaptera. The term sounded like something siphoning off the land, an earth vampire. What do I know about fleas except that they ride into one's home on the backs of stray dogs and cats? Imagine this tiny little creature, born into a cocoon, hatching out, not much more than a millimetre long, wingless and blind. It avoids sunlight, lives in dark places—sand, cracks, crevices, bedding—jumps on and off animals and humans, lives solely to find blood. It eats blood, then breeds. Wreaking havoc. Larissa had owned cats all her life and I remember visiting her after she left to go away to school in Toronto, a few years ahead of me—away from her mother's clean house—in shared student apartments on Huron Street or Spadina. I'd pick fleas off her pets, pinching the insects between my fingers.

The first time I heard about the Flea Vector Denialists I was sitting in a diner one afternoon, eating a hamburger. The volume on the flat screen in the corner was cranked. Onscreen, two men of about the same age were arguing across an illuminated desk. One man's hair was combed directly back from his forehead; the other man's hair was combed directly forward.

Loud man: Flea Vector Denialists claim hair bleach and highlighting products have destroyed the immune systems of women and allowed a mutant form of rabies to thrive, making blonde women a convenient, but by no means exclusive, host population. Look at the outbreak charts showing clusters around Brentwood, Grosse Pointe, and the Hamptons.

Louder man: Wait! How can you discount Plum Island Animal Research facilities? Ten miles away from the Hamptons. Three hours from the first clinical evidence of the Blonde Fury in New York City. Just like Lyme disease, this disease is flea-transmitted but government-made.

Loud man: Conspiratorial thinking is easy, but it's not science. You want answers fast, and when science caters to fast answers, people die.

Louder man: People are dying now. People are being killed.

Loud man: AZT was rushed to the market. They skipped testing, and it was proven to cause more harm. Right now the quick answers are social, not medical. Educate. Inform. Shut down the hair salons.

For some reason, this silly conversation galvanized me. I finished off the coleslaw and pickles and went back to room 306 at the Dunn Inn, where I phoned Information and asked for the number of the clinic the post-airport doctor had mentioned to me. A computerized voice read out the number in a clipped tone.

When I called, a woman with a deep Queens accent booked me an appointment. I should expect to be in their offices for three to five hours, she said, for blood work, a pregnancy test, medical history, ultrasound to determine my dates, discussion of my options and their risks and benefits, and the procedure itself if I decided to go ahead with it. Once they completed the procedure I would need someone to accompany me home. I wrote down the address and time at the top of the bloody-looking *National Geographic* map of North America.

———

An hour or so before my appointment at the clinic, I was standing on a Midtown street in front of an American Apparel store. A transparent photograph of a woman in a one-piece gymnastics suit, her arms thrown up above her head as if she was about to do a handstand, had been affixed to the window. In the window on the other side of the door was the same girl in a similar position, slightly turned. She was layered over the headless mannequins that had been pushed into gold lamé leggings by some patient window dresser. Decapitated figures wore items of clothing I couldn't identify as either shirts or dresses, complete with zip-up purple hoodies. On the wall inside, more plastic torsos—headless, legless, armless—hung from a metal grid, zipped into New Arrivals. I was early for the appointment, which was just beyond double doors to the right of the American Apparel store, through the lobby and up ten floors.

Someone was standing behind me, assessing me in the reflection. I turned and it was Kovacs. We both breathed a sigh of relief.

"That is you. Good, good." Kovacs swept a hand out and we shook, like colleagues, as people streamed around us on either side.

I had forgotten that my hair colour had changed since our meeting. Kovacs's own hair caught the light. It surprised me. I remember how I couldn't stop looking at it: spun sugar. She was the first blonde I had seen in at least a week. In the September breeze, her hair didn't budge, just sat on her shoulders perfectly, like a long golden helmet. On closer examination, I realized it was a wig, cut and styled. She must have shaved her head, but then vanity overtook her.

"Dr. Kovacs—" I began.

"Wanda," she said. "Really, let's not be formal at a time like this."

I thanked her for coming and said it went beyond the call.

But Kovacs wasn't looking at me. She was blinking in the window, fussing with the mascara on her eyelashes. When she finished, she said, "Pardon me," and flicked her fingers and frowned at the mannequins. She was dressed more casually than the last time we had met, but still expensively: a dark sweater and jeans, a cashmere scarf that might have been Hermés draped loosely about her neck, though it seemed to me we were just barely out of summer. I wondered if there was a designer collection out there inspired by "What to Wear to a Young Woman's Abortion." It occurred to me that she had probably spent as much on her day-off sweater as I was about to throw down at the clinic.

I marvelled that people in my age group were supposed to be the demographic for the store in front of us. I gestured to a figure in a chambray jumpsuit—a strapless top and a cinched elastic waist. It would flatter someone only if they were five-eight and a hundred and ten pounds.

"Can you see me in that?"

"No, I do not think so, dear. Leave it to the undergrads. They still need some regret in their lives." Then Kovacs asked if we had time for a coffee, or should we get me upstairs to the suction room?

I couldn't tell if she was being funny or mean, or if the two were always one and the same with her. Maybe she and I were more alike than I wanted to admit. Maybe Karl dated the same woman again and again. Around us, morning traffic surged and honked. To make myself feel better, I imagined Kovacs taking a shit. This is something I do sometimes when I feel nervous around people. It's better than imagining them naked, you know. I started doing it when I was in high school. When I confided in Larissa, she told me it was the sickest thing she'd ever heard. She told me I must have a fetish, which just for the record is not true. I've never gone there. I've hardly gone anywhere. Larissa did try my technique once though—at an art event where she felt like everyone was "scads" older and more important than her—and she admitted that it had worked. Part of it is about posture. The posture a person might adopt when alone. There are some people you imagine sitting very tall and upright, hands tightly clasped. Others you imagine slumped with hands between the knees. The secret posture of shitters. We all do it, right? At one point in university I switched it to imagining people's sex faces, but that had a strange effect on me. I became sexually attracted in third year to a lecturer whom I really didn't like—one who always said, "So what does this tell us?"—and it was mortifying, even though I kept thinking about it. So I went back to the taking-a-dump exercise. I decided that Kovacs was a chin-clutcher, like *The Thinker*, and felt a bit better. Don't get me wrong, I was happy she was there. It's just that she was such a pill. It's old-fashioned, but that's the word for her.

We hit the café two doors down, where she ordered an Americano and biscotti; I snagged a bottle of water in case I needed to drink something for the ultrasound, and paid for all of it. Kovacs did not reach for her wallet that time. She knew very well the favour she was doing me.

Aside from the shops at street level, the building housed a number of physicians and clinics—physiotherapy and psychotherapy—as well as design firms. I joked that I had thought there might be protestors, and Kovacs told me that it was no joke, we were lucky. This wasn't Canada, where maniacs were polite.

As we rode the elevator to the top floor, we stood side by side looking straight ahead, not at each other. I remember Kovacs slurped her coffee loudly and it made me think of her as more human.

Before the doors could ding open, I turned to Kovacs and said, "I really do appreciate it—I hate to put you out this way. It's only because I don't know anyone else in the city."

"Here I thought it was because we got on so famously." She smiled and stepped out into the hall. The place smelled of rubbing alcohol and Froot Loops. As we walked toward the clinic door, she asked me to please stop with the apologies and self-consciousness or we would never get through the day. If I continued in this manner, she said, I would only remind her how she could be at home doing her pilates or walking Tallulah. Then she stopped abruptly, her shoulders drawn back.

"My Westie," she amended, but the name of her dog wasn't what had made her halt.

The health clinic was closed. A sign had been taped to the glass:

SIPHONAPTERA HUMAN VIRUS ("BLONDE RABIES")
HAS CLOSED THIS OFFICE TEMPORARILY.
FOR YOUR OWN SAFETY, WE ARE NOT SEEING CLIENTS TODAY.
WE APOLOGIZE FOR THE INCONVENIENCE.

IF YOU HAVE AN APPOINTMENT, PLEASE BE ASSURED
SOMEONE WILL CALL YOU TO RESCHEDULE
WHEN WE REOPEN ON TUESDAY.

There was a phone number scrawled in blue pen across the bottom, in case I was in emotional crisis. It was for a children's helpline. A stack of pamphlets for the same organization had been dropped sloppily on the floor to the left of the door.

I registered the meaning of the sign, but found I couldn't move. I wasn't quite ready to leave. Perhaps I thought that if Kovacs and I stood outside the clinic door a little longer, something would change. I could feel my nasal passages becoming inflamed. I so did not want to cry in front of Kovacs. I swallowed and said I couldn't imagine being thirteen or fourteen and dealing with something like this. I tapped the note, indicating the number. It was something to say. The burning subsided.

"I can't imagine being thirteen or fourteen. Period," Kovacs said. Her face had taken on a sour look. It was as if she were more put out by my inability to access the clinic than I was. She tried the door handle. It twisted but didn't open. "There's blood on the carpet," she said.

It was true. Someone had pulled down a shade inside the glass, but it stopped partway. On the blue-grey carpet, there was indeed a bloodstain—about the size of my hand. In spite of the lights being out, the stain was unmistakable.

"That's why they didn't phone you—they shut down hastily. They've had an attack. Check your phone," Kovacs commanded. It was as if she honestly couldn't believe what had happened and required proof.

I pulled out the phone, but there were no messages.

"How dreadful," Kovacs said. "How dreadful."

She squatted and put her hands around her face, peering in the window, the slim curve of her buttocks hovering above her square-heeled shoes. Then she stood again, and turned to me. She asked if I thought it had happened the day before. The hardness had fallen from her and she looked genuinely lost. Clearly, this was the closest she'd been to an attack.

A woman came out of an office a few doors down and headed in the opposite direction. I called to her and asked if she knew anything.

Reluctantly, the woman came back toward us. I noticed she still kept her distance, as if she thought we might be infected. She was wearing scrubs. The door she'd come out of was a dentist's office, I think.

"Police, ambulance, it happened around five last night. Just thankful it wasn't us. But you know, women's health care—there's bound to be more risk."

"Perhaps you should try somewhere else, dear," Kovacs said to me, and she seemed more like herself again. "Just to be safe." She patted my elbow with something between friendliness and formality.

"Good luck," the dental lady said, and moved off down the hall.

"But Tuesday," I said. A door opened and closed in the distance. "Tuesday or Wednesday?"

The question hovered between us.

Kovacs peered down at me. She said that she simply couldn't do it, that she was leaving the continent—and none too soon, it seemed. "This outbreak. I've made plans to fly to Mumbai from LaGuardia. I told you this on the phone. Research." She made finger quotes around the word *research* as if she didn't care that I knew she had other reasons for going. It wasn't until the following week, but she was going to be packing and frantically making arrangements.

Yes, her decision was cold. I thought it then, and now . . . well, I assume she's safe, after all. So how can I blame her?

We waited for the elevator, staring at the illuminated red Down arrow. I felt sick to my stomach. I put my palm against the wall to steady myself. I remember Kovacs tossed her coffee cup into the trash can, and ran her hands up and down her knit scarf, held on to its ends like she was weighing something.

"I am very sorry, but you are on your own."

We boarded the elevator, and as it took us down, I felt like its bottom was dropping out.

We exited into the lobby, then out to the street, and we both turned toward the American Apparel store before pausing, realizing we should be sure to walk in separate directions. We stood in front of the twin images of the spandex-clad girls with their arms up.

Kovacs put her hand on my arm again. "Phone Karl," she said from beneath her shiny synthetic bangs. "He has the money. He can fly in for this appointment if you make him."

"Do you think he'd leave Grace?"

"Grow up, Hazel," Kovacs said, her voice rising over the din of rush hour. She squinted into traffic. It had become too hot for her scarf, and she unwound it and shoved it into her bulky black purse, her fingers scrabbling. "He has been with that *bitch* ten years." The word *bitch* emerged from her lips as if she relished putting her mouth around the shape of it. She leaned in and embraced me stiffly, which took me aback. She smelled of talc and bitter coffee. She kissed my right cheek and then my left, and before I could thank her or kiss back, she turned and stalked off, past the clothing store and the mannequins without hips or breasts or heads.

I haven't seen her since.

EIGHT

AFTER GRACE AND I LOST THE TV SIGNAL HERE, she went on a jag. She said a red wine hangover was a bitch, but what else was there to do? She drank and talked about the outbreak, pontificating like someone who worked in television—which she does, or at least did—parroting things she'd read or seen as if they were her own opinions.

Meanwhile, I read books of Karl's that he left here on who knows which getaway. Or maybe he brought them here in boxloads—things Grace didn't want around their condo. Occasionally I got up and did the yoga position the Child for a minute or two. Grace called it a "supine" pose. I couldn't tell if that was a nice way of saying "doesn't require a lot of effort," but then I decided that Grace isn't nice enough to cast about for the gentle word for things. Sometimes I do the Cat and the

Cow too, because those only involve getting down on hands and knees and flexing my back.

One of the books of Karl's that I was reading last week was *Willing Seduction: The Blue Angel, Marlene Dietrich and Mass Culture.* I came to this passage: "Once the source of endless pleasure, the female voice has stripped Rath of masculine authority, effected its crisis and uprooted him from his class. Unshaven, unkempt, and dressed in tattered clothes, misplaced and displaced in the cabaret milieu, he is the tragic shadow of his former self."

It gave me an odd sense of déjà vu. I put the book down for a second, then picked it up again. I'd heard Karl say these words. I closed my eyes and tried to remember where. I had watched the film with Karl here in this cabin, but—looking around—I knew it wasn't here he'd said them. I was supposed to watch *The Blue Angel* for that first symposium I took with him, but somehow I had missed doing so. Karl said he couldn't believe he'd let me pass the course—and he made me watch it with him.

Then the memory came to me, like a perfect snapshot: the long table that ran down the middle of the symposium room. It was my first class and everyone else's third. Dr. Mann. I remember I sat there looking at him while he spoke. I had believed the words he was saying were his own. This was a couple of months before anything occurred between us. He was standing, and everyone else was seated around the table. I remember thinking, *Yeah*, when he said "stripped of masculine authority"—yeah, maybe I could take this course. Maybe Dr. Mann would make a good adviser.

I remember it was a cramped, narrow room, and yet Dr. Mann seemed so apart from the rest of us. He closed his eyes when he spoke, like he knew what he wanted to say, like he was listening to a piece of music only he could hear and was trying to identify it. I envied that separation, that ability to be so caught up in an idea. His face was made of lines. I could draw it for you. There was a set of brackets around his eyes, and another around his mouth. There was a double T-shape across his high forehead. Short, thick brown eyebrows sat above his square metal glasses. Vertical lines of tendon ran down his neck. Later he sat at the long table with us, and under the table, his feet bounced up on tiptoe, his dress shoelaces dangling, even as his voice went calmly on. He seemed like two different people, one below the table's surface and one above.

"The CIA is behind this," Grace interrupted my reverie, and I lowered the book, unsure what she was talking about.

I was beginning to worry that if I went into labour with you, I wouldn't be able to drive myself, and Grace wouldn't be sober. I worried that even if she were sober, she might go into some kind of spontaneous vengeful state and just let me bleed out, or she might panic about the disease and I would be left bleeding even if she *didn't* intend it. I mean, we humoured each other, and there were occasionally acts of kindness, but she was erratic, that's for sure. That's one thing you can count on in an alcoholic.

I told myself not to dwell on it—but here we are, my little cub. It's morning, day four on our own now, and I'm here with Larissa's dead vehicle, and Grace Pargetter is not.

———

After the missed appointment at the clinic with Kovacs, I lay in bed and tried not to think about the money sitting in my bank account. The thing about the first months of pregnancy is that they're almost incapacitating. You incapacitated me—like a vampire. I'm not exaggerating. I felt as limp as if I'd lost blood. Even the smallest errands exhausted me. I feel no animosity toward you now, my little parasite, but really, truly, it was as if you planned it, this tactic.

I remember one night I dreamed you were scratching me, clawing your way out through my abdomen, and eating my innards on your way. I turned over onto my stomach and went back to sleep. Yes, I dreamt that. I'm not going to lie to you. People pretend otherwise, but motherhood is scary shit, girl.

When my computer was ready for pickup, I used some of the money from Mom and Richard to pay for it. As I walked to a nearby café where I could sit and get wireless, I passed a small assembly of people. They were positioned at the edge of the sidewalk, where normally one might find vendors of sunglasses and scarves. Across from the small crowd was a sign that said WORSHIP BEGINS AT THREE. It stood beside an open doorway. I peered in at stairs that must have led to a walk-up second-floor church squeezed above the storefronts. I stepped over a long orange extension cord that snaked between the sneakers of the onlookers and connected to a pair of buzzing clippers. The man wielding them had a hard, pocked face, cruel as the moon's surface. In the thick sunshine of midday, he was wearing a black suit. He held the clippers above the head of a girl covered in a smock. I wondered why she wasn't in school. She looked no more than fourteen.

"This hair-borne illness," the man shouted, and without meaning to, I stopped to watch. "This hair-borne illness"—he grabbed a hank of her seed-brown hair—"has been sent from God. That's right, sent from God as a punishment for vanity. A punishment for promiscuity! A punishment for those who worship false deities! A punishment for pride!" He kept going, coming up with new reasons for the punishment.

An assistant in a teal dress held up a handful of the hair, then cut into it with a pair of scissors. The girl in the smock watched it fall. For a moment, she looked like she might cry. Then you could see her face rearrange and compose itself. Some people hooted and clapped.

Someone else muttered obscenities and dodged around the group. Deking between people, he expertly cut a trail for me.

I've always felt uncomfortable with religion—with the exception of Catholicism, which is so creepy it's almost admirable. Besides, Catholicism is a requisite for horror movies. When I was growing up, five out of ten of my classmates were Catholic, but when I asked Mom about our religion, she just said, cigarette hanging from her lip, fingers flying over her friend Ruth's hair as she snipped, "One rule, Hazel: do unto others. That's all you need—one golden rule." So I always visualized religion as an object: a ring, a coin, or even a gold filling, something with weight and value that you could use if you really got down on your luck, but that, at the same time, was fairly useless.

This little assemblage was surreal. I don't know what denomination these people were, if any. As I walked on, I heard more clapping and the rattle and buzz of the clippers. When I looked back, the hard-faced man was taking a strip off the side of the unhappy girl's head. Locks littered the sidewalk and bristles appeared at her scalp. Like brown leaves, the clippings rolled away in the breeze, out into the street. Car tires rolled over them. As the two figures moved around her, continuing to snip and clip, coils rained down on the girl's shoulders and smaller wisps floated on the air. The man commanded her to smile, his voice thundering. "You have said, 'No to vanity!' 'No to promiscuity!' and 'Take that, pride!'"

At the wireless café, I found an email from Moira's friend waiting for me. I had emailed her before turning to Kovacs for help. She apologized for the delay, saying she'd had a scare when she thought her mother had contracted the virus. Thankfully it had turned out to be food poisoning. She'd been with her mother in the hospital for two days, and hoped I'd managed all right with my appointment. She asked me if I'd heard from Moira, said she had seen on Moira's website that she was supposed to be back in the city for another show. Like the woman in the dental scrubs at the medical centre, she closed by wishing me luck, as if things like life and death were decided by the stars.

There was an email from a women's organization whose newsletter I had signed up for late one night in a bout of lonely, political earnestness. *Blame the disease, not the women!* their headline proclaimed. Their newsletter attacked the language being employed by the media and prophesied the impact of the disease on women's services as well as pink-collar workers.

There was also an email from Karl, and I left this one until last. He wrote that he had only just realized I might have been caught in "that madness at the airport." He was quite emotional and signed off **Love, Karl,** but I noted how the email had come a full week after I'd been expected home. I considered writing back, but when I looked into the bottom of my cappuccino cup, I found only foam.

I didn't know then that this would be our last correspondence: love from Karl; and from me, silence.

New York's cineplexes got shut down, which is how I found myself the following day in an artist's warehouse space in Williamsburg for a showing of three films layered overtop of one another—three versions of *King Kong* playing at once. The artist was French, from Paris; her name was Camille Henrot. It all added up to layers of ghost, blonde and beast, city and jungle. I watched cars driving through close-ups of faces. I had always felt an overpowering empathy with the beast: I *was* Kong. *The King Kong Addition,* it was called. It made me imagine art as an equation—an addition and subtraction of empathy, understanding, what the viewer brings to a cultural work just by being present. I'd thought the filmmaker would be there and I wanted to ask her about her interest in icons and if she could tell us what was happening with the plague in France, whether it was impacting her current work. But she wasn't there, or perhaps I'd got that part wrong. When I asked the couple sitting next to me about this, they told me the King Kong work was several years old and had been sent over for a single screening, without the filmmaker.

Watching those beautiful blonde actresses—Naomi Watts layered over Jessica Lange layered over Fay Wray—I thought of Karl's face. It was a man's face, but it was also a face full of clouds. I had seen him fully naked only twice. Once at my apartment, and once here at the cottage. It hurts if I think of it too much. My favourite part was the place where his hip bone jutted against his skin—that, and the divot at the base of his knotty throat. Ours wasn't much of a relationship, but it was mine. Karl was the kind of man who would walk out into a storm thinking he could beat it, then find out later he'd been skirting a tornado just twenty miles north and was lucky all he'd got was drenched. He made you feel fiercely protective of him. Maybe that was also why I hadn't told him about you; maybe the hesitation wasn't just my anger. The clinic hadn't phoned that Tuesday when they'd said they would. When I'd checked their website there was a message across the homepage saying they were very sorry but the city had stepped in and shut them down "due to gyno-threat." I squinted at the movie screen and tried to see only one layer. I swallowed down my queasiness. I concentrated on Fay Wray.

When I walked out of the art space, afternoon sunlight dazzled me. The couple who had been sitting next to me on folding chairs began to bicker on the sidewalk about where to get dinner; they were thirtysomethings and were similar in their manners, hairstyles and dress—masculine/feminine versions of each other. One was tugging on his blazer and the other was trading spectacles for prescription sunglasses. They looked like worn-in shoes, turned toward each other, creased and faded. I envied them their choices. Putting my hand along the ridge of my glasses, I shielded my watering eyes.

It was time to go home and face Karl. I planned to fly out of New York again—or attempt to—and Larissa said she could pick me up. "But it's going to be hard."

I thought at first that she meant hard on her—geographically, schedule-wise, or maybe even emotionally—since she'd been stuck at the Toronto airport waiting for me when the JFK disaster was announced. I told her I'd get a commuter flight at a reasonable time so she could get Dev from daycare on her way from her job at the gallery.

But she said to hang on, and she covered the phone again. In the background I could hear the cadence of Jay's voice.

She said distinctly, as if her hand had slipped from the mouthpiece, "I'm not going to tell her that," and then after another moment, to me, "Uh-huh, Jaichand says to rent a car and drive if you haven't bought your ticket. Or even if you have. Don't fly. You'll be lucky to get in." She said the military was running the airport now. "Jay read that they'll definitely make you do a carpet-and-drapes test." She was always flipping back and forth between Jaichand's real name, and his nickname, Jay.

"A what?"

"Apparently they're making women show their pubic hair."

"That's so . . . wrong."

"I know! They say they have to be able to assess your risk level before they let you into the country." There was a dull flick-flick in the background.

"You didn't start smoking again?"

Larissa sighed. "My son still doesn't know me. He says I'm not his mom."

Remembering Kovacs, I told her to get a wig. She could find a good one if she was willing to pay for it.

"It's not just because of the hair, it's I've been crying a lot. Dev's a little kid, he's confused by strong emotions in adults. He's just not used to them."

"What's going on, Lar?"

This launched her into a prepackaged panic. She said she could tell I was only reading American news. I'd thought I'd been following along pretty well, but she commanded me to read the CBC and BBC websites. "It's really intense. They're predicting a ten percent population drop in Europe if things continue. International travel is one of the main ways the disease is spread: we're such globetrotters these days. Scientists say it originated with fleas, possibly in California or Florida—"

"I know that. I thought the Netherlands—"

"Regardless," Larissa insisted, and I could hear her dragging on the cigarette, "the main point is that they *don't know* how it's reacting with melanin. I mean, what do fleas and melanin have to do with each other? I'm with the Flea

Vector Denialists on this one. Really, they have no handle on this. Yes, we can shave, we can wear wigs, but you think they know what's happening? They don't. They have *theories*, that's all. New York is teeming with cases—they say because of its population and because it's a hub for the rest of the country, travel-wise. There are cases here in Toronto, but mostly they're trying to keep it out. Today there was a headline proclaiming 'The Blonde Death.'"

"That's terrible."

"Everything is." There was a quaver in Larissa's voice.

"You don't have to pick me up. I'll see about renting a car and driving through Buffalo," I told her resolutely. I clicked off and lay on the bed with the phone, staring at it. Larissa and Jay had married at city hall to avoid a large wedding while she was pregnant; she was my first married friend, and this had made her seem instantly ten years older than me instead of one. She and Jay lived in a condo building with advertising on the side, a bank ad proclaiming that we all had more money than we thought we did. The development was positioned strategically with access to the expressway, a view of the CN Tower, and a short walk to the St. Lawrence Market. They had a beautiful child, and beautiful clothes, and a small but beautiful living space with colourful, delicate things inside it made of glass, paper, and hard plastic.

All week, for a living, Larissa made phone calls and sent emails to international donors. She wrote grant applications explaining why the work done by her gallery was making an important contribution to the country's cultural environment and exactly how the gallery engaged the public in diverse ways. She had pretended to be an artist throughout her youth, and had become an administrator. She didn't need the income really, but chose to work anyway. On the advice of lifestyle magazines, she spent money on what she called "experiential investments" for herself and Jay and Devang—activities, classes, shows, restaurants, travel. Sometimes she paid for me, and I protested only a little. She kept a Full Life Diary with special sections earmarked for *Health, Relationships, Meaningful Work, Recreation, Spirituality*, and *Personal Goals*. She had worn various Indian camisas and pyjamas throughout her pregnancy and looked radiant. She had learned to cook curries so that Jay wouldn't have to make his own lunches. She became good at them, the way she was good at almost everything she put her mind to.

Every day Jaichand aimed an extensible light into people's faces and watched them squint and open their mouths like babies. He put a mirror inside them and looked for barely visible holes. Sometimes, if he used gas, people disclosed things they wouldn't otherwise. He did root canals and put crowns in for businessmen who confided they had piercings or tattoos in unseen places, and for condo wives who confided they were having virtual affairs. He took wax between his gloved fingers, positioned it between their molars, and said, "Bite down."

Jay made jokes about these things at parties. Larissa made jokes about how landing a dentist was a better deal than landing a doctor. Neither of them meant these remarks; both of them meant them.

I'd first met Jay at a party just like that. I had been flipping through a fashion magazine on our host's coffee table because I was never good at small talk. I stopped at an ad spread for Fructis shampoo. It wasn't the image but the slogan that caught me: *No one makes your hair stronger*. I thought the personification was interesting, *no one* not *nothing*. As if the product were your best friend. Or maybe a higher power.

"The word *shampoo* comes from India. It's Hindi," Jaichand told me. He told me shampooing had originally meant a scalp massage with oils, and when it caught on in Britain, the word eventually evolved to include washing with soap-flecked water and herbs. I'd known the first marketed shampoos had surfaced around the turn of the century, but hadn't known this. I asked him how he'd come upon this nugget, and he said, "Don't I look wise?" and mugged a face as serious as a mountain. Jay knew a lot of obscure facts that had nothing to do with dentistry.

I was the person who introduced him to Larissa when a little group of us went to see a movie. It was shortly after I'd first moved to Toronto and Larissa and I were figuring out how to be friends again, grown friends, friends in the same city as opposed to high school friends. We'd been away from each other during our undergrad years. Now we were friends who didn't tell each other about our sex lives, friends who didn't admit to feeling crazy or depressed. Instead we called each other up and complained about public transit; we had brunch or went to dinner together at restaurants; we caught a concert or an art show together. By the end of the movie night, Larissa and Jay had swapped email addresses. At first I thought she was interested in him because she thought I liked him. I *did* like him, but not romantically—the idea was ludicrous. Men like Jaichand—good-looking, accomplished, well-off, intelligent, funny, sexy men—were not interested in me. It made me uncomfortable to think about both ideas: the idea that he might be, or might have been, interested; and the idea that she might be interested in him as a way to best me.

But now, I think Larissa took my introduction as a recommendation. Like a letter of reference: he came through me, and she trusted my opinion. It wasn't love at first sight, but they fit together. They got married quickly. And she got pregnant even more quickly. Some people might have said she was trying to "land" him, but I wouldn't say that. Larissa came from a better home than I did—her dad worked at Windsor City Hall. She had gone to a rich high school, and she was smart; even when she slacked off she still made honour roll. Larissa could have had anyone she wanted. She didn't need to "land" anyone.

The first time I saw Larissa she was sixteen and sitting on the bumper of a car, under a street light in a parking lot down by the Detroit River. She was wearing a blue-and-white sundress, very Shaman Shack, this fair-trade store in downtown Windsor that I always walked past but, at fifteen, hadn't worked up the courage to go into yet. It was just after sunset, but not that dark yet. Dusk. The July long weekend. Detroit and Windsor always partnered for Fourth of July/Canada Day fireworks.

I was in a foul mood because my mom hadn't let me ride my bike downtown to the Freedom Festival. My mom was dating Pete then. He came between Gary and Ray—and all of this was years before Richard. Pete wore an open golf collar even though his chest hairs were grey; he wasn't that much older than Mom, maybe forty-five, but he had a lot of grey curly hair, which seemed to be everywhere on him, like soot.

There was nothing my mother liked better than a man with a suntan and shining silver hair. Although her steady customers were mostly women from the neighbourhood, she had one male customer who insisted on dying his hair. I remember my mom would Scotch-tape a bit of the grey fringe around the front down to this customer's cheeks and forehead, dye the rest hawk brown, and then flip the silver strands backward overtop for a "natural" look. It was about as natural as drinking orange juice after brushing your teeth. The guy looked like he had walked out of the 1970s and into the 1990s.

Pete's hair was almost all grey—no dye for him. Mom really liked Pete—she said he was built, which maybe he was for an old guy. He had his own place and sold used lawn mowers from a lot out near the racetrack. I didn't care one way or the other about him. When I was leaving the house after her command not to ride my bike to the festival—"You know there'll be drunk Americans out driving tonight"—I must have given my mom a sour look, because suddenly Pete wanted to be my buddy.

"Wait, gotcha somethin'."

He went to his gym bag, which meant he was planning to

stay over, and pulled out a single roman candle. He handed it to me, along with a black plastic lighter with the words *Johnnie Walker* on it and an image of a man in boots with a top hat inked on the side.

I took the objects tentatively.

"That there's a collector's item," Pete said of the lighter. And, "Don't set anything on fire." He opened his wallet and handed me ten bucks.

Later I was wandering up and down the river, between families with lawn chairs and teenagers who were half-corked. I was holding the roman candle in my hand, trying to decide if I would set it off, and whether I was going to stay out.

"Hey, Firecracker!" the girl on the bumper yelled. She threw her arms up in the air and crossed them, waving them back and forth. "Hey, you, Firecracker Girl!"

I braced myself and waited for the insult. She was with two guys, both older. One had a ponytail and was wearing jeans and a long-sleeved shirt even though it had been a hundred degrees all day. The other guy was better-looking, with spiky bleach-blond hair, a white T-shirt with tattoos peeking out from the sleeves, cargo pants, a length of plumbing chain at the throat. The kind of gaze that made me worried. As my mom would've said, "Handsome as hell and don't he know it."

But they weren't making fun of me—they wanted something.

"You got a light?" the girl called, jumping off the car and jogging across the lot to me.

A silver ankle bracelet made of bells chirped with each step. She put the cigarette in her mouth and held her hand out. She had on a clingy white T-shirt beneath the sundress, so that she looked half hippie, half La Senza. She was tall and her arms were long and gold.

"I don't smoke," I told her.

"But you have a light for that—" She gestured at the roman candle I was holding.

At her command, I dug into my jean shorts and retrieved the Johnnie Walker lighter.

"I'm Larissa," she said around the cigarette as she sparked it like a pro.

She wore her hair long and iron-straight, parted down the middle, no bangs, one side tucked behind an ear. She walked back to the car with my lighter and I followed her.

"Hey, Molly," the bleach-blond guy said, putting his hand out for the lighter, which Larissa passed him, "who's your friend?"

"Hazel," I said, not wise enough to take the cue that she hadn't told them her real name.

"Nice," he said, flicking the lighter. "You drink Black Label?"

I shook my head. He passed the lighter to his friend.

"What about beer?"

"That's a stupid question," Larissa said. "Everybody drinks beer. You don't get sick on it."

The other guy handed me back the lighter, appraising me as he did. "She's not old enough to drink," he said.

"That's Rob. Don't listen to him."

"Fuck off, Derek. It's Robert," Rob said. "How come you only have one?" He gestured to the roman candle, then turned away from us to gaze out over the river, expelling the cigarette smoke.

"That's—that's all he gave me," I stammered.

"At least they sold to you," Larissa said.

I had gone up a notch in her eyes: she thought I'd bought the firework.

"You want a beer?" Derek nodded to the back seat of the car. I forget what kind it was, just an ordinary car.

"Not here," Robert said. He clearly had moral misgivings about the fact that he and Derek were in university and Larissa and I were minors. Either that, or he was worried about getting caught.

Larissa began edging around the car in a floating, shuffling little dance; a few cars over, someone was playing music. She was waving her cigarette up and down. It reminded me of a firefly, her head dipping and her hair following, her arms weaving, and the glow of that cigarette arriving at her mouth again and again. When she came back around, she looked at me and winked. She was a thick girl, like me, maybe a little smaller, size twelve or so. But she was tall, which makes all the difference between stacked and stout. She had a heart-shaped pixie face with a sprinkle of freckles across it, the kind of face guys automatically love. She step-danced in strappy sandals, leather flowers encircling her toes. She yanked open the back door of the car and climbed in. A decision had been made.

"You should sit up front with me," Derek said, draping a hand over the open door and placing the other on the car roof, peering in at her.

"Nuh-uh," she said. "I sit with my girl."

Suddenly I was not just a stranger but her friend. I was going with them. Because I had a lighter. Because I was a girl and there were two guys.

"Unless you let me drive," Larissa sang, leaning her head to one side, her hair shifting.

"You got a licence?" Derek asked. He looked up and glanced over the car at me like I was in on the whole thing. His eyes were so blue that his gaze made something pool low inside me. He had more pronounced eyelashes than I did. He was wearing eyeliner, I realized. It was hot.

"Got a permit . . ." Larissa cajoled.

"*Rob–ert*," Derek drawled, "get in the front."

Larissa rolled down the window and tossed her cigarette butt out. I couldn't believe she had sat in their car smoking without even asking if it was okay. She had such nerve.

No one had ever asked me to go for beers before. I got in the car.

As we headed away from the crowds downtown, out along Riverside Drive, Robert rolled down his window and stuck his head out like a dog. Like he couldn't be bothered to talk to us. The sound of the wind clipped the conversation between the front and back seats. I watched his ponytail fly around. It was sweltering and I was glad for the breeze. I leaned in toward Larissa's ear and asked if she knew these guys.

"Anh," she said, making that waffling hand motion that my school's French teacher always made when she said *comme ci, comme ça*—so-so. "I've seen them around. How well does anyone know anybody, man?"

"I have to be home by midnight," I told her.

"Don't worry about it." She shrugged. "He seems like he likes you." She indicated Robert behind his back.

I told her I thought the other one was cuter.

"Yeah . . ." she inclined her head. "But I think I might be in love with him."

I remember being impressed that she believed in love.

By the end of the night we'd stolen a canoe from a dark house along the waterfront, from someone the guys vaguely knew. It probably wasn't a smart thing to do, but we paddled out to Peche Island, an uninhabited bit of land shaped like a crooked question mark, floating between Grosse Pointe and Windsor. Larissa went off into the woods with the gleaming-haired Derek, leaving me alone with a beer-breathed Robert, who didn't seem that happy to be stuck with me. We sat on a thick log of driftwood embedded in the sand, looking back toward the low beaded lights of the Windsor skyline.

"What do you think they're doing?" I was already a bit light-headed but I tipped back some more of the beer. I hated the taste and smell of it—it reminded me of my mom—but there I was and it seemed like the thing to do.

"Them? They're probably banging boots by now," Robert said flatly.

I'd never heard the saying. It reminded me of someone kicking the side of a house to get mud or dog shit off his shoes.

He asked me why I'd come out there, and I said I didn't know, and he said he didn't either. Then he slid over next to me, and even though I'd never been kissed, I knew he was going to kiss me, so I set down the beer in the sand and licked my lips. He looked me in the eyes and leaned in, and then his mouth was on mine and his eyelids flicked closed. He kissed me once, just a peck, and then I said, "Glasses," and took them off and held them in my lap. His long hair hit my face, which was kind of nice, and I could feel him breathing, then he pried my lips open with his tongue and put his hand on my boob over my clothes, just like that. Either I stopped kissing him, or I leaned back enough that he got the idea I was sort of done with the moment.

"How old are you really?" he asked, pulling away.

I didn't lie. He and Derek had five or six years on us.

"What about Molly?"

"Isn't her name Larissa?" Then I held up the roman candle, because I thought you could stop a boy kissing you if you gave him something else to do. "Do you want to light this?" I asked.

Later Larissa told me everything that she and Derek had done in detail. She said Derek totally wasn't worth it. She was wild. She would have laughed if I'd told her she would one day keep a Full Life Diary. Larissa didn't need a diary then. She went after the whole experience, the full life, and I kept her secrets for her.

After our phone call ended, I lay back against the motel pillows and wondered what it was that Jay had instructed her to tell me. It sure wasn't long, baby, before I found out.

NINE

WHEN I FIRST ARRIVED HERE at the cottage, I really thought everything would be okay. I remember steering into the drive-way, which was thick with snow. I figured Karl had been here for some time and hadn't shovelled. I didn't know that the snow could collect that way overnight, blowing, filling in the tire grooves. As I neared the cottage I could see Karl's Mini Cooper under the carport. A stupid car for Canada, but it lit something inside me to see it again. My hands shook as I killed the engine. When I got out, snow squeaked beneath my soles. I pounded three times on the cherry-coloured door. My knuckles turned red as I waited. My breath went in and out. I called his name. The wind seemed to take it from me.

You know, of course, that it was Grace who answered. She pulled open the door slowly, after about half an hour, when I had already circled the place, sinking flesh-deep into the snow and getting it somehow under my pant legs and inside my boots. I was standing on the deck in the back and peering through the sliding glass doors. The place was aglow, and because it isn't large, I could see most of it from there. The back of that couch, the old-fashioned record player, the king-size bed tucked into the alcove to the right where Karl and I did it that first time, not even separate from the living space. The only things I couldn't see were the kitchen and the bath. I was about to resign myself to the fact that in spite of the car, no one was here, when I saw the boots. Sitting on the stone tile to the left of the door. When I went round front again, I pounded and yelled, her name this time, interchangeably with his: "Grace! Karl! Karl, it's Hazel! Grace, let me in!"

I remember Grace cracked the door and all she said was "What do you want?" Her face peered out from underneath a turban, her narrow nostrils quivering. The turban was a thin white scarf, and it gave her the appearance of wearing a bandage around her head. I thought she might have been bathing, but she was wearing makeup. Her eyebrows had been stencilled on.

"Is Karl here?"

She looked down at my torso. "What do you want?" she repeated.

That first night with Grace was the longest. She was so reluctant to let me in, and when she did finally allow me inside to warm up, she watched me constantly. Every time my eyes came to rest on some object, she would follow my gaze, then look back at me, as if she would be able to tell whether I recognized things inside this space. We barely spoke at first. She simply said, "Fine," and held the door open for me to enter. She went into the kitchen area and put a kettle to boil on the antique stove. We waited for the water, and when it was hot, she tripped past my melting boots with a glare and set down yellow mugs of steaming lemongrass on the coffee table.

I knew where the bathroom was, but asked anyway, and she brusquely told me. When I returned she had sunk into Karl's cowboy chair, a low glider on old springs. That left the sofa to me. I sat in the middle of it, my shoulders hunched. I remember I was getting a pinched nerve from having been out in the cold. My body has become a foreign place—muscles just kind of seize up, without provocation.

I was too short for my feet to touch the floor, and I remember that night, especially, feeling like a little kid, trying to sit up straight on Grace's couch, my legs and toes hanging out awkwardly. My bump, you—even more awkward.

She sipped at her tea and stared at the wood stove as if it were the television. The TV itself was grey and blank. Grace's face was not the face I remembered from the day I'd glimpsed her far off down the hall at the university, what now seems like an eternity ago. At the time, her hair had been wrong for her: short and spiky, emphasizing the points of her face rather than lending it softness.

I remember Grace's face was hard that night, as though she were made exclusively of bone, and yet her mouth was wide, and in the light I could see that if she was smiling, she would be a striking woman. She *is* a striking woman, even without her hair—perhaps more so without it. Her forehead is large, her cheekbones pronounced, her eyes catlike. As cold as she was, she was comfortable in her stillness, which made me even edgier. All of a sudden, I had no idea why her husband had slept with me. It was like a joke on the chubby girl. Grace sipped her tea silently seven or eight times in a row, and it seemed like a signal to me to say something. She was accommodating, but it was clear she didn't want me there.

"I'm one of Karl's students . . ." I began.

She put her mug down on top of a magazine on the table. *American Cowboy: Guns, Guts & Glory.*

"I know who you are," Grace said in a way that dared me to say anything more.

But I did say something more. "Where's Karl? Will he be back here?" The Mini, of course, was Grace's—I'd realized it the moment I saw her boots beside the door. Karl just liked to borrow it.

Grace stared at the sofa I was sitting on. If I had to describe it, it's kind of a nothing colour mixed with green plaid. Like faded Christmas. On the end table was a small ceramic wagon train. "You know," she said after a minute, "all this cowboy stuff—after a while things go past irony, and then you wonder if you've become someone with bad taste. I think maybe I'll rip out the wood panel and paint the place yellow. Just something nice. Maybe ecru. Ecru and cranberry." The mug clicked on the wood table as she missed the magazine.

"Grace—" I said, feeling her name catch in my throat. "Where's Karl?"

"Hazel." She unwound her scarf from her temples and hung it over her chair back. She looked at me again with a kind of question in her eyes, as if waiting for me to confirm who I was.

I nodded and, like her, set my teacup down.

Grace leaned back, rocking in the chair. It made that soft, hazy sound that it makes when I sit here, gliding and talking to you. You know the one.

"Hazel, Karl's dead," she said, and the chair went *swoosh, shush, swoosh.*

Grace wouldn't tell me how it happened. There was part of me that didn't believe her. You have to understand, I wanted to cry right then and there. But how do you cry about someone else's husband in front of her? Especially when you have no facts. We sat in silence. The wood stove creaked and popped, and the chair swooshed and shushed, and Grace sipped loudly.

"Too many people have died from this," I told her, as if trying to justify the expression on my face, or that my eyes were gleaming.

"A relative? Someone close to you?"

I nodded.

"That's a real shame."

Swoosh, shush, swoosh went her chair. Karl and I had necked in it, awkwardly. At the cabin almost everything had been awkward; it was not like being high in his office with him.

I remember I asked Grace again how Karl had died, but she didn't answer.

She rubbed at the wooden arms of the chair. "Maybe I could paint this ivory," she said. She patted the cushions. A little bit of dust sprang out of them. Karl's dust. Skin cells of Karl's that had been shed and left there. "When this thing has passed I could have these reupholstered. I think about these things here. There's not much else to think about." Grace ran the same hand that had thumped the cushions over her nubby scalp. Her eyes were like polished glass. "You look tired. Maybe you'd like to lie down," she said to me, not unkindly.

I thanked her and said if she didn't mind, that would be very nice. She pointed at the bed, put on her boots, took my car keys, and brought my bag in from the car. When she came back, I was lying on top of her bed, on top of the bedspread where Karl and I first did it. I felt very vulnerable there. I couldn't cry because this little cabin is essentially all one space, divided visually by two walls but no doors. I listened to Grace plunking about in the kitchen where Karl had made me sweet-potato ravioli one night, and cowboy-style chili another. My eyes watered into Grace's pillows. At one point, I bit into one to stay silent. I kept wondering if she knew. But of course she knew. I'd known about and been able to find the place, hadn't I? She'd said my name. She'd said she knew who I was. And there was you— the big round proof. I was practically an explosion of boobs and butt and hormones, a *Venus of Willendorf* in comparison to Grace, whose body was like an exoskeleton. She couldn't exactly overlook you. You stuck out like an extension on a house.

She continued banging things around in the kitchen. Sharp instruments—I was sure they were sharp—clattered in a tin drawer in the vintage cabinetry. I listened very carefully. And gradually I ceased thinking of Karl at all. I wondered what Grace might do with me. Out here, with no ID, no one knowing where I'd gone, the world in chaos—I'd never be found. There were knives, an axe outdoors to chop up kindling, probably rat poison and other things. Grace worked in television. I recalled Karl telling me she'd worked on some great programs—some truly fine series—but that these days she was supervising a show about murders that had been solved by psychics, because the money was good. I assumed she'd collected all sorts of facts through her crime show—information squirrelled away, both useful and sinister.

Eventually she came around the corner. "I've made some nibbles," she said flatly.

After I struggled to a standing position, she looked me up and down again, as if reminded of your existence. You bulged out from under my shirt, which, in spite of being a blousy thing when I'd bought it six months before, left half my midriff bare when I turned too much. I'd thought the bump was the reason for her kindness, for her offering to let me lie down. But her eyes narrowed, and she turned her back to me and disappeared into the kitchen. You twitched as if you were sending me an SOS signal, but I followed Grace anyway.

We sat at the Formica table and she asked me questions while we ate. We had olives. She put whole olives in her mouth and pulled them out again as pits, which she laid along one side of her plate. I inspected the sandwich she had made for me, but not having any detective skills aside from a long history of movie-watching, I decided to bite into it. I wasn't supposed to eat lunch meat while pregnant, but the meat itself was less likely to poison me than Grace was, I decided.

"Karl was your adviser?"

It seemed safe enough to agree.

"How well did you know him?"

I ignored the question and swallowed the first bite of sandwich. I had been working it around my mouth for a full minute, unable to get it down.

"This is very good, thank you. It was a long drive."

Grace changed tack. "It must have been excruciating to drive with only one good lens. Karl wore glasses, but his night vision . . . fucking terrible. He just abhorred driving after dark."

I did know this. He had let me drive the Mini once because of it.

"Let me see," Grace said, moving her tongue around an olive. She continued working it gingerly as I unfolded my glasses from my face and extended them to her. They shook in my hand. She nimbly held the goggles up. Those glasses were one of my favourite things of all time. I had paid sixty dollars for them in a vintage store and got my optometrist to put my prescription in. The frames reached over the top of my eyebrows and all the way round to the sides of my face. They were brown marbled with pink, and they were cumbersome, perfect for balancing out my generous proportions. My mom called them my Big City Glasses—long before I went to New York. Grace gazed through the one lens, twisting in her seat. All her movements are stiff, you know, like she's measuring them.

"I wonder." Grace got up and stalked away from the table, holding my glasses. She went into the bathroom. "I wonder if they're close enough to Karl's prescription for you to wear his . . ."

I pulled in a breath.

"Oh," she said from the other room, "I don't think so. His are much stronger. Like pop bottles."

She laughed as she came back to me, her hand out. She smiled cunningly, sideways, an olive still pressed in her cheek. She laid Karl's silver rectangular spectacles on the table between us.

I stared at them. A car passed in the night, down on the road, sounding like an airplane in the silence.

"Take them away," I squeaked. "Please. You're upsetting me."

She expelled an olive pit into her palm and set it on her plate next to the crusts of her sandwich. She had—and has—that uncanny female ability to take bites and chew only when you aren't looking. She wiped her hand with a butter-coloured napkin. Her eyebrows were shaved off because of the virus, but she raised the bumps of flesh where her eyebrows once were. The drawn-on facsimiles of hair jumped like exclamation points.

"And you don't think you're upsetting *me*?"

She swept her own plate off the table and opened a tin garbage pail, and dumped the bits into it. The plate clattered into the sink and she began to scrub it under the faucet.

"Are you going to finish that?" she asked, nodding her angular face at my sandwich.

I remember staring at the curls of shaved turkey. I had taken three bites. Grace swept it off the table and into the old-fashioned refrigerator.

"Did—did you have a service for Karl? What was it like?" I inquired, my eyes falling again on the glasses.

She placed the single washed plate upright in the dish rack and turned back around. "No, of course not. I've got him out there in the fucking shed."

My eyes had started to tear up, and then rivulets ran down my cheeks. I couldn't help it. You have to understand: I had never thought about encountering Grace all alone. I had assumed the two of them might be there, but then I'd have Karl to smooth the situation. Wasn't it his situation, really, to deal with—not mine? I felt like I'd shown up to a funeral where the only person I knew was the deceased.

Grace watched me cry. She drew herself up to her full height, kind of indignantly, as if she were disgusted by the show—yet she didn't look away.

I started to hiccup, and I placed my hand over my mouth because the sound was so loud in this little space it practically reverberated off the hood of the oven and the stone flooring. I clamped my teeth shut and tried to stop, but I couldn't. My nose ran and I wiped it on my sleeve. The longer Grace looked at me, unmoving, just hovering in that stillness of hers with those icicle eyes, the more I sobbed.

"Of course I buried him," she finally said, and sat down

in the chrome chair across from me again, pressing her hands to her brow as if I had fatigued her. "My husband. What do you think of me that you believe he wouldn't have a proper fucking service?"

"The sch—schoo—" I just couldn't get the words out.

"The school? Not every asshole at that university needs to know just yet. The few who needed to be informed were. It was a private service," she said more quietly. "I wanted . . . I want discretion. Some dignity for him."

She refused to tell me what she meant by that. As long as we sat up, she wouldn't say anything more about Karl. I couldn't tell then if his death was truly horrible, or if she wanted it to herself—or both.

Eventually she took his glasses away, but she didn't bring mine back. I figured they were in the bathroom, or perhaps in the pantry, but when I thought to look for them in the middle of the night while Grace was sleeping, I couldn't find them.

For the first week or two of our cohabitation, she played little tricks like that, saying and doing things that would completely disable me. But I slept on the sofa anyway, staying because I had to. She was as close to your father as I could get, and I had nowhere else to go.

It's funny to think I once imagined there might be somewhere safe, somewhere to escape to.

I remember it was after my strange phone call with Larissa, and after I had made the reservation for a rental car, that

Moira reappeared in my life. I was standing behind her at the Dunn Inn, waiting to check out as she was checking in. I wanted to say hi, put out my hand and touch her, but it had been a couple weeks and I didn't know if she would remember me. She stood very erect, a habit of hers I had forgotten. Her head bobbed when she talked. She leaned forward to fix something that she had missed on the hotel form. Then she turned and saw me.

"Oh . . . you!" she said. My name had escaped her in the two weeks she'd been gone. She put out her hand to shake, then, looking at me, laughed and clutched me warmly around the neck, my laptop a wedge between our abdomens. I think she hugged me because we were fellow travellers.

"Hazel," I supplied.

"Yes! Hazel Hayes. I knew that," Moira said, stepping back. "It was in there somewhere." She knocked on her head using the leather wallet. "You're still here."

"I'm going," I said. I set my room keys on the counter for Natalie. "I'm driving back today. Through Buffalo, actually."

"Too bad. I'm playing tonight. It would have been nice to have a familiar face there." Moira seemed genuinely disappointed.

A boy came in just then, a young guy. He sometimes covered shifts during the day. He dodged between Moira and me without apology and whirled himself into the booth, where he and Natalie began shuffling papers and trading off shifts.

"And things are . . . ?" Moira's voice trailed off.

"Things are what they are."

We stood nodding, our heads aglow beneath the spotlight that hung from the ceiling. Then Moira bent and wrapped her fingers around the handle of her music case and picked it up.

"Listen," I said before she could go. The room key hung from her finger. "What's the border like?"

She said she wished she could update me, but she was coming from the south. "Good luck," she said.

I turned, but still didn't let her go. "Do you go home after this?"

She said she did, the next day, and I asked how she was travelling.

"Bus," she said, like it was a dirty word.

The boy who had taken over the check-in desk pushed a form at me and asked if I wanted to run it on my card or pay cash. I noticed my room key was still sitting on the counter where I'd set it down. It occurred to me that company on the drive would be a good thing.

I put the money back in my wallet and reclaimed my room key. "I could drive you," I said to Moira.

On the way to Moira's show I remember we walked past a big, sleek chain clothing store that had substituted the word *wearing* for *troubling*. Its display proclaimed: MAKE THE MOST OF WEARING TIMES. Then we passed a wooden barrier where another ad had been erected, one in which a man and woman dressed in black clothing were stomping around sulkily on a white background, their small shadows thrown behind them, hunched like chimpanzees. In another image, a man and woman clung to each other, embracing almost desperately, her shirt-tail riding up over one buttock. Every bank of pay phones seemed to have a row of posters for a TV special, its title simply *Emergency*. Men and women in uniforms, holding up cellphones and walkie-talkies, their mouths open, ran toward or sometimes away from explosions. Bodies littered the backgrounds. Flame fluffed like candy floss across the paper sky.

"Were these planned months ahead of time?" I asked. "I know they're not a response to the outbreak, but . . ."

Moira was matter-of-fact. "It's fall." She shrugged. "Everything's new."

I remember she was wearing heels and tight jeans, and with each step she clicked. The day was clear, the late afternoon sun turned bright.

She was right, of course. The television shows were making their debuts, and the ads were for fall and winter fashions though it was still sixty-five degrees outside. As we headed through Washington Square, we dodged a group of students who looked very much like they had just climbed off a bus from some small town, they were all so fresh-faced and starched. The girls wore knee-length plaid shorts and jean skirts, T-shirts that didn't look as though they'd been washed yet, tiny cardigans it wasn't cold enough for. They moved slowly, like tourists, then paused, deciding which way to go. A couple of them were wearing wigs. We passed someone in a jaunty hat like TV's Blossom would have worn, and another girl had a silk turban with a brooch. Hats and scarves seemed to be everywhere. I saw a girl wearing a flamingo-pink T-shirt that said, in black lettering, *Blondes still have more fun.*

Then I felt Moira's fingers wrapping my wrist.

Across the circle was a baby in a posh-kid mini-adult outfit. She was climbing on the rim of Washington Square fountain. A few feet away, near an overturned stroller, the mother stood with arms stretched out, not as if she were reaching for her child, but as if she were keeping the blonde toddler away. Two tourists loaded with backpacks had stopped nearby. Stupid and happy, the woman fed the man blue liquid from a water bottle. At the edge of the fountain, the pale toddler began to screech.

Moira was pulling me away, hard.

"She *has it*," Moira snapped. She jumped up and then over a concrete bench in spite of her high heels. I felt my stiff, injured knee jerk as she pulled me over it.

At a safe distance, we looked back. There was another high-pitched screech. The small blonde child had turned and run at the man with the backpack. We watched as little fingers clutched at his knees and teeth dug into the muscled white thigh below the hem of his shorts. The toddler's dress exposed a pull-up diaper. The man stumbled about, exclaiming in another language, attempting to grasp and dislodge her. His girlfriend dropped her sports drink; as the man bent and thrashed, the camera that had been around his neck smashed to the concrete.

We both turned and ran out of the park, me galloping on my bad knee and Moira sprinting in her heels, her glockenspiel case clutched firmly across her chest.

When we slowed a block or so later, I begged for a rest, my chest heaving. But Moira said, "Let's just get to the club." She let the music case fall to her side, one fist wrapped around its handle. She brought her other hand up and used her delicate scarf to mop her brow.

"Your leg," she said then, pointing.

There was blood on my jeans. I must have torn a stitch.

I asked Moira if she'd seen attacks before, but she didn't answer. A cop car zoomed down the narrow side street past us, siren warbling, toward the park. It paused at the light, then surged on.

Moira acquiesced to my demand for rest, and then we continued on, but slowly.

"This is it," Moira said finally. We were standing at the base of a flight of stone steps outside what looked like a house. It had the sign we were looking for. "It's too early," Moira said. "I always arrive for shows too early. It's part of my process." She sank down on one of the steps. There were other people sitting on the stairs as well, two guys, one a few steps up from her and one a few steps down. One was smoking, the other reading a book. Moira asked the reader if he knew what time the bar opened. He shook his head. I thought it was funny, that she had asked the one who was engrossed in something rather than the one who was just sitting there. Then I realized the guy she'd asked was probably better-looking.

We waited for half an hour. Moira pulled a compact from her purse and retouched her cover-up with a sponge. She closed the compact and said, "Damn." She was staring at the building across the street, but when I looked over at it, I couldn't see anything remarkable. It was a red-brick tenement. I looked back at her.

"Now I don't want to play," she said.

I asked her again if the attack in the park was the first she'd seen.

She shook her head.

I thought about the backpack man, his gnawed knee, and whether men could be asymptomatic carriers. One of the reports I'd read had seemed ambiguous on that point. I asked Moira what she thought.

She pushed her hair back. "The women. I saw a whole ward of them down south. They have them all in one room and they strap them down."

"You're kidding."

"I'm not. The sounds they make. They can tranquilize them, but—" She shuddered visibly, and the cords in her neck popped out. "My dad's an administrator at a private hospital. It's been pretty harrowing for him. That's why I was down there."

A group of politicians had walked through the hospital, legislators who wanted to see "the real face" of the disease, she said, an acid note in her usually calm voice.

She described a big room, with beds on either side, a post in the middle, and wicker chairs grouped around it, aiming toward the beds. "Like you're going to sit down and have a heart-to-heart with someone in that situation," she said. "Seriously, there was this grouping of chairs like you might find in a hotel lobby, and then there were these women tied down. These raging animal noises on the one hand," she said, "and then these chairs . . . I went only once, but I thought of those chairs when my dad told me about the politicians. I could just see them in their suits, sitting down and quietly observing, someone taking notes, some photographer snapping pictures."

The smoker on the stair below us gave us a look. He had long ago butted out, and now he got up and loped off.

The victims were mostly women of privilege, old-money wives and trust-fund students, Moira said. Their husbands or fathers cried in the hallways and signed forms for any test the doctors asked for.

"Didn't you worry about catching it?"

Moira tilted her curly head and threw her arms out as if daring me to look at her. "It isn't airborne," she said, staring unseeing at the building across the street again. "It's spread through saliva and blood. That's why they turn psychotic, like animals with rabies. If they go into a frenzy they're more likely to bite or scratch someone and the infection can jump to a new host. A lot of them self-destruct before they can spread it because they're just raging out, don't know what they're doing. A part of me thinks that's a good thing . . . and that makes me feel sick."

She said there was a code of secrecy among the rich. They called it "gone to the spa," rather than telling people their wives or daughters were in danger. I said I couldn't believe that. Moira just raised an eyebrow.

I said I didn't know a lot of wealthy people—that academics

are just good at faking it. I asked her what happened to the women. Was it true that they eventually died?

"I don't know," she said, and she crossed her arms and put her head down on them in a way that told me not to ask any more about it.

We'd waited an hour when dusk settled on the sidewalks. The reader on the steps above us stood up; his friend had arrived. The two debated other bars before leaving.

Down the street a man whose back was to us shouted into a pay phone, "Nigga, if I say I got nothin', it means I got *nothin'*, nigga. You ask around. There ain't nothin' to get. It don't help that half the world's closed down."

"Oh god." Annoyed, Moira said, "Let's just go in."

She got up, gathered up her things, and pulled on the bar's door. It opened into an art centre. There was an office and ticket booth on the first floor, but they were empty. We went upstairs and looked around. A steel garage-style door was rolled down over the bar where Moira was performing. She had played there before, she said. She set the glockenspiel down outside the space, then turned and continued up to the third floor. I followed. Inside was a dance-and-theatre space with hardwood floors. Two women were fussing with costumes and hangers in the far corner. They looked up when we walked in.

"I'm playing at the bar downstairs. Do you know when it opens up?"

"Only about fifteen minutes before our events," a woman holding a pink crinoline said. "Our event doesn't start for another hour. Do they know you're coming?"

"Maybe not. I'm an import," Moira said.

The women gazed blankly at her.

"From out of town, but my show's on the website," Moira elaborated.

"Good for you," the woman said, but it wasn't meant to be congratulatory. She and her friend turned back to their costumes.

We exited and camped in front of the roll-down steel door on the second floor, inhaling wafts of urine cakes from the men's toilet down the hall. I excused myself to use the women's, and when I came back, Moira was peering into a closet off the hallway. It was full of beer cases.

"Empty?" I asked.

She pulled one from a carton and held it up. It was full. She let it slide back into the box with a papery thud. "Watch them walk in this minute," she said with a laugh. She closed the closet door. "If they don't show up though . . ."

There was one chair beside the corpse of a pay phone that had wires springing from its mouthpiece. Moira let me have the chair, my back to a large antique mirror. I didn't argue. I rolled up my jeans and examined my knee. A stitch had popped, and the wound looked like a Cheshire cat grin. I had three stitches where I was supposed to have six. There's a scar there now.

I remember Moira sat on the floor, cross-legged. The walls of the place were painted red and black. The hall was narrow and dark. If anyone had come in, we'd have startled them. Moira slipped one shoe off and rested her foot on top of her opposite jeaned thigh. Her toenails were painted blue-black.

I remember thinking how beautiful they were, how amazing it was she didn't have any marks on her feet even though she wore impractical shoes, how nicely done the pedicure was, and how I'd never had one. Take this as a sign of the times, baby: a man had been mauled in front of us by a child who behaved like a rabid dog, and I was thinking about pedicures.

The start time for Moira's show came and went, but neither the bar owners nor curious audience members showed. The steel door remained in its rolled-down state.

"That's it for me," Moira said at last, and slipped her shoe back on.

"You don't think they're opening?"

"I don't think they're opening for my show or the one upstairs. These days I don't count on anything or anyone."

She stood up, stuck her hand into the closet, and pulled out the same bottle she'd shown me earlier. Just the one. Then she looked at me and smiled, and grabbed another.

When Moira and I left New York the next morning in the rental car, it was like leaving the known world. She directed me as I drove through Manhattan, which, with her shouting out instructions, was not as difficult as you might imagine. It didn't hurt that we were driving in the opposite direction to most people: out of Manhattan while everyone else was trying to get in. We got to New Jersey and were feeling triumphant, buzzing on caffeine, when we realized we'd taken a wrong turn and were off route.

We curved around and pulled in at a two-pump gas station. I put gas in the car and Moira went in to the station to use the bathroom and get directions.

When she came out she handed me a map and said, "Let's go." She got in the car and slammed the door.

I asked her if she'd paid.

"Absolutely. Let's go."

There was an urgency to her voice so I did what she said. This time, she didn't bother to give me directions. I just drove back the way we'd come, hoping she'd pipe up if I was doing it wrong. We weren't far down the road when she leaned her head back against the seat rest and gave a growl of frustration.

"What the hell happened back there?" I asked, slowing down.

"'Kay, pull over here," she said, and gestured to the side of the road, where I parked us and put on my flashers. A car passed us but otherwise there wasn't too much traffic. We were clearly still off-route.

"This woman in there is working the cash." Moira turned toward me in the seat, her hands up, palms toward me as if she were waiting for a volleyball. "I ask her for directions and she says, 'Who's your friend out there? Is she naturally blonde? She looks like a blonde.' And she's peering out the window at you. I mean, she was a nasty woman." Moira shuddered, her hands falling into her lap.

"Oh," I said. "Well, that's okay, Moira. I don't mind." I was about to put the car back into drive but she still seemed upset.

"It was just so rude. I said, 'I just want directions to get back on the highway.' I get out my wallet to remind her that we're buying gas, and she rings it up, but she just keeps watching you out that curtained window. She takes the money and I ask for the directions again, and she says, 'I see you got New York plates. Why don't you tell your friend to just turn around and go back there.'"

I tried to calm her down, but Moira was really upset. "You don't understand," she said. Her eyes were glassy. I told her the woman hadn't said anything mean about her, she'd said it about *me*, and not to worry about it, not to let it spoil the day. So the woman was afraid of possible blondes. Everyone was afraid of blondes these days. I joked that my skin tone *was* the colour of veal.

"That's not the point," Moira insisted, but she unfolded the map and after a few minutes we found our route. We'd shot off-course by ten miles.

I gave Moira control of the stereo and she plugged in her iPod. I asked her questions about every song, partly because they were by bands I'd never heard of, and partly because when she talked, it seemed to help her forget the experience at the gas station.

We'd been back on the freeway for half an hour when Moira kicked off her pumps, slid her seat back, and put her toes up against the glovebox. That was when a car ahead of us veered into the divider. It scraped the concrete, left behind a stripe of paint, then bounced back across two lanes.

"Jesus!" I shrieked, and hit the brakes and pulled hard on the wheel, steering us into the lane the other vehicle had just vacated.

Moira flew forward, then back. Thank god her seat belt was on. The other car plunged off the right shoulder and through the grass down a low grade. I pulled into the right lane and slowed down. I felt like I'd done fifty sit-ups—my heart was racing that fast. But I'd done everything right and we were safe. I was still watching my speedometer and checking my rear-view. I couldn't see the car that had gone off the road, but the vehicles behind us had slowed right down.

Even though we'd made it through, Moira was gasping and I could feel thin rivers running down the sides of my cheeks. I put on my turn signal, checked my rear-view, and pulled over.

With shaking hands, Moira dug through her purse and pulled out a package of cigarettes. She got out of the car, leaving the door wide open. She walked around the back and leaned against the trunk, shielding the cigarette from the breeze with one hand as she lit it. I scooched over, across the gearshift, to get out her side of the car because it was safer, and when I joined her against the trunk, her head was thrown back and she was peering off in the direction of the accident, holding the smoke in her lungs.

"Are you okay?"

She nodded and the wind took the smoke from her lips.

"That was close."

She nodded again.

Cars roared past us, kicking up dust and lifting our hair.

Moira dug in her purse and took out the Salem package, extended it toward me. I gestured for her smoke instead and she passed it to me. I took one drag and passed it back. Even that gave me a head rush, and I went and sat back in the car on her side with my legs hanging out. What can I say, my little fetal syndrome? I'm sorry, but I still thought you wouldn't be happening.

I watched Moira's back as she stood, leaning on the corner of the car, her elbow tight against her body and the cigarette held out. I looked down at my hands between my knees. They were shaking. I saw her pumps on the floor of the car. She was out there barefoot. I took the shoes to her. She tossed the cigarette butt into the gravel and toed the shoes on. We got in the car without saying anything more.

When we'd gone a little farther down the road, Moira said we should call in the accident. I told her someone probably already had. We'd passed a couple more cars that seemed to have pulled off like we had.

"What do you think went wrong?" she asked.

"He just lost control of his car," I said, tightening my grip on the wheel. "You don't careen around like that otherwise."

"It was a woman," Moira said.

"You saw her?"

"When you passed her. I mean, she was bald, but it was a woman."

"You think . . . ?" I didn't finish the sentence. "Was anyone with her?" I asked instead.

Moira shook her head.

EMILY SCHULTZ

Given our shakeup, Moira and I rested too long over lunch and our day trip began to stretch into an epic. Soon it was late afternoon and I felt numb from the motion of the road. Erik Satie was pouring out of the car speakers from Moira's iPod. She was turned away from me, toward the window. The sun was streaming in, and it was warm even though I had the fan on. She hadn't said anything for a long stretch of freeway, so I thought she might have closed her eyes.

We passed a white Mustang parked on the side of the road. No one was in it and the passenger door was open. In my rear-view, the smooth sneer of its hood disappeared as we rounded a bend. I didn't think much of it. I assumed someone had wanted to pee, let themselves out the safer side of the car, and climbed down in the ditch out of sight to do their business. But then we whipped past a guy jogging away from the car, up the mountain, in black jeans. He was on his cellphone.

"Hazel?" Moira said. Her head lifted. Her voice had a gravelly edge to it.

I was surprised she was awake and I glanced over at her. She turned, peering back over her shoulder. Then she said, "That was a nice car. Why would he leave the door open?"

"Maybe he lost something and he's going back over the highway for it."

But Moira told me to slow down.

The road was straight, and I couldn't see anything up ahead, but the tone in her voice had me peering intently.

"He was a long way from his car to leave it like that," she added.

I wasn't going more than sixty when, a few miles farther up the road, we saw the woman. She was still quite a ways ahead of us, just a speck on the shoulder, and at first I thought she was a deer, because we'd seen signs for them and she was wearing brown. As we got closer, I slowed down even more. She had on a beige coat and a brown fedora, and she was on her hands and knees, her head down, the hat brim over her face. We heard a siren, and a state trooper's car zoomed up on us from my left. Numbly, I steered over to the shoulder and brought our vehicle to a complete stop, about fifty yards back from the woman. The cruiser zigzagged in behind her and blocked our view.

Moira unbuckled her seat belt and strained forward in her seat, trying to see through the windows of the police car. The trooper got out. He stood there assessing the situation. He called something to the woman. I could hear both Moira's and my breath overtop of the Satie, still playing from the dash. The trooper reached an arm back into his vehicle, tugged out his radio, and said something into it.

"She's a blonde," Moira speculated, but she wasn't talking about the woman's hair colour. She meant the disease.

I didn't say anything.

The trooper planted the radio back in the car. Vehicles were still flying past in the left lane, but I had no intention of driving on yet. The trooper stood very still in the sun, staring out from beneath his hat. Then he leaned through his car window and pulled out a black shotgun, even though he still had his pistol on his hip.

I was watching him when I heard Moira say, "She's on the road . . ." and I realized the woman had crawled out from the shoulder into the right-hand lane. We could see her now, up ahead of the trooper's car, half-crouching, half-crawling. Her fedora was gone and the blonde bristles of her shorn head glinted in the sunlight. The trooper advanced, slowly, after her. His boots were black, his steps deliberate. The woman scrambled now, one back leg dragging. Horns bleated. Cars began swerving into the leftmost lane, some veering into what little shoulder there was, practically against the divider. The state trooper continued to walk calmly toward her. Maybe he was saying something, but we couldn't hear. The woman staggered, spun, and lunged at him. In one smooth motion, he brought up the shotgun and sighted it on her. The blonde's body twisted and jerked back, and at first I didn't realize he'd shot her in the stomach. There was an awful wail, and I thought it was her. I don't think I knew that it was me until Moira grabbed me by the shoulder. Knocked on her back, the woman scrabbled on the concrete as she tried to get up. Her head jerked up; her elbows still held her slightly off the pavement. The man stepped forward, shotgun in hand, and stood over her but didn't fire again. Slowly, the woman flattened.

The trooper nudged her with his boot two or three times, then he turned and walked back to his car. He bent at the waist and his head and shoulders disappeared inside. When he emerged, the gun was gone and he had the radio again.

Moira began cursing. Then she punched me hard in the

shoulder and said, "Goddamn it, Hazel, go!" and I saw that the trooper had walked out into the right lane between us and the woman, and was directing traffic. He was slowing down the left lane and signalling us to pull back onto the freeway, motioning with a cone flashlight, which he must have retrieved from inside his vehicle. I grabbed the gear shift and hit the gas and the car revved and we tore out into the space he'd made for us. I looked back in my rear-view, but by then I could barely make out the woman in the road.

We were a couple miles on when Moira instructed me to pull over again. I think she yelled at me, actually. I brought the car to an abrupt stop on the side of the freeway and she got out and came around and jerked open my door. The next thing I knew I was on the passenger side and Moira was driving.

We were insured only for one driver but I didn't think of that then. She had told me before that she didn't have a licence, that she'd let it lapse, but I didn't think of that either. She must have driven thirty or forty miles. She'd taken us past Binghamton, New York, and onto Highway 17. We were at a place called Endwell when I finally thought to mention the insurance and the license. At first she said it didn't matter, but soon after that, she did take an off-ramp.

The sun was starting to sink. There was a hotel—a Super 8 or a Red Carpet Inn—and I said, "Let's stop," and Moira didn't argue.

TEN

I'LL TELL YOU, MY LITTLE HAMSTER IN A WHEEL, I thought
I'd lose it that first morning here with Grace, when I went into
the bathroom and saw Karl. I thought I'd really lose it.

I hadn't noticed the photo the night before because it was
dark and Grace had taken my glasses. But the next day I went
into the bathroom, and there he was, framed on the wall in
close-up: a beautiful lifelike print of him, wearing a brown
cowboy hat, maybe the one from his office. He was looking
at the photographer, a wistful smile on his face. His eyes
full of secrets. When the time comes for me to show you a
picture of your father, it will be that one.

Grace hid the photo one day not long after that. I made
the mistake of commenting on it, asking if she was the
photographer, and she took it and jammed it into the back of

the entertainment cabinet, probably while I was out getting us more wood for the stove. I found it again later, of course, and now it's back up on the wall. She didn't like sharing him, and that's understandable. Except that she kept saying she didn't care. I never had a sister, but I imagine that in some ways we were like two sisters arguing over an item of clothing.

Perhaps I should consider myself lucky that all Grace did was play mind games. I remember Grace setting down a plate of scrambled eggs in front of me and saying, "I can't stand to fucking look at you in that garb."

She swore a lot without thinking about it—probably from working in television. But at that time I didn't understand that swearing was her habit, and the criticism struck me as being overly harsh. She hovered, appraising me.

"Those clothes are ass-ugly. You look like a bear in a circus."

"I have—have some others," I stammered.

"If they were better you'd have them on, wouldn't you?" She folded her arms across the flat chest of her white housecoat. "What did your hair look like?" She cocked her head, her chin pointed at me and my bald head. "You must have had very beautiful hair . . ." The words sounded wistful. Her mouth pinched around the edges, showing her age. What she meant was: I must have had beautiful hair for her husband to make the mistake of sleeping with me.

I didn't correct her. I didn't tell her my hair had always been my worst feature.

"We're going to have to do something about this situation"—she used her fork like a magician's wand, waving at my top half as if she could transform it—"if I'm going to have to look at you every day."

"Are you letting me stay?" I'd barely slept all night between nightmares of her murdering me as if I were Sharon Tate. Although—it had occurred to me that she could just put me out in the snow and achieve the same result.

"Are you going to eat those, or shall I put them in the fridge with yesterday's sandwich?" she asked. She picked up her own plate and ate her eggs leaning against the counter, as if she didn't even want to sit at the same table with me. When we'd finished breakfast, she reached into her housecoat pocket and produced my glasses with the one remaining good lens now splintered. "I'm very sorry. You must have dropped them on the bedroom floor—I stepped on them this morning. I'm lucky I didn't cut open my whole damn foot."

Aloud, I surmised that without them I couldn't very well drive away.

"You can borrow my fucking husband," she said, scraping the plates, "but I would never let you borrow my car."

Maybe she was grieving in her own way.

There were other little games Grace played to get back at me. That first day, she fixed the spigot on the shower so that it bled so little water I felt like I could have bathed more thoroughly underneath a water pistol. I know that she did this, because when *she* bathed, I could hear the water gush as if she had opened up the tap. I think she wanted to test whether I knew how to adjust the water pressure. I did. Karl had shown me. The next time, to get a better shower, I turned it partway, and before

I got out I reset it to where she'd had it. I didn't dare open it all the way. Not at first. Although eventually I did. I guess I played some games too. I pretended I'd never been to the cottage before, when we both knew I had trespassed—in serious ways.

Other games included Grace moving the few possessions I had brought with me. Occasionally, like the glasses, things would turn up ruined. Other times, they'd simply find their way back into my bag as if they'd never been gone. My alarm clock, even though I had no real use for it, wound up taking a vacation of three days, and when it reappeared its hands no longer moved. Considering how small our space was, these acts worried me. I couldn't figure out how or when they occurred, and it seemed that Grace was expending an awful lot of energy completing them in secrecy. I feared these little crimes against me would escalate; everything else seemed changeable and unpredictable, after all. That first night, when I'd thought she was beautiful, her skin had been white-almond, but after that, it turned more gold every day. Either she patted on more blush, or she was using the bronzer featured on the infomercial (*Break Out and Get Your Glow!*) on the flat-screen TV we watched only when Grace stamped it on, her long nail on the remote button.

Over the first few days, we established a pattern: We took two meals a day civilly together. The rest of the time, Grace watched the flat-screen TV, sitting on the couch or in Karl's chair. She would spend half the morning on hair removal and making herself up. Then she would stare at the news reports the rest of the day. Even then, she sometimes had the tweezers and a hand mirror beside her, as if she thought SHV might jump right out of the TV and into whatever lip or chin hairs were left on her. We ignored each other, unless laundry needed to be done, in which case I asked Grace what needed doing and collected it and tottered into the pantry to complete that task. It gave me something to do that allowed me to be in a different room from Grace.

We were eating breakfast one day when I decided to confront our situation. I pointed to the pepper and, in mid-gesture, asked her to forgive me for sleeping with Karl. It was the first and only time I said those words: that I'd slept with Karl.

Grace passed the pepper. I waited. She asked if I was going to fucking use it, or did I just want to make fun of her? She had a haughty way of saying the word *fuck*. We hadn't showered yet and so she'd not yet gone through her strange ritual of putting on her face even though there was no one except me to see her. She tried to raise an eyebrow, but she had no eyebrow, not even a fake thin line of brown. It made her face, which was usually so defined, look hollow. I told her I didn't want to make fun of her.

"That was never my purpose. I didn't even know you then."

"No, you didn't. And you fucking don't now," she said, and she took the pepper back and shook it over her eggs before stabbing them with her fork.

I watched her shove the lumps of them into her mouth. She had four long horizontal lines in her forehead. It wasn't until her plate was empty that she said, "Contrary to what you might think, I don't actually care that you fucked Karl. I knew he was doing it. I even knew it was you. I could tell you the dates and times." She stared down at the ceramic plate, which, like everything else in the cabin, bore a washed-out plaid pattern. On her face was a defeated look, one I hadn't seen before.

"What I resent is *that*—" She picked up her knife and fork and gestured at my belly in a way that made me wary. "He didn't tell me about *that*." She rose and turned and put the dishes in the sink.

She left them for me to wash, which I did dutifully, combing off the specks of pepper using a scrub brush. I stared at the blue bathroom door. The pipes groaned as she adjusted the water pressure.

I remember the hum of the water through the wall of the bargain hotel Moira and I stayed in during our escape from New York. I lay on the bed while Moira showered. I kicked my shoes off and I waited for the sound of the shower to stop. The day's coffee and you pressing on my bladder had left me feeling bloated. The thrum of the water continued and I got up. I remember opening the door to the bathroom. Moira didn't turn toward the sound.

"Sorry," I squeaked as I entered.

I could see her vaguely through the curtain, which was thin and pink. The room was warm and steamed, and smelled like bleach. I sat on the toilet. My pee was loud. I said sorry again.

"Don't worry about it," Moira said, and I heard her punch in the shower tap to cut the stream. Her hand came out from behind the curtain and wandered over the rack, then pulled a towel into the shower with her. She stepped out, towel-wrapped, and left the room without looking at me.

When I joined her in the main room again, she was lying on the bed in the towel, her eyes closed. Her legs still had droplets of water up and down her shins, but she didn't seem to care. Moira must have heard me moving around, but she didn't say anything or react. I dug through my bag for some things, then left her there alone and took my shower, which I didn't rush. It was like we both needed to get the day off us.

When I came back into the room, she had yanked on a pair of jeans and a shirt, and was still lying on the bed. She had pulled her hair back in a bun. It made her look tired. We lay beside each other on the bed for a while, a foot of ugly comforter between us.

"I want Chinese," Moira said, sitting up.

She ordered the food and then phoned someone who I guessed must be her boyfriend, twice. She was sitting right next to me and I had no place to go to give them privacy, so although I flipped through muted TV channels, I didn't pretend not to hear. I watched the solemn faces of the American president and the Canadian prime minister at separate press conferences but the TV remote was so old I couldn't figure out how to turn on the closed captioning.

Meanwhile Moira had her two phone conversations. It took a half-hour before I realized the calls must have been to two different men. I asked her about it afterward, but she shrugged her shoulders. She said she wasn't romantically involved with either of them—they were just friends. "We just spend a lot of time together."

I wondered what that was like, to have a boy *friend* and endless hours and days of being with someone without some dread hanging over your head. It sounded pretty good. It sounded like something I was supposed to have done by my age. I wondered whether each of Moira's friends knew about the other, and if either thought he was having a relationship with her.

She seemed to know I wanted to ask, because she said, "Really, it's not like that. We just go to coffee shops in the afternoon, and shows and stuff." Then she pointed at the TV and said, "Can you change it? To something dumb. I don't know about you, but I can't watch the news right now. I need to come down."

When the takeout arrived, even though there was a table, we ate the food cross-legged on the bed holding the Styrofoam containers under our chins, as if it were safer there.

Later, in the middle of the night, I woke up crying. Moira was awake too, and I asked her, "Why did he shoot her that way?" In spite of everything I'd seen, I couldn't stop thinking about that cop, standing over the woman, holding a gun.

Next morning, I didn't have time to feel embarrassed about waking up bawling in the middle of the night. It helped that Moira got up and immediately did sit-ups. It put a distance between one day and the next. It had never occurred to me to do such a thing in my life, and I watched her, a little bit in awe. I tramped down to the lobby and brought us back hot beverages. We both fought with our hair for a bit and I put on some foundation to cover my freckles and avoid an issue at the border. Then we shoved our things into Moira's big pack and my suitcase, and left. We weren't very far from Buffalo, it turned out— about three and a half hours. Moira must have known that, yet she'd let us stop. Maybe she'd needed to, as I had.

"I think I should go with you all the way to Toronto," she said when we were on the road. She was sipping at her tea and staring at the plastic lid between her fingers when I glanced over. The day was grey and the passing scenery flew by greyly too.

"I'll be all right," I told her.

Moira said that with two of us travelling, we would think smarter, react quicker. We should also take the Lewiston border crossing, she said. It was just a little farther on from Buffalo, but it was smaller—maybe there'd be less hassle.

"If you come with me, you're still stuck," I protested.

But she said she had some musician friends in Toronto and she'd always wanted to play there—she would see if she could hook up a gig "to make up for the bomb-out of the last one." She gave a weak smile. If anything, she said, I was still doing her the favour.

I wondered if she had a third boy *friend* there, but then I felt bad for thinking it. I knew I was just envious she didn't have my problems.

I phoned Larissa on my cell and told her to make dinner

for one more. "She works with artists. You'll like Larissa," I told Moira after I clicked off.

She asked how I knew Larissa, and after I'd told her she said, "So you just, like, met her around, and the next thing you were transferring to her high school?"

Something like that, I told her. I mentioned that I'd had to lie about my address in order to get into the school; I also had to take a bus across the city.

"You must have had a real connection."

"I guess so," I said. Glancing in the rear-view, I watched my own forehead scrunch.

"I'm just surprised," Moira said, rearranging her things in the bag on the floor. "It sounds like you picked up your life and rearranged it for someone you didn't know that well. Is that something you do a lot? I mean, like with this guy—" She meant Karl.

I cut her off. "It was—it was a good school," I explained. "Larissa lived in a better area of town than I did. They had a full arts program there."

"Oh, I see." Moira nodded. These were reasons she understood.

She put the radio on and cruised the dial until she came to some disco.

"No," I told her. "This is my mom's music."

She laughed. "What?" She'd grown up on jazz and classical, then gone to school for jazz and classical.

She thumbed the buttons. A talk radio announcer stated, "With more than a hundred thousand new infections, not to

mention the Canadian prime minister's statements about
SHV last night, tensions are bound to be up. How can people
prepare themselves psychologically for what's happening?"

I put out my hand for her to leave it, but she had already
settled back into her seat.

"That's a huge rise," Moira said, her brow furrowed.
"A hundred thousand. That's really *up*."

"Well, Dane," a guest expert said to the host, "it's normal
for people to be afraid of what they don't understand. The
threat here is something we can't detect immediately. I mean,
it can take hold of a woman at any time and the only cues we
have are behavioural. Reported cues are 'looking bad,' 'looking
in rough shape,' or 'not being herself,' but what does that
really mean? So immediately, there's a paranoia that sets in.
The threat becomes abstract, and the fear is almost as intense
as the disease itself."

The host, Dane, sputtered that there had been a surge of
cases of women with highlights, women who were not natural
blondes, and that that was bound to increase public panic.

The expert—I guessed she was a psychologist—responded
that, yes, certainly, there had been *some* cases among women
who dyed their hair. "But SHV is still largely a preventable
virus. If you are a blonde, or even a fair-haired woman, and
you feel like you have a cold or the flu, the thing to do is to alert
a relative or even a co-worker—someone—that you are feeling
rundown, and *don't go to work*. Don't go out to pick up your
kids from daycare. Don't go to yoga. Simply make alternative
arrangements on the off chance you do have SHV. Everyone

should be washing and sanitizing their hands regularly, and also limiting social activities. Avoid needless errands and outings in order to limit exposure. We can't prevent the virus once it has taken hold, but we can prevent its spread—"

"Yes," Dane cut in, "but the second point is that some women who are bleachers aren't protecting themselves by going to a darker shade. Why is that, Doctor? Because they're afraid they'll look bad?"

"Partially, but also because we don't want to admit we might be susceptible. And so on the one hand there are women with lower incomes who are natural blondes, who simply can't afford to dye their hair. We're not talking about one box of dye, we're talking about ongoing hair maintenance. And on the other hand, for women who *are* bleachers, we're talking about making a break with a history of behaviour, which is always hard for people to do."

"In the long run, we can't afford *not* to."

"Exactly."

Dane interrupted to say he was speaking to Dr. Janet Rosselli, and they'd be back shortly with more tips for readying for the next wave of SHV. *"Also up next: How Americans will be affected by our neighbours to the north and the hard stance they're taking toward SHV."*

Moira changed the dial. The hum of the highway began to weigh on me. The sky streaked hieroglyphs on the glass, which the wipers erased.

"So are you going to tell this guy?" Moira asked again, meaning Karl. "I think he should take some responsibility."

"Responsibility. What does that really mean?" I asked her.

But now that Moira had me talking, I was forced to admit that Karl wasn't very responsible. Take that book he was supposed to send back to one of his former students. I remember that was the first time I wondered if he'd been involved with her too, if she was one of the girls Kovacs had meant. He'd got the book down off the shelf the day I signed up for his course, but it had sat there on his desk for weeks. He never mailed it to her like he'd said he would. I found it again on the shelf above his desk later, when he and I were involved. When I asked him about it then, he said he had sent it back, and when I pulled it out and showed him, he said, "Oh no, I bought that second-hand, to replace it." But I'm pretty sure it was the same copy.

When I confessed this story to Moira, she pursed her lips, the way she often did, and put her lime-green Keds up on the glovebox. I noticed she wore more practical shoes that day, as if she thought she might need to be prepared after the previous day's ordeals. I hadn't seen her in sneakers before.

"I think you're too smart for this guy," she said. I remember she kept calling him a "guy," which struck me as comical. "I think you're trying to punish yourself."

I laughed. "You're Oprah now?"

She gave a short grunt. "Maybe for sleeping with him the first time."

"*I* seduced *him*," I told her, but she remained unconvinced. I could see the disbelief in her broad, stern face.

I switched the windshield wipers to a higher speed and

drove a little faster, as if we could leave the conversation between two sets of exits. Far back from the highway the trees were dark with rain and blurring at the edges of my vision. Among those still holding their foliage was a copper one, with a hole where the leaves had fallen from it. A wind came up and shook it, and I watched it pass into my rear-view where the whole thing seemed to float, frail and yellow as antique lace.

Even at the small crossing at Lewiston, the line for the border was jammed, and when we finally crept within sight of the guard stations a full hour after arriving, Moira and I could see why. In addition to the usual border guards, patrol with rifles stood at the ready. Moira and I exchanged glances.

"I'm not a musician," she said. "They always stop musicians, so make sure you don't say that I am one." She turned around and tucked her trench coat around the glockenspiel case in the back seat so it wouldn't show.

"I don't think they care about musicians today."

She smiled weakly.

I asked if she thought my brown hair looked natural. It looked natural to me, but I was used to dyeing. She said that she could see my freckles through my cover-up, but that she couldn't imagine they were performing the kind of tests Larissa had told me about. At the same time, she handed me her tube of mocha lipstick and I swiped some on my mouth in an attempt to look less like a natural redhead.

When we got to the next-in-line position, a patrolman with a rifle came up. I sucked in a breath and rolled down the window. He bent and looked in. He gave Moira little more than a glance but looked me up and down thoroughly.

"Your vehicle has been selected at random for an additional security search," he told me in an even voice. Did I understand?

I said I did, since I didn't expect I could refuse the check. He asked for my passport. Once it was in his hand, he retreated and gestured our car into an empty space between two guard houses.

"He didn't take yours," I said to Moira, who was still holding her passport in her lap. I pulled the vehicle ahead.

Then a different guard was at my window, a woman. Because of where they'd pulled us over, we weren't quite under the station roof. She had a big black slicker slung over the shoulders of her tight blue uniform, and even though it was noon, she seemed to shine under the station's lights.

"We're just going to ask you a few additional questions, if you don't mind." She looked like a Barbie doll after its hair had been cut off. I turned off the engine so we could hear each other. "Where are you coming from?" she asked, and when I told her New York, she said to wait right here, please, ladies. In spite of her congenial demeanour I noticed the patrolman stood close by. The woman disappeared into one of the stations and came back with a map and a black umbrella open overhead—to keep the map dry, I realized as she unfolded it. "Now if you can, I'd like you to show me where you were staying."

The tines of the umbrella squeaked, scraping the hardtop of the car as she leaned closer and tried to get the map spread where I could see it.

I pointed roughly to the area of the Dunn Inn. "And my friend too," I told her.

"Oh, you're fine, ma'am. We don't need any information from you today," the guard said, nodding to Moira. "But we do have to run your passport inside," she said to me. "It will only be a minute, and then I'm sure we can get you on your way." She asked me how long I'd been outside the country. I told her, and she presented the map again. "Due to recent events, we must be thorough, you understand. I'd just like you to point out any other areas of the city you may have visited."

The map was blocked into distinct sections, which were different colours, like a climate or agricultural map. It was not unlike the *National Geographic* map of the disease I'd been looking at—except this one had been painted by hand with marker, rather than professionally done. The veins of Manhattan throbbed with orange, brown, and green streaks. It made it hard to tell which streets were which, and I had to look closely.

"No one's behind you—take your time, ma'am," she said in a chipper manner, even though I knew a whole bridge of cars waited, idling. Armed Canadians were an eerie enough sight, but armed Canadians "please and thank you, ma'am-ing" me did nothing to bolster my confidence.

I indicated only the two areas closest to the hotel. One was green, the other a mud green. They looked like safe zones.

"All right, then," the guard said.

I glanced at Moira again. Her shoulders lowered a little. Then she looked past me and through the window on my side. I followed her gaze. Another guard had come out of the little hut. He was carrying my passport. I smiled and wiped the sweat off my palms onto my jeans.

The new guard pressed my passport into our guard's hand. He said something to her quietly.

She folded the map back up and leaned back down to the car. She gave me a hard look, like I had tried to take something from her. "JFK," she said. Her tone had changed dramatically. "You had a ticket and cleared Security there on the eighteenth of September."

It wasn't a question, but she hovered there, expecting an answer. "Yes," I admitted.

She lightened a little. "Given that, ma'am, we're just going to ask you to come inside for a moment and fill out some paperwork. We only need to ask a few questions about what other areas you may have passed through recently, and if you don't mind, we'll conduct a little test or two."

The rain pulsed over the car top, and I looked at Moira. The dark freckles on her nose and cheeks stood out.

"I'll ask you to step out of the car and come this way, miss."

I unfastened my seat belt and put my hand on the door handle. Moira's expression was uneasy, but she nodded at me to do as requested. Not having any choice, I got out of the car into the rain.

The male guard who'd brought out my passport took it back, along with the umbrella from the female guard. He touched me by the elbow and guided me.

"I'm going to need you to vacate the vehicle also," I heard the woman guard say to Moira behind me.

When I looked back, Moira was unfolding herself stiffly from the passenger side as the wind pushed her hair back from her face.

Then we were at the station and the male guard was saying, "Step this way, please."

The door hit me in the shoulder on the way in because I was looking back at Moira, who was standing on the sidewalk as two officers appeared from some other station. With gloved hands they arranged a plastic netting over the car. They hooked it to a tow truck that had appeared as if it had been grown there by just adding water.

I entered the office in a fog. Our things were still in the car. How would I find Moira when I was done? I glanced around that hut—just a single desk and computer, a rack of maps, a wall calendar, a box of latex gloves, and a small folding screen set up in one corner. My government had duped me with pleasantries. Moira would be sent back to the U.S. side, and they would deal with me separately. This was goodbye. I could still feel the car door handle between my fingers and the rain on my shoulders where the umbrella hadn't reached, and I hadn't thought to touch her or say a word to her before I went. How long was quarantine these days? Three days, four, a week? They wouldn't make her walk back over the long bridge past all that idling traffic to the United States, though, would they? I couldn't believe that.

She would be waiting for me, I told myself, in one of the other stations. I took off my corduroy jacket and hung it over the chair the guard had indicated. My laptop bag was still in the car with my cellphone and all my ID besides the passport.

"I'm going to conduct a private test with you, or if you prefer you may request Officer Howe, who questioned you earlier," the male guard was saying. I noticed that even as he hung up the umbrella, there was a hand on his hip not far from his holster. The rain dribbled off the umbrella onto a rubber mat on the floor: *drip, drip, drip.* He smiled amiably and gestured to the screened corner of the room. "It's just a formality. There's nothing to worry about, Miss Hayes. It's a standard procedure, and not invasive in any way. If you could just step to this side of the room and we'll get your paperwork taken care of right after. Leave all of your clothing in place, please, and simply lower your pants and underthings to your knees. I'll step around the screen when you're ready. It will only be a second."

But I knew that second would be my undoing. My blazing bush was not going to pass inspection, and the likelihood of my seeing Moira anytime soon was slimmer than the chance that I'd be able to keep my appointments in Toronto.

PART THREE

ELEVEN

GRACE ISN'T COMING HOME tonight, either. That's pretty clear. As awful as she could be, dealing with her games and jags and binges was preferable to this—this feeling of isolation. It's been five days and five nights now since I woke up and she was gone. Everything is dark out there again. The bushes are just little flames of grey against the snow, and the trees are a black wall. I'm going to sleep in her bed. That's what I'm going to do. I'm going to sleep in her bed and I don't care if she comes back and finds me there. I *want* her to come back and find me.

I've already decided that if she doesn't return at all, eventually I'll go too. I don't want you born here, all alone, because if something were to happen to me, what would happen to you?

There's a calendar here and I'm counting the days on it. When we get to eight months, exactly, that's when I'll leave. I know if I go outside, I might be able to find the North Star, like I was shown. But where will I walk to? To town, and from there, our fate will depend on who I can find to help me. We have another two weeks until then, although we may have to go sooner, depending on the food. When Grace came up here, she stocked the pantry pretty well, like this was her bomb shelter. Nothing fancy. Cans of beef stew and chicken soup, tinned pears and mandarin oranges, beans and corn, bags of rice, granola, canned milk, potatoes, dry pasta, salt, and olive oil. But she didn't plan for two of us, and she certainly didn't stock up with the idea of meals balanced enough to grow a healthy baby.

She may not have planned well enough to last the winter herself. It is easy to imagine Grace under the fluorescents of some Price Chopper, snapping up items as they came within sight and slinging them into the squeaky-wheeled cart without tallying the prices or considering their long-term value. I don't think she made a careful inventory.

In contrast I remember when I made that drive here with Karl, that one and only time. We brought little delicacies with us. He was really trying to woo me, I think. None of this camping stuff. The cottage was a hideaway. Even though he walked around the place nervously, putting away things that were too personal, too Grace. Even though he avoided waving to the neighbours and wanted to stay indoors. We went down to the water, but we went at night. It was cold and still, and we looked out at the glass sheet of ice and the black tarp of the sky for about two minutes, then kissed and headed back. No wonder I thought I was the first. When I think of it now . . . It was as if—Oh god, it wasn't that I was his first affair—it was that I was the first one he brought here. Into a place that was theirs. Oh.

When I made that little getaway from Toronto with Karl, it was early on, you understand. We'd had that one session in his office, and then we ignored each other for about two months. I worked on my thesis, and I thought I'd done a pretty good job. I'd come up with the title and a reading list and the first four or five pages. I had sent the lot to him via email and he'd told me to come in and we'd talk about it. The meeting was at one-thirty in the afternoon, so I understood what message he was sending me. Purely professional. I remember his hair had started to grow back a little then, and he was getting that slightly crazed professor look, the one the other students had told me about. His glasses were greasy and his hair tufted up from his forehead in a silver-brown horn. He was standing behind his desk with his hand drawn up to his chin, over his mouth, and I was waiting for him to tell me what he thought. I really couldn't read him then. Maybe what we'd done had obliterated my ability to read him.

"I think—" he said. "Hmm. Well. I'd like you to try—" He came around the desk and braced his hips on it, leaning, or sitting, the way he'd done that first time we messed around. He laughed nervously. "Try—" He held his fist up and made a pulling-down motion. It looked like a very earnest dance move of decades past.

"You want me to go deeper?"

"That's it, Hayes," he said, placing his hands on his knees, blinking behind his glasses. "See if you can. See if you can go deeper."

The next week I ran into him in the hallway. Meaning, we literally collided. As if he'd planned it. I was coming out of the department office with some papers from the students I was TAing, and he was turning the corner sharp and fast to go in there. I put my brakes on, and he grabbed me by my elbows, and then we were chest to chest—except that he was taller, so we were technically chest to gut.

"Oopsy!" he said, which was comical, except for the way he looked down at me. Behind his rectangular spectacles, his eyes were bright, desperate. "Could you . . . ?" he asked. "Just a moment while I get this in?" He ducked into the department office.

I stood there, shifting from foot to foot. But when he came back, I wasn't ready for what he said to me. He walked me to the end of the corridor, and when we turned the corner we were alone, just for a minute in the middle of the day. He seized my hand and looked at me, then, fearing someone would come by, dropped it. Just that little beat of skin. We didn't go into his office. "I have some extra time next week." His tone was placid but his eyes were bright. "My wife, Grace, is going for three days on a press circuit in New York for a television show she's been working on. Yes . . . it will just be marvellous for her, such an opportunity," he said, his voice suddenly rising animatedly as a pair of students rounded the corner and passed us. He said he was thinking of going up north for a few days. A little escape. "Who can think in the middle of the city?"

The students turned the corner to another wing, and a door opened and closed in the corridor we'd just left.

"It's—it's nice that you have that escape," I stuttered. I wasn't sure why he had waylaid me for this.

"You could have it too, couldn't you?" he said, glancing down. I remember I watched his lips saying the words. "You just need a place to go to."

Maybe Moira was bang-on in her assessment of me. I didn't protest. I didn't walk away. I could have.

He stepped back and pushed his hand up through his hair. He rubbed at his chin. "How's that thesis coming along?" he asked as another professor, Dr. Webber, edged between us and continued on.

There was something really dirty about crossing all the lines. I'd been alone most of my life; you would think I wouldn't need to have a secret. When you're alone, your whole life is a secret, isn't it? In any case, that was how we wound up pretending to be lovers, in love, driving north in December with a shopping bag full of expensive cheeses and a plastic tub of sundried tomatoes, and brown-paper-wrapped sausages, and bottles of wine with trendy labels.

My memory of it was that after that day in the hallway I had tried to forget what he'd said to me. Then I was standing in my shower at home and I closed my eyes and saw his mouth again, moving around the words, and the next thing I knew I was remembering kissing him the previous fall. I wanted to be wanted, even in a cheap way.

Then just like that, it seemed, we were on the highway. Half a year before you were conceived. The sun was slanting down and little flurries of snow caught the light. It was before the holidays and Karl had finished his marking. For someone so inept he could be awfully organized when it came to deception. With the exception of the hand-squeeze in the hall, there hadn't been a single touch between us since that night in his office, when I lay across his lap and he stroked up under my skirt. To suddenly be riding in his passenger seat made me feel light-headed. My stomach felt like a fire pit, scorched and empty, as if something had already burned there and might again.

We were passing a Levi's outlet mall about an hour beyond the city when Karl looked over and said, "Hayes, it's good to see you here in my car," as if I had been instantly beamed there like a character on *Star Trek*. Hayes—he was still calling me by my last name! "It's good to know there's more and more to you."

I don't know that there *was* more and more to me. I feel that in the past year there's been less and less of me. I've been reduced to leaving behind everything I know, fleeing to New York, the purpose of my study about as legitimate as Wanda Kovacs saying she was going to do research in India at the height of the epidemic.

I want to be a better person. I want to think I will provide a better example for you than anything in my past might suggest. Maybe that's why I'm sitting here, sorting it all out aloud. So I won't have to tell you when you get here, my little amoeba. So I won't have to tell you any of it.

———

The border guards informed me that the Canadian government had declared a state of national crisis, and quarantine for at-risk travellers was eight weeks. When I asked them if I would have access to health care, they told me to get on the bus, please. When I told them I didn't need to enter Canada and could I please remain in the United States on my student visa, they told me I was being taken to a quarantine building outside of Hamilton, Ontario, where clean bedding and meals would be provided for me at the expense of the government, and did I understand, *ma'am?* I said I would like my cellphone and my computer and my belongings, please. I said that they couldn't impound my rental car, that it had to go back to the rental chain or I'd have legal troubles to the tune of $30,000 or whatever the price of the vehicle was, and that this was the last thing I needed right now on top of my student loans, on top of being stuck in limbo, on top of—They said, calm down, Miss Hayes, we're going to ask you to just calm down.

They put me in a room with nothing in it but a couple benches that were affixed to the floor. Eventually there was a group of us, all glaring at one another. The guards loaded us onto a bus, and off we went. *Fuck*, I thought, *Hamilton!* I leaned my head against the window and tried to remember Moira's music. She'd played me some of it the previous day, her iPod plugged into the car stereo. I had one or two little licks caught in my brain and I played them to myself as if on repeat, the chime of her mallets a soundtrack, as I watched

Ontario-green flash past. It was futile to be home. I could hum the music for you. It goes *hmm-hmm, hmm-hmm, da da da. Hmm-hmm, hmm-hmm, da da da.* And that's all that's left of Moira.

The quarantine area was actually a brand-new grade school, one level with a flat roof, save for the gym. It was only a stone's throw from the main road and tucked behind it was a subdivision that no one had moved into yet. Hamilton has quickly become a satellite city to Toronto, but I guess it had started developing too fast, and this part was still deserted—unsold. The homes looked alike, tall and thin as supermodels, in various shades of sand and slate, with garages that shot out in front on the right sides. The driveways hadn't been poured. They all had gravel with wood beams set in the sod, curving up to the houses, like mouths that were missing teeth. At night, I would gaze across the field and see two or three houses with their lights on, a good distance off, through the twisted cul-de-sacs, and the rest black peaks against the night sky. But when the guards first unloaded us, I had no idea why they'd chosen the place.

The bus pulled through a chain-link fence and let us off in the parking lot. There was already a truck there, and workers were unloading army cots, which they carried through the double doors of the gym.

"Isn't this cute?" an older woman in a blue blouse with a yellow rope design on it said when we were marched into the school and assigned to our classroom: room 8. The cots had been set up around the walls and the core of the space contained an informal area with a rug and chairs in a size better suited to teddy bears than adults. Outside room 8, desks were stacked along one hallway, right side up and upside down, clean and gleaming, unused, ungraffitied, fitting together like dentures. The classroom whiteboards still had plastic over them. There weren't any textbooks. I walked over to the shelves that ought to contain them, and took my jacket off and threw it on a bed, using the only possession I had to claim a space for myself beneath a window. We were told—for our own protection, and to prevent the spread of SHV—we weren't to leave room 8, and there were men positioned in the hallway who would stop us if we tried. Bathroom breaks would be assigned and we would go in groups.

Periodically throughout that day, more buses brought more women. We were all women, of course, and I noticed that all the soldiers were men. It made sense, really. They weren't at risk of active SHV. Room 8 seemed intent on sticking together. We'd glared at each other at Customs and on the bus, but now that there were others arriving, people began talking, pairing up, making friends, and staking out space for themselves. We had status as the original load in this particular quarantine. A small group shuttled off to the bathrooms under stern supervision from two uniforms. The women came back tittering and moaning at the size of the toilets, the dividers that didn't reach their eyes. In a fog, on the second bathroom run I walked with the other inmates, which was how I thought of the lot of us. I noticed we passed a library with a spine of unfilled shelves down its centre. The fluorescent tubes for the lighting hadn't been put in yet. There were just some plug-in construction lamps lying around. Then we were in the ladies' room, and the men were hollering, "Hurry up, let's go, let's go!"

There was another redhead in room 6. Unlike me, she'd left hers gleaming, a bright Popsicle orange. The rest of the women were blondes or grey-hairs. Apparently, the elderly were more susceptible to SHV. All of us were white, except for one woman who had high cheekbones and an eye shape that indicated she might be First Nations, or partly so. Her hair had been dyed pitch black, but there were natural gold roots along her part. It didn't matter—by the end of that first evening, all our hair was gone.

By late afternoon, the guards had turned the library into an impromptu lab. Under the new institutional glow of fluorescents, a weedy-looking private with a scarred lip greeted each of us silently with an extended hand. He shaved our heads and bagged the hair samples, marked them, and filed them. His latex fingers jerked my head around, and the clippers bit and pinched, but I didn't cry like some of the others did.

"This is a jug fuck," the private said grimly over his shoulder to the soldier who'd brought me in. "This whole place. Wait and see."

"What? You don't like the split arse?" the other soldier shot back, grinning.

"It's not that . . . But that SHV is going to tear through here faster than a shack hack."

Two female soldiers in spacesuits were brought in to

supervise while we shaved our own pubic hair. They were the only women we'd see, besides one another, the entire time we were there.

That night, the women in room 8 gathered in the miniature circle of chairs, some sitting on the piece of carpet, some at the ends of their beds. It was harder to remember their names and keep straight who was who after the shaving. We all looked like clones, just fatter or thinner, with longer noses or bigger teeth. Needless to say, I didn't attend this impromptu meeting, although I could certainly hear it from my bed. We'd been labelled high-risk, and I had to assume that many of them were higher risk than I was.

Back at the border, when I told Customs I'd been pronounced clean after the JFK incident, they told me they would look for my paper trail from my time at the clinic with the other pregnant ladies. "In Jamaica, Queens," I told them, "outside the airport." I hoped they'd clear me soon, and I didn't want my chance to get out mucked up by hanging too closely with this lot. In the end, of course, my request would be lost, like everything else. But during the initial week, I still had hope.

The first order of business was the food. As at the airport, we'd been brought fast food and this was not sitting well with the older women, some of whom had dietary restrictions. It seemed like almost everyone was older than me—Karl's age, but further away, sociologically speaking. These women were thinking ahead and they knew they didn't want to eat hamburgers for the entire eight weeks we were to be there.

"Haven't you seen *Fast Food Nation*, dear?" the ropey-bloused woman—whose head shape, it turned out, was pool-ball round—said to a mawkish teenage girl who had been picking her hangnails and seemed to be alone. Later I'd find out she'd been travelling between divorced parents. She was ten years younger than me, but I felt closer to her than any of the others.

The second order of business was bathing, a difficult proposition when all we had were birdbath-sized sinks. And the third issue was that of contacting family members.

A great number of suggestions were raised at the third point, but none of us knew what to expect during our incarceration and we wound up saying, "Let's make a note to ask about that."

We had a lot of security and two health-care workers on hand. One woman kept going into the hall to try to talk to the men stationed there. They were gruff and treated each of us as if we were akin to the disease itself. The inquisitive woman was about thirty-five, and had arrived at the detention centre with a crew cut. When she came back, she said she'd got some answers because the major liked her. We'd heard his answers through the door and they'd sounded like grunts for her to get back into her room—but in her defence, she did relay some useful information.

She told us that there were other quarantines, and that we were lucky to have a whole school, with only fifteen of us or so to a room. Others had been bused from the U.S.–Canada border to a new outlet mall that was as yet unoccupied. The government had leased it and the school. They called these newly established centres Women's Entry and Evaluation, or WEE. The outlet mall WEE didn't have nearly the facilities we had, the woman said happily. I couldn't understand how she would consider anything a triumph at that moment. She was one of those glass-half-full types, and I would've been ready to choke her at the end of the eight weeks if someone else hadn't actually tried. But I'm getting ahead of myself.

The woman's name was Michelle Morell. I knew the names of all the other women while I was there, but, consciously or subconsciously, I've blocked most of them out now.

I fell asleep that night to a hollow wind and the sound of strangers sniffing and coughing and turning over. There were no curtains on our windows, but there was no moon either, so I stared up at an opaque sky and wondered how Larissa had reacted to my absence. I'd done it to her again: said I'd be coming, then disappeared.

The first illnesses came two to three days in. They took out a woman in room 3, tied down to a stretcher. I was outside on the playground at the time. The others told me that her mouth was foaming, and that they'd collected her sample bags of hair and taken those out with her. She was trucked off someplace else for observation, and/or tests, and/or—it was rumoured— termination. Room 8 buzzed with conspiracy theories and speculation, each as plausible as the next.

I decided afterward that the playground was a good, safe area, since the soldiers granted us a couple hours of outside time daily. The other women ignored this privilege and tended to stay indoors, or clustered in small circles up by the building. I spent time outside regardless of the weather. After a few days, one of the soldiers brought out a basketball. I didn't know if he'd located it in the gym or brought it from home, and he didn't tell me. He showed me how to do a foul shot, and also an outside shot without using the backboard, before returning dutifully to his post. It was one of the few humane acts I'd experienced there.

The only other time I saw the soldiers acting like normal teenagers—which some of them were—was when they were typing frantically into their iPhones. They weren't supposed to use them while on duty, but once we heard one of the soldiers laughing quietly and telling his buddy about how he had just texted their commanding officer, "What's up, sir!"

Michelle Morell tried and tried to persuade this fellow to allow her to borrow it to send a text or check the Internet for news, but whatever mirth he'd been showing before she entered the hallway disappeared quickly. He just snorted and pocketed the phone. "That one's a hard, mean thing," Michelle said when she returned. "But I *know* he'll come around." None of them ever did, though.

I've never been very skilled at sports, but I got pretty good with the basketball as long as I didn't try to do anything ridiculous, like a layup. The soldier who gave me the ball was named Augustus, and he told me to call him August. I let

August do the layups, although he'd usually get only one or two in before he had to go back to his post. He must have liked me to break protocol like that, and that was fine by me because it meant I had one non-risk person I could talk to. I didn't know why he liked me—although, now that I think about it, my chest had expanded two sizes in the three weeks since the pregnancy test. I had bought a couple new bras in a bigger size when I lost my bags at the airport, but already my cleavage was spilling out over the top of them.

Soon there was another outbreak in room 5: a woman didn't get up one morning, and everyone said she had menstrual cramps. Then, at around 2 p.m., she suddenly stood up, lurched out into the hallway, grabbed Michelle Morell by the throat, jammed her against the wall, lifted her off the ground, and shook her. The army took the woman down in about two seconds, and carried her out. I remember the sound of the footsteps: the private running back into the library to gather the woman's sample bags, and then chasing after the stretcher with them. Michelle Morell was treated on premises, mostly just tending to bruises and some counselling alongside a lot of blood tests and saliva swabs. The soldiers put her in a storage closet in case fluids had been exchanged in the attack, and after that, whenever I passed her in the hallway she bragged about having her own "room."

I had told August about my pregnancy that first time he brought out the ball, but he said he didn't know what to advise me. He asked if I'd talked to either of the medical staff, and I told him they'd promised to see what they could do.

"Well, then," he said. And he arced the ball with one arm over his head right into the basket. There weren't any nets; it was just the metal hoops. It had been two days since I'd visited Health Care about the pregnancy and nothing had happened.

"Can you help me?" I asked again.

August dribbled the ball around, turning his back to me like I was supposed to take it from him while he guarded it. He jumped and turned in mid-air, sinking another. "I don't believe in abortion," he said. But when he saw my face he said, "But I hear you."

I went back to Health Care, even though I was afraid. It seemed to me to be a more high-risk area for SHV. No one knew if I was susceptible or not. Red was an in-between colour. There had been only one highly publicized case involving an infected redhead, although there were possibly others. The Health Care unit was in the principal's office. There was an outer foyer where an assistant would have sat if there had been one. But since the school hadn't been wired for Internet or phone lines yet, the foyer was being used as a storage area. A desk was covered in stacks of bandages, bottles of peroxide, and boxes of gloves.

The soldiers used the staff room across the way as a break spot, and as I waited my turn to talk to a nurse, I could hear a couple of them in there. Normally they were stone-faced, angry, and bored. But out of sight from us, they were cracking jokes about how you'd think being in an isolated place with a gang of suddenly single women would be more fun. That was probably the nicest thing they said. The rest was tougher in tone—one part repulsed, and one part lustful.

There were two nurses in the principal's quarters. The one I was there to see was Nurse Ben. He called me into the VP's office and said casually, "Sit down, Hazel."

No one had called me by my name in a week, even though Augustus had asked it. Nurse Ben had an amicable manner that disarmed me. "Here's what I've got for you," he said. He opened my file. "I understand you're pregnant and you believe you're in the eleventh or twelfth week?"

"I didn't think anything was going to happen."

"You know this isn't a hospital. We have to get the equipment and we're going to get an ultrasound technician out here first to accurately determine how far along you are." Nurse Ben said that's where they had to start things, and unfortunately, he couldn't make any promises about which day that might happen. He made some notes and closed the file, so I stood up. But Nurse Ben told me to have a seat again, please. He said he was going to tell me something I didn't want to hear.

I never like it when people do that: prep you for bad news. It only makes it worse, because you have this horrible apprehension while they wind themselves up to it. I could practically feel my blood pressure rise—at my age! I remember I stared at the shelf above him, which, given his height, seemed positioned so that he'd hit his head on it every time he stood up or sat down. It was jammed with plastic bins containing assorted paper packets and bandages. He whistled to get my attention and I realized he was my age, no older. His face had turned very pink, like mine always does, and I knew that whatever he was going to say was hard for him. I looked him in the eyes because I thought it might make him feel better, and as soon as I did so, I relaxed more than I had thought I would, and listened.

"You should prepare yourself to have this pregnancy. Mentally. It's possible we will be able to get you the procedure, but the country has declared a national state of emergency. No one, at any level, was prepared for this epidemic. It's possible, and we will do everything we can for you, but I do have to tell you it's not probable."

There was an uncomfortable silence. I leaned forward in my chair. Then I leaned back. Ben pushed a box of tissue at me, even though I wasn't about to cry. When he realized I wasn't going to, he said, "I know that's not what you want to hear, and if you want to yell at me, I won't blame you."

I still didn't say anything. I stared out the window and Nurse Ben shifted around on his chair. There was a Tim Hortons coffee shop across the field on the highway, in a little plaza that hadn't opened yet. I could see it from his window and I could usually see it from the playground area too, even though my window in room 8 faced the back way. The shop's big red sign shone in the sun even though it wasn't lit up, just a scrawl of lettering on the squat brown building. The windows underneath the sign were always black. Like everything else out there, it had been built too soon.

Nurse Ben followed my gaze. "That's my view," he said. "Looking at that every day really sucks."

"Yeah," I agreed.

"I just want to walk across the field and find a steaming hot cup of coffee in my hand," Nurse Ben continued, telling me we were certainly not the only Canadians stuck in quarantine, and human rights groups were lobbying for better conditions for us. It might result in actual catering, he had read. Something more healthful.

I knew someone out there cared about us because even though we had no access to media, we were given clothing donations from the Goodwill. Garbage bags full of clothes had been trucked in and dumped in the gym. Brand-new packets of underwear were at a premium, and these were judiciously allotted. There wasn't a lot of nightwear, so we mostly slept in our clothes, or the bolder ones in just T-shirts. There was a janitor's mop closet where we showered on a strict schedule. SHV could be transmitted by blood, which meant that menses and all associated garbage had to be treated as if it were industrial waste.

Another two women got sick. They were both from room 3, the room the first frothing woman had been in. There was debate among the women in room 8, but eventually we decided that it was more likely they'd become sick here than arrived sick.

After that, everyone was on edge. We began to limit our social activities. One woman had a deck of cards, and before that point, there had been some marathon games. After, no one wanted to play.

I didn't mind. I was never much good at cards anyway, never having had anyone to play with growing up except my mom, so I continued to limit myself to basketball. Most of the time now, Augustus didn't join me, but just watched from his post.

Room 3 was the first and only room to go. Four of the women were taken from it, and then, one afternoon, the guards realized it was going to spread to all of them. I heard one of the uniforms in the hallway say, "It's looking bad. They're looking ugly down there," and another said, "Don't talk in front of the blondes"—by which he meant us, all of us, the women.

The school was L-shaped and room 3 was around the corner and halfway down the other branch. I don't know what the soldiers did. We didn't see it and I'm grateful, but we heard it. A lot of shouting and hammering. Then we saw a couple soldiers come in the main doors by the reception-cum-medical area lugging welding equipment. Off they went down that hallway. I guess the outside windows had already been sealed. I won't tell you what happened, but it was a dreadful din that seemed to have no end, and I hope you never hear anything like it in your lifetime.

Eventually, we were brought a bag of orange industrial earplugs. When the soldiers cleaned up the mess, they locked us in our rooms, and we thought they'd seal us in too. One of the older women in our room, her skin like turkey flesh on her bones, said she was going to break the window and run. She probably would have broken a hip if she'd tried. But she didn't, of course.

Through that same window two days later we watched the hazmats arrive, and we caught sight of them going in and out with carts full of bags, bags, and more bags.

By the end of the week a truck arrived bringing better food, as if any of us wanted to eat after what had happened with room 3. But at the same time, we *did* eat. In fact, we ate a surprising amount, as if to remind ourselves to stay healthy and keep living. The government had caved to public pressure and we were brought top-notch stuff from a company whose truck had a film slate stencilled on the side and the name Take One Foods. We heard the soldiers complaining that our food was better than what they got.

As I ate an egg focaccia sandwich and drank urn-spewed coffee with brown sugar from a paper cup made from recycled materials, I wondered if I could fake a heart attack. That would get me on an ambulance and out of there. The soldiers might buy it after all the fast food we'd been given. I even gave serious thought to throwing myself into a psychotic episode, pretending to have SHV, but I was worried that would land me in a ward where I'd be at greater risk, if that were possible.

After a second cup of Seattle's Best, blood firing, I decided to give the ultrasound one more day. If it hadn't happened by Tuesday morning, on Tuesday night I would climb the fence and walk out. By this time, I want you to know, it wasn't that I was so determined to be rid of you personally, but I wanted to choose what to do, and I could feel that choice being taken—day by day, hour by hour—from me.

The men were intimidating, but I knew they'd acted as they did because of the dire circumstances in room 3. I don't think they were expecting any of us healthy women to attempt to bust out. What would they do, shoot me? They might have, of course, but I wasn't thinking straight at the time. There was only ever a half-squad (six to eight soldiers) on duty at night. I thought that at worst, they'd run out, grab me, and bring me back. At best, I'd slip past, they wouldn't notice, and I'd walk or hitch to a hospital in town.

TWELVE

IT'S COLD OUT THIS MORNING, but the snow has stopped. Two days now without a flurry. You've woken me up, and even though it's early, there's nothing to do now but get up and eat something. You keep moving around, making that swimming motion down my side. My little remora. I can feel your squirms more when I haven't eaten, as though you're tugging on my sides, going, "Gimme my D vitamins and my morning sugar fix, bitch!" For a couple months when I felt you it was usually a distinct kick, but now the motion is changing. You bump more than kick. You flex, or pulse. The space you're in is getting smaller around you, and I feel you when you roll over or swipe your arm this way or that. Of course, I don't know if that's what you're really doing; I only know what it feels like. It feels like you're doing a slow dog-paddle or maybe a front flip through water. Sometimes, if I rub my fingers up and down my abdomen, it seems as if you float toward the touch and push against my belly button to feel me stroking you through the skin.

I remember having dinner at Larissa and Jay's way back when she was pregnant with Devang. At the time, she must have been experiencing the first kicks and taps. Jay told me that the motion of the fetus in the uterus as it's first felt by the pregnant woman is called "quickening," and that "quick meant alive," or showing signs of life. Jaichand was always reading thick nonfiction books from the library: cultural primers, biographies, whatever had recently come out that seemed important—the kinds of books that got reviewed in the Sunday news. In ancient times, Jay said, the fetus wasn't considered living until that point when it could be felt by the mother.

I read in the WEE pamphlets that I should get exercise, like brisk walking, but avoid strenuous activities requiring balance and agility, such as riding a bicycle. Out here I have no bicycle to avoid, but chopping wood probably falls into a similar category. And I've chopped a fair bit of wood in the last little while.

When I realized that Karl had told Grace about our affair, I felt so ashamed and my face flamed so furiously that I put on my boots and walked outside. Thinking of it even now, my face gets hot and I feel light-headed. Out at the woodpile I chopped furiously, even though I knew my balance wasn't so spectacular that I should be wielding a heavy instrument over my head. I brought the axe down on the stump where the log stood upright and you squirmed when it split, as if you were nervous. I wielded the axe again and again, until I'd broken a thorough sweat and my muscles ached. I had thought, up until that point, that Grace had known about the affair by intuition, or by reading our emails, or by whatever other evidence married people leave for each other when they want to be caught at something. I had never considered that Karl might have told her outright.

I came back into the cottage and restocked the basket, where we keep the fuel for the stove, but I'd brought too much wood and it rolled over the floor. I remember I bent down to pick it up, but I was plump and winded, and the amount of time it took me to complete the task made Grace exhale impatiently from the couch and turn up the volume on the TV, where two talking heads were debating the development of a vaccine for SHV. We still had the TV signal then.

"Even if the vaccine can be developed," one of the experts was saying, leaning over a gaudy illuminated desk that looked like it would better suit a sports commentator than a political one, "what we're hearing is that people may have an allergic reaction, or possibly contract a mild version of the virus."

"I'd like to know what a mild version of this looks like . . ." Grace huffed.

That little exhalation of Grace's fired off a series of images in my mind: I imagined her making similar impatient sounds when Karl had told her about me the first time—months and months before I turned up on her doorstep, calling her husband's name. It bothered me that he may have told her our intimate details, down to the words, down to the sounds, down to—whatever you can go down to on that stuff.

"I'm going for a walk," I informed Grace. "I need some exercise. I'm going to go to the lake." I hadn't been to have a look at it since I'd arrived, but I knew it was a walkable distance.

Grace looked up from her remote control, startled. "You're not going anywhere." She put out one hand like Moses must have when he parted the Red Sea. "Not unless you plan to walk all the way out on the lake and fall through the ice. Why do you think we're holed up like this? It's safe. If you go out there, you could bring the SHV back with you."

I waited, prone on the couch, until Grace put out her bedside lamp that night. Although she'd given me an old toothbrush of Karl's to use, there was no way she was going to let me sleep on his side of the bed. In my opinion even the couch wasn't far enough away. Grace decided when the lights went out and when they came on again in the morning, when showers were taken, and when food was eaten. The only thing she didn't decide was when you were going to kick me in the kidneys.

"Grace . . ."

There was silence.

"He didn't know. About the baby. I never told him."

I couldn't hear her breathing anymore. The room felt tight and narrow. Then she said, "You dumb bitch."

An hour passed in darkness as I tried to interpret that comment. Before I could, I realized the breathing in the room had changed. There was that high-pitched whine that sometimes occurred when Grace exhaled. She was asleep.

———

I remember the window in the girls' bathroom at the WEE was smaller than I'd expected. It was also over my head, which is always awkward, pregnant or no. I'd stowed away a plastic butter knife from the catering truck earlier that day, and with this makeshift screwdriver, I flicked the latches on the screen. I had thought about using the window above my bed, but it didn't open far enough, and even if it had, it was way too risky to use with fourteen other women sleeping nearby and a man out in the hall. So I'd settled on the bathroom as an escape route. It had taken me two bathroom trips just to get the room to myself, and that had also meant lying to the man in the hall about indigestion. Of course he believed me. What with the pregnancy I was irregular at the best of times.

By 3 a.m., I was still waiting for the night to settle. It had been excruciating—lying in the dark listening to the other women cough, my stomach knotted with nerves. Once in the bathroom it became clear to me that sound was going to be my biggest giveaway. When the screen fell, I instinctively grabbed it before it could clatter its way to the ground outside. I pulled it up against the brick wall with my palm and twisted around so I could get a better grip, then swept it in through the window, turned it on its side, and stashed it quietly behind a toilet. The questions facing me now were, Could I fit through the window? And more important, could I do it without making a shitload of noise? And how much time could I spend in the bathroom, before one of the men came looking?

I snapped off my glasses and put them in my shirt pocket for safekeeping. Then I grabbed the window frame, braced one foot against the sink, and jumped up. I kind of hung there, wedged, the bottom of the window frame pressing into my belly. My head was out, but not my shoulders. But I could see the blur of field and the highway just beyond the playground fence. The air smelled clean, sweet, kind of like whisky and clover. That was when I knew I was going to fit through that window—my size be damned. I could hear a whooshing sound: traffic. I couldn't locate the headlights, but it was the sound of a car far off. I was going to have to be extra quiet. Quieter than I thought quiet was—if the sound could carry that far. I twisted to get through. The first shoulder was easy. The second caught and I felt the sting of what would develop into a long red scrape.

My hands searched against the building, and found if I stretched I could reach the roof. Coming through that window backward now, I walked my hands up the building and wriggled until my hips were braced on the ledge. One hand caught the roof, which jutted out from the building. Then the other. I jarred my hip bone inside on the windowframe and there was a rattle from the impact. I stopped. I breathed. I told myself, "Don't breathe."

Using the roof, I angled myself. I glanced back, and remembered my tenth-grade geometry, how I learned that you can take a measured space and fit various items within it depending how they are arranged, even if their dimensional value is the same. I knew my stomach was squishy and would give no matter where I put it. My butt was the problem. There was some heft there. There was also the giant glowing question mark in my brain about what would happen if another woman walked in to use the bathroom. I sucked in my gut and gently rocked this way and that. Once I almost lost my grip on the gritty shingle and then, just like that, when I was most afraid of falling, my body gave and I was free.

Out came my legs and I dangled, butt out, my shoes still braced against the window's edge. Down, I decided. Time to go down. One shoe fell off and hit the asphalt below me. It made a little *wallop*. It occurred to me that I would make a lot more sound when my whole body went. I flicked off the other clog and it fell. Then my sock feet hit the concrete and the jolt went into my knees and I remember I nearly ruined everything by yelping in pain. The knee with the stitches in it buckled and I went down and felt concrete under my palms. It was two or three feet farther to the ground from outside the window than it had been up to the window from the floor inside.

It was colder than I had expected. I hadn't been out at night and we were now well into October. But I was out, I was out, and this was no time to worry about popping one goddamn stitch. I snatched up my shoes and ran with them in my hands. I didn't look to see if there was anyone on guard; I just concentrated on the fence. Without my glasses on, it was barely there: a grey lattice about a hundred feet out and six feet high, and I raced for it, half sprinting, half hobbling, in socks over cement and stones. My chest was heaving from the effort—running while pregnant, even a few weeks pregnant, was an entirely different thing from regular running, not that I was ever good at that either. I threw one shoe over the fence, then the other. They clunked on the other side. I felt the wire between my fingers. It was cold and it clinked under my ring, but the chain-link was new and it didn't jangle or waver much. Rambunctious kids had not yet bent it down. My sock feet stuck in between the diamond spaces, which hurt without shoes. My toes hooked in. I hadn't done this sort of thing in ten years or more, but up I went. At the top, one leg, then the other, then I dropped without looking for a toehold and fell. It was a longer drop than I had thought and I landed on one of the shoes and my ankle went, then my knee, and I went down again. Then I saw a shape over by the building and I grabbed my shoes. I didn't even put them on. I just pushed myself off the ground and went, grass and twigs flying under my feet.

I heard the fence rattle. The soldier must have hit it harder than I had. He yelled, "Stop!" It was August's voice. Oh Christ. But I didn't have time to think; I just kept running in spite of the pain. Thing is, I'm not in the best shape, never have been, never was.

"Hazel!" August hollered. "Hazel!"

I stopped and looked back. He was still on his side of the fence but he had a hand up on it. I bent over, breathing hard. Was he giving me a head start? I knew I couldn't beat him even so. I looked at the road, a fuzzy blue ribbon still a long way off. Longer than I'd thought. Away from the schoolyard lights, everything was gradients of grey.

"Don't make me take you down!" He sounded like he meant it, the way that some men sound when they get drunk and angry. I wasn't sure what he meant by "take you down." He had a gun. Did he mean he'd use it?

I caught my breath and then, without thinking, started running. It was the only thing to do.

I heard August vault the fence easily. *Boom*, he was on the ground just like that. But I ran as hard as I could and I didn't look back.

He kept calling my name as if I would stop again because we were friends. But every time he called my name I knew where he was behind me. He was gaining fast, so I started to weave. I remembered this tactic from grade-school games of tag and outrunning bullies. You can't go as quickly but you're harder to catch. I could hear his boots on the rutted ground. I dropped one of my shoes and kept going. I sank through mud, I stepped on a thistle, I whined, I kept going. I straightened out to go faster and try to gain some ground. That was when he took me down, tackled me around the knees, and my body skidded to the ground. I had a grass burn down one side, an object sharp under my ribs, and a mouth full of weeds. One front tooth impacted with something hard.

I still didn't know what he would do with me. I saw his eyes roll up to look at me—and my arm shot out with all my might. I punched him in the face, right in the eye. I kicked him in the chest. I almost scrambled away but he took barely a second to recover. Then he had me again and he climbed up my body from the knees and pinned my arms down with his.

He weighed more than I could have imagined and all that weight was on me, pressing down. I could barely breathe, let alone scream, but I did manage to yelp, "You bastard! You fucking bastard!" I gathered up what little energy I had left and spit in his face. I tried to knee him in the groin, but he put his own knees on my arms on either side of my head. I tried to buck him off using my body, but I couldn't shake him. He didn't say a word. He just breathed hard above me.

I thought that maybe I would miscarry after being tackled, because of the fall, but I couldn't feel anything happening. I couldn't feel anything at all.

After a few more seconds I realized August's crotch was in my face, and there was blood in my mouth, and I couldn't move. I knew I wasn't going to jostle him loose, and I gave up trying. I thought I might run again when he let me up, but by then someone else was at the fence, calling out, "Do you need help out there, major?"

"No!" August yelled like it was a matter of pride. "You knew I would catch you. Why didn't you stop?" he asked me between hard breaths, like he was truly perplexed. My glasses were in my pocket but he was close enough that I could see his face. He moved one knee and it hurt, fastening me down. I thought my shoulder might be dislocated. I started to tear up. His own eye was red where I'd punched him, and I could see, even in the dark, that it was going to swell.

"Let me go," I begged him. But it was too late and we both knew it. The other soldier had jumped the fence in spite of being told not to. We could hear him jogging over, boots pounding the earth. "You could have—" I told August. "You could have let me go."

My arresting officers took me into the school between them, waking up both nurses, or "Band-Aid techs," as they called them. Against August's protests, one of them made him read an eye chart on the wall, which he did fine. The nurse gave him an ice pack and said, "Major shiner"—which I guess was a joke, although no one laughed—before going back to bed.

Nurse Ben cleaned the cut on my lip—my teeth were fine. So was my shoulder. I located my glasses in my shirt pocket, and found that one lens had been crushed and splintered. That was what had been under my ribs. Later, I would break the lens into a garbage can and keep the frame so I could at least have the one good eye. Nurse Ben swabbed the bottom of my foot where I'd run through the picker and put ointment on it. He handed me an ice pack for my ankle. Then he pulled up my jean leg and made a sucking sound in his mouth.

"How long have you been like this?"

"A couple weeks." I told him about the two stitches I was supposed to get that I didn't, then about popping another one while running during the fountain attack in New York.

"You finished off the job tonight. It will scar. But I can sew it back up for you," he said, swabbing at it. It stung and I winced. "You're lucky it's not infected. You haven't been treating it with any kind of antiseptic. Why didn't you come see me about this?"

I could feel my face turn red, and I started to hiccup more than cry. "I had . . . other things . . . on my mind."

"Yes." He pushed thread through a needle. "That's clear. Hold still, and don't cry until it's done."

Michelle Morell was ordered to get up and go take my bed for the night, and they put me in the stock closet. As I lay there, I was glad she'd had extra tests done, because no one offered me clean linens.

"What's going to happen to me?" I said aloud to myself, because I was in my own room and no one could hear me, and I didn't care if they could. "What's going to happen to me?"

The next day, after only a few hours' sleep, August looked like I'd really pounded him. He had a black streak under his eye like a football player and his cheek was as swollen as an apple. He was not a small guy, and I hadn't known I possessed that much strength. I must have gone crazy. He bit his lip when I walked by, as if there was something he was trying to keep in. I didn't apologize.

One of the other soldiers glared at me when I was hobbling to the library for my regularly enforced head shave. "He should have lit you up, bitch," the guy seethed as I passed. His tone gave me a good indication of what it might feel like to be riddled with bullets.

The private who cut our hair always jerked me back and forth with his needle fingers, but that morning it felt as though he was doing it all the more. The clippers had fangs, and my shoulders throbbed from where August had pinned me. My body hurt in strange places, places I didn't know a person could hurt, like my elbows, the muscles under my armpits all the way into my boobs, my hip bones, even the front cords of my neck. I watched the red dust of my hair powder the inside of a plastic bag, like swept-up grass trimmings in the wrong colour. I didn't wear my broken glasses and everything was blurred.

After the head shave, the commanding officer, with whom I'd never spoken, stuffed the door of my little room. He went up one side of me and down the other, at the top of his voice, it seemed—although truthfully his voice never seemed to reach its full volume; there was always another level it could hit. The wooden door had been left ajar so the others could hear. He informed me that I had not only disobeyed the rules and regulations of the Women's Entry and Evaluation centre to which I'd been assigned, but also broken the laws of my country by attempting sedition. In trying to leave the quarantine, I had knowingly put my countrymen at risk. There would be serious consequences to my actions. I would be punished, and my privileges taken away. The federal government of Canada had invoked the Emergencies Act—this was a time of natural disaster, and how could I think that any one person should exist above the law? The invoking of this act by the Cabinet and by Parliament had been given full and total consideration. Did I know better than the fine men and women serving on those bodies? Did I really think that my individual rights meant more than the safety and security of my countrymen and our nation at large? Did I? *No, sir.* Did I believe I had the right to assault an employee of that nation, an employee who had been engaged to follow orders, to do everything within his power to serve and protect?

I didn't say "No, sir" that time. The commanding officer closed the door for effect, trapping me with him in that closet space. I remained seated on the cot, which made me feel even smaller. This man, he had eyes the colour of a mountain. He lowered his voice, which made him even more frightening. He asked what I would have done if I had managed to escape, and reminded me I didn't even have a health card. He told me he understood my thoughts, and he was not wrong.

"You mistakenly think the major was preventing you from receiving health care. This man was preventing you from contaminating others. This man has been trained and is paid to keep you here at all costs. This man was doing his job."

I must have said "Yes, sir," because I don't think he would have left until I agreed with him, but if I did, I honestly don't remember. I didn't have much voice at all by that point. And I was physically quaking at the idea that he might lay formal charges against me. My outdoor privileges were to be revoked. From then on, I could exercise only in the gym. I would be locked into the storeroom at night. The bathroom window would be nailed shut, and as if that wasn't enough of a security measure, henceforth anytime I had to shit or piss, someone would be there to listen.

Maybe it was a terrible coincidence, but the ultrasound arrived promptly that day at 10 a.m.

———

The ultrasound technician was a woman, and unlike us, she had hair. It was lush and black and piled up on her head under a paper cap, but I could see the curls above her ears threatening to escape. She squeezed jelly on me, which was cold and lube-like, and moved the head of an instrument around my belly button. It felt like some kind of rubber sex toy and looked like a barcode scanner. Nurse Ben had said I needed to drink twelve ounces of water for the ultrasound, but I didn't know how much that was, had drunk probably twice that amount from the water fountain, and needed to pee. The technician spoke gently and gave no indication of knowing about my escape, my desperation. In fact, she barely acknowledged our unfortunate surroundings.

We were in what was meant to become the kindergarten, and it had its own bathroom. The technician rubbed the juice off my belly with Kleenex and pointed, and said, "Go let a little out."

I did what she said, then I came back into the cloakroom, where we had set up to perform the ultrasound. I climbed back onto the table she'd wheeled in when she arrived, and she re-squirted and started rubbing me with the instrument again, moving it in circles across my bloated abdomen. I had gained weight at the WEE. Baby weight.

I couldn't see the screen. It was turned toward her. She asked if I wanted to see, but I didn't say anything, so she didn't ask again. We were in close proximity and she smelled like jasmine and honey. I remember that because, aside from the cleanser they used to scrub down the halls and the classrooms, everything—everyone—at the WEE smelled salty and sour. Beside me, and just behind her, were two rows of little pegs, one at knee-height, the other at eye level to where I lay, about four feet off the ground. The pegs had been painted barn red even though the room was institutional green.

"What's happening out there, in the world?" I asked her.

"Nothing so interesting as what's happening in here. Everyone thinks they're sick. But not everyone is, of course. The hospitals are full up, half with people who need to be there, and half with people who don't. Halloween is going to be something. There's a magazine in Toronto that's holding a blonde ball, or a peroxide party, or some such thing. I read a very controversial piece about it in the *Spectator*. You have to wear a wig to get in. Somehow it's very chi-chi—don't ask me. I guess maybe they're doing it in New York and now Toronto's copying."

"But . . . what about the rest of the world? I know we're in a state of emergency, but how are other countries reacting?"

She stopped talking, squiggling the device back and forth until it became clear she wasn't going to tell me anything more. Or maybe she was concentrating. I could hear clicking from the computer.

"This all looks fine," she said, as if someone had told her it might not. Her brow scrunched. "Ah, there," she remarked finally, in a satisfied manner, pushing down hard on my abdomen with the barcode scanner. "Hold it, that's it," she said, as if she were a school photographer.

After the technician was done, Nurse Ben called me in for counselling. He was grim. He'd lost his charm and sat awkwardly, as if he didn't know what to do with his hands. They lay there on his desk, long and white. He looked at them as though they were two fish that needed to be skinned and he wasn't sure where to start—head or tail. I would have trusted him if I'd needed a limb amputated or a bullet dug out of me. But with this, he was out of his element.

"Your pregnancy has progressed to fourteen weeks," he said.

"It *was* twelve—not even—when I came here. The outbreak makes this a special circumstance," I argued.

"You know I agree," he said, and stared at the folder in front of him without opening it.

"In a special circumstance . . ."

"Yes." But he did not mean *yes, he could help me*. He meant *yes, that was true*. Technically. "Have you been following legislation on this issue in the last three to five years?" Things had changed under the Conservative government, he said. And with the added burdens of the viral outbreak, he explained, our hospitals were overcrowded, overloaded. Medical personnel and almost every health resource was being used for other efforts. In other words, I was fortunate to have had the ultrasound. Then he said something I didn't expect: "I can put in an order and we can arrange to terminate it for you. But you need to know that it may not happen quickly—especially under this government, and especially given the current crisis. I can put in the request, but I cannot promise that we would see results this week. It might be next, or it might be longer. I want you to consider if that is what you want, and come back to see me tomorrow. If it is, I will put in the request—and then, we wait some more and see."

Through the window behind him, I could see the orange orb of the basketball lying at the edge of the painted blacktop court. It blurred, but this time not because of my missing glasses lens. I watched it lose and regain its shape, softening and then coming clear again, as the minutes passed. I knew I should ask him to put in the request, but I also knew that I couldn't. I had waited too long already—and that part was no one's fault but mine.

As a kid and then a young adult, I had wondered what my mom wanted from me, what she wanted *for* me, why she'd brought me into the world. I remembered slamming my bedroom door at age twelve, hollering, "Why did you even have me?" Now I know there was no big dream. She just wanted to see me grow.

Lying on my cot in the stock closet that night, I thought about my mother and everything she must have gone through to give birth to me—alone, or mostly alone. I thought about how tired I was every minute of every day, and how I had been weary from the moment I first found out about you. I thought about my own mom going through that fatigue, and the nausea, every second of every day for months for me, and how I never knew that and never respected her—and I wished now that I had. I wished I could take back every mean thing I'd ever retorted, every time I'd rolled my eyes or hadn't listened.

Her hands would shake when she was counting money out to store clerks, as if she were afraid she would come up short. I remembered her hand when she touched the back of my head when I was a little girl. With the flat of her palm she used to stroke the hairs down behind my ears. She was always rubbing at me, like I was some kind of goddamn worry-bead, and at the time I thought she was trying to change me or make some adjustment to my appearance. Bills would pile up, unopened sometimes, because she couldn't stand to look at them. I can recall her slapping them down on the kitchen table and then pushing them off to the side when we ate; I remember the smell of booze on her breath at night when she tucked me in. The men she dated always had cars; we never had one of our own. I learned to drive in random vehicles belonging to men my mom was dating. At the time I thought there were any number of reasons for the alcohol and for the men, but lying in detention with no window, no view to the world, I knew the truth: it was because raising a kid was hard, especially when you had no help from anyone. How she had suffered without anyone to tell. It was that—more than Karl, more than Grace—that I had been avoiding. It was this truth that scared the bejesus out of me.

The next day, Nurse Ben opened my file and began to pass me pale blue pamphlets about the stages of pregnancy I would go through. All of the women in the photos were beautiful. All were in their early thirties. All were trim, the only fat on their bodies the round perfect hump at the abdomen. None of them had purple hair or shaved heads or Mohawks; none had tattoos or nose rings or Avril Lavigne eyeliner; none wore ugly vintage dresses or Birkenstock sandals or slutty super-stretch jeans or Chuck Taylors. They were all dressed in crisp office wear, or pastel T-shirts, or white flowing dresses. They were all being embraced from behind by clean-shaven men who looked like they'd stepped out of car commercials—men who were older than the women, sure, but not substantially so. They were all smiling. In one picture, the man's hands were positioned to make a heart shape overtop of his wife's bulging bare belly. I didn't know anyone like these women and didn't feel anything like them. Motherhood, I thought, should have a better PR campaign, one that was more inclusive.

Larissa had told me just after her son was born that being pregnant was the happiest time in her life. I sat there in front of Nurse Ben and waited to feel pastel, and crisp, and clean, and happy. The feeling didn't come.

Ben passed me a blue-lined sheet of the diet and vitamins they were going to give me. I could see that he had written it out himself. I focused on the word *legumes*, its letters stitched together neatly, slanting as if Ben was a lefty trying his best to write clearly. I was no longer allowed to eat lunch meat from the caterer because of the chance of listeriosis. I was allowed my morning coffee, though, and I considered that a small wonder.

He asked me if I could read them, and I said, yes, I'm nearsighted.

"Do you want to see the pictures?"

I nodded dumbly and he passed me the ultrasound pictures. There were two images—not photographs, but images on regular paper as if they had been run off a Laser printer. Because I hadn't seen the screen, at first I couldn't identify you. I couldn't tell my insides from your outsides. You were just a black-and-white blur, something colourless, made out of static.

"Here is the head. This little bright spot in the centre of the image is the heart." Nurse Ben pointed to a blank spot.

Then he turned the file around and showed me that your heart rate had also been noted. He pointed at some measurements and said they were of your brain. He told me your heart rate was 146 beats per minute.

"What will it be?" I asked Nurse Ben, without looking up from the shapeless shape.

"It's very early yet, but in this case the technician has noted that there is little doubt. Do you see the three parallel lines?" he asked, and I squinted. "They mean female."

THIRTEEN

I REMEMBER THE DAY GRACE DECLARED the majority of the fresh foods gone. She called me a porker, said I could really put it back now that I'd got over my nerves. She asked me if I was carrying a beluga calf in there, and told me she'd seen on some nature program that they're born at nearly five feet and weigh as much as a full-grown man.

She pulled packaged hash browns from the freezer. "Now we're fucking camping," she declared. "It's this and canned soup from here on in." There was more food available than that, of course, but she was old and well-off, used to being a gourmet.

We didn't talk about what I'd told her—about Karl not knowing about you. But I felt as though something had changed in Grace's attitude toward me. She stood on a chair and pulled down the ladder from the attic. I hadn't known there was an attic before that. She went up there and eventually called to ask if I could help her. Her face appeared at the top of the ladder. She peered down.

"No, there's no way," she said. "If I pass it to you and you drop it, it'll crush the baby." She paused as if considering that, then said, "Okay, forget it. I've fucking got it." She came back down the ladder and tugged something down after her, grunting, the muscles in her shoulders ridged beneath her sweater. I watched dumbly. She staggered on the last step and set a case down heavily on the floor. It turned out to contain an old sewing machine.

"Karl bought this for me—thought it was quaint. Antique crap. I wonder if it still fucking works. How the hell—?"

Grace scratched the lagoon-blue Formica table loading the machine onto it. I'm willing to bet Karl paid top dollar for the table, which was in pristine shape, but clearly Grace didn't care or even notice what she'd done. She pretzelled and contorted her fingers, and eventually she had the machine threaded. She commanded me to take off my pants. She wrapped a tape measure around my bust, her thumb and forefinger holding it there, just over my nipple. She looped it again around my hips, and noted the measurement. Then all afternoon, she stitched and cursed, and by evening, she'd put new panels into half my clothes.

At one point, she climbed up into the attic and threw down a box of musty fabric, most of it cowboy print. You'd be surprised how many different cowboy prints Karl had collected:

silhouettes of horses, prints of boots and guns, white-on-red polka dot, a pony print. She said they were for an abandoned project. I wonder what he'd thought he would do with them. She also found a box of old T-shirts and sweatshirts of Karl's that she said I could wear. Men's large is a surprisingly good look for me and the bump, aka you. The funny thing is, I never saw Karl wear a T-shirt or sweatshirt in the time that I knew him.

I reflected that in spite of Grace's explosions of profanity, she seemed to be adept at everything. When I thanked her and asked if she'd ever made maternity clothes before, she said, around two pins held between her teeth, "Some things a woman just knows, and the rest is improvisation."

I never learned to sew. When I ripped my jeans growing up, my mom would slap an iron-on patch over the tear. If she sewed on a button, it was hairy with thread. There were a lot of hairy buttons and patches that came loose again like snakes shedding their skins, but she never seemed to get better at these tasks. At the time, I'd blamed the beer. But maybe such skills just didn't run in our blood. How my mom managed to cut hair so well, I don't know. Then again, her clients at Head Start were mostly middle-aged women and students. Cheap cuts for people seeking a deal. She learned only one or maybe two new styles a year.

Grace told me to launder the clothes before I wore them. When I looked in the full-length mirror in the bathroom, I saw someone who was part old-me, wearing last year's wardrobe, part Karl, and a big part you. I felt like a Mrs. Potato

Head doll stuck together by some indiscriminate three-year-old. I think I had gained an extra five pounds in my boobs alone, and they were never small to begin with. I didn't recognize this weird physical amalgam. I certainly didn't look like the women in the prenatal pamphlets that Nurse Ben gave me.

After my escape attempt, I was at the WEE for another six weeks, and during that time you grew fast. It was only a couple weeks after my first ultrasound that my belly popped out and began to look, if not like that basketball of August's, at least slightly volleyball shaped. I could tell I was showing because sometimes women who didn't know me, women from the other rooms, would apologize and let me use the toilets first. According to the pamphlets, by then your arms were almost as long as they will be when you are born, you'd developed bones; and by sixteen weeks, your eyes inside me could move. You got your fat, though hopefully you've inherited Karl's fat and not my fat. You began to hear my blood move around you, my digestion. All these things happened and more, and yet as much as everything changed inside me, not much changed at all. I still felt exhausted, ugly, and uncertain.

Once or twice, I did get a pastel, happy feeling—the one that women like Larissa talked about. But when it came, it crept up on me almost like an attack. It must have been hormones. I would find myself sitting, dazed and euphoric. But I had no reason to feel happy and nothing to channel my happiness into, so it felt as if it were not so much an actual emotion as a physical state. It was like being a little high, or drunk, or just plain sleepy. It came only now and again in a short surge. And like the nausea in the earlier days, it passed fairly quickly.

I filled out forms indicating where the Canadian government should forward my possessions when they were done with them. I chose Larissa's address for stability. Before going to New York, I'd sublet my apartment in Toronto and I didn't know how dependable the student I'd rented it to was, whether the rent would still be paid without my checking in, or even whether she'd still be there when I returned. I filled out forms, and followed my diet, and took my folic acid and calcium and B6, and slept an awful lot.

I couldn't decide if it was ethically right that I hated August for standing in my way that night. He was, as the commanding officer had said, doing his job. But, right or wrong, through all the weeks that remained, I couldn't bring myself to speak to him again. I noticed at some point that the basketball was gone from the post outside. I heard the men playing with it in the gym, thumping up and down on a break one afternoon, skidding in their boots on the finished floor. I wondered if school kids would one day attend that place, play in that gym, learn to read in room 3. I wondered whether they'd tell ghost stories to each other about the things that happened there long ago, or if they'd be a new generation, more innocent than mine, shielded somehow. If they will be . . . If you will be . . .

It was around then that news of the death of the singer Shelbee Brown hit. We knew of it almost immediately, although it was one of the few news items that reached us in that place. We knew because we heard the men's reactions. We heard an exclamation echo through the hall: "What the fuck!"

Women stuck their heads out of doorways, and the men who would normally wave them back inside their classrooms had gathered around a single guy with an iPhone who muttered, "Jesus, not her. Not her!"

Two guys were looking over his shoulder while others pulled out their own devices and scrolled through them. Even the private from the library came out and said, without emotion, "What is it?"

August was there and he looked up and said, "Shelbee Brown died."

The private, who was normally so expressionless, crept farther into the hall.

"She contracted it," one of the men said. "Her family and managers kept it from the media, but she was down for days before expiring. That's why they cancelled her last two shows saying 'exhaustion.'"

"How? An attack?"

"Her hair," one of the men said. "She always said it was part of her show. She kept it for the fans."

"Fucking artist."

"I saw her last July. Only music me and my lady could agree on."

"The world just lost some prime pussy."

"Shut it. I feel like somebody ripped my heart right outta my chest and you're all, like, pussy this, pussy that."

"She was something, man. I just can't believe it."

The men were depressed all week. We heard them talk-singing under their breath while they were standing guard, *Nobody feeds you like your mama, You may think they're gonna, You may think they wanna, But no one will, no one will, Yeah, yeah, yeah,* lyrics that seemed deeper or sexier or more earnest when they came from the mouth of a woman with a big blonde bouffant and a skinny, overexposed, over-tattooed torso. I didn't mourn her, but I knew her death was serious: the disease now had a publicist.

A few days later, one of the men came in with an image of Shelbee tattooed on his biceps. He rolled up the sleeve of his uniform to show the others. "Now it's permanent," he said.

August transferred before I was released. I guess it was in week seven of the WEE centre and week nineteen of you. One day he was there and the next he was gone. When I asked one of the other uniforms, who'd seemed to be a friend of his, the guy glared at me and said that August had been moved to another assignment at a different WEE, that they'd got some new rentals (meaning reservists) coming in—but what the fuck did I care anyway?

If the men hated me, though, the women were kinder. I don't know if it was because of what I was going through specifically, if they would have been so kind in the event of an ordinary pregnancy. The illnesses had petered out. Our room was unsullied. That probably didn't hurt.

I don't believe there is a bond between all women. I don't believe that sisterhood is powerful. I believe just the opposite. I believe that these women were simply in the right circumstances to be kind. There was nothing to prevent them from it. We were stuck there, by this point more bored than terrified, growing more confident daily that we were going to get out, but feeling at the end of the world nonetheless. Every day we looked at the same damn field. Every day a small group played bridge. Another group collected the towels and bedding, even though it wasn't their job, and sent it off in an army truck to be laundered. One woman said the best thing about being there was that she'd kicked smoking after forty years. What else did these women have to do but rub my back and feet and offer advice?

The teenager in my old room 8 had a small set of binoculars one of the men had lent her because she was just a kid, I guess, and she had an interest in stars. From the window, she showed me Polaris, the North Star, and how the Big Dipper always pointed to it, almost like it was trying to catch it in its spoon. I could see them, but only through my one eye, the part of my glasses that still had a lens. I covered the other with my hand. She told me if I thought of the Big Dipper as a goldfish net trying to scoop up Polaris, I'd always be able to find it. That was how her father had explained it to her. And she showed me the Great Bear, which was an easy one, she said, because the Dipper made up its shoulder. She also pointed out

Cassiopeia—at least she thought it was, she couldn't be sure—Perseus, and Andromeda Nebula, the Chained Lady. But the Whale was hidden behind the edge of the roof and we couldn't see that one. Cassiopeia was Andromeda's mother. She bragged about her daughter's beauty so much that she incurred the wrath of the sea. To save his kingdoms, her husband, Cepheus, chained their daughter to a rock—for the sea monster to take her and devour her. But Perseus wandered by and freed her, killed the monster, and became her husband. The teenager said she wished her name was Andromeda, and would I call her that?

"Okay," I said. I couldn't make out all the constellations; they were just stars to me. I couldn't connect them in my mind's eye like she did. We had to sit right up against the window just to see, our knees pressed against the glass, leaning forward. I could tell I was getting bigger because this was awkward for me. Nurse Ben had been taking my blood pressure and my weight; I had gained twenty pounds, although without the WEE's catering truck I've not gained much since. I worry about that, actually. For someone who's always struggled with weight, it's odd that now I might suddenly be under what I ought to be for your sake.

"It's my mom's fault I'm here," the girl proclaimed, as I passed the binoculars back to her. "She *made* me go visit my dad. I didn't want to."

She looked as though she weighed about as much as a fence post and I was fascinated by the amount of hate contained in her small frame. There she was, away from both her parents, away from all her friends, in a terrible place, and instead of missing them, she spent her time cursing them. The girl said the stars in Andromeda Nebula—right at the knee, which I strained to find—were 2.7 million light-years away, the farthest object the human eye could see. For some reason, I remembered my mom's hands on my head when she cut my hair, the way her fingers were gentle and she tucked and lifted the sections of it along my neckline. The smell of smoke rising up behind me from her Virginia Slims, sinking into my collar. For once I didn't think about her boyfriends over the years, or her drinking. All of that felt as far away as this star that the girl, Andromeda, was trying to show me. She said her real name was—something lame by her own admission—Sandy, I think.

The next afternoon Sandy said she had an iPod Shuffle, but it didn't work anymore because she'd run down the battery our first week there. We could pretend, though, she said. We each put an earbud in and lay back on her cot, very close together because the cot was so narrow. I had to keep one foot on the floor so as not to tumble off it. She sang a bunch of pop songs I didn't know that had horribly cliché lyrics, and I nodded my head and felt old for the first time in my life. The only two songs I knew were "Hot N Cold" by Katy Perry and the Shelbee Brown song that the soldiers were always humming. I sang along to those two.

Sandy asked, didn't I hate having my hair taken away? She said she was glad no one important could see her. I told her I'd never liked my hair much anyway, and since it could kill me now, I really didn't miss it.

"You're so totally brave," she said.

She had a squirrelled-away bottle of nail polish, which she used to paint my toenails pitch black.

My midsection had grown so big that my toes seemed as if they were on the other side of a wall—far enough away that bending over to wash my feet in the shower had become awkward. Women from my old room started coming around the stock closet where I slept and touching me and suggesting names. The ultrasoundist arrived again. This time I looked when she offered to show me the screen. You resembled the brand of honey where the bottle is shaped like a bear: transparent with nubs in familiar places. When she showed me your face, I strained to figure out if you looked like me or Karl, but it was too soon. You wore an expression, but you simply looked like baby—and yet not baby. More like Ghost Baby. Translucent Baby. You were rolling around a lot, bringing your hands up as if you were at a dance party, which amazed me because I couldn't feel a thing. You were 323 grams. The technician reconfirmed that the smear of you, with its three parallel lines, was girl. This was your labia. The women had a heyday with the name lists after that. The younger women, in their thirties like Michelle Morrell, suggested trendy names that sounded like perfume brands. Names like Destiny and Serenity and London. The older women suggested names from decades past, names that seemed like they ought to come with polished buckles and bows attached. Names like Susan and Claire and Christina. I listened as if in a fog.

Nothing much changed until the last week of the WEE,

and then—that was when I felt you move. I was lying in bed the first time: you were like a sleepy kitten rubbing its ears against my abdomen. The feeling was so fleeting I thought I must have imagined it. Then, the next day, I was standing at the food cart, filling my coffee, and you kicked twice low down in my pelvis, a kind of knocking, hard enough that I said "Oh!" out loud. So hard it was as if you were trying to break out.

The day we were freed, the soldiers didn't tell us in advance. We had our breakfast and our showers, those of us who got them that day. They didn't send us for shaving—that was the only clue. Then the soldiers started coming around, barking that it was time to go. We all looked at each other, like, *Really?* We didn't believe they meant it. A couple women had been keeping calendars, charting when everything happened— who was menstruating when, how long we'd been there, which tests they ran and on whom—but even they were caught off guard. They had thought it would be the following week, but either they'd missed a couple days somewhere, or else the government had simply tired of paying for us.

There was only one shuttle we could take: into Hamilton. Many of the women were from farther-flung areas in Ontario— Owen Sound, Kingston, Ottawa; a couple travelling together were even bound for Winnipeg, Manitoba—but Hamilton was our only option. That was how far the government was willing to pay for us to be shuttled back to civilization. The soldiers gave us paperwork that said we'd been cleared by Canada

Customs. The teenager, Sandy, rolled hers up into a tube and made trumpet sounds through it.

"Dear, you're going to need that," one of the older women said to her, even though it seemed to me like a useless document now that we were free to go.

We were allowed to use the phone at the Hamilton armoury, where we were dropped. We lined up and one by one each took a turn, and one by one people came to collect us. When I dialled Larissa's number, I got a prerecorded voicemail saying the number was not in service. The same thing occurred when I phoned my mom and Richard. I tried to remember the numbers of other friends, like Addy and Jude from my university department, but I'd seldom called them, or if I had, it had been via my cellphone and I'd just hit the big green Phone icon and hadn't ever thought to look closely at the number. Desperately, I called Karl's cell, then his home number. I got a message saying that he and Grace were at their cabin. I wasn't sure if it was the same recorded greeting that had been there two and a half months before or a new one. This time I left a message.

"I've been at a Women's Entry and Evaluation centre," I explained, using the full name in case WEE wasn't commonly known, "I'm free to go. I can't get through to anyone, and I'm just desperate for a ride. *Desperate*," I stressed, and gave my location. I didn't apologize or make excuses for calling.

By late afternoon, the day was greying, and all of the other women but one were gone. Some lived too far for pickups, but someone had phoned someone who had phoned someone who . . . and they'd all been shuttled off. No one said goodbye, I noticed. Women just hopped into vehicles and sped away, knowing—hoping—they'd never see the others again. Even Sandy left without a backward glance. The one remaining woman was clutching her paperwork under her coat against her chest because she didn't want it to get wrinkled or blow away. When no one showed up to collect us, I told her I was going to walk to the Greyhound station. I asked her twice if she wanted to come, but the woman just sat there crying as if she hadn't heard me. I didn't know her—she was from room 1—so as heartless as you may think this was, I left her there. I did not want to get stuck at night in a city I didn't know.

Asking directions, I managed to get to the Greyhound Station, and there I did the only thing I could do: I begged. It was surprisingly easy. Even for an expert thrift-store shopper my charity clothes were mismatched, not nearly warm enough for the weather, and I was bald and pregnant, wobbling like a penguin. I had no ID, no money, no possessions to speak of. "Excuse me, can you help me? I've been in quarantine for eight weeks and I've just been cleared . . ." I held up my papers as if they were a diploma. "I have nothing and I have to get to Toronto."

"Get away from me," one woman said to me. She was blonde, and I remember being surprised that there were blondes still in the world.

The other passersby were more forthcoming. I put on the glasses with one lens so that I could make eye contact with people at a distance. There was a way to stand, I found, where I looked even more pregnant than I actually was. The women in the WEE had been able to tell, but they'd had nothing else to think about in that place. Strangers on the street, on the other hand, had many distractions. I undid my thin jacket, stuck my gut out, and placed my hand on my belly, and finally they noticed. Beneath the skin you kicked as if you were eager to participate. People are kinder to the unborn than they are to women themselves, and soon I had my ticket.

FOURTEEN

LET ME TELL YOU, BABY, when I got off the bus in Toronto at Bay and Dundas, I literally could have fallen to my knees and kissed the pavement of my city.

It was December and there were Christmas lights and advertisements for new gadgets just for him, and spa and tanning certificates just for her. Tanning salons and sun beds seemed to be the gift for women that year. SHOPPING, DINING, NIGHTLIFE, JOY! a sign declared. I had to pull out my glasses to see it, and I didn't care what I looked like, wearing frames with only one lens. Another sign read GET HER A GIFT SHE REALLY NEEDS—A GIFT FOR THE WHOLE FAMILY—THE DANCO RAZOR. Coffee shops were playing carols and lights blinked and shone above shelves displaying silver espresso pots. I watched a fat baby wearing a hat shove a brownie in its mouth, leaving chocolate smeared across its face. A man was standing outside the doors of the bus station, smoking, peering into the distance, just waiting for somebody. I couldn't believe how normal and goddamn beautiful it all was.

I used a precious quarter to phone again, finally managed to get through to Larissa's cellphone, and left a message telling her I had made it into Toronto and was on my way over. In the middle of an icy city, dark and bright, thronged with people in toques and turbans, scarves and mittens, I made my way to Larissa and Jay's.

As I approached Dundas Square from the west, I continued to admire the light show. The sky rained advertisements. Had I really been out in the country so long that Toronto's one-intersection attempt to mimic Times Square could seem so huge? People had protested against these ads, saying that they were gawdy and distracting, and that the city needed more art, but to me, at that moment, they were the most stunning things I'd ever seen. Neon, sparkling life.

On a two-storey screen, a nude woman with jet-black hair held a small twinkling light in her cupped palm, a wistful smile on her face as she lifted it above her head and let it float away from her, bright as tinsel. BLONDE MEMORY, the screen said, burning gold, a glass bottle appearing ghost-like around the words. BOTTLE IT. WEAR IT. FEAR IT.

Other ads were hyper-masculine, edging into the territory women's advertising had occupied for years, where women were portrayed as twinned naïfs, lover-like but without sex characteristics: pretty things fawning together over pretty things that could be bought and sold. A man with all the glam charms of the 1970s lay in recline. He was thickly muscled, his black hair frizzing out from his head, his lips overly red, a feminine choker lacing his throat, a black vest over his nude torso. Behind him sat his buddy, white-gold and gleaming with his shirt off, wearing only a cream-coloured knit scarf and a pair of jeans. Do WHAT YOU WANT, the top tagline read, and beneath the models' feet: NOW MORE THAN EVER and a logo. I think it was for jeans, or maybe clothing—the scarf did seem to stand out—but the subtext was that this was a better time to sleep with men than women.

I was walking past the Eaton Centre, laden shoppers ducking in and out of its opalescent revolving doors, when I stopped to watch a performance—a busker hoping for coins in the street. Painted on a placard were the words SILVER & GOLD. He had divided himself down the middle like the male–female hybrid of midways and boardwalks, except in this case both sides of him were meant to be female. He was silver and bald on one side, sparkling gold with a blonde half-wig on the other. His dress was shiny, sprayed stiff. He mimed and vogued on the one side, tousling his blonde wig. Then he turned to the other side and broke into his silver schtick, which included a rain of tears made of a foil streamer he released dramatically from his hand. Music from a beatbox accompanied him. I couldn't look away. Two teenage girls—both their heads shaven, wearing 1920s-style black caps with feathers in the front—approached, tittering, and dumped a handful of dimes and quarters into his tin. He winked and rotated and began his dance again.

The girls returned to a group. A friend of theirs had pulled her knit cap off her hair, which showed an alluvial history: the layers of colour she had attempted over the past few months. Black now was striped with brown and finally blonde coming back in. She ran her fingers through it. "Oh, I don't care if I get it," she bragged to a boy in a pea coat who would probably be a catch when he was old enough to shave. "I hope I do—at least it would be *something*." She smacked her cap against her thin leggings.

I must have been distracted and not watching where I was going, because the next thing I knew my body buckled and I was going down—fast. It was just a spot of ice, but my front was so much heavier than I was used to, and I realized immediately that I couldn't stop myself from hitting the sidewalk hard. A voice in my mind said: *Protect your head, Hazel!* And another one shouted out at the same time: *Protect the baby, Hazel!* And my hands hit the cold concrete and still I was going down too hard to stop. I managed to adhere to the commands of both voices, and rolled onto my right shoulder, which took the brunt of the force. As I struggled to sit up, my chest started to heave with small sobs—from embarrassment more than anything. No one extended a hand to help me up.

The silver-and-gold man had plucked up his sign and his money tin. He was heading across the street to continue his act in Dundas Square. The girls in their feather headwear had scampered closer to the shopping mall. Even the nonchalant girl with the cap and the hair like layers of sediment was watching me. Other people had backed away and were eyeing me warily.

Swallowing my embarrassment, I pulled myself up. I decided I wasn't hurt and walked on fast, watching the sidewalk to avoid another spill. But the spirit I'd felt was gone. As I passed St. Michael's Hospital, I saw the foyer was stuffed with people waiting for attention. I grabbed at a newspaper box and pulled out a free weekly. *I'll Have a White-Blonde Christmas*, its headline proclaimed. I stopped in the park outside the Metropolitan Church on Queen Street and leaned there, resting as I flipped the pages. The frontmatter gave me the statistics. A pandemic had been declared several weeks earlier. In spite of increasing campaigns on the part of the Canadian government, the editorial said, prevention efforts were simply not working.

"People feel very beaten down," a University of Toronto professor was quoted as saying. "It's hard to protect yourself when you're seriously depressed. On campus, we have poster campaigns to create awareness and free shave-and-dye kits, but it's just not enough." One in five people, the article claimed, had lost someone they knew to SHV, attacks, or acts relating to the virus. Around the world, cases had risen to a hundred thousand per day. There had also been a dramatic rise in instances of post-traumatic stress disorder. The number of women on anxiety meds had increased by 60 percent. Simply having a panic attack, the journalist wrote, could put a woman at risk, as the resulting behaviour—crying, acting emotional or paranoid, trembling, collapsing—could lead spectators to conclude that she carried SHV. A case was cited of a Halifax woman who had been tranquilized by officials during a public anxiety attack, but who did not in fact have the virus. Her family had filed charges against the city for putting her into a ward where she might since have been exposed.

Across the lamp-lit park, I heard rustling. Even though evening was falling fast, and the temperature falling faster, a group of men sat at tables that were painted with chessboards. I remembered having seen men play there in the summer, always from a distance. Some of them were ragged. Some of them were old. Some of them were speed players with a timer, snapping it down like the pros I had seen in New York. Some of them were there day and night. And apparently some of them were there even amid ruts of slush and with darkness creeping blue at their backs. They were watching over each other's shoulders, a serious huddle around one of the tables. With cramped fingers, I folded up the news weekly, rolled it under my arm, and continued down the sidewalk.

As I passed these men, though, I realized it wasn't chess they were watching at all. They were frozen around their own table, the rooks and kings still in place, but their heads were turned to an adjacent chess table. A woman who looked like she had drifted into the church park for the charity dinner or for shelter was sitting there, her head lolling. I had to turn my own noggin to focus, because of my missing lens. I saw the word *Juicy* across pink track pants riding low on her hips, her back hunched. A smile-shape of skin was exposed. Her hair was half blonde and half brunette, the dye long ago having grown out. She was muttering to herself, swatting at things around her head with one hand; the other supported the glowing end of a cigarette. It was impossible to tell if she was homeless and mentally unstable, like so many in Toronto, or if she was one of the blondes.

The chess players assessed her, then one of the seated men reached out quickly, picked up his bishop, and moved it forward. His opponent followed suit and the clock was punched down again.

I had thought that coming to Toronto would be a homecoming—that I'd find myself on familiar ground, feel a sense of relief after so many months away. I wasn't expecting to find the fear of the Fury welling up in me only a few blocks from where I'd climbed off the bus. I zigzagged through traffic, not bothering to wait for the light in my haste to get away from there.

A couple blocks later, I slowed. An SUV idled at the corner. The woman inside it, all alone, wore a surgical mask. She was tiny inside the enormous vehicle. I remember that under the streetlight, the mask seemed to glow blue. The rest of the truck was dark and amorphous to me. She had a pensive look as she waited for the stoplight to change. I shivered and turned down Jarvis Street and headed south, past the Holiday Inn, St. James Cathedral, St. Lawrence Market, toward Larissa and Jay's condo, a little farther on, below the black snaking expressway along the lake.

———

By the time I reached Lake Shore Boulevard, where Larissa's condo was, the sky was between twilight and night, and everything seemed unfamiliar. I couldn't tell if I had been away so long that I had forgotten where things were. I walked twice up and down the stretch. On the Gardiner Expressway above, traffic roared. Ice creaked beneath my feet, which were freezing in spite of my wearing a pair of rubber boots I had found in my size among the donations at the WEE. They were rainboots, after all, with thin unlined soles. As I took in the numbers on the buildings, tires hissed beside me on the wet pavement, and spat things out at the gutters. I could see the numbers through my one lens, but they weren't making sense. So I walked through parking lots, right up to the buildings. All the condos looked the same to me, but still I knew Larissa's was missing. Sure enough, the numbers skipped over hers from one building to the next. I trudged back to the street and stood looking at where I thought her condo should be. There was just a vacant lot, a blue gap with Lake Ontario showing through under a blue-black sky, where the building had been. What had been a landscaped front and a concrete parking lot was now gravel.

Brand-new condo buildings don't get torn down, I told myself. People protest them going up—protest gentrification, changing a neighbourhood, blighting the landscape with their *sameness*—but they don't get torn down once they're *up*. Even if they go unsold, they'll sit empty, waiting.

And yet, the building wasn't there.

I'd told the government to send my things to this address.

I knew it by heart. But the address was gone, and the big white building it had been pinned to was also gone. The wind pushed in off the lake, cold, and I blinked back tears.

I returned to one of the other buildings and tried to get into the foyer, but the concierge wouldn't let me in. He wouldn't even answer my buzz. I just wanted to talk to him, ask him what had happened to the place next door. He looked at me through two thick layers of glass with dull eyes and distrust. It was a long way back to my old apartment in the west end.

The key didn't fit my lock any longer. I could hear someone inside my apartment and I banged on the door four times, but no one answered. Finally, I went downstairs to the mostly empty Thai restaurant. They knew me there. When I walked in, one of the servers made a face and sat down abruptly in a chair, spilling the soup she'd been about to take to the lone occupied table.

"We—we thought you were dead," the server told me. "That is what the girl upstairs said."

My sublet had apparently sent me multiple emails and tried my cell to no avail. She'd made the only logical assumption. Canadians have no optimism. I told the server I'd been caught at the border, and her eyes widened. She must have heard about the WEE centres. She pushed the sloshed lemon–coconut soup toward me, urging me to take it. Then she went into the kitchen and got a new one for her table while I ate hungrily. I thought about how I'd lived upstairs and eaten there for two years. The server and I had said hello and whatnot, but we'd never even swapped names.

When she came back, she told me there were new people in my apartment. "They are a little . . ." She made a sign, rotating her finger next to her cocked head. I took it to mean cuckoo, but later I'd find out she meant paranoid. She said that after my sublet left, the landlord got a little scared and changed the lock. When I asked her why, she said, "You know, the SHV."

Then she left to greet new customers.

I opened up the news weekly I'd been carrying and skimmed through the pages as I ate. There were ads for products I'd never seen before, remedies like Blonde-Away and Blonde-Off—ointments, sprays, and skin tanners. I couldn't tell if they were meant to keep blondes at bay or take your melanin up a level for self-protection, but they promised "miracle results." The health columnist wrote of natural oils and their healing principles. Just a few drops in your bathwater or around your home would strengthen and purify you. Magnets, sewn into clothing, were also recommended, to achieve balance and repel the ions that supposedly activated SHV.

A syndicated sex columnist had coined a new phrase, *blonde-backing*, which was labelled a high-risk activity. The column confirmed that there were men who would pay ridiculous rates to have sex with blonde women. Sometimes they asked the women to perform as if they were crazy, sometimes to play dead, sometimes just to be their own "blonde and beautiful" selves. Just a few tricks would pay for a full semester at an Ivy League school.

There was a feature on holiday giving and making a difference. In lieu of giving "meaningless bric-a-brac," readers were urged to adopt pets or donate money to animal rescue groups in the name of their gift recipients. Since the pandemic was declared, families had begun to surrender long-loved pets, out of fear that they would transport fleas carrying the virus into their homes. British scientists had officially claimed that fleas weren't the vector, but in spite of that, animal shelters across North America were at an all-time high capacity and euthanasia rates were through the roof. A pie graph demonstrated how animals were being scapegoated—even though flea-prevention medications were available. I thought back to the Black Plague, to how Londoners were convinced that dogs and cats spread the disease. The animals were killed en masse and the rat population soon overtook the dwindling human one.

I thanked the server again and collected my mail from the box at the bottom of the stairs. The tenants had clearly taken in their own mail, but a handful of mine they had just shoved into an empty mailbox beside theirs. I found some letters from the university, loads of junk mail, and something official-looking from the City of Windsor.

By that point, I could smell pot floating down the stairwell, so I trekked back upstairs to see if the occupants had mellowed out and if I would have more luck with them. I banged on the door but again it went unanswered.

"I used to live here," I hollered. "Can you just open the door and talk to me?"

This time the door opened with the security chain in place. A wolfish-looking twenty-year-old eyeballed me from behind a beard and a bush of hair. His pupils were dilated. He said slowly, his words halfway between a statement and a question, "You aren't blonde?"

I told him, no, I wasn't blonde. That I was the original tenant, before the girl who had lived there before them.

"Before the girl who . . ." He seemed to consider that a long time. Then he said, "Right! Travis!" He said something to someone I couldn't see, and then another guy appeared.

"I just want to come in and see if any of my old things are still here. Look, I'm pregnant." I stuck out my hips and placed my hand on my belly for emphasis. "I'm no threat to you. Can you help me out?"

"Yeah, man, check it. She's huge," the bearded one said to Travis, who was lurking somewhere outside of my sightline.

It took them a second to figure out how to close the door and take the chain off. When they opened it again, I saw that Travis was holding a baseball bat. I ventured in slowly. Things weren't entirely the way I had left them, but many of my possessions were still there. My pink curtains. My IKEA kitchen table. The mismatched chairs from my mom's. My thrift-store four-seater sofa with the curved wooden legs. I sank down onto it without being invited. Travis glanced at his buddy, who introduced himself as Nicolas.

"You guys are really high, huh?" I said.

Travis stowed the bat under my coffee table. He called into my bedroom for a girl named Carrie to come out. The girl shuffled into the living room, shifty-eyed and stinking of weed. She was thin and dark, and sat down in one place and didn't move the rest of the time I was there. They were typical stoners. I asked them what year they were in and they said second. I told them my department and asked if they knew Karl. They took a long time to think about it, then said they didn't. One of them said that the place had been repainted before they moved in—I could see that—but that all the furniture had been stacked in the back. The landlord hadn't liked the girl who was there before, and even though he'd fumigated the place for fleas, he had still put the furniture out.

"She was high-risk," Nicolas said of my subletter, running an explanatory hand through his mane, stopping to twist the ends, "and the landlord just wanted to be rid of all of it."

I didn't need to ask what he meant by high-risk.

These three had lugged much of the furniture back in, up the fire escape, because they could use it. The dining area was now a makeshift bedroom, with sheets strung up to section it off, and the living room was both the living and the dining area. I wasn't sure how they managed to live that way, three of them in a space that was clearly intended for one.

I went down the hall into my bedroom. A bunch of my things were still in the closet. I found some better footwear and my winter coat, which, even though it wouldn't close up all the way, was worth taking. My bed was gone, replaced with someone else's, but it was my alarm clock on the window ledge. I didn't ask if I could take it—I just shoved it in the inside pocket of my coat. There was kitty litter on the carpet, although I didn't see the cat. One of the guys called out to ask if I was going to take anything they needed. And the other asked if I wanted to smoke with them. I said no to both.

In the kitchen, I ran my fingers over the counters. This was where Karl had come in that night I was making macaroni. I felt so strange and nostalgic, being in that space that was mine but not mine.

Then I went out back, down the fire escape, and found boxes with other possessions of mine—a big leather bag I could pack things in, some other clothes and trinkets and books that were all too wet and mouldy to bother with. There was a framed photo of me and my mom in the Head Start salon, and I grabbed it because even though it was a little weather-stained with one green wrinkle at the top, it was still snug behind the glass.

I went back in and tore back through the closet, pulling out more clothes now that I had a bag to fold them into. It seemed the girl, in spite of being a few sizes smaller than me, had an eye for good vintage. I was grateful she'd gone dumpster diving and saved my things from the weather. But now they were coming with me. I found a familiar-looking towel and rolled it up and stuffed it in too. By the time I'd finished, the zipper on the bag wouldn't close.

When I walked back into the living room, I left the bag in the hall so they wouldn't see how much I was taking. The two guys were lumped around the girl. She was in the same spot, sitting straight as a German vampire in a silent movie. Nicolas had his head in her lap and Travis was squished in behind her with an arm across her shoulders. They were staring at the TV, which was on mute. It was my TV, but it wasn't a good one. That was when I realized I'd taken the wrong stuff—I should have grabbed things I could sell. I had gone for the clothes because I was cold.

I sat down on the edge of the couch and looked around, realizing I'd never had much that was worth anything. The laptop was my only item with resale value, and of course, it was gone. There was an old stereo record player and speakers, but who listened to vinyl these days? It might be worth fifty bucks, but how would I carry it?

"Do you listen to that?" I asked, gesturing.

"That's the heart of the apartment!" Nicolas suddenly became animated. He sprang off the girl and opened the cupboard where I'd kept all my vinyl. He flipped slowly through the records, pulling out gems and presenting them to me as if they were his finds and not my own. "Isn't this cool?" He put on the Velvet Underground's *White Light/White Heat*. He had only just discovered it.

Listening to my records in my old apartment, I started to cry. I told them about getting out of the WEE and trying to find Larissa's, and how the building had disappeared. They were freaked about that. Their eyes got big and they started talking over each other.

"We have to help her find her!" Travis called to Nicolas as if it were a rescue mission.

"Go on the Internet." Nicolas gestured toward the hanging sheets.

They had a computer hidden away in the sheet bedroom. Using 411, I was able to locate Larissa. Her listing was in her name, not Jaichand's, and gave her address between Jarvis and Parliament streets, in the direction I'd just come from. Walking to her condo, I'd passed within three or four blocks of where she was now.

I called her on the land line that was listed online.

"Who is this?" Larissa said.

"Lara, it's Hazel."

There was a sound like she had dropped the phone.

"It's Hazel!" I said again, in case she hadn't heard me.

"Is this . . . a joke?" she said haltingly.

I told her how I had been in quarantine for eight weeks with no outside line. I told her how good it was to hear her voice.

"Keep talking," she said, "so I can tell if it's really you."

Why would it be a joke? I asked, but it probably didn't help that the stoners were trying to croon along to "Stephanie Says" in the background.

"People play jokes on me these days," Larissa said, her voice flattening to a hard edge.

"Larissa, it's me." I told her to come get me at my old apartment. "Then you'll see. You want to see me, don't you?"

"I don't know if I can drive," she said. Then she changed her mind and said, "I guess I can. I'll be there in ten." And she hung up. I reflected that she hadn't once said that she was relieved to finally hear from me. It was kind of a weird reaction, I thought. But then, it occurred to me that maybe, like the people at the Thai restaurant, she'd thought I was simply gone—dead. Maybe she was in shock.

I picked up my bag and came back into the living room to thank the inhabitants of my apartment, which was when the girl saw what I'd taken. For the first time, her stoned eyes seemed to focus on a single object. She squinted.

"What do you need all that for? That black one," she said, raising her arm slowly until she was pointing dramatically. "That one," she said, her finger striking the air in the direction of the sleeve of a dress that was hanging over the side of the bag. "It isn't even going to fit you anymore."

I looked down at my gut. I pulled the dress out of the bag and held it up, tried to fit it across me. She had a point. I tossed it to her. It landed on the end of my sofa, and Travis flipped it up on his socked toe and extended it backward over his head to her. It was the one I'd worn in Karl's office that first time we messed around.

"What about your records?" Nicolas asked.

I told him to take good care of them.

The Larissa I'd spoken to on the phone was not the one who greeted me when she picked me up. Her car practically swerved into the curb, and she was out of the front seat in no time and on the sidewalk with her arms around me.

"Oh my god, Haze," she said, looking down at my belly. "Oh my god! Look at you."

Tears ran down the sides of her face, and she had to fumble in her purse and find Kleenex while I loaded my bag in the back seat, hefting it overtop of Devang's empty baby seat. Then she grabbed me and hugged me again. She stood stroking my back in the middle of the sidewalk. She was wearing a bright white beehive wig, very Marie Antoinette.

"What's with this?" I asked, one hand creeping up to feel it. It was an extremely firm piece of equipment, and had gold trinkets fastened into it, dangling like earrings.

"It was a gift from an artist," Larissa explained. "She made it for me. She said if we have to wear them, why not go all the way, right?"

Sure, I said. We got in the car and drove. At stoplights, Larissa kept reaching over to touch my hand or my shoulder, or she would toggle my coat collar. Watch the road, I told her. I'd been through too much for us to have an accident now, even just a fender bender. Jesus, it was good to see her.

"I practically lost it when I couldn't get through," I said, "and then when I went to your place and it was just gone . . ."

Her face darkened. "Isn't that crazy? There was an explosion."

"What?"

"In the middle of the night. Some woman down on floor four had SHV, and I don't know what she did, but, she blew the windows right out of the place. The building was in danger of collapsing. We all woke up, and Jaichand and Devang and I ended up down on the street in the middle of the night in our dressing gowns."

"Wow, that's serious," I said. I asked her if she'd got my message on her cell. I told her about trying to get a pickup.

"Oh," she said, "my cellphone, it's . . ." Beneath the white heaps of fake hair, she got a cloudy look on her face. "It's—I left it at work," she said decisively. Then she smiled in a way that seemed to me broken, disingenuous.

I wondered if maybe she was on some kind of medication, but then I dismissed the idea, telling myself I was suspicious only because I'd just been around three very stoned people.

We pulled up at the apartment and it was unlike any place I'd ever expected Larissa to live. She must have seen my look, because she said, "Yeah, a lot has changed. We had to take something really fast after the explosion. But they've got other condos partially built, and they're supposed to relocate us all eventually."

It was one of those old buildings where people seem to be living on top of one another. I protested, saying I was just surprised because I was so used to seeing her in her other place. I had begun to think of it as her "house."

"Well, so had I," she said toughly as she took me in through a grubby stairwell, and from there down a concrete hall.

"When I looked at the unit, a nice carpet ran through here—" Larissa gestured to the hall floor, and I saw on closer inspection that black streaks over the concrete were rubber and glue where carpet had been torn it up. "Fleas . . ." Larissa said with a sour face. "There weren't any, but no landlord wants to be accused of it. They fumigated my unit before I moved in. It's written into the lease."

The place smelled like soap and sausages. We took the elevator up, and Larissa shouldered my bag. She laughed and seemed to come back to herself, saying, "Look at you. How many months?" She touched me again. "That's great," she said, as if the whole thing were something I had planned on.

"I'm getting used to it," I replied.

"Listen," Larissa said before she opened the door, as if she were bracing me for something, "it isn't much. It's just all I can afford for now."

I told her if she'd been where I had, she'd think it was a palace.

We went in and Larissa turned on the hall switch. I took my new-old boots off and parked them next to a pair of hers. The boots were all hers, but I didn't think anything of it at the time. She went into the little kitchen and turned on the light there and asked if I was hungry. I said no and was about to go into my story—tell her how they'd fed me at the Thai restaurant, how charitable everyone had been, but she stopped me by saying, "That's good, because to tell you the truth, I don't have much. I meant to get groceries. Tomorrow. I'll do that tomorrow."

She told me she'd fix us some tea while I put my bag in on the bed. I went down the little hall and found her room. It was the only bedroom and it contained a double bed with her and Jay's beautiful spread on it, but the rest was pretty bare. There were two unopened paint cans from Benjamin Moore sitting on the floor with a clean roller, and swaths of peacock blue across the tops of the cans to show the colour, as if she planned to do some decorating but hadn't yet. There was a picture of Devang on the bedside table, but other than that, just a chair with a pile of clean clothes on it and a pile of dirty clothes in the closet, which was missing a door. There were no men's shirts or jackets hanging in the closet, no baby toys scattered across the rug the way I would have expected. No crib or change table.

When I went back through the hall, I saw that Larissa had taken off her wig and placed it on a Styrofoam head as if it were a hat that you removed whenever you went in or out. From wearing the wig, her hair now stuck to her head in some spots and jutted up in others. It was pitch black, about an inch and a half long all over, like she was trying to grow it out after having shaved it. The kettle was on, and she was pulling cups out for us. They were big, sturdy ceramic ones in a terracotta colour. I'd been with her the day she'd bought them and I remembered how much she paid for them—how I couldn't get over the fact that she would pay that much for a set of mugs, as if she had become a suburban housewife while still in her twenties. I watched her move in the kitchen, that natural grace she had, as if her limbs floated. She'd lost weight. It was that, I realized, not the big snowball wig, that had made her look different. More like high school Larissa.

She removed an already opened package of crackers from the cupboard and arranged them artfully on a plate along with a knife. Then she pulled a nub of cheese out of the fridge, sniffed it, and put it on the plate. She dug into the fridge and produced another morsel. It too went on the plate. I leaned in the doorway, bracing one hip against the frame. It creaked and she jumped, and the knife clattered to the floor.

"You scared me," she said sheepishly.

"Where did you think I was?" I asked her.

"The bathroom, I guess. I'm just jumpy here." She bent to pick up the knife. She rinsed it in the sink and then we took the things into a little living room off to the side, where we sat on one part of the sectional that had previously been in her condo. The other half seemed to be missing.

When she had set everything up on the glass coffee table, she smiled. We sat down side by side. One cheese, she said, was a smoked apple cheddar. The other was a blue cheese with an ash rind. She urged me to try it.

Overhead, footsteps flurried: kids racing across the floor. We both looked up, but she didn't comment on it.

"It's hard to get used to you without your hair," she said to me, and I laughed and said I could say the same of her.

I remembered once or twice in high school, Larissa had come to my mom's hair shop. Everyone wanted henna red hair one year, and Larissa thought I was crazy that I insisted on dying mine the opposite when I naturally had what everyone else yearned for. My mom gave her highlights for free, streaking her hair from gold to auburn—and later that year dyed it back to blonde for her. But Larissa wouldn't let Mom cut her hair. She was very particular about that. When I reminded her, she laughed and ran her hand over her short cut.

I remember I was worried back in high school that my mom would feel insulted by Larissa, but she hadn't been. Meanwhile I was walking around with my mom's practice cuts, "new" styles she would persuade me to let her try. Needless to say, in high school I was always growing out awkward lengths—until I too put my foot down and wouldn't let her touch my hair. There are two things women latch on to when they feel circumstances are outside of their control: their weight and their hair. I didn't care about the former; for me it was always the latter. But Larissa? She never seemed to struggle over anything. With her, my mother just smoked and smiled, smiled and smoked, abandoning the scissors in the vanity drawer. They both liked Virginia Slims and my mom let Larissa bum them if she promised not to tell. I recalled Larissa walking around that shop with the broken linoleum floor, the white wallpaper with the aqua-and-pink diamond pattern, the wood-grain vanities, a cigarette burning between her pro fingers . . .

Larissa laughed again, a forced chuckle. We chewed through a few crackers. They were a little stale. She didn't ask me anything about the day I was supposed to come, the day I was supposed to bring Moira, or about my time in the WEE, or about Karl and the baby. If she had asked me those things, I guess I would have been happy to tell her, to ignore the fact that her child wasn't there and there weren't any toys in the place. But she didn't, so I couldn't pretend.

"What's happened, Larissa?" I asked abruptly.

She picked up her tea and held it by the brim with both hands, ignoring the big handle she'd bought it for (because it would fit Jay's hands, I remember she said when she snapped down her credit card).

When she set the mug down, she said, "We might need wine for that particular story," and she got up and went into the kitchen. I reminded her I couldn't drink, and she said, "Oh, shit!" Did I mind if she did? I told her to go ahead, and heard her open the fridge. She brought a half-full bottle of red into the room with a glass. Larissa had been one of those people who pored over the wine picks in the paper. The Larissa I'd left a few months ago would never have put a red in the refrigerator. It was just wrong.

"Jaichand and Devang are in India." She poured herself a glass and sat back on the white leather sectional-half beside me. "We thought it would be safer. We all thought it would be much safer. His parents wanted them there," she said, leaning her head back, digging her way into the pillows. The flourescent kitchen light was not atmospheric to sit by, so I reached over and turned on a small table lamp with a paper shade. It was yellow, and immediately Larissa looked better and I felt better.

"Oh, right," she said. "I forgot you haven't had too many comforts lately. When it's just me, I sometimes forget and don't bother."

But I wasn't fooled; Larissa always bothered. It was the essence of Larissa.

"Will you join them?" I asked her.

"I would if I could, but I can't. Borders are still closed," she said, her lips tight.

I noticed now that she was wearing a shiny turquoise

camisole without a bra. I guess that was all she'd had on beneath her winter coat, but I hadn't noticed. It looked like something she would normally wear with a blouse or a blazer. I wondered if, when I called, I'd gotten her out of bed. She *had* said at first that she couldn't come. It was about eleven on a Thursday evening. I asked her when Jay and Devang would come home, and she said that was the part she wasn't sure about.

She drank some more while I told her about the WEE. She was horrified at everything, so much so that I left out all the really gruesome details and just talked about things like never having hot water for the shower because it ran out too fast.

When I brought up Moira, she said, "Oh, right, you were going to come here with a friend," as if it had completely slipped her mind. Of course, I thought more important things had happened between that time and now—like her husband and child going away, and having to move out of her old building.

I brought this up, but Larissa waved her hand like it was a bad smell, nothing more. "That explosion. I wasn't even there when it went off. I came home and the front of the building was charred, but I don't see how it affected the structure of the place enough that they had to take it all down. Thank god Jay and Devang had already left, huh? There are some small miracles."

"I thought you were all there," I said.

She swallowed the rest of her drink and looked at me as if I were silly. "You must be bone tired, sweetheart," she said.

I admitted I was.

"It's so good to see you," she said again.

"It's so good to see you," I said.

I felt like we were parting instead of going to bed in the same tiny apartment. The place was smaller, in fact, than the one I'd just left to the stoners. She said she could dig around and find some blankets and make me up a bed on the couch, but in the end, we just flopped together onto her bed, wriggled under the blankets, and passed out. Larissa's comforter was the softest thing I had ever felt.

I put my cold feet on her shins, and she laughed. "I had poor circulation too when I was preggers with Devang," she said. "It means it's a boy."

"That's just an old wives' tale. And only a Windsor girl would say *preggers*," I told her.

I fell asleep when my feet got warm.

FIFTEEN

YESTERDAY, I CLIMBED UP INTO THE COTTAGE ATTIC and went poking around. I found a box of old things up there. I went up very carefully. I want you to know that I am cautious, for your sake. Sliding the stairs down wasn't easy, but I worked at it slowly. I had to stand on a chair and I wasn't sure of my balance, but I had to do something. Without Grace, the days are longer than ever. It's dusty up there, and pink insulation runs all around the outside, fluffy as birthday cake frosting.

The box I found was full of photos of Karl as a kid in Alberta: the Diclicker homestead, which appears to be a very clean but no-frills farmhouse. The family was Swiss. There were his sister and mother done up in 1960s hairdos sitting on the hood of the family vehicle at what might be a rest stop; his father with thick black glasses and a cowboy shirt; Karl in miniature, about eight, holding a View-Master just below his face, as if he's been told to lower it for the picture, as if he were more interested in what was in the machine than wherever they were going. At first I thought the photos were of some other family—relatives, maybe. I didn't recognize Karl because he was so fair. He was blond as a child, and then, you can see from photo to photo, his hair darkened gradually.

It makes me wonder about you, whether you might be blonde when you're born. My mother was blonde, and it seems Karl was too—at least for a while.

I felt like I shouldn't be up there, opening things, peering in. Like it wasn't mine to do. But, my little kangaroo, you're here—you will be here soon, at least—and he was your father.

An old thesis of Karl's was up there. It must have been written during his MA. Hand-typed, but he'd had it leather bound. "The Grotesque in Early Cinema." I read ten pages of it before I realized he was talking about clowns. I was stunned to discover it was no better than something I'd write. But god, the attic was cold and the floorboards very hard beneath me. My muscles started to seize up and I couldn't stay there very long. I thought I heard a car far away and I stopped for a second and listened. But it was nothing.

I found Grace and Karl's—which is how I've begun to think of them, even though I used to think "Karl and Grace"—marriage certificate in a closed-up box with a bunch of other trinkets. It was folded, not even framed.

She retained her name after marriage, I remember Karl telling me the one time we came here. She retained it because she didn't want to take on a name that wasn't even originally his own, that he'd given himself. She said it felt like playing pretend, like becoming a fictional character from one of her own TV shows. Pargetter-Mann, she'd have been if she hyphenated. But she'd already started her career and didn't want to do that either, so she remained Grace Pargetter. I remember I asked Karl if he minded, and he said, "No, no, not that," as if there were something else that he minded. But then he rolled over and picked up the DVD case for a movie he'd wanted us to watch. It was *Ekstase*, a silent film starring Hedy Lamarr.

"Who's this Hedy Lamarr chick again?" I asked, flicking my thumb at the pounds and pounds of dark hair surrounding her face on the case's cover.

Apparently, in *Ekstase*, she acted in nude scenes where she approximated the female orgasm as if her young soldier lover were giving her oral pleasure.

"Interesting," I said.

"When Lamarr later married, her husband, a munitions manufacturer, attempted to buy up all remaining copies of the film to destroy it, he felt so possessive of her. Benito Mussolini retained his copy, refusing to part with it for any price."

"And who's this Mussolini guy?" I asked.

Karl tapped me on the nose and said, "Don't be cute."

He rolled away from me and I remember his thin, hairy buttocks. I remember the dark seams of him.

"'The last time I was inside a woman was when I was inside the Statue of Liberty . . .' Woody Allen," he proclaimed.

I covered my face and groaned, "*Don't!*" He was old, so old.

"The only difference between you and me," he said, picking his clothes off the back of the plaid couch, "is that I thought I was special at eighteen for seeing Woody Allen films in the theatre when they were first released, and when you were eighteen you thought you were special for finding them in the video store and renting them on DVD. The film is the same. The experience is the same."

I didn't tell him I had watched Allen's entire oeuvre as downloads. It was precisely because of observations like this I admired Karl. Admired, perhaps, more than loved. Although when I think of the way Grace speaks of him—spoke of him—I realize perhaps it was a kind of love.

I remember the night Grace made me the maternity clothes, she knocked back half a bottle of red wine from the pantry. "You still look a little clownish," she said, scrutinizing me. "But at least you're presentable."

I did look clownish, but I had to admit I was more comfortable than I'd been in months. "You have to understand," I told Grace, "since you crushed my glasses, I can't really see myself."

"Now, if I can just get you to shave your head more often . . . or maybe those eyebrows."

I noticed that she ignored my accusation about the glasses.

At that point, I'd never seen Grace drunk. Her body bent more. Her arms flopped out from her stick figure. I seized my moment.

"I don't know how many times I should ask you to forgive me."

She raised a hand like it was no big deal. It hovered, her elbow on the wooden arm of the chair. Her painted face reclined against the cushion. She closed her eyes, her mascaraed eyelashes standing out all the more on her hairless face—or maybe they only seemed to because I had no glasses.

"He had a ball sac like a jelly doughnut, didn't he?" she said through lipsticked lips.

I didn't say anything.

"But he won in the end. He really won the war."

Grace kicked the cowboy magazine off the table with her wool-socked toe. She had the TV on mute. We'd been waiting for a television series I abhorred to come on. Grace said it was "top-notch, production-wise, and very smart." I think she meant for Canadian television, but she didn't say that. The show was called *Fourteenth Colony,* and it was set on another planet where people had been sent to live after an outbreak wiped out much of the earth's population. They were rebuilding in a back-to-basics way, but with advanced technology. We'd watched one episode already and I'd thought that it was too on the nose, that the actors were like highly polished wood. Nonetheless, Grace insisted we watch. But before the program came on, there were commercials, then an on-the-hour news update.

There had been a riot in Toronto at the Eaton Centre shopping mall. Surveillance footage showed a faceless, shapeless herd of people. They rushed past the fountain on the lower level, shopping bags strewn everywhere. Another camera had captured what was happening a level above. An enormous Christmas tree, twenty-five or thirty feet tall, had tipped and was balanced precariously on the rail, threatening to fall. Ornaments had already dropped off, like small, bright bombs smashing on the tile below. **Boxing Day brouhaha leaves six dead and forty-two wounded**, the closed captioning declared in large letters. I could only make it out because I was sitting on the end of the sofa that was closest to the screen.

In spite of the calendar in the kitchen, Grace and I had missed Christmas.

In the next bit of footage, the newscaster was positioned against the same rail as the toppled Christmas tree, overlooking the fountain structure. Officials below her were attempting to clean it. The still water in its base was blood red. It seemed to catch both the uniforms and the newscaster off guard when the fountain shot up, geyser-like. The newscaster recovered quickly and continued with the broadcast, saying that a little girl had plunged to her death in the latest SHV attack, and that five trample victims had succumbed to injuries. Others were in hospital and being treated. Four blondes, an a cappella choir comprised of sisters, had been taken into isolation. I watched the newscaster's lips moving silently and the type parading across the bottom of the screen. I leaned forward, squinting to make it out.

"I stopped sleeping with him eight years ago," Grace said.

She'd drunk too much and wasn't paying attention to the TV. My mouth went dry.

"I just realized one day that I didn't need it, and that I still seemed to get everything from him that I wanted."

She volunteered this information easily, and I stared at the screen, trying to figure out if officials were pulling a dripping Santa Claus hat or a bloodied garment from the fountain with a net. Either way I felt sick. I was glad I didn't have my glasses.

Grace just kept talking, in her own world. "There were other girls before you, you know—plenty. But I think he loved me more after we stopped. He just did. He loved me more."

Grace sat up as the television flashed the photo of the little girl who had died. She was about four years old, with exaggerated dimples and brown eyes. Her name was Kami. Over the next two days they would show that picture about eighty more times—as if that little girl was the face of all victims of the virus. They didn't show a photo of the blonde sisters.

Grace poured herself another glass of wine. She was all elbows and knotted wrists. In comparison, I was shaped like a balloon. I watched her move. She got up and rolled the empty bottle onto the counter in the kitchen and came back, taking up her glass and sinking into the chair without spilling it.

"Let's watch TV," she said, even though I was already watching.

"You go ahead," I told her, and I got up and went to the bathroom. I heard her jack the volume up for the final minute of the news.

I have to tell you, my little water bug, there are so many things I wish I could change. I wish, for instance, that I had got up before Larissa on that one day in Toronto in particular. And I wish that I had thought to make a list of things I needed to do, like getting my glasses repaired, or making a doctor's appointment, or going to my bank and seeing about getting access to my account even without my card, or finding a contact who could locate my things from Canada Customs—because chances are, they're sitting in some little back office somewhere. There were so many things I should have done while I was in the city. But I thought I was going to be there longer.

It was Larissa who brought my attention to the letter from the City of Windsor. In the morning when I got up, she had put my things out for me on the coffee table. I guess I'd just dumped them in her hall when I walked in, like I owned the place even though I'd never been there. But that's what an old friendship will do to you.

"I didn't have any coffee, so I went out and bought us some," she said. "I'll do some shopping later."

The coffee was from Tim Hortons, the same brand as the empty store that was across the field from the quarantine. I kissed Larissa on the cheek and told her the story of how I gazed longingly at that distant building while captive at the Women's Entry and Evaluation centre. I wrapped my hands around the cardboard cup and breathed in the smell of the coffee.

"You should open those," she said abruptly, about the

mail I'd collected from my old place. "I'm kind of worried about that one." She indicated the government envelope. She told me that as the strip club capital of Canada, Windsor had become a war zone, that bleaching had reached an all-time high, and that officials were unable to deal with the fallout from the rampant virus. "My dad's retired now, but he tells me things about city hall and the stuff they're dealing with. They're basically bankrupt . . ." Her voice trailed off. Then she said brightly, "I'm going to take a shower," and she left me alone with the envelope.

The language of debt—of bills and collections—is colder than winter. As much as I could figure, the invoice the city had sent me was for the disposal of my mother's body. I owed them $5,243. This was, apparently, the "basic" service. I sat holding on to the edges of the letter for a long time. I could feel my heart beating in my chest like someone punching me from the inside, or maybe that was you. Eventually the shower stopped, and I heard flushing and then the hair dryer. It roared like the blood racing inside my skull.

When Larissa came out, she said apologetically, "I'm sorry, hon," without my having to tell her what the envelope contained.

"Where's Richard?" I asked numbly, but I wasn't asking Larissa. I knew he was the executor of my mother's estate, and the burden of her burial should have fallen to him. I'd never been particularly fond of him—my mother drank as much with him as she had before him—but he'd been well enough off and emotionally even. Or so I'd thought. Then I remembered my mom at the beginning of the outbreak, saying her business was going gangbusters. Still, she'd asked Richard if she could give me the money she put in my account. Possibly, he too had made the assumption I was dead, like my landlord had; maybe he'd taken whatever money Mom had and gone somewhere safer.

I shut my eyes and tried not to think about the risks my mother must have faced in the Head Start salon. The wallpaper and wood panel of that old place appeared behind my eyelids, unwilled. I could feel my mother's hands on my scalp, the way she used to wash my hair for me sometimes—in spite of my protests—in the big black sink. "What do you do to your head, Hazel?" she used to nag. "You've got ten fingers. Use them," and her fingertips would dig and rub, working in circles. She would massage down to my ears and neck like she wanted to excise something from me. Sometimes it was torture, and sometimes a kind of affection, the soap blooming in her hands like a ball of white lace.

When I opened my eyes again, Larissa's back was to me and she was fixing toast. There were only two pieces left in the bag and one was a crust. She gave them both to me, smeared with honey from a jar with a cloth-and-ribbon lid. They went cold. The coffee had also gone cold. I wished I could throw up, but I seemed to be past that part of the pregnancy. I went into Larissa's tiny bathroom. Her medicine cabinet was well stocked with bottles that sounded like anxiety pills, their meaningless syllables clumped around a big Z: zzzzzz.

In the end, I didn't take any pills. I wasn't sure what effect they would have on you, and when I laid my hand across my abdomen, you jumped. All of a sudden you seemed more important than anything else in the universe. Up to that point, I'd thought of you as a seedling in the wind. Something blowing past me that would inevitably find its place. Now, every gust of breath seemed vital to the direction you might travel. You were all I had, and you were just a shivering little star of flesh beneath my hand. I showered, not soaping, just standing still as the drops beat over my bald head and my belly.

"What do you want to do today?" Larissa asked when I came out, like she was glad we had cleared that other bit of business out of the way. She was over by the living room window in the sun, nibbling the toast I'd left.

It was the medication, I told myself, making her behave that way. I stared at her. Her expensive jeans had faded, but you could still tell by the cut that they had cost a lot. The children upstairs thumped across the ceiling even though the schoolday had already started. I asked Larissa if she had to work, but she smiled and said, "Not today," and, turning her back to me to look out the window, "I told them to make do without me."

Larissa left her giant headdress at home, and we went out shorthaired. She put on long earrings to compensate. She guided me to a brunch joint with a French name, as if it would make up for the shock of my suddenly being motherless. She said that I had to eat right for my little bundle, that Jay had practically forced her when she was carrying Devang, and now she would force me.

I followed her without protest. I didn't know what else to do. She glided into a sparkling green booth in the front window and ordered herself an open-faced sandwich, a *croque*, and when I just stared at the menu, she said, "Two, please," and held up two fingers.

She seemed almost like her teenage self, excited that we were together again, careening through the city. She grasped my hand across the table and whispered, "I didn't want to tell you this last night because everything was so *serious*, but I'm seeing someone. He lives in the building. He's incredibly good-looking." I squinted at her and wondered what part of the morning hadn't been as serious as last night.

She smiled and played with her hair, feathering it '80s-style with her fingers. She watched people pass by outside, the women in footwear that was still meant for November instead of December, stepping as though they were afraid they might slip. It was sunny but the ice hadn't melted. Everything dazzled and reflected. I asked her, "What about Jay?"

"Oh, Haze, we're all adults. I know you liked him," she said. "But he's gone. Fidelity is only as far as your area code."

She pulled her coat back on and excused herself. She said she didn't want to smoke around me given my condition. Through the window, I watched her bum a cigarette and a light for it on the sidewalk. She held it glamorously in the V of her fingers; she tipped her head back and expelled smoke. The light caught her face and I noticed how colourless her eyes were. The server brought our beverages. I drank and stared at the cigarette moving toward her mouth and away. Those fluttering hands. That was when I realized it: her long fingers were naked, no wedding ring.

Throughout the meal Larissa chattered at me about old times and I grunted in agreement. I felt like I should cry, but didn't, even though she was talking about when I had lived with my mom. I remembered how my mother used to say I was just a late bloomer. When she had said that, I got mad and walked out. Whenever I heard that phrase, *late bloomer*, I visualized bright orange mums in autumn, in pots outside a grocery store, their green leaves growing furry with dust stirred up from traffic. Something waiting to be bought and planted. I excused myself to go to the bathroom, where I dug my fingers into the bridge of my nose and the corners of my eyes to squash down the gathering pressure there.

When I came back, Larissa said, "I've got some errands I just remembered. We need to go right now."

"Sure," I said. I looked around for the server but she was in the back. I don't know why I was looking anyway—it's not like I had any money.

"It's taken care of," Larissa said. Our booth was so close to the door, she was already on her way out.

Around the corner and down the street, she worked a couple keys off her ring and gave them to me so I could let myself into her apartment if we didn't arrive back at the same time. We parted ways and I headed for Karl's office at the school. Now that I had Larissa to draw on for help, I hoped to take transit and save my feet, but when I patted down my pockets, the change I'd begged the previous day was gone. I had switched coats, of course, at my old apartment, but I thought I'd been sure to move the money from one pocket to the other. Even though it was only a couple dollars, I hadn't wanted to use it to ride the streetcar until I was certain I had a place to stay. Cursing my bad luck, I trudged to the university on foot. On my way, I passed a row of hoardings where photographs of loved ones and handmade posters had been stapled up. It was a wall of the missing. The paper layers roiled in the wind, revealing yet more smiling faces underneath—the word *missing* repeated a hundred times.

Karl's door was like a tombstone. It was cold and blue and locked. At least, that's how I think of it now. I knocked hopelessly before cruising around, seeking out anyone who could help me. The halls were open but deserted. It was finals, I remembered.

I rounded a corner and came across a prof I knew. She had two pens stuck into the back of her hair, which was coiled up on her head. All her greys were gone and it was a healthy-looking solid brown. It suited her. She was walking with her head down, reading a student paper.

"Ex—excuse me, Dr. Jacques," I said as she approached. "I was in your symposium, Gender and Genre, two years ago."

"Oh," she said, "yes. You're the one with the aesthetology thesis . . ."

I nodded.

"Hilda?" she guessed.

"Hazel."

She had looked at my thesis early on, but had passed on being my adviser when I approached her, months before I began working with Karl. She'd said it was "intriguing" but didn't fit closely enough with her own expertise. Also, she'd felt I was trying to "cover too much ground," and that perhaps my ideas lacked focus. I liked her, and it had seemed she liked me—in class anyway. I was stung— devastated, in fact—when she suggested I approach Dr. Mann instead. I had hesitated at first, unsure if I could bend the thesis to Karl's areas.

Now, Dr. Jacques casually tucked the hand holding the paper on her hip, and said it was good to see me. Where had I been keeping myself? New York, I told her, and she joked, "I'll bet your thesis has a whole new direction after that!"

I muttered that I didn't know, actually. That I was thinking of abandoning it. At this point, what could it matter?

"Academics will always matter. Eventually people will want the outbreak interpreted. We'll look back on this time and we'll want to know what it meant." Then she excused herself for being so brazen and said I must have other things on my mind right now. "I remember when I was pregnant," she groaned before I could answer. "I was so sick and my feet swelled two sizes. I was always making my partner run out to the store to buy me ice cream and Epsom salt. But it's all worth it in the end, you'll see."

I must have given her a doubtful look because she silently ticked her finger at me.

"I'm looking for Dr. Mann," I confessed. Dr. Jacques didn't blink. She asked if I'd tried his office but, before I could answer, said, "Come to think of it, I haven't seen him skulking about in a couple weeks. But we're all squirrelled away, marking."

I asked her if she thought he and Grace might be at their cottage. I used Grace's first name, though I don't know why. Maybe I thought it would make Dr. Jacques more likely to tell me if she knew, though it was pretty clear they weren't close companions.

"Maybe." She smiled, and her gaze shifted toward the paper in her hand, as if we were through our little confab.

Before she moved to pass me she stopped again, and said warmly, eyeing my belly, "I didn't even say congratulations. This time of year makes animals of us. Congratulations, Heidi!"

"Hazel," I said, nodding my head and drawing in a breath. No one had congratulated me on being pregnant before.

When I exited the building, I found a cold ledge outside it, where I sat trembling. If Dr. Jacques had taken me and my thesis on, you wouldn't have happened. I wondered if I would still be snug in my old apartment, if I would have paid more attention to my mother when the plague broke out and warned her against whatever may have befallen her. I ran my hands up and down the quivering bump of you.

———

Larissa wasn't home when I got back. There was a form Scotch-taped to her door. I remember I pulled it off without thinking and stepped inside. I opened it up and glanced at it before going in to sit down and take off my boots in an easier position. I placed the yellow piece of paper, three-folded, on the glass coffee table next to my city invoice.

Moments later I flicked my finger to open the letter again. *Sorry we missed you*, it said. It was from Social Services. It had her name hand-printed in blue pen at the top, her maiden name: Larissa Engle. *As per our last visit, a reminder that you are to complete the following* . . . There was a checklist of tasks, some typed, some printed under the category "Other": looking for work; seeing her therapist; filling out forms for Gardin-Lake, the condo company Larissa had claimed would re-house her; keeping her appointment at someplace called the Grief Institute. The times and dates for the appointments had been scratched in hurriedly by some social worker, probably in the hallway. *We will call again in ___ days' time.* A "2" had been penned into the blank space.

I folded the note back up. I pressed my fingers into my eyes. I went out into the hall and retaped it to the door. Then, as I was coming back inside, I moved too quickly and my bump hit something and I grabbed the object before it could tumble over. It was the artisanal wig. The Styrofoam head wobbled over my sock feet, rolling on the laminate wood floor. I was arranging the wig back on the head when a tag slipped out and hung overtop of the nose. *Malibar Costumes*, it said, and the price. Maybe Larissa had frittered away the last of her money on it, or maybe she had stolen it—but it certainly wasn't a gift from an artist. She wasn't even working with artists any longer.

I went into Larissa's bedroom and lay down on her bed.

Jaichand didn't seem to me the type of man who would leave his wife when she was struggling. Something had happened, I reasoned—something he couldn't abide, something he couldn't solve. How bad had things become? Had he left the continent with their child? Or were one or both of them dead? I saw the social worker's handwriting again: *Your appointment at the Grief Institute.* In the picture frame beside the bed, Devang was just an infant, maybe two or three months old. Dark, wet trails of hair bled across his scalp. His eyes were only half open and his mouth pulled down to one side, like he had deep worry for the world.

I thought back to the morning. Larissa had snagged that three dollars from my pocket and used it to pay for our Tim Hortons coffees, I realized. How had she paid for breakfast? Then it came to me: she simply hadn't. She'd orchestrated an elegant dine and dash. I remembered asking her about her cellphone, whether she'd got my message the previous day. She said she'd left it at work. But according to the yellow form, she was supposed to *look* for work. Meaning, she didn't have a workplace. I got up suddenly and walked through her apartment pulling open drawers. The cellphone was in the utensil tray in the kitchen among the forks. When I turned it on, no message icon came up. She'd received my voicemail and then shoved it away in there.

The blue glass clock above her sink had hung in her condo. I watched the hands move. It hit me that she wasn't supposed to drive. I was making her break rules. My being there was making her pretend to be someone who had everything under control when she was supposed to be trying to get it together. That's why she had been reluctant to come get me, even though I'd been just twenty blocks across the city.

I went to the living room window and looked down into the parking lot. All the cars looked the same, silver glints in the sun, the icy pavement beneath them like aluminum foil. I found my glasses in the bathroom, carried them back to the window, and peered through the one good lens. My breath sailed through me with relief: Larissa's car was there.

I found the keys on the coffee table inside a metal dish with some paperclips and a lighter. It was sitting next to the invoice for my mother's funeral. If Larissa suspected what the envelope contained, I reasoned, it meant she was still talking to her father down in Windsor. It meant someone would take care of her. I grabbed my things and pushed them into my bag. I left her a note saying that I had to go. Then I locked up her apartment and loaded myself and my things into her Honda, and in a short two blocks, I was on the expressway.

Karl, Karl, Karl, the wheels seemed to mutter over the slick asphalt. The cottage was a small brown square with a sloped roof and a cherry-red door, tucked around a bend partially obscured by a hill and maple and pine. At the time, that was all I could remember. How many cottages did that describe? In my mind I could hear Moira saying that Karl should take some responsibility, and suddenly I knew what that meant: food, shelter, clothing, health care, *money*.

It was the same kind of crisp, sunny day as when I had first made the trip with Karl, and I was cresting the city, passing into Barrie, before I thought to look at Larissa's gas tank. When I glanced up again, a transport truck printed with an image of a short-haired, blonde, smiling woman went by. She was wearing heavy black rubber gloves and holding up a vacuum nozzle. The company logo was scrawled below her in red letters.

KLEANTECH:

THE BIO-CLEANUP PROFESSIONALS.

WE DO ATTACK SCENE RECOVERY, CRIME SCENES,

DECOMPOSITIONS, AND FALLOUT FROM TRAUMAS.

YOU NAME IT, WE CLEAN IT!

Why was she blonde? Why was she smiling? I sped up and passed her.

I zoomed along, barely able to see the road ahead because of my one lens, desperate with hope. There was just enough gas, I thought, to get me there—if I could remember where *there* was.

And, as you know, I did find it—but what else did I discover? I found I could steal a car and leave my best friend all alone. I found Grace and a kind of silence I still can't understand.

SIXTEEN

AFTER WE LOST THE TV SIGNAL, Grace would sit in the chair, sipping away on her glasses of wine, and staring at the wood stove or out the window at the snow. Laying her head back against the chair, her thin white scarf wrapped around it, she sometimes looked like a cancer victim to me, especially as breath sang in and out of her lungs. She'd stopped bronzing by then, as if she'd realized I hadn't brought the threat of the virus in on me. At least she trusted me a little.

Then one evening, out of the blue, she perked up in her chair and said, "He claimed he didn't bring you here, but I know he did. I know you did it all over our furniture." Her lips had turned black around the edges with wine and lipstick. "He said it was always at your place, but I know it wasn't. He said you were loud in bed and you couldn't get enough. He really bragged about it."

I shoved on my boots and went outside. She must have assumed I was going to go out to the woodshed, blow it off, and come back. But I walked down the roadway until I could see the lights in the next cottage. It was about ten below freezing. I went up to the neighbour's door, plowing through their snowed-in driveway in my boots. I knocked, my fingers pink with the cold, but if they were there, they didn't look out or answer. I stood there, feeling like I could hear my breath whistling through my chest. I mean, why would they take me in? I was a stubbly in-between colour in the middle of a blonde outbreak and probably everyone in these parts was like Grace: paranoid and hiding out.

I thought about coming back to the cottage and telling Grace that Karl and I had done it only once here, and that it hadn't been that spectacular, but then I thought maybe she envied me. Maybe I had some kind of power in her eyes, and I should let her think whatever he'd told her. I wondered if Karl really had bragged about me, or if it was just her interpretation. It's possible he did use those words—it's possible he enjoyed those kinds of games—but I try not to think so. I'm all right with thinking of him as sad or selfish, or even self-loathing. But I don't want to think of him as intentionally cruel. I think of you now as your own entity, separate from him, but it still makes me feel better to try to think well of him if I can.

I trudged back to the cabin, and when I got here, I went around back to the woodshed. I tried to catch my breath. Sometimes it feels like you're upside down inside me, hanging like a bat from my lungs. I put my hand on the axe. I did. I remember the smooth, cold wood handle between my fingers. I lifted it and let it fall against the tree trunk.

When I came back, Grace was furious. She had locked herself in the bathroom and wouldn't come out. I had calmed down but I did tell her through the closed blue door that *she* should be apologizing to *me*. She never did, never once. She just yelled that I'd put her at risk by leaving and walking around out there.

"How do I know you don't fucking have it?" she hollered through the door.

"I am not blonde. I am forming coherent sentences," I yelled back at her, and fought to control my breathing.

"I took you in and this is how you repay me? You wobbling, fat, toad-shaped cunt."

"No wonder he slept around on you." At first I didn't think I said it loud enough for her to hear, but I must have, because the door flew open and Grace slapped me in the face.

I don't know if I failed to see it coming because I didn't have my glasses, or if she was just that agile. She was tall and long-limbed enough that she just reached through the door and clocked me. I stumbled backward and bumped into the fridge. I stood there, my face stinging. The blow was hard enough that it left a mark. She slammed the door shut again.

A few minutes later, I heard her throw up into the toilet.

EMILY SCHULTZ

I was on the sofa with the lights out by the time she came out and found her way around the corner to her bed.

The cottage wasn't big enough for us to avoid each other. We had to accept the grudges we held against each other, if we were determined to survive.

The next morning Grace was taking a bath and I was desperate to pee. It felt like you were standing on my bladder.

"Fine," Grace groaned, and I heard the water in the tub splashing, then the door lock click open, and then the sweep of the shower curtain rings along the bar. "Come in," she said.

I burst through the bathroom door and lifted the lid on the toilet, fumbling with my clothes.

"Shit," Grace said from the other side of the curtain, where I tried not to think about her being naked. "You might need to flush."

Inside the toilet were the trimmings of her pubis. Floating on the water, blonde-brown stitches. I tapped down the handle and they disappeared.

While I was peeing she said through the curtain: "So can you tell me if he was taking risks even then, or are you so young and super-fertile that it happened just like that, through a condom after half a fucking second?"

I sat on the toilet. The room was steamy and her voice sounded small and wobbly.

"Just young and fertile, I guess."

"Of course you would be, at your age . . . God, are you packing a Super Soaker? Aren't you done yet?" Her hand came around the vinyl curtain and she pulled it back slightly and peered out at me. Un-made-up, she had dark circles like tracks around her eyes. Her lips were heavily lined, the colour of raw cedar. I caught a glimpse of the slope of her white chest.

She looked me up and down. The fleece pants I slept in were around my thick, scarred knees.

"Wow, that's some tumour," she said, then pulled the curtain back in place. "What's the term for what I am to that? Stepmother? Mother once removed? Friend of the family? Aunt?" There was a quaver in her voice again and I'm tempted to say she was crying, but then she ran more water into the tub, so I couldn't tell.

I wiped, and flushed, and left her alone.

Through to the end of January, Grace and I listened to the wind outside and fell back into our routine of breakfast, dishes, bathing, waxing, and shaving. After that, she would sit in the living room. She cut back on the drinking a bit too. She showed me how to wax my "stumps," which was what Grace called my legs. The waxing made me wince and cry but it seemed to make her relax about the chance of SHV, so I humoured her. I didn't tell her that I'd been down the hall from a room full of women who'd gone out, and that if I were susceptible, I'd already have it. Working on a TV crime show had not prepared her for death.

Waxing was also something to do. It takes a hell of a long time when you do it at home, heating up that little jar in the microwave, trying not to let it get too hot, waiting for it to cool just enough. Grace gave me my own jar so our hairs wouldn't mix in the solution, which was sticky as molasses. She knew exactly how thick to spread it, and how fast to rip the paper strips, and in which direction to pull. When I did it myself I wound up botching it. It hurt worse and the hairs stood up like weeds but didn't let go. My mom had tried to show me how to wax when I was in grade nine or ten—she sometimes did lips and eyebrows at the shop—but at that age, I hadn't been willing to let her show me anything . . .

"When I was a kid, six or seven," I told Grace, "women would come into my mom's shop. It just amazed me, these strangers talking. What did they find to say to each other? They could just talk, and talk, and talk. My mom standing there, plucking away at their heads, tilting them this way and that, wriggling things out of them."

I remember the exchange of money. My mother took away their hair, shook it out of the vinyl smocks that covered their chests, swept it up with a black broom or chased it with a blow dryer turned on high across the floor of the shop. She stored the combs that groomed them in blue water, and they gave her dollars, counting the bills out into her palm because there was no counter to stand between them.

"The gift of the gab," Grace said, and took a strip off me before I was ready.

"I never had it," I squeaked. "Never learned it. Existed in

an entirely female environment and couldn't pick it up."

After a while Grace pulled her yoga mat out of a cupboard and showed me some moves. She asked how my round ligaments were feeling, and I told her that I didn't know what those were, but that everything was feeling pretty round.

She would bend over in front of me with her hands on the floor and her butt in the air. She was so vain, it was funny to see her in an old pair of black stretch pants, one buttock out like a primate, one hand up in the air, the other touching the floor beside her toes. Given my condition, I wasn't very good at yoga. She ran through the poses like a drill sergeant and I would watch her, attempting to wriggle my body into a contortion that looked similar to hers, but never quite getting it down before she moved on to the next one. "Warrior," then "Reverse Warrior," she called out. The only position I managed very effectively was the Child. You basically lie like an egg on the carpet, but with your arms out like you're praying to Mecca. It's getting harder now, actually, which must mean I've grown more, in just this week she's been gone.

Grace assured me that lots of pregnant friends of hers did yoga, and that it would loosen tight muscles and improve my sense of balance. She showed me another position she called the Pigeon, where she sat up with a leg flexed out behind her, toes on the floor. Her entire body was made of flat surfaces.

I don't know if I gave her a look, but she said, "What? Lots of my friends have been pregnant in the past year or two. I could still get pregnant and be a mom. Or, I could have been . . . with Karl. How old do you think I am?"

Contorting her body into some kind of balletic stance, Grace asked me if I had things for the baby. By *things*, I suppose she meant clothes, blankets, hats and booties, and gear. "I expect people will buy things for him," she said, letting her toe slide back down her leg to touch the mat again. She nodded at my gut—at you. "They always do."

Her voice was breezy. Perhaps she imagined I would go back to Toronto to find everything normal again, a baby shower magically organized, although I couldn't think by whom.

I hadn't gone to Larissa's shower for Devang. She'd told me I didn't have to, as if she thought I'd find it a chore. A lot of her work friends would be attending, artists and curators, she said—people she'd met during the years she'd been in Toronto ahead of me. I couldn't tell if she was trying to dissuade me from going or if she didn't want me to spend money I didn't have. She'd researched strollers and car seats and Björns and cribs and diapering options online for weeks. She'd registered at two different stores, a large chain and an eco-friendly boutique that dealt in organics. "So people have some choice," she'd said.

In the end, I went over to Larissa's after the shower. I spotted a plate with grape stems on it and I picked at the remaining fruit, noting how the gift bags had been folded meticulously for reuse. Larissa had laid tiny sleepers and sweaters across the dining room table. There were the newborn onesies with fleece feet shaped like animal faces. There were the white sleeping gowns made masculine with trucks and boats and dogs and dinosaurs printed on them. There were jacket-and-pant sets with snaps up the front. The clothes came in sizes small, smaller, and smallest. As if the child who would wear them already had an opinion, the clothes contained messages: *Beary Handsome, Strong Like Daddy, Bananas for Mommy,* and *I Love Hugs.*

I had brought Larissa a pair of Robeez baby shoes, well outside my budget. They were brown leather with pink cupcake patches on the toes—even though we both knew she was having a boy. I thought she would appreciate the subversion. She hugged me with tears in her eyes, and she said she loved them. After Devang was born I never saw him wear them.

What I remember most, though, was how Larissa looked at each item of clothing—with so much tenderness you'd think it already contained her son.

What will I dress you in, my new roommate? What will I wrap around you to keep you warm in this empty winter?

SEVENTEEN

WHEN GRACE ISN'T HERE, I feel your father more, in his things, in these walls, in the bed linens, though she's slept in them more recently than he has. In retrospect all her cursing lifted some of my grief. When she was here I didn't look at his things—*really* look at them. It's funny, but I feel like I've got to know Grace better now than I ever knew Karl . . . I slept with him, but I've lived with her.

No, that's not true. That's a lie. The two kinds of familiarity can't be compared. I did know him very well, in glances.

And besides, Grace surprises me too sometimes. There are many ways in which I don't know her. Take the dog. I guess it was early February, three weeks ago now, when it showed up. Grace was outside and I was in. She was bringing back wood for the stove, and taking a long time about it. I got up from the couch to find out what had happened and I saw her bent over. I didn't realize why at first, and I thought maybe she was sick. The wood was scattered all around her. She was wearing her big black coat, her behind in the air. Then I saw the blur of fur, and I was afraid she was being attacked. I could just glimpse a shape, and movement. I threw open the door and called her name.

She turned, still bent over, one hand out. "Look at this little hobo," she called.

Then I saw him, dirty yellow fur, pushing his head into her lap. Again and again, the dog would back up and then come to her, pushing its head against her, ramming her. Why, I didn't understand.

Her arm went around its head, its neck. She bent her nose to its ear and nuzzled. Her glove came off and went into her pocket. I watched her hand stroking the fur along its back, the way the animal leapt into her, whining, almost bleating, trying to make as much contact as possible, eager for touch. She laughed, rubbed it all over.

There was a ribbon of colour along its neck, a collar, but it didn't look like anyone had fed or loved it anytime recently. It was so skinny it barely resembled a dog—I guess that's why I'd thought coyote at first. The dog head-butted Grace until it pushed her over on her bum, then it climbed on top of her, all paws and wagging tail.

Then, after a minute, she pushed the animal off. She didn't pat its head again or reach down for the wood she had gathered. She strode toward the door where I was standing, pushed past me, and closed it, saying, "Fuck, fuck, mother-fuck."

I could hear the dog crying at the door for more love.

"What?" I asked.

"Fleas!" She was peeling off her coat and her clothes, which were wet and muddy from the dog, dancing around in her boots, getting slush everywhere, even the carpet. "Launder these. Right away."

"That's a wool coat," I said, skeptical of what would happen to it in the washer.

"Fucking now! I don't know what I was thinking—my arms just went out to it. Damn dog. If I die because of a damn dog . . ."

She was overreacting, but I took the coat, her shirt, and her sweater, and ran to the pantry, where the washing machine was. She stripped her jeans off without even removing her boots.

"Shit." She was standing there in a beige bra, the jeans caught around one giant booted foot. She stopped yanking to scratch herself all over, leaving deep red carvings behind on her dry white skin.

The dog was still whining at the door.

"Easy," I said. I went over and helped untangle Grace, but she kept scratching. "Calm down, Grace."

She began muttering to herself.

"What are you doing?"

"Nothing," she said. "I don't know what I was thinking," she repeated.

"Why don't you take a shower?" I proposed, hoping it would make her stop scratching. She was visibly shaken, and now the dog had started to bay.

"He wants food," she said as she headed past the pantry into the bath.

"Should I feed him?"

"*No!*" she shouted emphatically. She was so distressed she hadn't shut the bathroom door. I heard the spigot go on full blast, then rattle down to practically nothing.

"The laundry," I said, and ran over to the machine and stopped the cycle, and the shower came back again.

"Don't feed it, whatever you do," Grace said through the shower curtain. "It will keep coming around. Oh god, this is wrong, it's wrong. Forgive me," she said.

Twenty minutes later, the water must have run cold but she was still in there, and still muttering. I watched the dog, who hadn't given up and was still sniffing around on the porch, occasionally making eye contact with me through the window and giving plaintive yelps.

I didn't know anything about dogs. I didn't know whether they had fleas in winter or not. I just thought that the way Grace was acting, she must have felt a bite. I went to the kitchen cabinet drawer and yanked it open. There was a knife as long as a ruler. I stood looking down at it. It was my best weapon. I pulled it out and went to my sofa and hid it, flat beneath the cushion, in case. Then I went back to Grace.

I stood in the doorway of the bathroom and said, "If that's gone cold, you need to come out."

The water stopped, but she didn't come out. No one got SHV that quickly, I told myself: go in. Go in and get her out of there. I pulled her towel off the rack and yanked back the curtain.

Grace's eyes were tightly shut and she was holding her fists in front of her body. She was standing the way you might if someone had just poured freezing water on you. She was shaking. Her nipples were hard and there were goose pimples all over her. Because she removed all her hair religiously, she was more naked than naked, and I could see her you-know-what. I threw the towel over her, but she didn't grab it. I went to work drying her off. "Get out," I commanded, and she opened one eye and stepped out of the tub, leaning so heavily on my shoulder, I thought I'd lose my balance. Outside of the tub, she seemed to come around a little.

"Fucking animal, fucking animal," she said. She grabbed hold of the corners of the towel, pulling it around herself.

"Did you feel a flea bite you?" I asked, backing away.

Her teeth chattered.

"Go sit by the wood stove." I ran to the bedroom area and grabbed her bathrobe. I glanced out the window again. The dog lay on the steps as if he lived here too. When he saw me looking, he jumped up and gave a woof. I realized all the wood for the stove was out there on the lawn in the snow, getting wet. There was enough wood inside to last for a while, I decided, and we also had a small electrical heater, built into the wall, though it didn't project very much or very far. When Karl had brought me here, he'd talked about "the bones" of a cottage, kind of proudly, like he didn't care for all the things he had in Toronto, even though he completely did.

Instead of sitting in her usual chair, Grace chose my spot on the couch. She was sitting on the cushion where I'd just stashed the knife.

I made her a bowl of chicken soup, but she said, "I can't eat. I feel terrible."

I eyed her, my heart racing. Wasn't lack of appetite one of the first signs?

Then she said, "That poor fucking animal. Someone's abandoned it because of the pandemic. There's only so much my heart can take. I know I shouldn't have touched it, but it's going to starve. I want to feed it, but we can't feed it or it will come around here all the time, and it's been living outside, so it must have fleas, and we can't, we can't . . ."

I held the soup bowl out to her. She wiped her nose on her bathrobe sleeve, then took the bowl, her fingers shaking. "Fuck it," she said, and ate, a forlorn expression I'd never seen before on her face. When she finished she said, "You never had dogs, did you?" and I shook my head. "You were too poor, weren't you? Couldn't afford the extra expense."

I was kind of surprised that she could deduce all that from one fact about me. I sighed.

"Karl liked you because of it, you know. He said that you were a rotten academic, actually, but that you reminded him of himself. A ragtag little thing from nowhere."

I thanked her for the compliments, such as they were.

"Is the dog still there?" she asked.

"Down by the road. I can see his tail. He's going. He's gone."

I asked what kind it was, and she said, "Lab." She seemed to be back to her usual crunchy self, but I decided I would monitor her closely for a few days.

After a while, she confessed that she didn't actually know if a flea had bitten her, or if she'd just imagined a bite when she realized one *might*. But I wasn't sure if she was lying to me. I knew that if *I'd* been bitten, I might very well lie about it. The British claimed that fleas were not the vector, I remembered. But I left the knife beneath the cushion just in case.

I woke a few nights later with Grace hanging over me, a hefty flashlight in her hand, turned on, casting its light up at the ceiling, but poised as though she were going to strike me with it. I shrank back as much as I could, given my girth.

"What are you doing? Get away from me!"

I didn't need to ask twice. She jumped back. She peered at me, but in the dark and without my glasses I couldn't make out her expression. Plus, the flashlight beam was weaving around the room.

"Are you all right?" she asked, a steely tone to her voice.

I struggled to sit up.

"You were making sounds." Grace clutched the flashlight, which was the size of a baton, as if she still wasn't convinced.

"What kind of sounds?"

"Moaning."

"I wasn't, I—" Then I knew what she was talking about because the pain hit me again and I groaned. "Oh . . ." It felt like bad gas. I clutched my stomach and held out a finger for her to wait a minute. The pain kept coming.

"What is it?" she said. "What's happening?"

"I'm—I'm not sure." I struggled into a better position. "Maybe you shouldn't have scared me."

"Just wait," she told me. "Wait it out. This is way too soon."

She was right. I was only thirty-two weeks along. But your taps and jabs had become forceful, like you were eager to come out, and sometimes I could see you wavering beneath the skin, sending small ripples across my belly.

Grace turned off the flashlight and we waited in the dark. We didn't put the lights on. Grace sat in Karl's chair and said things like, "What's happening now? Are you in pain? Do you think it's a contraction?"

And I said things like, "I don't know. Sort of. No, not really. Wait—*erggggh*."

She got me a bag of peas from the freezer and I clutched the cold packaging against my side.

Eventually the cramps subsided and I fell asleep again. When I woke Grace seemed to have found her way back to her bed. Morning light was coming through the window like pale smoke. I rubbed my hand over my abdomen and you gave a half-hearted roll. I felt like you were still positioned at the top of my belly, like you hadn't turned over in the night or dropped, although really, how would I know? The last person who had told me what to expect about any of this was Nurse Ben back at the WEE, and his pamphlets didn't describe months seven and eight.

I took my opportunity to slip the kitchen knife out from under the couch cushions and back into the drawer. No need for Grace to know.

We saw our dog again, a couple weeks later. He was down by the road but didn't come up to the cabin.

"There's Alf," Grace said, which is what she had taken to calling him behind his back.

"Is that him again?"

"Think so," Grace said. "He looks better." I couldn't tell, but she insisted he was fatter and cleaner, like he'd been bathed. She said someone must have taken him in, thank god, otherwise we'd have seen a lot more of him; he wouldn't have given up on us so easily.

"I always wanted a dog, but Karl said it wasn't fair in the city, in a condo, and out here only a few days once every couple months," Grace said. She folded her long arms, still staring out. "They had a lot of dogs on the farm outside Lethbridge when he was growing up. I suppose they were treated like farm animals. They probably ate cheap food, and slept outdoors, and wandered out onto the highway, and didn't get their shots. They didn't live that long. Little Karl Diclicker definitely had his share of heartbreak."

I can't even imagine Karl as "little Karl," even though I've since seen photos.

"You could get one, when the epidemic has passed, when it's safe," I suggested.

Alf's tail floated like a dandelion seedling as he jumped through a snowbank and disappeared in the opposite direction through long, dark lines of trees.

"We could," Grace said. At first I thought she meant me and her. Then, by the faraway look on her face, I realized that she meant her and Karl, that she sometimes slipped into those words, *we* and *our*, without thinking.

Once, she told me that when he slept, Karl always tucked his heels together, then positioned his feet against her calves, facing away from her. I could see him in that position; he may even have slept that way with me the two nights we spent here, and it made me feel funny, to think of him curved against her back like that. Like a boy, Grace said, almost with longing.

There's one photo of Karl and Grace before they married. I found it up in the attic. They're at some event, leaning against a shiny bar. It must be back when she was still a student. She's wearing skinny black jeans and pointy-toed stiletto boots. A rough-cut shag haircut frames her face and she's posing, pouting into the camera. In that picture she can't be much older than I am now. In contrast, Karl is all in brown, faded, with the exception of a glimmer of shirt beneath his jacket, and although he's looking at the camera, he seems unbearably bored. He's younger, thinner even than the Karl I knew. His hair is thick, and there's much more of it, darting across his forehead like an animal. But beneath it, he looks sallow, swallowed, dazed maybe. I suppose you could pull up any photograph of any couple and use it as an indicator of their relationship and what it might say about them, but . . . Well, there aren't even any photos of me and Karl—not one—so what does that say?

It's not that I believe they brought out the worst in each other; I believe they just got lost from each other.

I remember Kovacs's mouth when she said "That bitch" about Grace, on that busy street in New York, the way it dripped out of her—and yes, Grace is, Grace can be, a *bitch*. But it's more than that, more than Grace alone. If there was one thing Karl was good at, it was waffling. He devoted himself to things, ideas, objects, obsessions, but not to people. He married Grace, but he still couldn't find it in himself to commit.

When Karl brought me here that first time, I remember it smelling like woodsmoke, coffee, and the mustiness of a place that's been closed up. It felt like something waiting, just for us, and I remember his long steps across the place to open up windows and air it out, to turn on a space heater to warm the room. He was jangly, nervous. I stood in one spot on the mat. I could hear him throwing framed photographs and other items into drawers. The place was very much him, but it was Grace too—and her touches stood out to me more then, before I knew her. A throw rug in the kitchen with a design of coffee cups on it. A framed print titled *Birds of Northern Ontario*. Some decorative plates hanging on the panel above the kitchen window. These weren't things that fit with Karl.

I can't—oh god—it's hard for me to say this, especially looking around this space and remembering him moving through it a year ago. Long, long ago. Before I showed up and found Grace here. Your father—I'll tell you this now because Grace still isn't back—well, he did something I've come to think of as a suicidal act.

The night Grace told me how Karl's death happened, she had switched from wine to the whisky. We were sitting before the blank, useless TV, and she was whisking one fingernail up and down the chair's arm.

"I never should have taken him from Wanda, the same way you never should have taken him from me," she said.

You were unusually jumpy and I wasn't paying attention to Grace at first. It took me a second to realize that when she said "Wanda" she meant Dr. Kovacs.

She must have interpreted my surprise as denial that I'd, indeed, taken him, because she set down her glass and said, "You left him. It might have been different if he'd tired of you. But now, you'll always be the last one. He was ruined, you know."

I hadn't understood he liked me that much. There was the time in his car—well, Grace's car, actually—when he cried, but I had believed it was more over her than me. That he felt guilty for what he was doing to her. We'd been driving around talking about my going to New York. He hadn't seemed to care. He'd said decisively—and I remember this so distinctly— "You're young. It will be good for you. You should go."

I remember so vividly his hands, his knuckles on the wheel, the glint of the little hairs on them. The way he palmed the wheel when he turned it. I remember him complaining about Grace, but she was a different Grace then, one I didn't know, and I don't recall what he was on about. It was like the phone conversation with the teaching assistant when I had first entered his office so long ago—it didn't seem very important, and now, of course, it does. I wish I could remember. But I do recall him saying, "You don't know what it is to get old, Hazel."

He pulled the Mini over to the curb on a side street. There was no one around and the sun was going down, glinting off the glass of buildings. He said we weren't far from his condo, and I thought he might take me there. I thought we were driving around with that idea—of going there. Then he asked me to park with him, and to touch myself for him. It was summer dusk, but we were visible on a city street. This wasn't the kind of parking Larissa had told me about as a teenager, where you could find a pull-off from the highway or some rural route, or head down near some old railroad track or beside the Detroit River. This was Toronto, a city of eight million, at nine-thirty at night.

"But you're going away," he pleaded.

At the time, it seemed like a teacher's power play. Now, it seems so desperate. In the end, I made him climax. It was fast and awkward, and my wrist cramped, and I felt sick, and some people came out of a building nearby when it was almost done, but I didn't stop because the Mini's windows were tinted and I could tell Karl was near the end and I just wanted it to be over.

Afterward, Karl opened his eyes and stared out the windshield, and said, "That's my wife."

I didn't see her. I saw the top of her head behind a door that opened and then closed. We were parked outside the door to their building, but I hadn't known it. I'd known one of the buildings nearby was where he lived, and I'd made the logical assumption that we were several blocks away. I saw a spike of hair, then she was gone. That was when he started to cry. His shirt was folded up and there was ejaculate pooled on his belly and a stain hardening onto his pants.

I still don't know why he parked there. Had he wanted us to go in and have Grace catch us, but he couldn't work up the nerve for it? Had he wanted her to walk by and see? Had he wanted to orchestrate the three of us together? Or had he simply misjudged? Perhaps he'd meant for us to go in but lost his nerve. Perhaps he hadn't thought Grace was anywhere in the vicinity.

Karl and I had one more time together after that. We met at a boutique hotel. It wasn't glamorous, like you might think. The room was nice enough, but it was daytime and we were sober. I don't know about sober sex. It's not really something I've conquered. It seemed strange to be there, walking around the big clean bed, looking out the windows at the dirty city. The sex itself felt anonymous, dutiful, hurried, mechanical, and sunlit. I remember I was flattered he had spent the money on the room. I think it happened only because neither of us wanted me to go to New York on that other note.

I remember he asked if I would miss him, and I asked, did he want me to? To which he said faintly, "Of course."

"He lost it a bit when he thought you'd been caught in the outbreak . . ." Grace's lips pulled down and her voice trailed off. "When he never heard back, he tried to call Wanda to find out about you, but then, she was gone too. He—he felt responsible. Thought he'd played a part in your going away and whatever you came into contact with. He became quite manic, as if he wasn't up and down enough already. It was grief, but not a normal grief . . ." As Grace talked, she stared over my shoulder at the dead television screen. "More compulsive than normal. Obsessive.

"He went to *them*," Grace said. "He died in a hotel room, surrounded by the blondes. I knew he was doing it, but I couldn't make him stop. He told me only once, but he did it more than once. Whole gangs of them. He started selling things he'd collected over the years—rare books, prints of films—fucking collector's items. He had so much. He would package it up in his office at school so I wouldn't see him doing it. I didn't know. I realized what he'd done later, when I went to his office and there was nothing much left. He wrapped his stuff in kraft paper and plastic and he Purolator'ed it, and with the money he bought the blondes."

Grace said that he'd confessed to having five at once. She said she asked him not to do it again, "but . . ." and her voice faded. She told me he was an addict, and then she picked up her drink again. I remember the cabin had become dark, and Grace flicked on the light above her.

"He got a bad posse," Grace said. She laughed, but it was a hiccup of a laugh and set the amber liquid in her glass shivering. "One or two of them must have fucking had the disease. He had to have known it would happen, but he wanted them so bad—"

What did it mean, she asked me, to desire so much? She said that before she got married, she'd had a checklist for the man she wanted. Looks were on the list, but there were other qualities of Karl's she'd ranked higher. Like intelligence, financial stability, job security, talent, a sense of style, a sense of humour. She asked me why I'd chosen him and not some cute young thing my own age, but she didn't give me space to answer. She wasn't sure she'd ever known what desire was.

She ran her hand back over her head. "I never should have been so afraid. I never should have shaved it," she said, and she set her glass down. "At least then, I might have been enough for him. Or I'd have gone out with him, or maybe before him."

I hadn't thought I had any tears left for your father, for Karl, but here they are again. I've got this image in my mind of him in that photograph, the one I took. It now seems so long ago and lost, the one where he's looking up into the light above the bookshelf. I remember him in his office, saying, "I suppose I'm going to put these over here for a while and then I'll forget to move them again. They'll fall on my head one day." His carelessness wasn't how he felt about *things* so much as . . .

I told Grace she shouldn't blame herself. It kind of blipped out of me. I struggled under the weight of you.

My words, feeble as they were, seemed to relieve her. "Karl's mother," she said, and then she couldn't say anything more for a minute. "I had to tell her how it happened. I had to tell an old lady how her son died."

Grace picked up the glass and downed what was left in it, which wasn't much. She said his parents, who were elderly, flew in from Lethbridge for the small service. His older sister had refused to come. The parents stayed about five minutes, then got up and left, abandoning her to deal with the room. There was a casket, she said, but truthfully she didn't know what was inside it, and didn't want to know. Officials had told her it would have to be closed, and she was fine with that.

She'd wanted a prescription but didn't dare go see a doctor at the height of the pandemic. She'd holed up in their condo for a few days—I noticed she talked about her and Karl's space as if he were still there—she'd holed up there until a woman one floor up got the virus and threw herself off the balcony. Grace said she hadn't seen the woman fall, but she'd heard it. When Grace looked out the balcony door, she felt like she was looking at herself down there on the pavement. "The awning was torn and flapping where she'd hit and rolled, and then in the courtyard . . . It could have been anyone, and I thought, *I'm next*. That was when I figured I'd better haul ass someplace—any fucking place," she said. She set down her empty highball glass with a click on the long wooden arm of the chair. She said she'd been at the cabin for four days when I came hollering.

So I'd made it back to Toronto only to miss Karl by a week. I sat with that information, not moving, even though you were.

"I think I'm in shock," Grace said, touching a hand to her eyelashes. "Is it possible to be in shock for two months? What the hell is shock anyway?"

Then she got up and went into the bathroom. When she came back, I saw she'd retouched her makeup. Because she was a little drunk, she put it on crooked, and even without my glasses, her eyes seemed to float outside their shapes.

"Please don't name the baby after him," she said, looking down at the wedge of you.

"It's not a boy. She's a girl," I told her. "Or supposed to be." I was surprised I hadn't told her that before. I hadn't realized I'd been keeping the knowledge to myself.

"She'll be at risk, then. Like the rest of us," Grace said, and laughed wryly. Then she was thoughtful. "That first night—when you came here, you said someone close to you died. Who was it?"

I startled. I hadn't thought I'd told Grace anything about myself, but she did have an uncanny way of reading between the lines. "My—my mother."

"What was your mother's name?"

"Mary." There was a knot in my throat. I didn't know who it was for—Karl, my mother, Grace, me . . . you.

"Mary Hayes. It's a good name, solid. Name her that," Grace said.

That night I dreamt of hazmat suits carrying bags and bags down the hallways and out of the Women's Entry and Evaluation centre. They were also carrying the bulky black vinyl sacks down the narrow green stairs of the Dunn Inn in New York. I woke up in a sweat, sleeping at an odd angle around the lump of you, and I knew it was some other corridor, some other hotel, and it was Karl in my dreams inside those bags.

I sat up and the cottage was very still. I was alone, as if Grace too had been carried out by my dream.

EIGHTEEN

LAST NIGHT I WOKE AT 4 A.M. It may have been you who woke me, or a sudden cramp, or the tingling I get sometimes in my extremities—a kind of falling asleep in my limbs that prickles and aches. Or maybe it was just the buildup of sadness, as if sadness were something solid enough to shake me from a dream.

I could hear rain pattering on the roof, and I thought: *My mother is dead.* I thought it again, as if trying the words out on my tongue, although I didn't say them aloud: *My mother is dead.* Of course I had thought of it often, but because I learned of Karl's death and my mom's in the same day, his eclipsed hers—after all, I've had Grace beside me reminding me that his was real. My mom's passing still feels impossible. As I lay on my side in the dark, I saw my mom's face in my mind, from a long way away—through the windows of her shop, surrounded by the white fluorescent light from the overheads. I turned my face into Grace's pillows and sobbed, and when I stopped, it seemed as though the rushing wet sound continued. I realized again that it was raining, and I listened to the tiny arrows of it and imagined them pelting the snow and the sharp divots they must be making there.

I remembered that my mom's boyfriend Richard has a sister—Kristi—in Winnipeg. And it occurred to me he may have gone there. That *National Geographic* map left the Plains looking like one of the safest places to be. I resolved to look her up the very minute I am able, to see if Richard is there, if either he or his sister can tell me more about what happened to my mom at the Head Start. Kristi's married name floated into my brain, Kostelanetz, and as soon as it did sleep returned to me.

My biggest regret is that I didn't have a chance to tell my mom she would be a grandmother. But then, I didn't know. I also regret how I treated Larissa, that I left her in that terrible state of mind, in the same way that I have been left all alone here by Grace. The difference being that Larissa is my best friend, and to Grace I am just . . . well, who am I?

Then this morning, I looked out the window and discovered this: glimpses of green, just at the edges of the yard. Even without my glasses, I've seen so much. From this window in the past week I've seen five hawks—blurred but I can tell by their glide—three jack rabbits, two raccoons, and just this morning one small red fox. I didn't speak when it showed up—didn't want to risk scaring it. It was too far away at first for me to be sure of what it was, but when it came beyond the trees it moved like a streak of fire across the snow. It crept close to the cabin, flexing its legs and padding through the last patches of ice, every step like a pact. This creature—something between canine and feline—slunk low to the ground, snouting scents, its pointed red-black ears twitching. It was crouched out there in the snow near the porch on those flexed, always-ready-to-run paws. I watched its mouth open, its black nose, muzzle, and tongue tunnelling under the lattice, hunting a bird's nest, thieving a stone-coloured breakfast. It came out with the egg tucked between its teeth, unbroken.

The fox moved swiftly, in spite of the fact that it thought itself alone, shaking the snow loose with its bushy tail, sending buds wobbling on that bush, though they're barely there, green as the first day of March, which is today. The light was hollow and white and there was no wind. Then the fox was gone—just like that, prize still clutched tenderly in its mouth—darting across the yard and disappearing between the trees.

I've lived through five major incidents and I am unscathed. I count them on my fingers and feel like I'm counting my blessings for whatever little sidesteps allowed me to steer clear of danger: the Eugenia Gilongos subway attack; the day at JFK; the little girl near the fountain in Washington Square; the woman on the side of the highway; room 3, just one hundred yards down the hall at the WEE. This is how I used to count kisses; the course credits I needed to graduate; the number of pages in an essay; the number of music shows I'd gone to or films I'd seen in a month.

In some ways, so much has been taken from me that I haven't even begun to fathom it. In other ways, I'm grateful just to be here, to have made it this far. I feel guilty saying that, guilty to have what I do. To have a bath and electricity, warm bedding, and a place to heat up cans of food. Even as the soap runs low, even as the cupboard supplies dwindle, even as I wonder whether the electricity will be turned off without Grace here—although I assume it's paid automatically from some account of hers and Karl's. I know I should think about the future, what will become of me, of you, but every minute is very long. Behind the sound of the kitchen clock, the minutes seem to tremble.

When the fox left, I sat very still at the kitchen table for a long time, watching the branch move, naked, where it had been, hoping it would come back.

Things come to me in bits and pieces, just impressions. It's like being in the WEE all over again, minus the company. It's like being in lock-up. Sometimes I feel that you're very real, and that talking to you is like talking to a dog or a cat who's in the room with me. Other times I feel that talking to you is like talking to my ass or my elbow, or even that can of sardines in the cupboard.

My mother used to insist that women were motivated by

the three Ms—men, money, and more men and money. Then she'd laugh like it was a terrific joke. Every year when she styled for prom, she called it "Do and Douche" season. These were girls, she said, who would lose their virginity in exchange for a limo ride. She wasn't looking down on them, she was just pinning their hair up. She said she was no better; it was the way of the world. These were her truths, and certainly there was truth in her words—it's just that I didn't want those truths. I wanted to believe in a prettier picture. At the same time, whenever one was presented to me, I pushed it away.

The last email I had from Karl was signed **Love, Karl.** He said that things had been so crazy he couldn't tell me about them, that he missed me terribly, and that perhaps he had been wrong to have sent me away.

Except the truth is, he hadn't sent me away.

I had downloaded the forms for my grant months in advance of my leaving. And I went away. I went to the biggest city I could find, hoping it would take me far from what I'd done, accept me, gulp me into its belly.

I wish I had my computer now. I wish I could remember every word Karl wrote to me. I remember reading his last message in a Manhattan café after the attacks at JFK. I remember that it was grey outside but warm, and the breeze picked up dirt I couldn't see and blew it into my face. That a girl was having her head shaved on the sidewalk. That there were sugar granules, and the way they felt beneath my thumb as I turned it across the surface of the table, collecting them.

That the café owner seemed impatient, as if I'd been there too long and hadn't paid enough for my time. I remember the whipped milk clinging to the bottom of the white cup. But the words—they've evaporated.

Listen, there's a car coming, driving through the pitch black out there. I can hear it, but I can't see the lights. I know it's not just in my head. Have I talked myself silly? I've been alone before. I've been alone my whole life. But you're with me, my little barnacle. You can hear me, can't you, through the skin? Can you hear that car sputtering out there a long way off? Yes, you can. There—its lights. I wish I could see . . . Karl's glasses! They have to be better than nothing.

Ah, it's closer, it's closer. They're round headlights, I think. Yes, they are. It's turning in! It's the Mini.

Grace thinks I'm crazy for talking to you, but she really can't hear my words over the engine and the wind. She has to think about driving. There's a hospital in Collingwood where you and I, little one, can get our vaccines. Grace had hers last week. There's no guarantee to them, but early reports have been good. Grace didn't want to come back until she was sure. She didn't want to write a note in case she didn't come back, she says, because it might have affected my actions. I might have waited for her beyond the point of reason. She checked into a hotel and waited to see if she'd have side effects. She said she tried to call the land line at the cabin but the phone lines are down. Beautiful Grace, amazing Grace, Grace as I've never seen her, with a half-inch of fuzz sprouting all over her scalp. Grace who came back for us when she didn't have to. Expect nausea, she says, lethargy, and some congestion.

When I asked her why she's doing this, she said that there was nothing else *to* fucking do, that she hadn't wanted to wake to a bloody mess one day, and find the progeny of her dead husband "getting shit out into the world all over her sofa." That's Grace, that's just how she talks.

I told her it would be an excuse to change the decor, but she didn't laugh at that joke.

You're snug under my hand. You might yet be born, properly, in a hospital, or at least somewhere with someone to catch you, someone to trim the umbilical cord down to a thorn-like nub that will fall off and become your belly button.

When you're born, I won't tell you this story. I'll kiss your forehead, what will become your eyebrows but will at first be just a cloudlike wisp. I'll wiggle your toes, which will be minuscule and pink, like mine but unfathomably small. You'll grasp my finger in all five of yours, and you'll hold it so hard, Hazel Junior, like you're hanging on to the world by a wire. You'll be like a baby in a toilet paper commercial. I'll name you. You'll close your eyes and you'll dream whatever babies dream.

I'll tell you that I don't know where you came from—you, strange small thing. I'll tell you that you just happened. I'll tell you all those beautiful lies—that a stork delivered you, not that you were washed into the world on a torrent of amniotic fluid and blood.

What? Oh, but Grace says: Don't lie too much. Don't lie too much, or she'll turn out to be a monster. Lie just enough, kiddo.

ACKNOWLEDGMENTS

I would like to thank St. Martin's Press and Thomas Dunne Books for giving this work a home. Immeasurable thanks go to Thomas Dunne, my wonderful editor Marcia Markland, and Quressa Robinson. I am grateful to James Iacobelli for the stunning cover design. Thanks to Margaret Atwood, Stephen King, Helene Wecker, Emily St. John Mandel, Peter Orner, Ben Loory, and Andrew Pyper for their wonderful words of support. Thanks to Kelsey Lawrence, Justin Velella, and the publicity team. Special thanks to Kathleen Carter Zrelak.

I am also deeply indebted to Lynn Henry and my agent Shaun Bradley, both of whom nurtured this story. Thanks to my family, especially Mom and Dad (always) for patience and support, and Vicky and Mike Davis. Thank you to my husband

Brian Joseph Davis and everyone at *Joyland Magazine*. Some of the articles, films, and art pieces this novel references are real sources—they are used here to function within a fictional world. Thanks, too, to the soldier who provided tactical advice and helped with jargon while we talked a four-hour flight away.

To blonde friends and readers, I quote Louis Aragon: "Blond everywhere: I surrender myself to this pitch pine of the senses, to this concept of a blondness which is not so much a color as a sort of spirit of color blended with the accents of love."

A NOTE ABOUT THE TYPE

The Blondes has been set in Scala, a type family created in the late 1980s by Martin Majoor, a book typographer and type designer based in The Netherlands. The principle forms of Scala are derived from humanist faces such as Bembo and Fournier, yet feature lower contrasts and stronger serifs—ideal for modern electronic book design and typesetting. Of particular note is the rare balance and compatibility of the serif and sans serif. Originally designed to address the peculiar challenges of setting multiple levels and weights of information within a music concert programme, Scala is named after the Teatro alla Scala in Milan.